The Angel Street Assassination

A Bennett & DeMarko Mystery

Aaron S Gallagher

INDIES UNITED PUBLISHING HOUSE, LLC

The Angel Street Assassination ©2020 by Aaron S Gallagher.

All Rights Reserved.
Published by Indies United Publishing House, LLC All rights reserved worldwide. No part of this publication may be replicated, redistributed, or given away in any form without the prior written consent of the author/publisher or the terms relayed to you herein.

All rights reserved. No part of this book may be reproduced in any form or by any electronic or mechanical means including information storage and retrieval systems, without permission in writing from the author. The only exception is by a reviewer, who may quote short excerpts in a review.

Cover designed by Aaron S Gallagher

This book is a work of fiction. Names, characters, places, and incidents either are products of the author's imagination or are used fictitiously. Any resemblance to actual persons, living or dead, events, or locales is entirely coincidental. -Aaron S Gallagher

Visit my website at *www.aaronsgallagher.com*

Printed in the United States of America
First Printing: August 2020

ISBN 13: 978-1-64456-167-6
Library of Congress Control Number:2020943017

INDIES UNITED PUBLISHING HOUSE, LLC
P.O. BOX 3071
QUINCY, IL 62305-3071
www.indiesunited.net

This book is dedicated to Jennie Rosenblum

Editor, mentor, fan, Jersey girl

CHAPTER ONE

Friday 11:30 p.m.

A moonless night, dark and cold and silent. Outside the windows the wind tossed weightless flakes of new snow into the sky. A light flared in the darkness as the door of the refrigerator opened.

The light illuminated a tall man wrapped in a warm flannel robe as he reached into the inviting white interior and removed a glass bottle of milk. He closed the door as he twisted the cap from the bottle. He drank from the nearly full container. He emptied almost a third of it with a sigh. He glanced around the kitchen, still holding the milk. The clock over the stove told him it was almost midnight.

The milk soothed the heartburn that had awoken Sal D'Amico. He burped quietly, one cadaverous hand covering his mouth. He sipped again and turned to look out of the kitchen windows into the dark, cold night beyond. At first all he saw was his reflection: tall, thin to the point of gaunt, hair standing up in a crest on one side of his narrow skull. The hand went again to his mouth and he smoothed the thin mustache under the slightly hawkish nose. His stomach gurgled. He winced and swigged from the bottle again.

Sal went to the window, peering out into the night. He sipped the milk a third time, staring at the lazy, almost slow-motion spill of snow in the air. He leaned closer to see if the birdbath outside the window had frozen over.

Movement behind him in the reflection drew his eye. He turned. "It's all right, Bill. Just some indig-"

The figure in the doorway wasn't his bodyguard, Bill

Higgins. Too thin, too short. He couldn't see the face. Wary alertness gripped him.

"Who are you?"

No answer.

"Who sent you?" Sal's voice was firm, resigned.

Silence.

"You've got a lot of nerve, coming into my house like this. You know who I am?"

"Yes," the figure answered.

D'Amico glanced around the kitchen. Too far from the knives. He hadn't bothered to drop the little .32 into his robe pocket on his way out of the bedroom. The cooling allure of the milk had called too strongly.

A costly mistake.

The figure in the doorway of the kitchen took a hesitant step. Sal's eyes caught the hesitation and knew what it meant. He raised a hand. "Look, you don't want to do this."

The thumb pulled the hammer back. The mechanism of the gun was loud in the semidarkness. "No."

Sal's mouth compressed into a thin line. Eyes on the gun he growled, "You'd better not miss. You don't get a second chance."

When the hand started to rise, Sal took his shot. He heaved the milk bottle in an overhand that Sal had practiced a thousand times- forty years ago in the streets and empty lots of Brooklyn. His aim had diminished, he saw, but the bottle tumbled end over end and shattered against the doorframe next to the gunman. The explosion sent shards of glass and sprays of milk in every direction. The gunman flinched away and Sal took his chance. He darted left around the kitchen table and through the narrow hall that led to the sitting room off to one side. He heard the gunman stumble after him.

Sal D'Amico had been many things in his life:

Gambino underboss, gentleman, construction company owner, pimp. He was not a long-distance runner. More, he was never going to see the sunny side of fifty years old again. Heart thudding in his chest, Sal darted through the sitting room. He knew his rooms well, fortunately, because the scant light in the kitchen did not penetrate this deeply. He heard the gunman behind him. As he crossed the threshold of the sitting room into the foyer, he heard his pursuant stumble in the dark and a tight grin stretched his lips.

He hurried across the foyer, ignoring the front door. The cars were all in the garage, and anyhow the snow was two feet deep and he was in a robe and slippers. Besides, he had a better idea.

Through the second hall he went, until he came to the second door on the left. He put a shoulder to it and twisted the knob. It stuck. He reared back and hit it again. The door squealed and burst inward. Sal rushed into the room, feeling the hand of his assailant brush the back of his robe.

He stumbled through the room, slippers snagging on the bare plywood of the floor. The walls were skeletal and there was plastic draped on two of them. The plastic seemed to breathe as the wind billowed them, the outer shell of the walls of what would become a game room were not airtight. He jammed his left big toe against a stud nailed to the floor and fell headlong, arms flying out before him. He crashed to the floor where his wet bar would be when the room was complete. He scrambled to get to his feet, the wind knocked from his lungs. At the same moment he struggled upright, the gunman crashed into him, tackling him to the bare floor once more. They fell hard, Sal's breath still gone, the gunman's own breath exploding from his lungs as he landed hard on his ribs. Sal heard the gun skitter across the wood floor.

He rolled onto his hands and knees, climbed to his feet,

and started to run. He crashed into a pair of sawhorses. A single sheet of plywood across them made a rough table, upon which a large toolbox lay. The whole structure collapsed as Sal bumped it, and the toolbox clattered to the floor, scattering piles of tools.

Sal hit the floor a final time, and this time he screamed with sudden agony as he fell onto a crowbar. The tines of the hooked end punctured his thigh. He recoiled and hit his head against an upright beam, hard enough to see stars.

His assailant, meanwhile, had clambered to his hands and knees, frantically searching for the gun. Unable to locate it, he turned to face Sal.

D'Amico writhed, rolled, and curled in a fetal ball, clutching his injured leg with both hands. Blood pulsed between his fingers. His eyes met his attacker's eyes, and for a second they just stared.

Sal moved first, groping for the crowbar, snarling a curse.

Fear widened his attacker's eyes, and he reached for the first thing he saw.

Before Sal could raise the heavy crowbar, a hammer came crashing down, shattering the delicate bones in Sal's right hand. He screamed again and jerked his hand away, cradling it to his chest. The air was loud with gasps and grunts of effort as both men struggled to catch their breath. The hammer came down again on Sal's knee and the brittle crack of metal on bone was almost louder than Sal's miserable, breathy screech. He collapsed sideways on the floor, trying unsuccessfully to drag himself away from his attacker.

The figure stood, the hammer dangling from one hand. He stared down at Sal D'Amico, who stopped his frantic scramble and turned. They regarded one another.

Sal cleared his throat and forced a laughed. "Y-you got me good with that thing. You got lucky, y'know?"

The heavy gasping for breath had subsided. The figure stared down at Sal. "No," he whispered. "I did not. That is why I am here."

"You don't h-have to," Sal stuttered, regretting the whine that crept into his voice. "I have money. I can get you anything you want. Name it."

The attacker advanced. "You cannot."

Sal raised his good hand. "I'm telling you I can do anything you want! Get you anything. Just don't! You got a choice here!"

The man raised the hammer over his head and whispered, "No, I do not."

CHAPTER TWO

They pulled up to the curb, shut off the engine, and sat in the darkness listening to the wind whistle outside the warm confines of the car. The house was unassuming, if you didn't look too closely. Bordered on all sides by other houses, the yard buried beneath a soft blanket of snow. But the cul-de-sac was narrow, and it was impossible to approach without being seen, at least by car.

He watched the sides of the house carefully, looking for telltale glints of light or movement, but saw nothing. They sat in the cooling interior of the car, watching.

Finally he said, "All right. I'm gonna go."

"You be careful, Johnny."

He gave her a devilish smile. "Ah, babe, I'm always careful."

"Bullshit." She shook her red hair back from her brow. "You're usually an idiot."

"Okay," he agreed. "But I'm also careful."

She raised an eyebrow.

"And lucky. I'm an idiot, but I'm careful *and* lucky."

"You better be."

He leaned in and kissed her and she gave it right back. She smoothed his dark hair away from his cheek and touched it with her hand, cupping his face.

"You better be," she repeated.

He touched her hand and smiled, that crazy, devil-may-care smile she'd fallen for. "Easy-peasy. In and out."

Her beatific smile faded as he took the gun out of his pocket. It was too long, with a fat attachment to the barrel. He slid the clip from the handle and checked the bullets again. He snapped the clip back into the gun, racked the slide, and pushed the safety through.

"Five minutes, in and out," he repeated. "And it's easy street from here on. No more scraps. The big leagues."

She stared at the gun. "You're sure you-"

"We've been over this, babe. It's gotta be this way. This is my shot."

She nodded, eyes still downcast.

He lifted her chin and smiled at her. "Come on. You knew what I was when you married me."

"Yeah."

"You knew I was an Outfit guy. I'm always gonna be an Outfit guy."

"Yeah."

"You said you were in, no matter how bad it got."

"I did. I am. But-"

"But what?"

"I didn't think I'd have to... to watch."

"You don't have to. Just wait here until I get back. We'll get some food, and then we're gone, back to Chicago. You'll be home by tomorrow night. And not a minute too soon. This city is nuts."

A ghost of her smile appeared and vanished. "I like New York."

"Nothing makes sense here. It's too dirty and close."

She shrugged. "It's cozy."

"Naah. It's too close. I mean, look at these places." He gestured through the windshield. "They're on top of one another. Barely any lawn. It's crap. If you're gonna be apartments, be apartments. Don't pretend."

"Where we gonna eat?"

"I dunno. We'll find something. They say the pizza's good here. I mean, I don't buy it, but we can sample some if you want. It's a long drive, and we gotta go across the whole city anyhow." He pushed his hair back out of his face. "Think it over. I gotta go do this."

"You sure he's alone?"

"Sure as I can be. Our guys say he's down one bodyguard anyhow, and his other guy lives next door." He pointed at the smaller house on the right. "He should be all alone, tucked into bed. I go in, zap zap zap, I'm out in like five, and we're getting a pie to go in fifteen. Yeah?" he asked.

She nodded. "Okay."

"All right."

"Love you."

"Love you too, Shootin' Starr," he told her with a grin. He put a hand on the door and opened it. The chill night air cascaded into the car and she shivered. He didn't bother with the coat. He wore a dark button-down shirt, dark slacks, and his nice leather shoes. His hair whipped around in the wind as he closed the door and trotted across the street. He slid into the shadows around the side of the bigger house and she lost sight of him. She scrunched down, out of sight until just her eyes and hair were visible above the dash. She took a deep breath and started to count to herself. "One Mississippi, two Mississippi, three Mississippi, four..."

She closed her eyes and continued counting to herself, and soon the warmth of the car, the dark, and the mindless counting helped her drift into a light doze.

Some time later she lurched awake, heart thumping crazily in her chest, thinking she'd heard a-

A second shot rang out in the quiet night, unmistakable and echoing. Her hand clapped to her mouth. Gunshots. For a second she thought it was Johnny, but then she realized she shouldn't hear any of his shots. Johnny had the suppressor on his-

She saw him stagger out of the shadows into which he'd vanished, clutching his arm and grimacing. He slid across the snowy street and angled to her side of the car.

Heart pounding, she slid into the driver's seat and

started the engine. A third shot rang out and she saw snow kick up from the road near his feet. He clawed open the door and slumped in, yelling, "Go! Go!"

The engine roared as she turned it over and tromped on the gas. Johnny scrunched down in the passenger seat and slammed the door closed. She dropped the gearshift and they were fishtailing out of the narrow cul-de-sac. Another shot rang out and the rear window exploded in a shower of fragments. The windshield starred as the bullet passed through the cabin.

She screeched and swerved, almost lost control, and righted the car. A final shot missed the car completely as they rounded the corner and sped into the night.

Johnny craned up over the seat to see behind them.

"What happened?" she half-yelled. "You said it would be-"

"J-just drive, babe," he grunted, collapsing back into the seat with a hiss. "Just drive."

She frowned over at him as she eased up on the accelerator. Rule one: don't draw attention. She settled into traffic oozing onto the main road. Even this late, traffic in Queens was thick, people bustling to and fro over the bridge into Manhattan. She joined the line.

He took his hand off his arm and held it up. The blood was bright red, shining in the lights from outside the car.

"Jesus! Johnny, you're shot!"

"Yeah," he said. He grinned at her. "Just a wing. N-no big deal."

"We gotta get you to-"

"You know better," he grunted. "GSW. We need to curb that shit right now."

She nodded. Doctors, hospitals, they all reported gunshot wounds. Law. But there were ways around that. "So, a drug store?"

"Yeah. We need bandages, stuff for sutures. I'm gonna

keep leakin' if we don't do something," he said, teeth clenched.

"A-are you okay?" she asked, biting her lip. "I mean, you're not gonna die on me, are you?"

He grinned. "Hell no. This? Just a flesh wound."

The wind howled through the hole in the windshield and the gaping back window.

"We gotta get off the road," he said. "Cops'll bird-dog us with these holes. Good as a confession."

She nodded. "All we gotta do it make it out of the city, get over to Jersey. The junkyard-"

"Can't," Johnny said. "Can't leave yet."

"What?" she hooted. "We gotta get you outta town, Johnny. You know they're gonna come looking. You know who you just-"

"I know, Starr," Johnny said. He struggled upright, grunting with the pain of moving his arm. "But there was- it's complicated. We're not leaving yet."

She turned to stare at him. "Complicated?"

"I said I can't leave yet."

She fell silent.

After a moment of shock her business sense kicked in, and she worked the problem. "If we can't go home, and we can't stay on the road, we need to find a place to lay low. A place we can get you some help," she said. "We need a new car, and we have to regroup."

"Yeah," he said, wincing. He pressed harder, and realized that the bullet had passed through his arm. He had an entrance and an exit wound. "Shit. It went through. I'm gonna need a doctor. Maybe there's a vet's office or something around here. I got no contacts in this city. The Outfit doesn't keep anyone here."

"We need a new car, Johnny," she said again.

"Yeah, yeah. Let me think, will ya?" Abruzzi muttered. He pressed one hand to his forehead. His ears had started to ring, and the cold wasn't helping the ache along his side. "We need someplace with cars. Someplace not lit up. We need a place no one's gonna notice this piece of shit for a couple days."

He stared out the window as the wind whistled through the cabin of the Buick.

"What about a cab?" she asked.

"Can't wait around, can't leave this car just anywhere, and no cabbie's gonna pick up a bloody fare," he said.

"Right. Sorry."

"Don't be sorry. We need ideas."

She peered out of the windshield, looked around, and pointed. "What about there?" she asked.

The building she'd picked as a dingy, stand-alone brick building that had three or four cars parked in a lot alongside of it. He frowned. "What is that?"

"Porno theater," she said.

He raised an eyebrow. "Why?"

She grinned. "No one's gonna look hard at the car here. If it's anything like Chicago, they pay the cops not to hassle the customers. We can leave the car here a day or two 'til we have a better plan."

"Okay," he said, considering it. "But we still need another car."

"Got that covered too. We just need to wait for a guy who's married."

"What?"

"Someone'll come in or leave, and they'll have a wedding ring on. We take his car. What's he gonna do? Report it stolen from a porno theater?"

"Doubt it. Not bad, babe."

She pulled the car into the lot and took the last spot in the corner, far away from prying eyes. She said, "Gimme your gun."

He handed her the little automatic.

"Now we wait."

She kept the heater on full while they sat, and it kept them from freezing, but the wind through the holes in the glass bit deeply.

After almost an hour, headlights illuminated the interior as a car pulled into the lot. "Here's hoping he's an asshole," she said. "Be back in a minute."

He nodded. She slammed the door behind her and vanished into the swirling snow. He shivered violently. The man who got out was furtive-looking, casting glances all around him. Before he got to the building, Starr stepped out of the shadows. Abruzzi couldn't hear what she said, but the man tried to brush past her. She hit him in the head with the gun, and he fell over. She bent down and put the gun to his head, and he produced a set of keys. He got out of the car with a grunt of pain. He looked over and she was pressing the gun to his head harder, demanding something. After fumbling for a second, the guy produced a wallet. She took it, rifled through it, and took something out of it. She dropped the wallet on his chest and said something to him. The guy nodded frantically. She stood up, looked around, and trotted to the guy's car, a Pontiac with rust on the bumper. Abruzzi caught up with her as she started the car. He slid into the passenger seat with a groan. She handed him the gun. He set it on the floor.

"Good to go?"

"Better than good," she said. She started the Pontiac and cranked the heater. Johnny looked around. "Not bad," he said.

"It'll do." She pulled onto the road and put some distance between them and the theater.

"Did you have to rip him off?" Abruzzi asked.

"We needed the car," she said.

"No, the money you took. I've still got a couple hundred-"

Starr laughed. "I didn't take his *money*," she said. She fished in her blouse and took out a square of plastic. "I got his license."

Abruzzi frowned at it, and then grinned. "He *was* married."

"Indeed he was," she chuckled as she dropped the license on the seat.

"Good thinking, babe," Abruzzi said. They drove for a bit before she turned onto the main thoroughfare for Manhattan.

John took his hand away from his arm, winced, and pressed it back. "We need to do something fast, babe. This isn't getting any better."

She steered the car onto the Williamsburg Bridge. Her mind raced as they crossed over the East River into Manhattan. She followed the signs and turned north.

"W-where are you going?" Johnny asked.

"You need help, right? Well, I know a place. It's around here somewhere," Starr said. She read off the signs as the bridge merged into Delancey. She made a right onto Bowery and a left on Houston. Almost immediately she made another right, and he saw they had turned onto Elizabeth Street. It was a one-way street, one of those weird anachronisms left over from the merging of the past and the future. It had originally been an alley, he saw. The left side of the street was the backs of the buildings on the next block, but the right side held apartments and a few businesses. Starr slowed the car, killed the lights, and pulled up to the curb a short distance away from the one business front still lit up. It looked like some kind of office. Johnny saw movement inside.

"They must still be awake," Starr said. "Good."

"Where are we?" Johnny asked.

"It's... well. I've never been here, but it's a private detective. This is his office," she said.

"What the hell are we doing here?" Johnny demanded. He grabbed her arm. "I need help, not an almost-cop!"

She pulled her sleeve out of his grip. She bent down to look at his arm and when she touched the edges of the wound he jerked again. Blood from his shirt spattered her. She pulled back. "Trust me, babe. They're gonna help you here. Okay? Trust me."

He hesitated, but gave her a nod. He had started to shiver.

"I'll be back in a minute, okay?"

"I'll be here," he promised.

CHAPTER THREE

The phone rang. That wasn't unusual. Even this late, the phone would ring four or five times an hour. Not unusual at all. Sammy was a bail bondsman and kept odd hours.

The call wasn't for Sammy.

Sammy Evans handed the phone over to Bobby. Sammy went back to what he had been doing, which was the Times crossword. It had been a slow day. Sammy shifted his considerable bulk in the chair, which groaned in protest. He scribbled out the beginnings of 'consistent.' He scratched his head. "Ten letters…" he mused. "Steadfast. Fuckin… what the hell."

Bobby turned away with a grin on his face. He was tall and thin in a leather jacket zipped all the way up against the cool of the office. He covered the mouthpiece and said, "Dependable, Sammy."

Sammy stared at the crossword, the crease between his eyes deepening. "Doesn't start with a C, Bobby."

"And seven down doesn't *end* with a C, Sammy. You need to read more. 'Exercise your mind. It will get hungry just as your body does,'" Gold quoted.

As Sammy's face darkened as he scrubbed the second set of letters away, Bobby said into the phone, "Gold."

Sammy heard someone on the other end of the line saying something, but he was frowning down at the crossword again.

"Yeah. That's me," Gold said.

Sammy tapped the pencil on the paper, his eyes scrunching up as he thought.

"Say that again?" Gold asked into the handset.

Sammy pursed his lips. "Coffee," he said to himself.

"That's what I need."

"When?" Gold asked. His seamed, careworn face had faded, gone cheesy, whey colored. The fist gripping the phone closed tighter, the knuckles crackling.

Sammy heaved himself upright, stumbled across the half-walled office, and grabbed the pot from a hot plate He turned to fill his cup, but Bobby's voice stopped him.

"*How?*" he demanded of the voice on the other end of the line. "How did it-"

Sammy looked up at Bobby. The side of his face was all that Sammy could see, but it was enough. The milk-pale skin was bad enough, but as Sammy's eyes widened, the tears that spilled from the corner of the eye he could see coursed down Bobby's cheek.

"You're lying," Bobby whispered, his voice hoarse and clotted with disbelief. "You're lying."

Sammy stared at his friend, remembered the pot, and set it back on the hot plate. He waited, watching.

"That's doesn't make any sense," Bobby said, one hand running through his curly hair. Sammy saw the hand shaking. "That doesn't make any sense at all."

Bobby listened.

"Look, man, I'm telling you-"

Sammy saw the shoulders under the jacket slump, all the strength running from him, it seemed.

"O-ok," Bobby said. "Okay."

He stared at the floor as the voice said another something in his ear.

"Thanks. Thanks for calling."

Bobby let the handset fall to his side as he stared at the floor, through it, at nothing at all.

"Bobby?" Sammy asked. "Bobby, what the hell's the-"

Bobby looked up, wiped at his face with his free hand, and turned to Sammy. He handed him the handset and turned to go.

"Bobby, what's going on?"

"Nothing," Bobby mumbled. "I just- I need some air, you know?"

Bobby found his way to the door of the shabby office, yanked it open, and stumbled over the threshold into the late afternoon chill.

Sammy watched Bobby stuff his hands into the pockets of his jacket and start walking up the street out of sight. He stared at the hand set, put it back on the cradle. "What the hell was that about?"

CHAPTER FOUR

It was close to midnight, and she was thinking about locking up when the bell over the door chimed. Sandy looked up from her book. Her perpetual smile widened. She sat up straighter on the stool and said, "Well, well, well. Mr. Bobby Gold. How the hell are *you*?"

Bobby stared at her. The smile faded a little as she saw his eyes. They were... empty.

And then some semblance of light came into them, and he seemed to animate, all at once, with a slight shiver. He smiled at her, a sunny, bright smile that didn't quite reach his eyes. "Sandy. Sandy... Redmay, right?"

Sandy's cherubic face brightened. "You got it in one. What can I do you for, Bobby Gold?"

Bobby looked around. A glimpse of his usual sardonic half-smile perked up one corner of his mouth. He gestured at the store. "I was in the market for a good book."

Sandy put one hand on her hip. "Sorry, babe. This's a liquor store."

"Well, then, I'll have to do the other thing. 'I am only myself when I am drunk. Liquor makes me human.'"

Sandy game him a puzzled frown. "Huh?"

"Gilbert Parker. Doesn't matter." Bobby drifted down the main aisle. He stared at the bottles without seeing. His hands cast out almost of their own will, snagging two bottles of whiskey, one of Jack Daniel's, and one of Cutty Sark. He looked longingly at the rows of liquor, but turned his back and walked to the counter. He set the bottles down.

Sandy whistled. "Party?"

"Naah," Bobby said. He jammed a hand in his front pocket and hauled out a roll of bills. "Nighttime. What do I owe you, Sandy?"

She rang him up. "Call it eighteen." She stashed the bottles in a paper bag for him.

He nodded and gave her four fives. "Keep it."

She frowned. "Why?"

"Beats me. A tip?"

She raised her eyebrows. "Uh huh." She studied him. "You okay, Bobby?"

"No," He told her. He picked up the bag. "I guess I'm not."

"Wanna talk about it?" she asked. "You're free to hang here. I'm closing up in a bit, but we got a back room."

The ghost of a grateful smile crossed his lips. "I appreciate it, Sandy. I figure I'll just go bug Toni. She's a good drinker."

Sandy pursed her lips. "Uh... you remember Harry's back, right?"

"Crud. Right. The big hero."

Sandy said, somewhat archly, "What's *that* supposed to mean?"

"Sorry. I didn't mean it bitchy. Just she talked him up pretty big. In my experience, people tend to underwhelm their legend."

Sandy threw her head back and laughed gaily. Bobby smiled at her, bemused. "What's funny?"

Grinning, she said, "Honey, you have no idea who you're talking about. Harry'd be the first guy to tell you you're right. That he's nothing special."

"Maybe he's right."

"You're an idiot if you think so, Bobby Gold. Look..." Sandy considered. "You think Toni's a good girl, right?"

Bobby nodded. "Best I've ever met."

Sandy hesitated, squinted at him, and asked, "You sure you're not sweet on her, are you?"

"No," he said. "She's a good friend. I don't got many

of those left."

She nodded, clouds clearing from her face. "Okay, good. Because you'd be stupid to try it."

"Yeah, I know."

"It ain't Harry you'd have to worry about-"

Bobby grinned. "No, I wasn't talking about Harry. I've never met him. I meant *her*."

"Got it in one guess," Sandy said. "She'd rip you apart."

"Don't I know it," Bobby muttered. His bruises had faded from their encounter with Terry Shoulders, a living mountain of a man he, Toni, and their associate Keen had gone after. In Bobby's opinion, the bounty hadn't been worth the hurt. But what Toni did to a guy that outweighed her by at least a hundred, maybe a hundred fifty pounds had proved what he already believed: that she wasn't anyone to trifle with.

"And she's more than just a good fighter. She's one of the best people I know."

"Yeah, she is." Bobby had been living on her floor for a couple days before the Terry Shoulders incident because he had nowhere to go. And Toni, having known him for a couple of days, hadn't hesitated to offer him that floor. She'd acted like it wasn't just an option, but the *only* option.

"Well, she thinks she's not good enough for Harry."

"That's stupid. 'Reason is the first victim of strong emotion.'"

Sandy waited.

Bobby muttered, "Herbert. Doesn't matter."

"Uh huh. Well, that's how she feels, stupid or not. That's how good Harry is. He makes everyone around him better. And he has no idea he's doing anything other than just being himself. But that's the thing, Bobby. Harry being himself?" Sandy shrugged. "It's effortless. He's just… he's just that kind of guy. The last of the stand-up guys."

Bobby raised an eyebrow. "You make out like he's some kind of a saint."

Sandy bristled. "Listen up, Bobby, because you need to know this. There's a thousand people in this city that would die for Harry. FBI guys hang on his every word. Detectives ready to do whatever he asks. Us ordinary people are the same way. Me, Mikey, Keen… hell, there's *bums* in this town that would go to the mattresses for him. Pimps, hookers, Mob guys. He's *that* kind of guy. This is a guy who killed three people because they were hurting women. A guy who went to jail for a murder he didn't do just because it was the right thing to do. He almost gave up his whole life just *because*. They were gonna throw the scene, Bobby. Did you know that? His cop friends. They would have let him walk. Because he's *Harry*. They didn't just ask, Bobby, they *tried* to get him to let them throw it. Tried to get him to just walk away. And he refused. Because he's Harry. He had us, and Toni, and everything he could want, and he wouldn't take it except on the right terms. I never met *anybody* so good. So don't you tell *me* about Harry DeMarko. You haven't seen anything. I *promise* you that."

Sandy's volume had risen a little, and her normally cherubic face darkened.

"All right, all right," Bobby said. "Peace. I'm not knocking the guy. I just wanted to have a drink with my friend, that's all."

Sandy took a deep breath and let it out. "Yeah, well."

"I'll just find somewhere else to crash out," Bobby said. He shuffled the bottles to one arm and reached into his pocket. He came up with a couple of subway tokens. "Maybe I'll go for a ride."

Sandy's irritation dissolved. "You got nowhere to go?"

Bobby shrugged one shoulder, uncomfortable about his situation, at least to this woman. "I got places. I'm gonna go get drunk. Maybe I'll stop by there. I just... I just wanted to have a drink with her. Maybe talk about some stuff. But with Harry there..."

Sandy studied his face closely, and seemed to find what she was looking for. She said gently, "Go on, Bobby. Go see her."

"Naah." Bobby stared at the floor. "She's got her hands full. Harry-"

"You go on now, Bobby," she repeated. "It doesn't matter Harry's there. See if I'm not right. Besides, you'll understand when you meet him."

"What, is he some kind of mystical guru, gonna have me staring into my navel and chanting?"

Sandy glowered. "That's my friend you're shitting on, Gold."

He held up a hand. "I'm not, I swear. Just... he's that nice a guy?"

"Actually, he can be a prick," Sandy said. "But he's *good*. Just... he's good. That's all."

"And he loves her?" Bobby asked.

"Man, you *wish* you had someone love you the way they love each other," Sandy said.

The color drained from Bobby's seamed, careworn face. He clutched the bottles tightly. "Yeah, well."

Sandy saw something in his face she couldn't name. It was... he was devastated. She could see the pain in his eyes.

"Bobby, you don't-" she said, rushing her words out. "It's not that you're not a nice guy. It's just Toni and Harry are-"

"Yeah." He knew what she was thinking and didn't bother to explain. "Look, thanks for the booze. I'll see you, Sandy."

He kicked open the door. She bit her lip. "Bobby!"

He looked back at her as the door closed.

"Go see them," she called. "Just go see them."

He gave her that half-shrug again, and the ghost of his smile. His eyes glittered in the store lights as the white flakes of snow swirled around him. She watched him reach into the bag and take out the Cutty. He awkwardly spun the cap off and took a swig. Then another. And a third. Sandy frowned, got up off the stool, and started for the door, but he capped the bottle and dropped it into the bag. He seemed to consider his options, and without a backward glance into the store or at her, started to walk. She almost called him back, but he turned right, and she breathed a sigh of relief, because she knew he was headed to Elizabeth Street.

CHAPTER FIVE

Saturday 12:10 a.m.

The fist on his door brought Hendrick out of a sound sleep. He was up instantly, heaving his huge frame upright before his eyes were even open. He grabbed the automatic off the nightstand without looking and stalked into the front room of his tiny apartment. Outside the windows, the streetlights seemed to flicker with whirling snow.

He thumbed off the safety as he approached the door. He didn't stand in front of it, didn't put his eye to the peephole.

"Yeah?" he called.

"Bruno, man, it's me," a familiar voice said through the door. "Open up."

Hendrick frowned. He knew the voice, but-

"What're you doing here?"

"Come on, man, this is a emergency! Open the friggin door, man," the voice called, and a fist thumped against the wood again.

Hendrick considered. He reached up, shot the chain, the deadbolt, and the flimsy handle lock and opened the door, stepping back. It swung wide, and Hendrick brought the gun up.

The man who stepped in and slammed the door was almost as tall as Hendrick, but his skin was the complete opposite of his. Where Hendrick was Irish-white, pale and pallid, the other man's skin was smoothly dark, a rich shade of brown. His head was shaved bald, and his heavy coat couldn't hide his muscled build.

"Fuck you doin' here, Cheddar?" Hendrick groused

"It's late."

Darius 'Cheddar' Cheeseborough shrugged and said, "I tried your number, but-"

"I took it off the hook," Hendrick said, eyes narrow and suspicious. "I didn't wanna be disturbed. I had a late night last night."

"Yeah, well," Cheddar's silky voice was full of none of his usual charm and rhythm. "You shouldn't have. Been trying to get ahold of you since nine."

"Why?" Hendrick slipped the safety on the automatic, but he didn't put it down. Cheddar had never come to his apartment. He didn't even know that Cheddar knew where he flopped. Something wasn't right. Cheddar's downcast face sent an alarm through him. "You better start talkin', Cheddar."

"I came by for Bill."

"Higgins? What's he want?" Hendrick asked.

"Same thing I want. Same reason you shouldn't have unplugged your phone, man," Cheddar breathed. "It's Sal."

Hendrick had Cheddar by the throat, the gun pressed against his chest. "Watch what you say, Cheddar," Hendrick breathed. "One wrong thing, man. You know Sal's my uncle."

Cheddar's eyes were wide, the whites bloodshot and a little yellow. He grunted, nodded, and said in a curiously gentle voice, "That's why we've been trying to get in touch with you. You deserved to know as soon as you-"

"Know what?" Hendrick growled, pulling Cheddar's face close. Hendrick's breath was redolent of whiskey and sleep. Cheddar tried to breathe shallowly.

"What happened to Sal."

Hendrick shuddered as though shocked by an open electrical line. His grip faltered. "What-"

"Someone got to him, Bru," Cheddar said. His eyes held sympathy and fear. If he wanted, Cheddar had no doubt Hendrick could tie him in a knot.

Cheddar's feet touched the floor as Hendrick's grip loosened. "What do you- what're you talking about? I just left him a couple hours ago. Sal's... he..."

The look in Cheddar's eyes told him.

To Cheddar's surprise, Hendrick's eyes watered, tears gathering along the bottom of each lower lid. He looked away.

"What- what happened?" Hendrick choked out, his throat tight and hot. "Was it the-"

"No idea," Cheddar said. He was waiting for Hendrick to put a fist through him. "I don't know anything other than he's... you know... gone. I got a call from-"

Hendrick was already moving. He shucked out of his undershirt and rummaged for a clean one. Cheddar watched as Hendrick dropped his trousers and changed. He put on all dark clothing, jeans and a dark button-down. He gave Cheddar a sidelong glance, opened a drawer in the closet, and took out a set of leather straps. A shoulder harness. He shrugged into the harness and picked up the gun again. He jammed it into the holster and got his sport coat on.

Cheddar swallowed. "Well, I mean... that's all I came for. I'm gonna-"

The gun was in Hendrick's fist again, and a huge thumb pulled the hammer back. Cheddar stared at the gun.

"What's it to you, Cheddar?" Hendrick asked, his voice deadly quiet in the small room.

"Uh..."

Hendrick raised the gun and pointed it at Cheddar. "Asked you a question, asshole."

Cheddar raised his hands, staring at the muzzle of the gun, and the dark, dark hole from which his end could come before he could flinch. "Hendrick, man, what-"

"I *said*," Hendrick growled, "what's it to you? You

ain't family. You ain't Gambino. You're a nothing pimp. Just another whoremaster *nigger*. What's-"

Cheddar's head snapped up and his eyes blazed. "Fuck you, Bruno! You know goddamned well Sal was my man! Gave me a good job, promoted me- trusted me to run his strings right!" He bared his teeth. "He gave me responsibility, gave me a place. He didn't care I wasn't Italian, didn't care I wasn't *white*, man. And Goombah or no, Sal *never* called me 'nigger'! I'd have taken a bullet for that man, and you fucking know it, you Wop fucker! I ought to-"

Hendrick lowered the gun and holstered it. "All right, all right. Relax, Ched. I'm sorry. You know I don't give a shit about what color you are. Me'n you's tight. But you know what they say: whoever comes to you with the news is the one who made it."

Cheddar's breath was coming fast, his chest heaving. He rolled his shoulders and cracked his neck. "Man, I oughta fuck you up for that shit."

Hendrick chuckled then. "You're welcome to try. But save it. I wanna find out what happened. I wanna find out who got Sal. And when I do, I'm gonna find 'em. And you'n me?" Hendrick gave Cheddar a chilling smile. "We're gonna make sure they know how we feel."

Cheddar nodded to himself. "Yeah. I owe him at least that much. Maybe more. Come on, I left my car running. Uh, Hendrick?"

Hendrick stopped tying his shoes and looked up. "What?"

"I... I hate to have to ask, but... with Sal gone, I'm out a job. Lotta money. You... uh..." Cheddar shrugged. "I'll help you no matter what. Sal was my friend. But after-"

Hendrick nodded. "We'll talk about after *after*. I don't got a lot of pull, but I'll do what I can."

Cheddar smiled. "Thanks, man. Let's go get this son of

a bitch."

Hendrick clapped him on the shoulder and opened the apartment door. Taking a last look around, he snarled and slammed it behind them.

CHAPTER SIX

The house was lit up like a Christmas tree. Every light in the place was on and all the shades were drawn. It looked almost festive, like a house party.

Hendrick and Cheddar stumped through the snow to the front door. Hendrick hammered on it with a fist. Their breaths plumed in the frigid air. The shade pulled back from the window, and a pair of piggy eyes peered out. Spotting Hendrick, the shade fell back and the door opened. Sal's bodyguard, Bill Higgins, opened the door. He was wary, and he had his gun in his hand, Cheddar saw.

Better get used to this, he told himself. *These fuckers are gonna go to war. Unless Sally was dirty. If it was the Gs then it's gonna all blow away. But if it* wasn't, *they're going to burn down the city.*

"Hendrick," Higgins said by way of a greeting. Higgins's face was drawn and he looked haunted. He stood aside and let the men into the house. Sal's front room was nicely-appointed, with a sitting area to the left and a poker table to the right. Higgins closed the door and led them into the kitchen. The lights were on and there was coffee. Milk had dried on the wall and floor and there were shards of glass scattered everywhere. Hendrick looked around.

"Bill, where's Sal?"

Higgins picked up a cup, drained the coffee, and set it down. "Hen, listen." His voice was shaky. "It's… I wanted to warn you, like. It's-"

"Where is Sal?" Hendrick demanded. "I'm not playing with you, Bill. Is he upstairs? In the tub? What?"

Cheddar had scooted into the corner of the kitchen, leaning against the counter. He crossed his arms and kept his head down. He wanted no one to use him as a scratching post.

"He's in the... well, it would have been a pretty nice game room." He gestured vaguely to his right. "He's... it's bad, man."

Hendrick strode across the kitchen. "I seen worse than you can imagine."

"Yeah, well, I have too, now." Higgins muttered at Hendrick's back Cheddar didn't want to follow, but he did. He owed it to Sal. He couldn't help, but he could bear witness. He followed after Hendrick, through the hall, and into the bare-stud room under construction. In the center of the floor lay a twisted, narrow body under a bloody sheet. Hendrick stood over the body, his fists clenched.

Cheddar approached, but Hendrick said, "Stop."

Cheddar froze, seven or eight feet away from the fallen man. "What's up, Hen? I'm not scared of blood."

"Not that," Hendrick said. "Clues or whatever."

"Oh," Cheddar breathed. He nodded. "That's... yeah. The cops are gonna-"

Hendrick glared over his shoulder at Cheddar. "Cops? You fucking kidding me?"

"You ain't gonna call the cops?" Cheddar asked.

"Maybe. Eventually. But I want a head-start on 'em. I wanna know who did this. First thing cops'll do is arrest us all."

Higgins joined them, not coming into the room, just standing in the doorway. "What's the score, Hen?" he asked. "What do we do first?"

Hendrick looked around. "You see anyone?"

Higgins nodded. "Yeah. I came across cause I heard some shouting."

Cheddar frowned at him, and Higgins explained, "I live next door."

"What'd the guy look like?" Hendrick was still staring at the body.

"Couldn't say. It was dark. I caught up with him outside, between the houses. I took a couple shots at him. Hit him at least once," Higgins said. "Arm, I think. He jumped in a car and they took off. I put some holes in the car. Windows. But if they're smart, that car's already on fire somewhere."

Hendrick nodded. "What'd it feel like to you?"

Higgins said nothing for a while. Then he said, almost apologetically, "Amateur hour. This didn't feel like a pro. They chased him through the house, man. I think they startled Sal in the kitchen. The milk. Sal had that stomach thing, you know. Always bothered him at night. He drank almost a gallon of milk a day."

"Yeah, I know. It runs in the family."

"Anyhow, they scrapped in here. You can see there's, like, scratches and stuff on the floor. Sal gave 'em a run." Higgins stuffed his hands in his pockets.

"Why didn't he just shoot Sal?" Cheddar asked. "In the kitchen?"

Hendrick shrugged. "I'd say it was a message. This kind of hit usually is, except it doesn't make *sense*. It's amateur hour. No backup, Sal got the drop on him with a bottle of milk of all things... they fought here..." Hendrick scanned the area. "I think they must have fought some more. Maybe our doer dropped his piece. Bill, you look around?"

"Yeah, Bruno. I didn't see anything. There's no gun."

Hendrick glowered at the disarray of the scene. "Bill, walk me through it. What happened?"

"I came through the kitchen-"

"No," Hendrick snapped. "Start at the beginning. You were home, right? Start there. Go slow. I'm gonna ask questions."

Higgins frowned, but nodded. "Okay. I was watching the news. My porch... I can see into the kitchen from there. I saw the fridge open. Sal was drinking milk outta the bottle. He's been having that stomach thing lately, you remember. Anyhow, I was about to go to bed when I saw someone else. They-"

"What'd they look like?" Hendrick asked.

"I dunno, Hen. Tall. Thin. Didn't get a good look. At first I wondered if Sally was taking a late meeting. But then he threw his milk bottle. That's when I saw the guy had a gun. So I jumped up and ran for my piece."

"You don't wear it?" Hendrick asked. "You're Sal's bodyguard."

"And when I'm with Sal I'm covered every second. I got kids at home, Hen," Higgins reminded the larger man.

"Still, though. With Terry Shoulders in the joint, you shoulda been better-prepared," Hendrick scolded.

"Woulda coulda. You can't think of everything. Anyhow, I ran for my piece. It's upstairs in my safe. I hadda grab that. I ran for Sal's. I saw the guy chasing Sal through the porch. I ran to the kitchen door. I heard…" Higgins hesitated. Hendrick raised an eyebrow.

Higgins blushed. "I heard screaming. Like, agony. But no gunshots." He gestured to the limp form of Sal D'Amico stretched out on the floor. "I guess that's why. I came in here as the guy was running for the front door. I shouted and chased him, and he doubled back through the back. I ran after and got off a shot. I'm pretty sure I tagged him in the arm. He got around the front and ran into the street. I shot at him a couple more times. He jumped into a car, driver was waiting, and they took off. I put one through the back window, but they were gone. Didn't see the plate. And I came back in. Nothing else to do. I covered up Sal, called you, didn't get you, called Cheddar at the bar, and told him to go after you. And I waited for you."

Hendrick nodded. "You chased him, you shot him."

"Yeah. At least one hit."

"Describe him."

"Like I said, tall, thin. Wait… long hair. Like shoulders or so. Black. Musta worn a hat, because I didn't see that in the kitchen. Dark jacket. Dark pants. Came dressed for it. I didn't see his face. Oh, gloves, I think."

"You think?"

"Yeah," Higgins said. "Like, those skinny leather driving gloves. They were tight, not bulky."

"You saw his hands clear, but not his face?" Cheddar asked, from across the room.

Hendrick frowned at Cheddar, and looked at Higgins. "Yeah. Good point. How's that work?"

Higgins shrugged. "I didn't see his face, Hen. I told you: he had long hair. But when I was running after him, I saw his hands. The streetlights. You know."

Hendrick nodded. "Okay. Bill, lemme see your piece, would you?"

Higgins nodded and took out his handgun. He reversed it and handed it to Hendrick. Hendrick examined it. "Sal let you use an automatic?"

"He gave me shit about it, sure, but it's a good piece," Higgins said. "The 1911's good enough for the Army, it's good enough for me."

"Sal hated autos." Hendrick slid the clip. He counted. "You got off four shots?"

"Five," Higgins said. "One in the pipe."

Hendrick nodded. He slid the clip home and racked the slide. Raising the gun, he sighted at Higgins over the barrel. "Tell me the truth, Bill."

Higgins' eyes popped. Cheddar glanced from Hendrick to Higgins and back, but said nothing.

"What the fuck, Hen? You nuts?"

"Tell me the truth," Hendrick growled, and he thumbed back the hammer.

Higgins raised his hands. "Hen, what-"

"Who paid you to sell out Sal, huh?" Hendrick's voice was devoid of emotion, the implacable voice of a man who had resigned himself to a course of action. All that was left were details.

"Hen- Bruno- I swear, I wouldn't do that!" Higgins' eyes focused on the barrel of his own gun.

Cheddar stared at Higgins, anger boiling over. "You lousy some of a bitch," he ground out. "Sal was a good guy. Honest, fair. He never forgot his friends. What the fuck did you do?"

Higgins' eyes flicked from the gun to Cheddar and back. "That ain't what happened. I'd have died for Sal. I didn't- I swear on my kids' lives, Hen. I didn't do nothing!"

Hendrick's finger tightened on the trigger. Higgins watched aghast as the knuckles whitened. "Last chance, Billy."

Unable to speak, Higgins stared, transfixed, as the trigger twitched.

"Come on, Bill," Hendrick whispered. "'Fess up and I'll let you live. For your kids."

Higgins' eyes never left the barrel of the gun. "Hen, *please*. I swear! I swear! I didn't do anything! I didn't!"

"That was your last chance." Hendrick closed his left eye, aimed at the bridge of Higgins' nose, and finished pulling the trigger.

The snap of the hammer seemed loud. Cheddar's eyes flicked down to Higgins's pants. A dark circle of urine began to spread. Hendrick snickered. He tossed the gun to Higgins. The startled man fumbled the handgun, dropped it, and flinched away, fearful. The gun failed to fire.

Hendrick put a hand in his pocket and fished out a handful of loose bullets. He walked across the room and grabbed Higgins' left hand, dropping the remaining four bullets into it.

"I believe you, Bill. Sorry. Had to ask." Hendrick pushed past Higgins and went back into the kitchen.

Cheddar gave Bill Higgins an apologetic smile. "Man's thorough. I wouldn't have thought of that." He passed Higgins, trailing after Hendrick, who had gone to the fridge to get a beer. In the kitchen Cheddar and Hendrick shared a beer. Passing the bottle back and forth, Cheddar asked, "What's the play, boss?"

"I'm not sure. We gotta keep this to ourselves for now."

Higgins entered the kitchen, still prickly after Hendrick's interrogation.

"You hear me?" Hendrick asked him. "You keep your mouth shut."

Bill Higgins frowned. "What'll we do with him?"

Hendrick shrugged. "Keep him covered up. We can't keep him forever. We got maybe two days before it gets bad. But before that, we need to be out on the street, listening. Whoever it was you clipped, they're gonna have to get some help. That means a doctor or a nurse, or someone like that. And that means people are gonna know. People talk. They always do. Someone's gonna talk. And when they do, we'll know. We need to know who this mutt was. If it was business, we'll know fast. If it was personal… well… that might be harder. If it was a grudge or something, chances are still likely that it's someone in the rackets. Your average citizen doesn't usually have it in 'em to go at someone with a hammer. Someone somewhere wanted Sal dead. This ain't random. It wasn't a drive-by. But it's not a pro either. It wasn't professional, like. This was real messy. Personal. We need a cop or something. Someone who knows how to find someone who'd do this."

Hendrick squeezed the bottle of beer until Cheddar

feared it would shatter. Higgins asked, "We're going to the cops after all?"

Cheddar and Hendrick both glared at him. "Don't be stupid. Of course we're not going to the cops." Hendrick snarled.

"But you said-"

Cheddar overrode the man's protest. "He didn't mean a *cop* cop. He meant someone who thinks like them. Who knows how to do what they do. Someone with access to-"

Cheddar broke off and turned his head to Hendrick. Their eyes locked. They shared the thought without speaking, and Hendrick nodded. "Yeah. I was just thinking that myself."

Cheddar said, "I'll go."

"No. I'll do it. I don't have any time to waste. They need to take it serious." Cheddar bristled but didn't argue. Hendrick said to Higgins, "Where's Sal keep his mad money?"

Higgins frowned. "I can't just-"

Hendrick snapped, "I ain't got cash. I'm gonna need grease. Where's his kick-around?"

Higgins pointed at the cupboard. "In the cookie jar."

Hendrick snorted and fetched down the wide-mouthed jar. He dumped the chocolate chip cookies out of the ceramic urn and a plastic bag tumbled out after. Hendrick set the jar down and took it up. He removed the roll of hundreds from the bag and stuffed it into his front pocket "What's Sal's schedule like the next couple of days?"

Higgins frowned in concentration. "Uh… nothing tomorrow," he said. "Today, rather. Day after tomorrow he's got a meeting at the club. With Ducks."

Hendrick considered that. "Nothing else?"

"No."

"All right. You stay here. Don't touch anything in that room unless you wanna go down for it. We got maybe three days before he's missed. Cops are gonna come, but we'll clean the place out first. Cheddar, you're on the street. Go find me something. I wanna hear all the scat. Anything, no matter how small. Get your girls out there. Any of your guys. We gotta use everything we got."

Cheddar said, "I'm on it."

"Hen, you're gonna leave me here?" Higgins said. "With, like, a fucking rotting body?"

Hendrick crossed the floor with deliberation, and Higgins's eyes widened as he got closer. Hendrick put a finger on the smaller man's chest. Cheddar saw the wince on Higgins's face, and the man fell back a step from the pressure. "You're gonna stay fucking put. You're gonna start cleaning the upstairs. Wipe down everything. Do it good. You answer the phone if it rings. Anyone asks, Sal's in the shower. Or on the shitter. Or taking a nap. You don't give anything out you don't have to, and you ask everything you can. You understand me?"

Higgins nodded. "I gotta run home and-"

"You leave this house and I'll bury you next to Sal," Hendrick ordered. "I don't give a shit if your place is on fire and your kids are screaming out the windows, hear?"

Hendrick grabbed Bill Higgins around the throat and dragged his face close enough that their noses touched. His voice became a ragged, torn growl as he snarled, "You don't leave my Uncle Sal alone. He isn't gonna be left like some cat in the street. He ain't a body. He ain't a nobody. You treat him with respect or I'll gut you and leave you dead beside him. Hear?"

Higgins nodded. "Yes, Hen. I won't leave. Can... Can I call Cheryl? Let her know where-"

"You don't call out. They'll have records."

"Hen, I've called over to my place hundreds of times-"

Cheddar gave Higgins a withering stare. "Not when there's a body they need to find out when they died. Jesus.

You stupid? If the owner of the place is dead and they got a phone call going out, who the fuck do you think they're gonna believe made it? The body?"

Hendrick thought about it. "But they can't record the calls…can they?"

"No, you dumb fuck," Hendrick snapped. "But they'll sure as hell stop by your place when they find out that's where the call went."

"Hen… I live next door. And the cops already know I work for Sal."

Cheddar stared at Higgins with horror. "God… you *are* retarded. Even if they know it all, you still play dumb. Or in your case, act natural."

Higgins sneered at Cheddar. "Who the fuck you talking to, boy? You keep your pimp mouth shut and-"

Hendrick pinched the bridge of his nose with two fingers. Without looking up he said, "Bill, I'm a second away from killing you just to shut you up. Cheddar's got brains. You're just muscle."

"I'm smarter than this piece of-"

"If that was true you'd know when you was talking out your ass." Hendrick's patience snapped and he slapped the man across the face. It was a hard enough blow that Higgins staggered. "And don't you talk to my friend like that. His head's in the game. You're wasting our time. Do what I told you. Get a fucking apron on and go clean. And it better be perfect. You don't leave a single thing that'll help the cops out. But remember: don't go near Sal or that room. Not until I tell you."

Higgins sullenly nodded, eyes downcast. His cheek was already red and hot. He rubbed one hand along it. "I got it, Hen. Sorry."

"Just do what I tell you and nothing else. I'll be back. Come on, Cheddar. We got shit to do."

He left the kitchen, headed for the front door. Cheddar

gave Higgins a middle finger and a grin before following after.

On the street, Hendrick slid behind the wheel of the car. Cheddar passed over the key without a word. Hendrick threw the car into gear and they headed back into the city. Across the bridge, Hendrick headed north to the poolhall Cheddar used as an office. "I'mma keep the car," Hendrick said. It didn't sound like a request. "I don't have time to dick around."

Cheddar shrugged. "Ain't mine. The paper's in the glove box. I got a guy works the long-term lot at JFK. He gets me rides whenever I need. You need to burn it, burn it. What's John Citizen gonna do? Complain his car got boosted?"

Hendrick smiled. "Smart. Sal trusted you and he wasn't wrong. You ever do anything heavy for him?"

Cheddar knew what he meant. "Middle-weight stuff sometimes, if he was strapped for people, or he needed a face no one would recognize. Couple beatings, some collection. I was a temp, like."

"Ever get wet?"

"Not yet," Cheddar said. "But I'm all in on the idea now."

Hendrick liked that answer. "Good man. Look, we worry about today today. We'll worry about tomorrow when we got today sorted. Stick with me, don't pussy out, and I'll put you under my wing much as I can. I'll take care of you. Maybe not as cushy as Sal, but-"

"Hen, I said I was all in. Let's find the bastard. Worry about details later, like you said." Cheddar told him, almost shyly, "Sal was a good man. I want this as much as you."

Hendrick put out a fist and Cheddar bumped it with his own.

"I'm outta here," Cheddar said. "Let me work for a

couple hours and then check in. Say around noon. That should be long enough to put out feelers."

"Be careful," Hendrick warned. "Don't give it away."

"You kidding? I'll feed 'em the usual bullshit. Someone's looking to shake the tree and the boss wants to know all. Business as usual. Done it before. It won't look strange."

Hendrick nodded. "I know you know your shit. But we get one chance. Once it's out it's out. We'll have the Family, hell, maybe all the Families. The cops definitely. And the Feds, too. It's gonna be a three-ring. I want this guy before they even know Sal's gone. They go looking, I want 'em to find *nothing*. Sal would want it that way, even if we don't."

Cheddar smiled. "The man loved fucking with the Feds."

"Yeah, he did," Hendrick said. "Hey… I tell you they're still watching the Aces?"

"The Feds?" Cheddar cocked his head. "What for?"

"No idea. When Sal moved up, he made the place legit. But he let me and a couple guys hang out there, looking suspicious, carrying packages. You know the drill. They put a van down the street. Been there for a couple weeks, gathering snow, looking abandoned."

Cheddar's eyebrows climbed. "They're stupid enough to leave a spook truck in the same spot for weeks?"

"Not that stupid. They had it booted. Covered the windshield with tickets. It's clever. Took us a while to spot it. Now whenever we go outside near it, we cover our mouths and talk about baseball."

Cheddar snorted laughter. "You gotta be driving those dinks *nuts*."

Hendrick chuckled. "Sal said string 'em along, we're stringing them along."

"Man was mean, that's for sure," Cheddar said. "That's

just mean."

Hendrick nodded, seemed to remember something, and his grin faded. "Get on it, Cheddar."

"Keep the faith, brother," Cheddar said. He climbed out of the car. Before he closed the door, he said, "The guy even on the street yet? He's been gone, what, three-four months?"

"Yeah, he's back. Sal was keeping an eye on him. That beef they threw at him didn't stick. He got back a week ago. He's back with that little whore you used to run."

Cheddar nodded, then said, "Word of warning, Hen: that chick's got skills. And I don't mean on her back. She's as hard as *he* is. Watch it around her. She's really mouthy. She'll find your buttons and hammer on 'em. You're gonna wanna punch her mouth, but it's a trick. Puts people off their guard. I think she likes to push people. Angry people spill more."

"Ain't it the truth. I know what happened to Terry Shoulders. And you know… Sal told me almost the same thing. He liked her, I think. Thought she had more balls than a lot of street guys we know."

"More'n Higgins, that's for sure."

"After this is over, I think old Bill's going away." Hendrick's voice was cold as stone. "Even if he was smart, it still happened on his watch. I don't forget that, and I won't forgive it."

Cheddar said, "I'll help with that, too. Say the word."

Hendrick gave him a long, silent, appraising look. He gave Cheddar a minute, tight smile. "Jump on it. I'm gonna go see the Detective."

Cheddar gave him a thumbs-up and slammed the door. Hendrick put the car in gear and headed west. Cheddar watched him drive away. He shivered in the chilled morning air. "I'd love to be there when *that* conversation happens."

Then he turned toward the pool hall and went to work.

CHAPTER SEVEN

He tugged off his shoes and set them by the door of his apartment. He stripped out of his clothes as he walked into his small bedroom. By the door was a hamper he dropped his shirt, pants, boxers, and socks into it. A second hamper by the closet held his everyday clothes, but the one by his bed held his work clothes, and never the two did meet. He wouldn't even wash them in the same machine. His landlord thought he was nuts for having two washers and two dryers, but he didn't know what Gene knew.

Eugene Kaminski was a careful man. He kept himself as clean as possible, but he also took no chances. He spent all day up to his elbows in dead people and refused to entertain the possibility of contaminating himself or his wardrobe. He padded naked into the bathroom and took a quick shower, hot as he could stand, and scrubbed himself with the heavy bar of caustic soap. He washed his curly brown hair three times, rinsed, and got out. He took a new towel off the rack and dried himself.

As he left the bathroom and went into the bedroom, he pressed play on his answering machine. The tape rewound, it clicked, and he heard the familiar voice. He sighed as he dressed.

"Eugene, it's your mother. I'm calling again because you apparently forgot how to dial my number. It's perfectly okay, of course. God knows I don't deserve a call after how I treated you. My terrible life, working two jobs to put you through school, making sure you had enough food, plenty of money for books. I understand I neglected you by always being at work, but it would be nice if you would occasionally call so I'll know you're not dead in a ditch somewhere."

Gene sighed again as he pulled on a pair of sweatpants.

"It's no big deal, of course, but it would be nice to know you're still alive. Oh, and I'm going to have dinner Sunday for you and a nice girl I met from synagogue. Her parents are accountants for the supermarket across the way, and their daughter is a checker there. She's very excited to meet you. Call me back, Eugene. Love you, even if you don't love me back. See you Sunday. Oh, and bring some cannoli like you brought last week. You know the ones I mean."

Click.

Gene pulled his NYU sweatshirt on and shuffled into the kitchen. His stomach was growling but he didn't have anything good in the house. He set the coffee pot to boil and scanned the list of takeout menus on the fridge. He found one he liked and called.

Forty minutes later he settled in front of the TV with a cold beer and four boxes of noodles, Kung Pao chicken, rice, and veggies, happily into the first act of a Bond film.

The ringing phone woke him. He blinked and looked around. The television showed a past-broadcast-day hissing snowfield. A half-empty container of fried rice lay in his lap. He closed it and got up with a grunt. He made it to the phone by the third ring, his legs tingling with pins and needles.

"Hello," he muttered, scrubbing a hand along his cheek. Gene's eyes popped open. Delight filled his voice. "Harry! How you enjoying being back, eh? Glad to hear from you! I don't even care how late it is." Gene glanced at the clock in his kitchen, frowned, and said, "It *is* late, Harry."

He listened, the grin fading. "Well, *that's* got to be some kind of record, even for you. It hasn't been a week. What's going on?"

The urgency in Harry's voice chilled him. "Are you-"

Harry explained, and in the background Gene heard a rhythmic thumping. Gene cradled the handset between his ear and shoulder and looked around. "I'm getting my shoes on now. You used up a years' worth of favors this month, DeMarko. You *better* have coffee."

Harry sounded distracted.

"See you," Gene told him, and hung up.

He found his shoes, looked down, and decided to change into something resembling actual clothing. He shed his sweats on the way to the bedroom, grabbed a fresh shirt and a pair of jeans from his dresser. He tucked his shirt in, buttoned the jeans, and pulled on socks. Before he left the bedroom he looked up at the top shelf of his closet. His ME bag waited patiently. He sighed, grabbed it down, and clicked the light off as he went into his living room. He stuffed his feet into his sneakers, slid his coat on and took a look around. He turned off the TV before he left, patting his pockets for his keys before the door slammed shut.

In the lobby he nodded to his doorman. "Evening, Fred… or morning, I guess."

Fred Stokes, the night doorman, gave Gene the once-over. "Kinda late, isn't it, Doc?"

"Duty calls, Fred. Can you grab me a cab?" Gene asked, zipping up his coat.

"Give me a second, Doc." Fred clutched his long coat closed, stepped out into the windy, snow-filled darkness. A moment later a shrill whistle pierced the air. The door opened. "Got it."

Gene patted him on the shoulder as he passed. "Thank you, Fred. Go get warm."

"Hope it isn't a bad one this time, Doc."

Gene grimaced to himself as he climbed into the back of the Yellow Cab. "Me too," he muttered. To the driver he said, "Elizabeth and Bleecker."

"You got it, pal." The cabbie dropped the car into gear. Gene sat with the bag on his lap, both hands on the handle, wondering what he was getting into.

CHAPTER EIGHT

"Coming to bed?" she called.

"Yeah," he said, bent over the desk. "Just putting it all back together."

She heard him grunting as he shoved and muscled the desk into place. In the week since he had come home, they'd spent a lot of time in bed, a lot of time talking, and a lot of time *not* talking. The Monday after he'd come back, he had contacted Sal D'Amico's construction company and arranged for a new window. They had put in the window but the office was in disarray. He and Toni had gone on a date to let them work. When they'd come back, she just knew he wouldn't be able to sleep until it was all just right. It took him a while to sweep and mop; the front office was so small he had to do it in halves, shoving all the furniture to one side while cleaning the other, then reversing the process. And of course he had to get the new window just right. He'd had to clean off the tape and wash it inside and out, making sure every speck of lint and dust was wiped away. The clock struck three as he adjusted the nameplate on his desk, eyes aching with fatigue. But it was done. He'd gotten it the way he'd left it.

"Don't be too long," she called. "I'm getting sleepier by the second."

"Me too. I'll be right in. Shut the door, you'll let the heat out."

She smiled at him fussing with his chair, and let him fuss all he wanted. He'd been gone a long time, unsure if he'd ever come back every single day. He needed to touch familiar things.

He's already touched me a couple times, she thought, and a shiver of delight ran through her. *Hell, maybe I'm not* that *tired yet.* She closed the door. She was sure that he knew she wouldn't sleep without him.

He stood back to evaluate, sipping some coffee. Even the burned coffee was idyllic. With a last look at the desks, he reached for the light switch.

A tapping on the glass brought him up short. He turned. A woman was tapping on the door. She frowned, cupped her hand over the glass, and peered in. She was a redhead, he saw, with delicate features. She looked to be in her mid-to-late twenties. She wasn't wearing a coat, just a thin blouse. She had to be freezing.

He sighed, but there wasn't any possibility he'd ignore her. He opened it and she pushed past him into the office. "Sorry," he said. "We're closed right now. If you want to-"

She looked him up and down. He'd lost weight in prison and his tee shirt and jeans were a little loose, but he looked wiry and more than a little disreputable with his fading bruises and the half-healed cut over one eye. Disreputable, maybe, but formidable.

"You're Harry, aren't you?" she asked, and a dusky, sensual voice crossed the room and crowded right up to him. He blinked. He thought she sounded like Ann-Margaret. *Looks like her, too,* he thought. "Yeah. I'm Harry DeMarko. Who are you?"

She moved closer to him, reaching one hand out. She ran a fingertip along the side of his arm, where the muscles bunched. He shivered at her touch, gooseflesh springing forth.

"Hey, wait a-"

"You're much more handsome than I expected," she purred, blinking huge green eyes at him. Her long eyelashes seemed to take a long time to flutter closed and open. He stared down, dumbstruck. "*Far* more handsome And I *expected* handsome."

"Uh, thanks, I guess. Can I-"

"A drink would be lovely." She batted her eyes at him again.

"I'm sure it would. Look, miss-"

"Call me Starr," she hummed, leaning in to give him a whiff of her perfume and a dizzying look down her blouse. He started to look away but stopped. He squinted closer.

She had spatters of blood in her deep cleavage.

"If you have whiskey, that would be grand," she murmured, pressing closer.

"No," he said, trying to pull away. "That's not a-"

"You... *bitch*," Toni spat from the open doorway of the apartment. Harry's head snapped up. "You unbelievable *bitch*. Get the hell away from him. He's *mine*." She stalked into the room clad in a long shirt that covered her, but just.

"I didn't see a stamp or initials," the redhead purred. Her eyes traveled all the way to his shoes and back up. "But I haven't seen *everything*. Have you marked him? Where'd you *hide* it?"

"I told you- I *told* you- if I ever saw you again I'd kill you where you stood," Toni growled. She lifted her hand. Her backup .32 was cocked and she aimed down the barrel at both of them. "And *you*, DeMarko. You've got some goddamned nerve, feeling up this hussy with me ten feet away."

The redhead pressed her back against Harry, raising her arms to protest. "No, you can't have him. He's *mine!*" Her voice rose to a shrill yell. "We're in *love* and you're not keeping us apart any longer!"

Toni took a single step, the barrel of the gun steady as granite. "Love?" she snapped. "*Love?*"

"Don't kill him," the redhead pleaded. "Please! You can't. I... *I'm pregnant!*"

Toni froze.

Harry stared down at the woman pressed against him. He looked up at Toni, horror etched on his careworn, confused face.

Toni beamed at him, a merry, sunny grin of delight.

His mouth dropped open but no sound emanated. Toni eased the hammer on the .38 back down. "Don't worry, Harry." She waved the pistol in the air "It's not loaded."

The redhead said, "It was saying I'm pregnant, right? Pregnant went too far? It felt like it was too far."

Toni assured her, "No, no, it was perfect. Starr, what the hell are you doing here?"

Harry shook himself. "What-"

Toni set the gun on the desk. "Harry, This is Starr. Starr, this is my Harry."

The redhead turned around and aimed a beatific smile at him. "Nice to meet you, Harry."

Harry said, "Wait. Wait. What… what's happening right now?"

Toni slung an arm around Starr's shoulders. Side by side, Harry realized they had the same nose. Toni said, "This is my little sister. May I present Estrellita Marie Bennett."

The redhead scowled. "Watch it, *Antonia* Marie."

"Shut up, bitch," Toni said, and they laughed together.

"Besides, it's not Bennett anymore." She showed Toni a ring. Toni oohed.

"It's gorgeous. Who's the poor bastard you-" Toni broke off, staring into her sister's eyes. The grin on Toni's face faded. "Estrella, what are you *doing* here? Why didn't you call?"

Starr bit her lower lip in a familiar way that made Harry's dislocation even more off-setting. "I'm in trouble, Toni."

"Okay," Toni said, her face growing serious. "Whatever I can- *we*- can do, Starr. What's the trouble?"

"It's my husband," she said. "He's in the car. He's-"

A hand thumped against the door of the office. A tall,

skinny man with long black hair kicked the door in lieu of knocking. Harry opened the door and the tall man stumbled over the threshold. He wore an expensive, dark button-down shirt and slacks, light leather coat. His right hand clamped his left bicep hard, and blood oozed through his white-knuckled fingers.

"Cold…" he gasped. "N-needed to… to…"

"Toni, call an-"

"No!" Starr and the man both snapped.

Starr said, "Don't call anyone! We… we're in... it's bad. We're in bad trouble, Toni."

"Okay." Toni shot Harry a look. He shrugged and said, "Family, huh? What are you gonna do?"

"Thank you, Harry."

He winked at her. "Get him inside. I'll call Gene."

Starr turned, alarmed, but Harry said, "He's a friend of mine. And he's a doctor. We need him. He'll keep his mouth shut. I promise."

Starr nodded, and went into the apartment. As they went, Starr said, "Toni, this is my husband Johnny. Johnny Abruzzi."

Toni swung the door shut behind them. Harry locked the office door and pulled his address book out of his desk. He found Gene's home number and dialed. After a moment, the line connected.

"Gene, it's Harry." He drummed his fingers on the desk.

"Gene, it's not a social call. I need your help. Now."

He listened. "Bring your work bag to our office, would you?"

"Not me. It's a… a friend, I guess. Look, I don't-" A fist hammered on the door of the office. Harry turned. A gigantic form hulked outside the door.

"-have a lot of… uh… Gene, just get here when you can, okay? Please?" The hulking shape seemed familiar.

A sinking feeling gripped his stomach. He said almost absently into the phone, "Yeah. "I have coffee. See you in a bit, Gene."

Harry hung up, went to the door, unlocked, and opened it. After a moment he realized he'd seen the hulking man before and it hit him in a rush. The warning in prison, the problems he'd caused. *This bill always comes due,* he thought. *What are you up to, Sal?* "Come on in, Hendrick. It's Hendrick, right?"

The last time Harry had seen Bruno Hendrick, he'd been one of the three anonymous lumps of meat in Sal D'Amico's employ at the Four Aces jewelry store, one of the men Harry had questioned about Toni's kidnapping. When Sal moved out of the Aces, he'd left Hendrick in charge of the store. Hendrick stomped into the office. "DeMarko." His voice

"Look, I haven't been home long-"

"I heard you was out again. Sal and I-" Hendrick choked. He snarled. "Sal and I heard you were out."

"Yeah," Harry said, worry creeping up his spine "Look, I was going to talk to Sal-"

"I don't care," Hendrick said and he yanked his right fist out of his heavy coat. Harry considered the .32 on his desk but realized it wasn't loaded. Hendrick shoved the fist at him.

It wasn't a gun.

Harry stared at the rolled-up wad of cash. He looked up. "Hendrick? What-"

"I wanna hire you," Hendrick rumbled.

Harry raised his hands. "I- I don't-"

Hendrick narrowed his feral, reddened eyes. "I wanna *hire* you."

"O-okay," Harry said. "Sure. For what?"

"Sal's dead," Hendrick spat.

Harry's skin prickled. "Sal? What-"

"We found him a couple hours ago. He was- he's dead. It's a turf thing. We *think*. We don't *know*. No one's claimed it. But his bodyguard got off a shot. I wasn't there. I was doing something else for him. Bodyguard thinks he might have winged the guy who did it," Hendrick said. "But he got away."

"Uh…"

"We want *you* to get him before the cops do," Hendrick said. "Since it was your woman's fault he was down one guard, I figure you should feel *extra* responsible."

Harry licked his lips. "Okay… Look, I-"

"Here," Hendrick said, and shoved the roll of bills into Harry's hand. "Five grand. Get him before the cops do or he gets outta town, and there's another fifteen. But get him to *us* before the cops get to *him*. Or there's no money in it. You don't get him to us, and it's the *other* thing. You get me?"

Harry stared at the money. "Right… okay. Uh… look, I-I need to get some information-"

"You come find me tomorrow," Hendrick said. "I'll be at the Aces. I got ground to cover tonight."

"Wait, what-"

"Find me *tomorrow*, I'll fill you in." Hendrick reached for the door.

"Wait," Harry protested. "The shooter. What did he-"

"Wasn't a shooter. No gun," Hendrick said. "He used a *hammer*."

A chill coursed through Harry, his scalp felt too tight. "A… a hammer?"

Hendrick gave Harry a look of unmistakable, unrestrained fury. "I wanna do the same to whoever did it. Sal didn't deserve what- he didn't- you *find* this mutt, DeMarko."

"Did his bodyguard get a look at the… the hitter?"

Hendrick nodded. "Said he shouldn't be too hard to spot. Said the guy was skinny with a lot of dark hair. Long, black hair."

Harry swallowed.

"Come find me tomorrow," Hendrick said again. He slammed the door behind him.

Harry walked to the door as if in a dream. He locked it, turned, and reached for the door of the apartment. He thought better of it, picked up the gun from Toni's desk, and opened her bottom drawer. He found the ammunition and loaded the gun. Snapping the cylinder closed, he shut off the office lights. He opened the apartment door and said, "Toni? Can I speak to you for a second?"

CHAPTER NINE

Bobby spun the top off the bottle of Jack, breaking the paper seal and tossing the cap into the bag. He shuddered at the first sip and immediately took a second. A third swallow and he walked for a while, feeling the heat of the whiskey warming his belly. He walked steadily, heedless of the drifts of snow that mounded the sidewalks. He followed Bowery down past Bleecker and didn't turn. He crossed Houston and didn't turn. The few passers-by he did come across stepped out of his way. There was no mystery to why no one bothered a wiry, tall guy in a leather jacket with a bottle of Jack Daniel's clutched in one hand.

He walked until the streetlights gave way to darkness and then turned. He walked west for a while, sipping from the bottle. By the time he'd made it to the halfway mark his head was swimming. He staggered, flung out a hand to catch his balance, spraying amber droplets in the snow and up the sleeve of his jacket. He cursed. A shiver ran up the length of his spine. Dropping the bag in the snow and the square bottle of Jack next to it, he zipped his jacket, tugging over the flashing to zip it to his pointed chin.

He retrieved the bag and bottle both. His stomach growled and he wondered if there were a decent restaurant anywhere around.

They won't even serve me, he thought. *Ain't wearing a tie.*

He looked up and saw a bar on the corner of the next street. He recognized the neighborhood. He stood at the corner of Houston and Mercer. The Crane was a bar, but they served sit-down food. He stared at the warmth and light emanating from the windows and his stomach flipped. He'd eaten here often enough and the food was okay. But the owner of the place... he owned and ran several places. A bar uptown, this place, and a bistro downtown. Les Halles. His old restaurant. Back when he'd been a young chef, invincible, piratical in his whites and his enormous knife. Back when the ring he still kept in his pocket had lived on his hand, and the woman who'd put it there was still his wife.

His stomach lurched. He grimly swallowed and held his breath, picturing a quiet field with a bubbling stream. He imagined a butterfly drifting down to rest and drink from a bright yellow flower. His stomach spasmed a final time, then stilled. *Damned if those fuckers at the hospital didn't know some tricks,* he thought. *Trust junkies to know how to keep from puking.*

He immediately followed his success with another swig, grinning at the burn. Another memory fell out of the hindbrain he tried too hard to keep anesthetized. Again, this place, but not the dining room. Not the kitchen. He'd covered shifts two or three times here and he happened to know there was a little alley behind the restaurant. The back door of the kitchen opened into a delivery cul-de-sac, free of prying eyes. This was good because although trash came out of the door and food deliveries came in, it wasn't just food they brought in from the alley.

Jets of saliva squirted into his mouth as he remembered the taste. That high, slivery taste that always seemed to impact right between his eyes. How you could taste with your brain he didn't know, but that's where he'd tasted it every time he spiked. He would never forget that banana-vanilla-nirvana taste, the electric-alkaline-bluish taste. The colors bursting behind his eyelids, the zing of power thrilling along his nerves.

Bobby Gold wanted another hit more than he ever had in his life.

Bob, you're gonna get clean or you're gonna die, her voice whispered in his mind.

"What's it to you?" he muttered. He sipped again, relishing the burn that even now was fading as he became numb from the liquor, the cold, or both. He kicked at the snow and walked, playing out his side of the old conversation. "You're leaving either way."

Either way, I'm done with you. Hope you don't die, she whispered. *See ya.*

"Liar," he croaked. "Such a liar, Nell."

He stumbled, almost dropped the bottle, and grabbed a lamppost in an awkward hug. He chuckled. "Crisis averted," he said to no one. He strode up Mercer in a wavering line, hugging the paper bag in one arm, dangling the bottle of Jack by its neck with the other. His knuckles were white and the fist shook with the strain. He trudged woodenly up the snow-choked sidewalk.

Liar yourself, Gold, Nell snapped, but good-naturedly. She'd always been good-natured, even at their worst. She had such a sunny outlook on life. *Liar, junkie, thief, cheater... where do you get off? What makes you so much better?*

Tears that crystalized at the corners of his eyes blurred his vision and he brushed them away with the back of his fist. He rewarded himself with another sip.

"Yeah," he agreed, "I'm all of those things. All of 'em and more. Never said otherwise."

You never gave yourself a chance to be anything else, she said. *You always led with that. Then you felt duty-bound to live up to it.*

"Didn't ask you, Nelly," he growled, crossing over Bleecker Street and headed north, headed nowhere.

Since when do I care? she asked him archly. *I decide to give you my mind, you get no choice. You may be a liar and a junkie and a thief and a cheater but I'm a woman of opinion. You live up to your label. I live up to mine. So knuckle up, Gold, because the ride ain't over 'til I say it's over.*

"Okay, okay. You say your piece, Nelly. T'were best done quickly."

You and your quotes, Nell chided. *You have so much to say. Why do you always use other people's words?*

"You can't top the classics," he said defensively. "My words ain't got anything on-"

There you go again. Knocking yourself down before anyone else can. Just like you introducing yourself. 'I'm Bobby Gold. I'm a liar and a thief and a junkie and a cheater. You're better off telling me to screw. But if you don't, we could have some fun. What do you say, gorgeous?' Such a line, Gold. What woman could resist that kind of bullshit? You practically challenged me to prove you wrong.

"But you did, didn't you?" he snarled. He passed the Mercer Street playground. The streetlights were on, the wide park empty. The blanket of snow over the equipment reminded him of skeletons, an elephant's graveyard of abandoned slides, merry-go-rounds, and swings. He upended the bottle of Jack and drained the lees. He looked around, lobbed it at a trashcan. It flew true and detonated inside the lip raining glass shards. He belched, grinned to himself, and kept walking.

Of course I did, she said. *You were a challenge. And hot as a June garbage fire. How's a girl pass that up?*

He snorted. "Such a turn of phrase, Nelly."

I lived with a writer for a decade, what do you expect? I'm practically T. S. Bernard fucking Shakespeare.

He barked laughter, stumbling over his own feet, and collapsing into the snow. He threw out his hands to catch himself and the unopened bottle of Cutty Sark flew like a football, spiraling easily in the night. It landed with a soft flump somewhere out of his sight, buried in the fresh snow.

He climbed unsteadily to his feet and brushed powder from his jeans. His hands were numb, his face was numb, his whole body was numb. His soul was numb.

"'It isn't dying young that's the tragedy. It's growing old and mean,'" Gold told himself.

At least it won't happen to me, Nell finished for him. *Who said that?*

"You're in my head. You tell me." He swiped again at tears.

That isn't how this works, Gold. You know that. I have to be me, *otherwise-*

He crashed a fist down on his thigh, twice, three times, four, his rage driving the punches into the big muscle. Even through the cold and the whiskey he felt the pain. He grinned, embraced it, and fought back despair.

"Yeah," he whispered. He started walking again. He didn't bother looking for the bag with the Sark. He knew his limits; he'd tested them fanatically. He could handle the Jack, especially with the exercise. But another bottle would put him into the black. And passing out in the snow would kill him.

"Otherwise, you're really d- you're really…"

Say it, Gold. You gotta say it.

"'We're born dying,'" he said.

Doesn't mean you have to help it along, Gold.

"What's the fucking *point*, Nelly?" he demanded. "At least you were *there*, over in Jersey. I could still dream. Now-"

Now you gotta strap on a pair of big-boy panties and get to it. Nothing else for it.

He sucked in biting night air. He coughed weakly. His breath plumed before him. He looked up. He was at the corner of Mercer and West 3rd Street. He looked left, looked right.

She can help you, Nell told him.

"Fuck yourself sideways, Nelly," he murmured.

You know it, too.

"I said fuck yourself," Bobby snapped. A passing pedestrian headed south gave him a wary glance.

"Not you," Bobby explained. "The ex-wife in my head's loud tonight."

"Nutjob," the man said, and kept walking.

Bobby Gold considered his options. Keep walking and hope he passed out somewhere warm, or he could listen to Sandy and head to Toni's.

Harry and Toni's, he corrected himself. *Ain't just the tough cookie there anymore.*

Does it matter, Gold? Nell asked in his mind. *You aren't sweet on her anyhow. She's a friend. And you've got too few of those as it is.*

"Can't have friends," he said, admiring his breath as it billowed in the air before him. "Too easy to let them all down."

Bullshit, Gold, she said. *The people you let down were all your junkie friends, counting on you to jump back in after rehab. You never let down anyone who* mattered *to you.*

"Except you," he snarled, desolate and tired to his bones.

She respond for a long time. He plopped down in the snow cross-legged, staring up at the street signs. They hadn't changed. He didn't shiver. He was so numb he wasn't even cold anymore.

"What do I do, Nelly?" he asked.

You get your ass up and you go ask your friend for help, she said. *It isn't time for you to give up. It never* was.

"What do *you* know about it?" he sneered, and immediately regretted it. Just like every time he'd actually crossed her and she lost that pleasant, amused demeanor and showed the fire below. That fire that had pulled him in, kept him warm, and scared the hell out of him all at the same time.

Bobby Fucking Gold, you know damned well what I know about it! I was there when you were a nothing hash-slinger in a shitty seaside diner. I was there when you learned to cook! I watched while you pulled double shifts and took classes at the CIA all day! I watched you bluff, impress, and cook your way to the top! Don't tell me *what I do and don't know about* my *man. You got a soul of cast iron, Gold. Nothing bad's going to stick to it. Nothing touches it that doesn't turn to something good. Now you get up off your lazy, fat ass this second and get walking, you little pansy. If you can handle a double shift and six hundred covers a night running low on everything, you can handle a little bump in the road like losing me all over again.*

He flinched as if slapped, and he was on his feet. He swayed, staggered, grabbed a light pole for support. Once steady he let go of the freezing green metal. He left skin and didn't feel it. He couldn't feel anything. He half-heartedly brushed snow off his ass and skinny legs and lurched into a semblance of a purposeful walk.

You get mean when you're worried, baby. That hasn't changed.

Maybe it sounds *mean, but it's always the truth, Gold. I never lied to you.*

"Yes, you did."

When have I ever *lied to you, Gold?*

"*When you said 'see ya',*" he barked. "You fucking lied when you said it."

The voice in his head was silent for most of a block.

Never on purpose, Bobby. Never ever on purpose. It broke my heart when I left, but I never expected it to be forever.

"Yeah, yeah," he muttered. "Sure."

Fuck yourself, Gold. What do you know about it?

"You gave me up because I was bad for you, baby. I didn't give *you* up. I never did."

What makes you think I ever gave you up, Gold? I had to stay away to stay safe.

"I never would have hurt you, Nelly," he whispered "Ever."

Then why didn't you kick when I asked you the first time?

He didn't speak.

Gold... we both know who you were when we met. You were always on the edge, looking for the next kick. And when you graduated to shooting I told you I wanted you to kick. What'd you say?

He stared at his feet, ashamed, afraid to look up just in case her eyes were there, watching his. But Bobby Gold had been confronting his demons for years, and he said, albeit sullenly, "I said I could handle it."

What did I say?

"And you asked me why should I be any different than anyone else," he whispered. He looked around. 3rd and Broadway now, headed west. He waited for a pair of taxis to blow past and crossed.

So you decided you could have the best of both worlds. And I couldn't be around that.

"So I wouldn't drag you down. I know, I know."

You fucking dolt! I left so I didn't have to watch*!*

He stumbled as he came to that realization.

Imagine if it was me, Gold. And you knew, you knew, *nothing was gonna stop it. And there wasn't anything you could do. How would you feel?*

He stared at the snow drifts marking the boundaries of the sidewalk. Big fluffy white mounds of snow. His nose twitched as he thought of the cold-hot snorts of coke in the walk-in, just a bump to keep up the old energy during the dinner rush. And again during the drunk-rush. Then a couple hours drinking in the bars. Then home around dawn and the waiting bennies and reds to put him into a black sleep for three or four hours, just enough rest to get up and do it all again. His day starting with the uppers to get him moving to the market for the day's fresh vegetables, fish, and meat. Then to the kitchen, where the first bump awaited before the lunch rush.

He could remember the taste of everything he'd ever smoked, snorted, or shot. He knew which drugs would make his nose run, or make him constipated, or just cause the shakes. He knew which two to pair to get the vivid, acid-like colors to spawn, but which ones not to cross, or he'd hallucinate flames or talking fish. He knew which ones would relax him, and which ones would give him that sharp edge, where he'd be inspired to create a new dish, combine flavors no one had ever tried.

He knew all that about himself, but on his *life* he couldn't remember at this particular moment what color Nell's eyes had been- green or brown. Or her hair. Was it black? Brown-black? And her skin. What did it smell like, fresh out of a shower, clean and pink and scrubbed until it glowed? He knew each of her breasts had fit into one of his wide hands easily, but not what cup size they were.

He swallowed. The need for oblivion rolled over him again. His fingertips itched, his mouth was dry, and he had the junkie shuffle playing in his nerves. He wanted to scratch both elbows at the same time, bite the ragged, chapped skin from his lips.

Instead, he resumed his walk, plodding solidly through the snow, hands shoved once again fisted in his pockets. "It would have been torture. And I would have had to let you go."

Why, Bobby?

"Same reason you cut me loose," he said. The tears had stopped now. Epiphany had dried them. Made him face a possibility that he'd never, in all his selfish days, considered.

Why?

"Because it would have killed me to watch you kill yourself, Nelly," he whispered. He came to another street sign and looked up. Lafayette. He half-grinned. Yeah. All roads, and all that shit. He turned right, headed south.

It almost did. That time they had to jump-start you was it for me. I couldn't watch you go away and not come back, Gold. No way in hell I was going to be left here. You couldn't kick the horse, Gold, so I had to kick you.

His steps were purposeful now. He put some effort into it, getting his blood up, getting the heat back.

He knew everything she said, of course he did. They weren't new words. She couldn't say anything new in his head because she wasn't actually there. And even though he'd heard her words before, that didn't mean that he'd *listened*.

He was listening now. The guilt of being a junkie, he'd found, had a way of cropping up at the most inconvenient times. And just when you thought you had it all squared away, you found yourself in the next battle.

One day at a time, they preached. *Easier said than done,* he'd parried.

That too, they'd said.

He didn't go to many meetings. It was rough, staring into the burned-out eyes of people who'd seen the ragged edge and were desperate to claw their way back from it. In a strange way, he felt bad for being there. All those poor bastards struggling to maintain, struggling to get a little dignity back. And good for them. But there he was, blazing away with a merry heat because he'd loved every fucking second of it. He'd loved every twisted, dark path he ever walked down. Like a broken-down quarterback or boxer who'd taken one too many hits, he couldn't suit up and play the game anymore; it would kill him.

But he desperately *wanted* to.

And that kind of love never seemed fair to the people in the groups. Those black coffee-addicted, donut munching, cigarette-sucking shells of people who wanted nothing more than to be people again. They had to sit there and listen to him wax nostalgic about that rush, that white-yellow halo his vision used to get. That burning clarity he always felt as the first drip of chemical mixed with his cerebellum, and the world seemed so simple, like tumblers in a lock that lined up, and it went click and the door swung wide.

He looked up occasionally and saw the longing in those red-rimmed eyes. And the loathing. But not for him.

For that feeling. For their personal feeling.

So Bobby Gold stopped going to meetings. He'd had a sponsor fresh out of rehab, a fellow junkie-turned-preacher named, if you could believe it, Othello. A skinny black man from Alabama, Othello had been there for Bobby, night and day. Made him go to two meetings a day, helped him find a cheap place to stay. One night, in an all-night diner, Bobby had told Othello exactly what he loved about heroin, exactly what he missed, and exactly what he thought about having to kick. He waxed loquacious, using all the powers of his love of words to compose a sonnet to junk right there in a greasy spoon diner over a plate of shitty eggs and half-cold hash. It was some of his finest composition, that soliloquy. And it must have had some juice behind it because-

-because Othello had turned up dead three days later, overdosed on the B train. Endlessly riding to oblivion.

Oh, the program people were quick to tell Bobby it

wasn't his fault. Everyone, they told him, was *that* close. Sobriety was a constant battle, and you'd lose as many fights as you win.

Bullshit.

So Bobby didn't go to many meetings anymore. The point was to share the load, share the burden. Support each other. But he didn't *hate* heroin. He didn't hate what it did. He loved ever fucking second of it.

Except for losing Nell.

When he came out the last time, he went home to find the locks changed, Nell gone, and his ass on the street. He'd never had a place of his own after that. After Othello OD's, he stayed away so long they re-rented his room at the halfway house. When he did turn up, his meager possessions had been given away. The couple who ran it were vaguely surprised but unapologetic. "Most of you that vanish never turn up alive. We just assumed you were dead."

He kept walking. The snow was picking up, flakes drifting more steadily down now. *It's beginning to look a lot like Christmas,* he thought unironically. *A week away now.*

He crossed Bond. Normally he'd hang a left and walk all the way to the end of Bond. All the way to Bowery, and a block south to CBGBs. The club was always full of people and music, good and bad kinds of both, and he could lose himself for a couple hours in the heat and noise. Not tonight. He rolled his shoulders, settling the jacket a little higher around his neck, and scrunched against the wind. He picked up his steps.

He'd stumbled into the job with Sammy, just like he stumbled into everything else in his life. One of the cooks he knew came running past him one day on 42nd street. He skittered to a halt when he saw Bobby and hissed *"Corra, amigo! Caçadores de recompensas chegando!"*

He knew a little Portuguese from his time in the trenches of half a dozen kitchens. He knew enough to know the cook was on the run. Bobby pulled him into an alley. "How much do they got on you?" he asked.

"*Dois Mil!*" the panicked cook hissed, crouching next to Bobby out of sight.

"Two grand, huh? What'd you do, man?"

The cook pressed against the wall. "*Eu esfaqueei um idiota batendo na minha garota,*" the wiry, darkly-complected man muttered. "*Eu o coloquei no hospital, cara.*"

"You did, huh?" Bobby mused. He thought about it. "He live?"

"*Eu duvido muito,*" the cook said, and chuckled. He mimed stabbing himself in the balls and grinned up at Bobby.

"Stabbed a guy in the dick for hitting on his girl," Bobby mused aloud. *Seems a little overzealous.* The cook reached back and tugged a six-inch kitchen knife out of his belt and stared up at Bobby. "Ela é a próxima, amigo."

"No kidding," Bobby said, less amused now. "Did she flirt back?"

"Isso importa?" the skinny cook asked. "A cadela não disse não."

"Kind of important, yeah," Bobby said. "Whether she said no or not's kinda important."

He looked up. At the mouth of the alley an overweight guy puffed into view, leaning on the wall, gasping for breath. Beside Bobby, the cook's eyes rolled, and he fingered the knife. Bobby looked at the fat guy, looked at the cook, and picked up the lid from the can he stood by.

Thirty minutes later he was in Sammy's office watching Sammy write a check for a thousand dollars.

"I chased him down, you put him out," Sammy groused. "We split it. Or I keep it all. Problem with that?"

"Not a problem at all," Bobby had said with a shrug.

"You a skip trace?" Sammy had asked, holding out the check. Bobby took it and looked at it. He considered how much white it would buy him, and remembered Nell was gone because of that. He said with regret, "I guess I am now. Gotta do something, right?"

He wasn't a great skip trace, but he was okay. His nose for the underground in the City gave him a pretty good advantage when it came to tracking down people who didn't want to be found, and most of Sammy's trade was tied up in the drug culture anyhow. A lot of the time he was able to give Sammy a street address as soon as he heard the name of the target.

In fact, he thought, *that's how I met Toni. Sammy's tip on Dexter Harris. Toni tracked him to that bodega, brought him down, and dressed him out. Even snaked him out from under me when I tried to swipe her prize. Then she cut me into that job, gave me a place to crash, and treated me like-*

He tried to quell that line of thought, but there was Nell again, big as life and twice as annoying.

Treated you like what?

"Shut up," he whispered. "You're dead."

Yep. So what? If you think *I'm here, I'm here. Treated you like what?*

He skidded to a stop at the corner. He didn't need to look up. Lafayette and Bleecker Street. He turned left. The next cross street was Houston. He was close now. And sober enough that his confidence in Toni's affection for him wavered.

Finish your fucking thought, Gold, Nelly all but shouted in his head. *I'm not giving you any peace until you do.*

He pressed a fist against his forehead and scrunched his eyes closed. He thumped himself between the eyes.

The Jack seemed to have evaporated from his blood; he felt sober as a Catholic judge.

Treated you like what, Gold?

"Like a friend," he whispered, broken-heartedly. "Like a friend. Like I deserved it."

Go on, Nell urged. *Keep walking.*

"Okay, baby," he said softly. "Okay. You're the boss."

Good boy, Nell told him, and for a moment he felt her hand on the back of his head, the way he had when he was sick or drunk, or, like that last time, in an ambulance after overdosing and having his heart restarted after a-fib. *Good boy.*

His eyes blurred from the tears that had again sprung up, and he staggered down the unplowed side of Elizabeth, that cock-eyed remnant of a former age that held both the backs of the Mott Street buildings and the fronts of the Elizabeth Street ones. Halfway down, almost in the center of the block, the single lit storefront on Elizabeth beckoned him. There were three cars parked in front of the former Chinese restaurant. One he recognized as the Chevelle Toni had... liberated. The owner of the Chevelle, a porn star and hooker named Steudel, had agreed to loan it to her until he got out of County himself. The other two he didn't recognize. One of them was parked properly, two or three lengths away from the office. The third was parked cross-wise in the street, and as Bobby watched an impossibly large slab of beef got out of that one and stalked toward the door of the office. He yanked it open and marched inside.

Brow knitting, Bobby slowed his walk again, concerned. *It couldn't be*, he thought, terror gripping his heart. *No way Terry Shoulders made bail. Not after jumping once already. He's in for the winter, at least. Please God let that not be Terry Shoulders.*

He lingered until the door opened and the slab of beef

climbed back into the car and revved the engine. He gunned the car up the street almost directly toward Bobby, corrected, and caromed up past him before the headlights snapped on. Bobby watched the tail lights disappear as the car turned east toward Bowery.

Bobby watched the front of the office for a few moments, not thinking anything, trying not to think anything. He purposely drove all thoughts from his mind and tried to find a center. It didn't happen. He grinned at nothing and wondered if that said something about him or about meditation, or if it meant nothing.

Headlights momentarily blinded him as yet another vehicle came up Elizabeth Street. The Taxi sign unmistakable on the roof, like a shark fin.

A strange feeling crawled up Bobby's back and nestled between his shoulder blades. They were popular tonight. It was… what? Three A.M. if it was a second. Why would they be so popular?

"Gotta be Toni," he said to himself. *That woman attracts trouble like a dog did fleas.* A smile flickered across his drawn face and vanished. If they were this popular, it stood to reason it was trouble. If it was trouble, maybe they could use a hand. His experience with Toni had been brief, but he'd come away with the firm opinion that she could never have too much help. He watched as the taxi stopped. A diminutive figure, almost the opposite of the previous visitor, got out and slammed the door behind. He hurried to the door of the office and swung it open. It wasn't locked.

He sighed. They likely had their hands full. Didn't need an extra burden. But maybe they could use an extra pair of hands that didn't shake too much. He shoved his hands into his coat pockets and trudged across the street as the taxi skidded and slid and gained traction enough to make the top of Elizabeth Street and vanish toward the west.

Bobby Gold put on his best easy-going, devil-may-care-but-I-don't grin, and walked over to the office door. He reached for it as he recognized the newest arrival.

CHAPTER TEN

Toni stuck her head out of the apartment. "Did you get ahold of Gene?" she asked.

"Yeah," Harry said. "He's on his way."

"Okay, good." She started closing the door.

"Give me a minute, would you?" he asked. "In private?"

She frowned and closed the apartment door. "What's up, Harry?"

"Who is he?" Harry asked.

Toni shrugged. "I don't know. I mean, he's my brother-in-law, I guess. Starr's husband. But I've never heard of him. But then," she said thoughtfully, "I've been out of touch with the family for a while."

Harry nodded. "He say how he got shot yet?"

She shook her head. "No. He's just dealing with the pain and waiting for Gene. He's looking a little peaked, Harry. I gave him some aspirins and a couple slugs of whiskey, but he needs that hole taken care of before he gets an infection."

"Yeah," Harry said. "So, nothing at all? He hasn't said anything? What about her?"

Toni studied him, eyes wary. "Look, Harry, it's not like I have the family over for Sunday dinner, but Starr's still my sister. I'm gonna help her. I know you're generally about doing things the law way, but-"

"It's not that," Harry said. "I get that part."

"Then what?" she asked. She propped her hands on her hips. "This is sounding an awful lot like an interrogation."

"It kind of is," he said.

She raised an eyebrow. "You're lucky you're fresh out of the joint, DeMarko. You still got some I-was-wrongly-accused-of-murder currency built up."

"What about the I-was-fucked-around-with-by-the-Bennett-sisters credit? How far does that get me?" he asked.

She was still wearing just a long tee shirt, and he watched with interest as she crossed her arms, making it ride up a little. Her smirk told him she knew it, too.

"Depends on how far you push the Jack Webb routine with me, Harry," she said. "I'll stand for a little more bullshit, but not *much* more."

He said, "Go ask him how he got shot, Toni."

She didn't move. She studied him. He almost grinned. He loved how quick she was. After a moment she said, "Okay. Be right back. I'll grab some pants, too."

"Don't go to too much trouble on my account," he told her.

She looked at him over her shoulder as she opened the door of their apartment. "You got a good reason for this, I'll take 'em back off for you," she said. She reached back and flipped up the hem of the shirt, giving him a quick flash of her bare rear before the door closed. He smiled to himself and poured coffee while he waited for her. After a sip he reached into the center drawer of his desk and found the small bottle of bourbon he kept for emergencies, such as running out of the bigger bottle in the apartment. He dosed his coffee with a decent slug of bourbon, sipped, and put the bottle away as the door opened and closed behind him.

She was wearing jeans now, but her face showed consternation. He didn't even need to ask. She said, "They're not talking. And now I'm pissed off as well as suspicious. Do I need to add worried to the pile?"

Harry shrugged. "Remains to be seen. Okay, I think I got everything from you and them, so now I'll tell you what the deal is."

"Good," she said. "I'm about ready to punch you."

"Yeah, well, hold off a second, I bet I can change your mind. Or at least change your target. While you were inside, we had a visitor."

"We should get a revolving door," Toni said. "What did this one want? If it's another case, I'm gonna start charging you overtime when you get arrested for stuff you didn't do."

"It's another case," Harry confirmed. He tugged the roll of bills out of his pocket and tossed it to her. "And they offered an advance."

She snagged the roll and examined it, eyes glittering. "There's gotta be, what, two, three-"

"Five thousand," he said absently, turning to stare out the window.

"Jesus. Did you say this was an *advance*? Against what? Finding the Hope Diamond?" she asked, still staring at the roll of hundreds.

"No," Harry said. His melancholy eyes watched her reflection in the window. "It's another murder."

She sighed. "Damn it. Who didn't you kill *this* time?"

"Sal D'Amico."

Her shocked expression and pale countenance snapped up to meet his gaze in the reflection. He turned to look at her.

"You're kidding," she whispered.

"I'm not," he said. "Bruno Hendrick was here. I thought he was gonna lean on me about what happened in Riker's, but that wasn't it at all. Told me Sal's been killed. Murdered, obviously. He wants us to find whoever did it before the cops do."

She swallowed. Her eyes fell to the roll of hundreds and rose again to his. "Nope," she said. "We don't need the money now that you can cash your pension checks again. Executive decision as your partner. We're out."

He didn't speak. She fingered the roll of money. He watched her thinking it over, watched her weighing his actions, responses, and his mood. She heaved a sigh. "It's not optional, is it?"

"Nope," he said.

"Shit. Because of Terry Shoulders, right?"

"That's one reason, yeah."

He watched her and his heart bloomed again with love for this fierce, feisty woman. He watched her weight the options, assess the damage, and he saw her decide she was all in. She came out swinging for the fences, and he loved her for it.

She dropped the roll into a drawer and hip-checked it shut. "Okay. First things first: what did he tell you?"

She was all-or-nothing on his side every time. He often wondered how he'd gotten so lucky.

"Hendrick was short on details. Said I should get to the Four Aces tomorrow for the full story, but he gave me a few tidbits. Whoever did it went after Sal at his home. They broke in and attacked him. Killed him. Fled the scene. His bodyguard, a guy named… uh…"

"Higgins," Toni said. "He didn't strike me as the brightest bulb that ever lit up a room. Is he dead too?"

"Not that I know of," Harry said. "He heard a commotion- small wonder- and came to investigate. Surprised the doer and chased him out of the place."

Toni absorbed this. "Why'd he let the guy get away?"

"Had a car waiting, as I understand it."

"That's two people," Toni noted. He smiled at her, a quick flash. "That's right. Doer and driver."

"Okay," Toni said. "All we have to do is call in a favor, right? Either Clara or Mills. There's bound to be prints, evidence. We wrangle a copy of the file, we can go over the-"

"Nope. They don't know yet. No one knows yet.

Hasn't been reported."

Toni blinked. "Are you serious?"

"As can be. Hendrick wants to wait as long as possible to give him a head start on this. Hendrick wants him before the cops even get wind of it. Rule two: don't give the cops anything, no matter what."

Toni nodded. "I would have figured that on being rule one."

Harry gave her a faint grin. "Nah. Rule one is 'money talks.' Family, loyalty, none of it's as powerful as money."

"Ah. Makes sense."

He waited, and she sorted the details in her mind before she asked, "Okay, so we might have to run prints ourselves, if possible. The killer drop the gun or take it with him?"

Harry said, "Wasn't a gun."

She frowned a little. "What then? Bazooka? Did they knife him? Or strangle him? If they strangled him, chances are likely it's an internal thing with the Gambinos."

"No, and no. Besides, Hendrick assured me it wasn't a family thing. At least, not *his*."

"Great," she said. "On top of everything else, now we got a Mob war."

"No idea if that's the case yet," he said.

"So how *did* Skinny Sal get his?" Toni asked.

"Hendrick says they used a hammer."

The animation drained from her face and he watched her swallow twice. She grimaced. "A hammer?"

"Yep."

She thought about it. Then she barked a laugh, which caused his eyebrows to climb.

"What's funny?"

"Come on, Harry. He got *hit*," she explained with a chuckle.

He didn't laugh.

"Okay, okay," she conceded. "Too soon."

He waited.

She sighed. "All right. Tell me what I don't know, Harry."

"Higgins says he took a couple shots at the guy."

Toni nodded. "Bodyguard. Figures he'd be heeled. So?"

"Says he's positive he hit the guy. Winged him, he told Hendrick."

Toni's eyes shifted color, darkening as she realized what he'd been trying to gently lead her to. She exhaled. "Well, shit."

"Yeah."

She appeared to consider it, head tilting to the side. "I'll go get answers."

"Just… be easy. If it's a coincidence you'll piss off your sister. If it's not… he's dangerous. And she is, too."

Toni picked up her gun from the desktop, checked the cylinder, and snapped it shut. She thumbed the hammer back, rotated the cylinder until she could drop the hammer on an empty chamber. She pushed the safety and put it in her back pocket.

"Good girl."

She beamed at him. "You're right about my sister. She'll be pissed if we're wrong. And he's not the only one who's dangerous."

"Think it will go better with me in there, or not?"

"We'll try it one way, and then the other," she said. "You hang back and keep an eye out for Gene, okay?"

He leaned forward and kissed her. She hummed against his mouth and pressed against him. They broke the kiss, and she smiled up at him. "Thanks for backing me, Harry. You didn't have to."

"I don't believe that at all," he told her. "If you're obligated, then *I'm* obligated. This isn't a sometimes deal we got, honey. If your mouth writes a check, my ass'll cover it."

"That's a good line, Harry," she said with a chuckle.

He shrugged. "It's the truth. Family or not. You want to help them, we'll help them. You don't ever need to ask me how I feel. You say it, I may as well be saying it too."

She reached up and held his cheek in her palm. "You're awful sweet for a guy that just got outta the joint. Aren't you supposed to be all hard and angry, ready to take out your rage on society and whatnot?"

He shrugged. "Maybe I wasn't in the right wing."

"You're sweet to me, Harry," she said solemnly. "Thank you for that."

"You get what you give. I owe you my life."

She shook her head. "You'd have figured it out, Harry. You didn't kill Messner. Somehow, it would have-"

"No, Toni. The alley."

Her face fell as she remembered that night, the night they'd met. He'd stopped a serial rapist from making her his next victim, and gotten shot for his trouble. It had ended his career. "Oh. That was-"

"-just another reason I love you," he said. "So don't ever worry about me backing you up."

Her eyes glistened, and she cleared her throat. "Okay, Harry. And it goes both ways."

"Good," he said. "I almost always need backup."

"You almost always need a *babysitter*, DeMarko," she said. She smiled. "And a crash helmet. All right. Time to go lean on Starr a little. Let me know when Gene gets here, huh?"

"Will do." He watched her go back into the apartment, tugging her tee-shirt down over the handle of her .38 as she went.

He opened his desk and took out a bottle of whiskey. He unscrewed it and tipped it into his coffee. It looked like it was going to be one long night.

CHAPTER ELEVEN

Gene suffered the cabbie's incessant bitching about the snow, letting the monologue wash over him, his mind filling in grunts and hums of acknowledgment in all the right places. He'd lived in the city since birth, and Brooklyn's cabbies and Manhattan's cabbies and the Lower East Side's cabbies and Harlem's cabbies all had the same spiel, they just used differing accents.

The lights were on, Gene saw as they pulled up. He grubbed in his coat, found five singles. The ride cost three-fifty. He dropped the bills in the tray.

"Keep it," he said as he swung the door open. There was gum on the door handle, and he grimaced as he felt the damp, sticky lump under his fingers.

"'Preciate it, pal," the cabbie grunted. "You need I should stay?"

"Nah," Gene told him. "I got no idea how long I'll be."

"Suit yourself," the cabbie told him, and dropped the gearshift before Gene had even gotten clear. The cabbie took off as Gene slammed the door. He gripped his bag and hurried to the door of the office. He tugged it open and bustled in. Harry was staring out the window of the office, his eyes far away.

"Harry?" Gene asked.

Harry DeMarko blinked, shivered, and turned to Gene Kaminski. He had a mug in one hand, Gene saw. Harry sipped from the mug. He seemed to take some psychic nourishment from the coffee and he shivered again, but his eyes lost the faraway look and snapped to life.

"Gene, thanks for coming," he said.

Gene nodded, and he dropped his bag. He stuck out a hand. Harry regarded it for a second before he held out the mug of coffee.

"No, you dope," Gene said with a happy grin. "I wanted to congratulate you."

Harry extended his other hand, bemused, as Gene shook it.

"Congratulations on getting out of jail," Gene said. "Glad you're okay."

Harry's face clouded. "Don't get ahead of yourself, Gene. I'm out, sure, but okay? I doubt it."

Gene nodded. He took the mug from Harry's hand and sipped. Harry started to protest as Gene's eyebrows popped up. His wide forehead wrinkled as he put on a shocked expression.

"Is that whiskey?"

"Yeah," Harry said. "Sorry. You were too quick for me."

"No, it's fine. Makes your normal battery acid almost pleasant," the smaller man said, and he sipped again. "But what's the occasion? You never drink except to celebrate or lament."

Harry nodded. "Yeah. Started out one, seems to be the other. Your patient's in the next room. GSW."

"Toni?" Gene asked, his concern immediate and gratifying to Harry.

"Hell no," Harry said. "I wouldn't have given you coffee first."

"Yeah, that makes sense," Gene admitted. "So what-"

The office door opened and Bobby Gold walked in. He pulled the door shut behind him and stamped his feet. He looked over the two men from his impressive height. Harry frowned.

"Sorry," he said. "This isn't a restaurant, and we're not open."

Gold said, "Mean Gene, thrower of the spleen. What's got you out of your crypt this late?"

Gene barked a laugh. He threw a thumb up at Harry's puzzled frown. "This guy. You?"

"I'm but a poor wandering traveler seeking a room for the night, some libation, and an ear." Gold's eyes settled on Harry's tired, drawn face. "Is that human wrecking ball hiding out in the back, or what?"

Harry began to speak but the door opened. Toni poked her head out. "Harry? Oh, Gene! Thank God! Come on-"

She broke off, seeing Gold by the door. She sighed. "Oh, hell. Gold, what are you- look, stay there for a sec. I have shit to do first. Gene, did you bring your-"

Gene picked up his bag.

"-great. Come on back." She pointed at Gold. "I'll be right back. Be nice."

Bobby pointed at himself. "Me?"

"You," Toni said. She stepped aside for Gene and closed the door behind them.

Bobby Gold and Harry DeMarko eyed one another. Harry said, "Coffee?"

"Please, thank you, and do you take IOUs?" Gold replied.

Harry smiled a little. "Cream, sugar, whiskey?"

"No, no, and hell yes, if you're offering," Gold said "Need some help?"

Harry studied him for a moment. "Sure, I guess."

Gold nodded, moved around Harry, and busied himself at the elderly Bunn coffee machine. He emptied the remaining pot into two of the ceramic mugs, filling both. He rummaged in the box under the stand for fresh filters and the restaurant-sized can of Folgers. He refilled the machine's chambers, topped the reservoir from a pitcher that sat nearby, and flicked the switches. He offered one of the cups to Harry, who took it.

"Thanks," he said. He didn't comment on Gold's familiarity with the coffee machine or their makings. He and Toni'd talked about Gold a little. Harry was grateful Gold had backed her up, concerned he seemed to be puppy-dogging her around, and completely confident that if Gold hit on Toni, she'd bend him into an interesting shape. He opened the top drawer of his desk and removed a bottle of bourbon. He topped his mug generously, did the same for Gold. Gold raised the mug.

"Long days, pleasant nights, and little to no lower back pain," he toasted.

Harry chuckled. "Amen."

They touched the mugs together and each drank. Harry sipped his; Bobby tossed half of the bitter, astringent brew back at one go. He let out a ragged sigh. "No pleasure so heavenly, no sin so pleasurable as a good cup of coffee."

"I can vouch for that," Harry said.

The door opened again as they were each sipping. Toni slipped out and closed the door behind her. She cast a critical eye at Gold. A glance at Harry got her a bland expression she couldn't read. She said, "Look... it's a little rambunctious in there," she said. "And I doubt it's gonna get any better. Bobby, if you're looking for a place to crash, I could give you some cash for a motel. We have-"

A strangled yelp from behind her startled all of them. Gold gazed at the door, looked at Toni, then at Harry. He said, "Sounds like a party. I'm going to go ahead and assume Gene's not here to have some drinks."

Toni sighed. "No, he's not. Look, just... Harry? You got some of that cash handy?"

Harry pointed with his chin. "In the drawer."

Toni nodded her thanks. She opened his left drawer, rifled in an envelope, and came out with a fifty. He noticed she didn't peel off any bills from the roll Hendrick had tossed at them. He wouldn't have either. Spending money before you earned it was bad luck. She handed it to Gold, who stared at it. "I'd give you the couch, but the inn's full up. Manger, too. There's a not-bad motel a couple blocks from here, off Bowery and Mitchell. Go crash. I'll talk to you later, when I got time, okay?"

He dropped the bill on the desk. "I don't need money, Toni. I needed-"

The office door behind them opened again and slammed.

"Jesus, I gotta lock that damned door," Harry muttered.

"You might want to brick it over, too," Gold said.

Harry snorted. He peered around the lanky form of Bobby Gold to see a young man panting and heaving, hands on knees as he leaned against the door. He wore a dark jacket and jeans, and had a black backpack on. He was dusky of skin, and wore a watch cap-style hat.

No, Bobby corrected himself. *It's a turban. Indian?*

"Farrokh?" Toni asked. She went to him. The nephew of their local shopkeeper was gasping for breath. "What's wrong? What happened? Is it your uncle?"

Harry was next to Toni like a flicker. Gold almost jumped with startlement. The man didn't look that quick.

Farrokh panted. He swiped at his forehead with the back of one hand, along the edge of his tightly-wrapped turban. "No," he gasped. "I… there are… please. Chasing- please help."

Harry looked up, head cocked. "Toni, get him in the back. Keep everyone quiet."

Toni nodded and helped Farrokh walk to the door of their apartment. She pushed the young man through, one hand on his backpack. She shoved him through and stopped to give Harry a look. She tugged the .38 out of her pocket and handed it to him. He nodded. She closed the door, and Harry and Bobby heard her shushing everyone.

Gold turned to Harry. "What-"

Harry handed him the .38 and brushed past him. He went to his desk and pulled his own gun, nestled in a clip holster, from the bottom drawer. He snapped it onto his belt, just behind his left hip. Gold stared at the gun in his hand. "What-"

"Pocket," Harry said casually. "And sit."

He pointed at the chair in front of his desk. Bobby frowned as Harry slid into Toni's chair and put his feet up. He picked up his coffee. "What-"

"Pocket. Chair. Coffee. Just a couple night owls. No one else here," Harry said with a flat stare that sent a chill up Bobby's spine. He attempted all three orders at once, and only fouled up on the chair. He almost slid off it onto the floor. He righted himself and picked up his half-full cup just as the office door opened again.

Outside, the first light of dawn was beginning to light the rooftop of the buildings that bordered the west side of Elizabeth. The three men who hustled into the office were burly, weaselly-looking and, in Bobby's estimation, dangerous. They were dressed almost identically, with heavy coats over denim jackets, dirty pants, and heavy black boots like Bobby's. One had long, stringy hair that he kept tossing to the side with little jerks of his head, the one beside him was shaved almost to the skull, and his ears and nose were bright pink with the cold. The third, standing in front of the others, was thinner in the face than his friends, a little taller, and his cheeks were covered in scruff. He had dark eyes and very bushy eyebrows. The trio looked over the two men casually drinking coffee.

"Hiya," Harry said. "Need something?"

One of the three approached Harry's desk. "Lookin' for a kid came running down this way. You seen him?"

Harry looked at Gold. "You seen a kid run through here?"

"I ain't seen shit," Gold opined, and sipped his coffee loudly. He smacked his lips. "Why? There a reward?"

Eyebrows grinned. "Yeah, there's a reward. You tell

me now, I give you fifty bucks. You make me beat it outta ya, you get a hundred."

Bobby shot a look at Harry. "We hard up for cash, or *very* hard up for cash?"

"You wanna take a beating for a hundred bucks?"

"Eh," Bobby shrugged. "I've taken worse. And I'm bored."

A flicker of a frown crossed Eyebrows' scruffy face. He shook it off. "Better fuckin' tell me now," he growled. "There ain't many places on this street he coulda gone."

"Did you try the apartment upstairs?" Harry asked. "I mention it 'cause it's full of hookers. Maybe whoever you're looking for wanted to tear off a piece."

"He didn't run up no stairs, man," Eyebrows snapped. "I'm almost positive he came in here."

"Well, you got to accen-tu-ate the positive," Bobby said, drawing the word out. "Cause right now, you're a hundred percent wrong."

Eyebrows stabbed a look in Bobby's direction. "You open your mouth again, I'mma cram my fist in it. Understand?"

Bobby hesitated, bit his lower lip, and without opening his mouth mumbled, "Mmms."

"What?"

"Mmmsss," Bobby hummed again, mouth firmly closed.

Eyebrows turned to Harry. "What the fuck?"

"He's trying to answer you," Harry said, and he sipped his coffee, "but you told him not to open his mouth."

Three rapid blinks from Eyebrows. "Where's the kid?" He snapped.

"Which kid would that be?" Harry asked. "You got a name?"

"Doesn't matter what the kid's name is," Eyebrows said. "You seen *any* kid this morning?"

"Which morning would that be?" Harry asked.

The color rose from Eyebrow's collar to fill his scruffed face in an alarming way. Bobby wondered if the guy would have a heart attack. "You… are you just fucking with me?"

Harry smiled lazily. "We've been sitting here all night drinking. Haven't been to bed in two days. For all I know, you guys are hallucinations. And I asked you if *you* had a name."

Eyebrows brought a fist down on the desk next to Harry's crossed feet. "I'm Cad. That's Ham and Def. We're with the 68s. You heard of us?"

Harry said, "Which 68s would that be?" and he set his mug on the desk.

Bobby snorted laughter. He slid one hand into his pocket.

Cad grabbed a fistful of Harry's shirt. "Now listen to me, you stupid son of a-"

Bobby had been looking and even *he* hadn't seen Harry's right hand duck down behind his back, pull his weapon, and press it into Cad's belly. His left hand grabbed the collar of Cad's jacket and held him fast.

Bobby very badly wanted to keep watching the show, but he knew his role. He turned his head and stared at the two other guys.

Cad's gulp swallowed his words, and he froze, leaning awkwardly over Harry. His eyes were wide.

"Now," Harry said in a quiet voice, "Cad. I don't know you. I've never seen you before. You may or may not know me. I'm Harry DeMarko. This is my place. I'm a private detective. And I used to be a cop."

Bobby heard Cad gulp again.

"And yes, I've heard of the 68s. And I know you're a little out of your turf. Not much. Couple of blocks, maybe. Right?"

Cad nodded once, convulsively.

"Yeah. And I know something else," Harry told him. "I know who runs this territory. And I'll go you one better. Do the Gambinos know you're moving H on their turf?"

Cad swallowed a third time. "W-what d'ya m-mean?"

"Don't screw around, junior," Harry said, and he dug the barrel of the pistol into Cad's belly. His finger wasn't on the trigger, but Cad didn't know that.

Cad's buddies realized something had gone amiss. They looked at each other, as if for confirmation. As they looked away, Bobby took out Toni's gun and laid his hand on the desk, the pistol pointed at them. "Hey, guys? Maybe you want to hold it right there before this party gets rowdy."

Ham and Def pondered this development, with oddly identical furrowed brows. Taking advantage of the moment, Harry said to Cad, "Tell them to be cool, Cad. If I've got to shoot them, remember who's in the way."

"Guys," Cad called over his shoulder. "It's okay. We're just talking."

The henchmen exchanged another communicative look.

"Better warn 'em again," Bobby cautioned. "They don't look convinced."

"Ham, Def, fucking don't make a move!" Cad barked. "It's all cool! I'm telling you, we're cool!"

Ham and Def settled back on the balls of their feet. "That's better," Bobby said. "Relax and let it happen, as the old woman once said."

Harry snorted laughter. He cleared his throat and his face lost all expression again. He stared up at Cad. He said, "I dunno who you're looking for. I don't much care. If I knew him, I wouldn't tell you where he was. If I didn't, I still wouldn't. If you had a goddamned bazooka, I wouldn't tell you if whoever you're chasing was on the other side of that door," Harry inclined his head at the apartment door. "Run on home. If you're feeling like you want to know how close you just came to getting your guts blown out, ask some people smarter than you about me. The name's Harry DeMarko. You're Cad, and the Glimmer Twins behind you are Ham and Def. Now I know who *you* are. And believe me, you don't want me knowing who you are. This is Gambino territory. And *they* do what *I* tell 'em to around here."

Cad's brow furrowed as he absorbed that nugget.

"So I'm gonna let you stand up, walk out my door, and keep right on walkin' back to whatever shithole you came out of." Harry pulled his feet off the desk with a thump, stood up, and pushed Cad toward the door backward, one hand on his collar, the other, with the gun, buried in his belly.

Bobby stood, his gun still trained on Ham and Def. He gestured toward the door and Ham and Def shuffled out. Harry released Cad's collar. He stepped backward and raised the gun to point just between Cad's impressive eyebrows. Sweat had beaded on Cad's forehead.

Bobby watched with one eye on the other two just outside the door.

Harry's face had gone blank again, and his eyes were remote, melancholy, and unnerving to Bobby, and he wasn't even on the other side of that gun.

"I can tell by the fact that you're running around in the snow at..." Harry glanced at the clock and back. "... almost five in the morning that you're not high up on the chain of command, Cad. By the way, open your jacket. Do it slowly."

Harry thumbed the hammer back. Cad's eyes widened as he slowly unzipped his jacket and held it open.

"Didn't think so," Harry said to himself. "No vest. You're not real 68s, are you?" Cad opened his mouth to speak.

"I don't care. You're not real. I could put you in a Dumpster and they might bill me for it, but I doubt it. You're paper soldiers. Now, if a real club member wants to come talk to me, he'll find my door always open and my demeanor polite. But you?" Harry thumped Cad in the forehead with the barrel of his gun. "If I *ever* see you on Gambino turf again, I'm not asking any questions. I'll just TCB. You understand me?" Harry's voice had gone cold and dead as a January blizzard.

Cad nodded. "I-I get it. I understand. I understand!"

"Vanish," Harry growled.

Cad turned and scooted out the door. He and his pals ran down the street toward Houston. When they were out of sight, Harry held out a hand.

Bobby slapped it and held his own out for the rebound with a bright grin on his face. Harry stared at him, those eyes still cold and hard, until Bobby realized what he'd wanted, and he placed the gun in Harry's open palm.

Harry nodded, checked both, and put Toni's in her desk. He slid the other into his holster. Bobby started to sit, and Harry said, pointing, "Lock that, would you?"

Bobby nodded and did so, shooting the bolt with a loud snap. He turned to see Harry refilling their coffee, and was gratified when Harry left room for another shot. He dosed both mugs and handed one to Bobby, who nodded his thanks. They sipped the hot, bitter brew in silence.

Bobby broke the silence. "So... I'd ask if it's always like this, but yeah. Questions I know the answers to I tend not to ask."

"Well... this is a little ridiculous, even for *us*," Harry said. He finished his coffee. "You're good backup. You handle yourself well."

Bobby shrugged. "It's easy to look tough. Harder to actually pull it off. All I did was what I always do: let someone else do the heavy lifting while I run off at the mouth."

"Yeah, well, half of all the work we do is just that," Harry said. "But you *know* that."

"That's bullshit right there," Bobby said. "And I know from bullshit. I've seen it."

Harry gave Bobby Gold a wan smile. "I know."

Bobby felt uneasy about that smile. "So... what was that about vests?"

Harry pursed his lips. "The 68s are a motorcycle gang that operate northwest of here. They're bringing heroin in. Those dim bulbs tonight said they were 68s, but no member of a motorcycle club would be caught dead without his vest. It's a uniform. No vest means those idiots were strictly wanna-bes. Nothing to worry about. No need to be diplomatic."

"You can be diplomatic?" Bobby asked.

"Sure I can. You don't get along in this town without being able to bend, at least a little."

"You learn that as a cop?"

Harry's eyes settled on Bobby's, and that melancholy stare caused him to review his words, revise his sentiment, and utter a retraction. "I mean- you know... about the 68s. Not about bending. I'm sure you were a-"

Harry grinned. "I'm messing with you. And yeah, the PD knows about the 68s. But they're hands-off."

"Too dangerous?"

Harry gave him a puzzled look. "That's kind of insulting. No, they're under the eye of the FBI and the ATF."

"For heroin?"

Harry suppressed an impatient sigh. *He's not one of us. He doesn't know how it all shakes out,* he thought. "No. Look outside."

Bobby did.

"What do you see?"

"Snow."

"Yeah. Ever ride a motorcycle?"

Bobby's face showed dawning understanding. "They're migrating. Like birds."

"Yes. They follow the weather. They cross the state line, it's out of the PD's hands. Then you're messing with Uncle. And Uncle *hates* it when people do that."

Harry crossed to the door, unlocked it and stepped outside. Bobby watched him look up and down the block, nod his head, and come back inside, rubbing his hands together.

"Friggin' cold out there," he muttered, locking the door behind him. He knocked on the apartment door and Toni opened it immediately.

"All clear," Harry said.

Toni nodded, looked up at Bobby, and back to Harry. "You being nice?"

"More or less."

"What's that mean?"

"I gave him a gun," Harry said. "We got a visit from a couple meatheads working for the 68s."

Toni grimaced. "I gathered as much from Farrokh. They had him running errands most of the night, and he got spooked. He ran off."

"Oh, man," Harry breathed. "That isn't good."

"It gets better. He's carrying a brick."

Bobby's radar twitched when he heard the word. The taste of it came back in a rush, and he licked his lips. Everything else about the night followed that response, and he looked like the wind had been knocked out of him. His narrow face had gone the color of whey. Toni, alarmed, went to him. "Gold? You okay?"

She helped him to the couch as Harry watched. He didn't say anything when she sat beside Gold and took his hand.

"Jesus, Gold, your pulse is going crazy. Are you drunk? If you puke, I'm gonna be pissed off."

"No, I'm… well, I mean, yeah, but not drunk-drunk. Just drunk. And tired. I…" his eyes flickered to Harry and back to her hand. "Can we talk? Alone?"

"Sure. Harry, you want to go babysit?" she chucked her chin toward the apartment. He nodded. "You get anywhere with your sister and her husband?"

"I got zilch. She ain't talkin' and he's out. Gene's working on him."

Harry raised an eyebrow. "It was just a graze, wasn't it?"

Toni's face became grim. "Go talk to Gene."

Harry took the hint. He said, "Your gun's in the drawer. You want mine?"

"Naah," she said, patting Bobby's hand. "I'll just throw Bobby at anyone who tries to get uppity. Look at him: his bony ass would make a good wrecking ball."

"Good enough. Holler if you need me," he said, and he went into the apartment, gently closing the door.

Toni smiled at the door and turned to Bobby. "So what's up?

"Well," Bobby began. He wasn't even aware the tears had started until Toni's shocked expression told him something was wrong.

CHAPTER TWELVE

Harry assessed the damage. Gene had Johnny Abruzzi on the bed, and it was soaking up blood. Starr was crouched on the other side of the bed from Gene, anxiously watching and fidgeting. Farrokh was in the bathroom, apparently.

"Gene, what's going on? Toni said there was trouble."

Gene nodded. He had Abruzzi's jacket off and his shirt cut away from his side. "The arm wasn't the problem," the ME said, concentrating. "He took a second shot. They didn't notice it because the arm was bleeding so badly. I'm trying to get the bullet out now."

"Can I help?"

"Nope," Gene said, tongue between his teeth.

"Okay." Harry went into the kitchen area and rummaged. They'd stocked up pretty well. The freezer was full of stuff, the walk-in cooler was topped up. He found some bread and meat and cheese and set about making a few sandwiches. While he was busy, the bathroom door opened and Farrokh Dahli came wandering out. His face showed exhaustion. Harry pointed at the wardrobe "There's some pillows and blankets in the bottom of that Get some and go curl up, Farrokh. We'll worry about the 68s later."

The youth nodded, eyes downcast. As he gathered the bedding, he asked, voice low, "Did they tell you, Mr. Harry?"

Harry nodded. "The basics, anyhow. Don't worry about that now."

Farrokh's eyes spilled tears, but he did as he was told. He shrugged the backpack off his back and put it in the corner. He built himself a pallet next to it. "I did not know where to go," he said, voice desolate. "My uncle-"

"I said don't worry about it. We'll sort it, okay?" Harry said. He brought the boy a sandwich. He held it out, then hesitated. "I'm sorry. I didn't think- do you eat ham?"

Farrokh nodded. "Yes, I can eat ham."

"I never thought to ask. Sorry."

"It is okay, Mr. Harry. We do not follow a particular diet." The youth took the plate, picked up the sandwich and took a bite. He chewed and swallowed. "Thank you."

"Of course."

"Thank *you*," the boy said, with stern emphasis. "I am indebted to you."

"You're not," Harry said. "It's all part of the package, Farrokh. Later on we'll give Kilburn a call-"

Farrokh paled. "No!" He dropped his plate and picked up his bag. "I-I must go!"

Harry put out a hand and said, soothingly, "Okay. We won't call Kilburn. Okay? We won't do anything until you say so. All right?"

Farrokh hesitated.

Harry said, "You have *my word*."

All doubt fled from Farrokh's face, and he lowered his eyes. "I apologize, Mr. Harry. I thank you."

"Just sit down before you fall over," Harry said. "Eat your sandwich. There's plenty if you're still hungry after."

Farrokh nodded, dropped his bag next to his makeshift bed, and sat cross-legged. He picked up the plate and began to eat again. His eyes, haunted and far-off, stared in the general direction of the floor, but Harry could see he wasn't seeing much through them. He was elsewhere, in his mind.

He took the pile of sandwiches to the table and sat. He watched Gene rooting around inside Abruzzi's side, eyes screwed up with the effort. He had a faraway look in his eyes similar to Farrokh's, but Harry was willing to bet

Farrokh wasn't visualizing the inside of a human being, navigating by feel.

Starr was shaking, her hands twisting together.

"Starr?" Harry called, voice pitched low.

She whipped her head around, eyes wide. "Huh?"

Harry could see she wasn't *much* younger than Toni. Maybe twenty if she was a day. She had that same girlishness about her that Toni still had. That curved, gentle, innocent look to her flesh that would fade in time, revealing the core of the woman beneath. "Come eat."

"What? No..." she said with a shake of her head.

"You a doctor?" Harry asked around a mouthful of bread and ham and spicy brown mustard.

Starr frowned. "Am I... no."

Harry gestured with his sandwich. "Well Gene is. Unless he needs your help, you're not going to be much use. Come sit with me and have some food. You look starved."

Starr stared at him, eyes shifting to the pile of sandwiches, and then back at Abruzzi.

"He's not gonna mind," Harry said. "And you're right here if he needs you."

She got jerkily to her feet and sat across from him at the table. She took a sandwich and set it on a napkin. "I'm terrified."

"I imagine you are," he said. He glanced at her chest. She had washed the blood off. She took a bite and chewed listlessly. "So, what happened?"

She gave him an opaque look. "What do you mean?"

"How'd he get shot?"

"No idea." Her face became a remote mask.

Instead of being upset, Harry just smiled at her. "I know that look. I've seen it once or twice on your sister's face."

Starr grinned, a fleeting, happy grin, and then it faded

"I bet."

"She never talks about herself. What can you tell me?" Harry asked.

Starr shot him a cool look. "No idea," she said with a hint of a smile.

He tilted his head, conceding the point. "You Bennett women are tough."

"Just like it says on the box, Harry."

"Man. It must have been hell, raising the two of you."

She arched an eyebrow. "Two? Two would have been a breeze."

"How many siblings do you have?" he asked, an uneasy feeling stirring in his belly.

"More than a few, fewer than a baseball team," she said. "All girls."

Harry leaned back, one arm hooked over the back of his chair and eyed her. "Not much of an answer."

"We're not much of a question-answering family."

"No kidding."

She pursed her lips and said, "She does that to you too, huh? Gives you the runaround when you ask questions?"

"I never asked."

Starr set her sandwich down and chewed the bite she'd taken, and swallowed it. "You never asked?"

"Nope."

"How long have you been together?"

Harry gave her a lopsided grin. "You tell me."

"Why would I know?"

"You showed up here knowing who I was, Starr. You knew my name. You're obviously not completely ignorant of her life."

It was Starr's turn to concede the point. "You're pretty sharp."

"I get by."

"Yeah, we've been in touch some. Not lately, but she

called this summer. She'd had a real scare, and wanted to hear a friendly voice."

He nodded and said nothing.

"This is the part where you protest," she said. "How you're a friendly voice, and all. Why isn't she talking to you, et cetera."

"She wanted to talk to me, she knows where to find me," Harry said.

Starr studied him with care, eyes narrowed slightly. "You're serious."

"We don't have that kind of relationship," He said.

"What kind is that?"

"The kind that doesn't work," he said.

She snorted laughter, but swallowed it when Abruzzi moaned on the bed. He thrashed a little, despite being unconscious. Gene dropped something in the glass on the bedside table. A small bullet rattled to a stop in the empty water glass.

"Got it," Gene said absently. "It was behind a rib. Must have spalled. Now I just have to pack it and close him. Hand me that alcohol." He didn't point and he didn't single anyone out. Starr moved before Harry. She gave Gene the bottle. "And that package of gauze."

She picked up one of the packages and opened it. Gene swore. "Damn it, I said hand it to me, not open it. Get another one."

She stared at the package in her hands. "What? Why?"

"Because I don't want to sew sandwich crumbs into his side, if you don't mind," Gene snapped. "Come on!"

Starr blushed and fetched another package. She handed it to Gene, who tore it with his teeth and extracted the gauze with one gloved hand. He rested it on Abruzzi's chest while he spun the top off the alcohol bottle with one thumb. It flicked off the bottle and rolled a few feet in the carpet before stopping.

He poured a generous amount into the hole in Abruzzi's side and pressed the gauze hard onto the wound. Abruzzi moaned, half-conscious. He pulled it away and dropped it on the man's chest. He said, "Harry, get gloves. You're gonna help me sew."

"I can-"

"Harry, I said. You're gonna sit next to him and hold his hand and pat his brow and keep him still while I put a needle in him. Got it?"

"Yes," she said. She slid onto the bed near his head as Harry found a pair of gloves. He slipped them on, held out his hands, and Gene doused them liberally with alcohol. Harry rubbed his hands together and dove into the case. He found a curved needle and some thread, both in sterile paper. He tore the needle open, held it out, and Gene splashed it. Harry opened the thread, found the easy-eye on the end, and dragged it through the eye of the needle. He pulled a length out, tied a quick knot, and held out a cupped hand. Gene filled his palm with alcohol, and Harry dragged the needle and thread through it. Then he swapped with Gene, taking the alcohol and handing him the needle. Gene nodded his thanks and waited. Harry doused the wound again, picked up the gauze, and patted the hole dry. Gene pinched the lips of the wound shut and started stitching.

Abruzzi moaned and tried to roll away from the needle, and Starr held him still. She took his hand in hers and squeezed it. Harry waited with the alcohol and gauze, but Gene was able to get it closed in a neat line of seven stitches. He held up the thread while Harry fetched the scissors and clipped it close. Gene took the alcohol and gauze back and doused it again, cleaning the wound. Then he stripped off his bloody gloves, put on new ones, and bandaged the wound. He finished and he and Harry cleaned up the medical debris and Harry dumped it in the trash.

"Better bag that and let me take it," Gene said. "Anyone roots through your trash they'll find it. I'll take it to work and put it in the incinerator. Someone twigs to what you're up to in here and all our efforts are for naught."

Harry nodded. "Okay. Thanks, Gene."

Gene glanced at Starr, grimaced, and said, "Can we talk outside?"

Harry glanced at the door. "No. Toni needed the office."

"Fair enough. You got coffee in here?"

"Nope," Harry said. "I got some orange juice."

"What kind of philistine are you? All right."

Gene followed Harry into the kitchen area. Harry glanced at Farrokh in the corner. The youth was deeply asleep, curled into a ball. Harry got the juice and poured them both a glass. Starr lay beside Abruzzi, one hand on his wrist, and closed her eyes. Harry watched her breathe Gene followed his eyes and jumped to the wrong conclusion.

"Aren't you a married man?" he asked with an impish smile. "Or at least close enough as makes no odds."

"Isn't like that," Harry said in a low voice. He edged away from the bed, as far as he could. Gene followed, confusion on his genial face. "I'm just waiting for her to fall asleep," Harry explained in that same quiet voice.

Gene nodded.

"Besides, she's Toni's sister."

Gene digested that nugget of information. Then he shrugged, giving Harry a wicked grin. "Doesn't seem to be an issue for Mike Brandt."

Harry snorted. "Believe me, he's welcome to those two. They're tame. I've got my hands full with one Bennett sister. Two would kill me in a week."

"Three days," Starr murmured from the bed. "Tops."

Harry sighed. "You need to sleep, Starr."

"I'll sleep when he's okay," she said through slack lips, eyes still closed.

"You see the kind of crap I have to put up with?" Harry asked.

"Yeah, I feel all kinds of bad for you, Harry," Gene told him. He sipped his juice with a notably sarcastic slurp.

Harry nodded. "Yeah, I can see that."

The apartment door opened and Toni poked her head in. Harry could see, even from across the room, her eyes were red. She beckoned him. He nodded and slapped Gene on the arm. "Come on, Kildare. I'll treat you to a cup."

He crossed the room. Gene trailed behind, setting his juice on the table. To Starr he said, "I'm in the next room if you need anything. Call out, I'm here."

She nodded without speaking, her red hair drifting over her face. He bet himself she wouldn't be awake ten minutes after they left.

With the door closed, Harry sized up Toni. Her eyes were red, her face puffy, and he knew when his woman had been crying. He glanced at Bobby, whose eyes were also red. He said nothing, because they didn't. Instead, he asked her, "Did you fill in your pal here?"

Toni shook her head. Her voice was hoarse. "No, I... we were talking about something else."

She stared hard at Harry and he gave her a bare nod. "Okay. I don't have to do it twice. Gene, have a seat. Who wants coffee?"

The sun was rising, and the street was almost fully illuminated now. Harry glanced at the clock. Almost seven. *Gonna be a long day*, he thought again. They all raised hands, although Bobby looked like it was the last thing in the world he wanted. Harry pointed at Toni's chair. She frowned at him, and he reiterated the gesture. Pouting, she sat, crossing her arms and grumping at him with her eyes. That was fine. It was more like her normal self. Whatever had happened between her and Gold had wrung her out. He hadn't seen that woman cry in forever.

"This is all amongst ourselves," Harry said. "It can't leave this room."

He looked from face to face. Gene, Toni, and even Bobby nodded.

"Last night... Sal D'Amico was murdered."

Bobby's eyes widened. Toni didn't react. Gene frowned. "I know that name, right?"

"He's a... a friend of ours," Harry said. "His construction company redid our office and apartment for us. It was in the nature of returning a favor."

Gene nodded. "Okay."

"And he's... was... a Gambino underboss."

Gene choked. "What?"

Harry nodded. "Yeah. It's complicated. Anyhow, he's dead."

"And that's... bad?" Gene asked. His face fell. "Oh. He was a friend."

Toni gave Gene a wan smile. Of all the people in that room, Gene would understand what that meant.

"Not like that," Harry said. "More like... more like a friendly adversary. Anyhow, if it was just a mob thing, all hands off. But it's not."

"You don't think it was a hit?" Bobby asked.

Harry sighed, and shared a glance with Toni. "No, I'm pretty sure it was."

Gene gave an exasperated sigh. "Okay. Simple, straightforward answer. Now give me the Harry spin."

"Come again?" Harry asked.

"Sorry, sorry," Gene said, patting the air. "I meant the *Harry-Toni* spin. Because Lord knows nothing's ever easy with you two."

"Tell me about it," Bobby said. He held up a hand and Gene gave him five.

Harry and Toni shared a second glance. She shrugged. "Better just tell 'em."

Harry crossed his arms and stared at her. "She's *your* sister."

Toni nodded. Taking a deep breath, she said, "One of Sal's bodyguards got there too late to stop it, but just in time to... to take a shot. Word we got is the bodyguard winged the hitter."

Gene's eyes widened. "Oh shit."

"Yeah."

Bobby frowned. He glanced at the apartment door and back at Toni. "You mean... the guy that whacked out a Gambino boss-"

"-married my sister, apparently," Toni finished.

"Oh," Bobby said. He considered this. The information belatedly registered. He raised one eyebrow. "Sister... Jesus H. Roosevelt *Christ*, what was *that* house like?"

"Right?" Harry agreed.

"Stow it, you," Toni growled, but she smiled at him.

"So, you got a sister, she's married to a mob hitter," Gene said. "Which Family? How bad is it?"

Toni bit her lip. Harry watched her face, surprised again at the family resemblance between she and Starr. Toni said, "I don't actually know. They're not from here. Last I heard, Starr had moved to Chicago."

The color drained from Harry's face. "Oh, you're *kidding* me," he muttered.

Remorse filled her voice as she said, "Last I heard."

Harry closed his eyes. "That means-"

"-we're screwed but good," she finished.

Bobby held up a hand. "Uh, guys? I'm a junkie chef. I don't know about the Spleeninator here, but I got zilch as far as having any idea at all what the hell you're talking about. Can I get some flashcards? Or subtitles?"

Harry opened his eyes. "The Five Families. You know that much?"

Bobby shrugged. "Gambinos? And... uh... Bonnanno. I know that one because the rumor is they're using Bellini's as a front."

Toni ticked off on her fingers, "Gambino. Bonnanno. Columbo. Lucchese. Genovese. Between them they control all of New York. All the boroughs. From upstate down to Jersey, and bits here and there till you get to Florida. Everything from petty robberies to full-on heists. Everything belongs to them, all the best money-makers, anyhow. Everything from construction to garbage."

"Okay, okay, I get it," Bobby said. "They're the power behind the throne. And your brother-in-law just took a boss out."

"Underboss," Harry corrected. "Like a vice president."

"Got it. And the... Families? They're gonna be upset?"

"Ordinarily?" Harry asked. "Not even a little. They love it when one of the other families takes a hit, either literally or figuratively. But there's one thing all five Families hate more than each other."

"And that would be?" Bobby asked.

"The Chicago Mob. The Outfit," Toni said.

"So, not one big happy mob?"

Harry snorted. "Not likely. It goes back to the twenties. Maybe further. Maybe it started in Sicily. But back in the day, Capone was the tops in Chicago. And the New York Families wanted Chicago. Or wanted Chicago in the Commission, so they could spread the wealth. Capone was making money hand over fist during prohibition. One man controlling all the action in a whole city? The Five Families wanted a piece. They tried negotiating, tried getting tough. Capone thumbed his nose at them. As the story goes, the Families here sent a team of guys to put out

Capone's lights. Capone was a showoff. Playboy. The newspapers all knew he was the man at the top, and he played it off. Everybody knew he was the Man. He was flashy, but he didn't get there being *only* flashy. He was ruthless. So when his sources told him there was a hit squad coming for him, he had his boy Nitti waiting for them. Nitti sent them back, and old Al told the Families to stay out of Chicago." Harry shrugged. "They've been enemies ever since."

"Sent 'em back?" Gene asked.

"Well," Harry hedged, "their heads, anyhow. With their cocks stuffed in their mouths. There was room, though. Nitti had cut out their tongues."

Bobby swallowed. "Okay, that's pretty much horrible."

Toni said, "That's nothing. They had JFK killed."

A startled silence settled over the room. Bobby, Gene, and even Harry gaped at her. She shrugged.

"That was the rumor, anyhow. They never proved anything, of course," she said. "Same as Castro."

Bobby said, "Castro?"

Harry nodded. "Yeah. When Castro took Cuba in 56, the Outfit was getting ready to open a bunch of casinos and stuff. Castro took Cuba away from them. Millions in potential revenue off American soil, gone."

Gene asked, "How do you know all this?"

"I was a cop for twenty years," Harry said.

Toni added, "I'm from Chicago."

Bobby studied her with a puzzled expression. "I thought you were from Queens."

Toni shook her head. "Naah. I just like New York better."

"Why?"

Toni looked at Harry. Bobby nodded. "Stupid question. I got it."

"Okay," Gene said. "If I got this right, the, uh, patient

is from Chicago. And he came to town to kill an underboss for the Gambino Family."

"Right so far," Harry said.

"Okay, so… you bring him in, patch him up, and now you hustle him out of town. I assume once he gets to Chicago he'll be safe?" Gene asked. "Safer, anyhow."

"You'd think that," Toni said. "But-"

"-because it's *you*-" Bobby interjected.

"-you'd be wrong," Toni said.

She flipped off Bobby, who merely shrugged and asked, "Am I wrong?"

"You ain't wrong," Harry said.

"So the problem is?" Gene asked.

"We got a case," Harry explained. "We got hired to find the hitter before the cops do."

Gene and Bobby looked at one another. "Uh-"

Toni said impatiently, "Sal's people dropped by right before you got here. They want us to find *him*-" she jerked a thumb at the apartment door, "before the cops do, because they want to kill him. And they're paying us a lot of money."

Gene looked skeptical. Bobby chuckled.

"Something funny?" Harry asked.

"Yeah. I don't know you," he said. He gave Toni a look of what Harry would have described as hero worship Bobby's eyes blazed, and the ferocity of his smile, more than anything else he's seen or heard from the man he found familiar. "But her? There just isn't enough money in the world. She wouldn't give up someone she *hated*, let alone family. So what's the catch? Because there's *always* a catch with you."

Toni grinned. "We find him before the cops do. We turn him over, and they kill him. The cops find him, or we don't find him and he gets away, they'll kill *us*."

Bobby nodded. "*There* it is."

Harry shot Gene a thoughtful look. "Been meaning to ask, but I figured you'd bring it up if it were the case, but… I don't suppose…?"

Gene said, "Nope. He's gonna be fine. The bullet passed through his bicep and into his side. That's why I thought he'd been shot twice, but it was the same bullet, luckily. The arm slowed it down, but it broke skin, a rib, and floated up under his ribcage. I don't *think* it breeched his peritoneum, but we need to watch out for infection. He's on some tranquilizers I happened to have from a wisdom tooth I had out a couple months ago. I can't give him anything stronger because I can't steal anything. I'll get caught, and I'm already-"

Harry held up a hand. "I know. You're already out on a limb. I appreciate everything you've done so far, Gene. We owe you. Huge."

"Don't sweat it, Harry. All I've done is fixed up a GSW, which by law I'm required to report to the cops or I could lose my license, maybe go to jail for a couple months, ruin my life, flush my career, and disappoint the hell out of my mother. Just another Friday," Gene said. The enormity of what he'd done seemed to weigh on him a little more heavily than before, and he leaned over, hands between his knees. "Whoo. Holy hell."

Toni went to him and put a hand on his shoulder. "You've done enough. Tell me what I need to do and I'll take it from here."

"He's stable, but I want to keep an eye on that infection. If he spikes a fever we need to jump on antibiotics. Those I can get easy. But I'm not a practicing doctor. I can't write prescriptions."

Bobby said, "Tell me what you need, I'll get it for you."

They all looked at him.

"I was a junkie. I've got connections."

"Can you get medical grade tranquilizers and painkillers?" Gene asked skeptically.

"If it exists, I can get it in under two hours," Bobby told him.

"Okay, okay," Harry said, raising his hands. "Let's stick to one felony at a time, huh?"

"Why stop at two?" Toni asked.

"Two?"

Toni mimed hammering in a nail. "Sal."

"Oh." Harry said. "Okay. Two then."

"At least three," Gene said. He ticked them off. "Murder, illegally harboring a murder suspect, not reporting a GSW, me treating him, you taking money from the Mob-"

"That's not a felony," Bobby interrupted. "That's just business."

"To find a killer and let them kill him," Gene said peevishly. "That's aiding and abetting at the least. Accessory after the fact. Maybe even premeditated murder."

"Conspiracy," Harry offered, then looked pained. He put a hand over his eyes. "At the least. Okay. Let's stick to…"

He took his hand off his face and looked at Toni, who said with a sheepish look, "Five, I think? Seven? Doesn't matter. After the first one you're looking at Federal time anyhow. Twenty years, fifty years, a hundred years… after a certain point, it doesn't matter. Seven? Eight? I don't know. It's late. Or early. I can't even decide which right now."

"Yeah," Harry said. "So let's leave a narcotics bust on the back burner until strictly necessary."

Bobby sat back and sighed. "Fine, fine. The one area I have practical experience in and you shoot it down. Be that way. Man. A couple hours ago I was standin' up fallin down drunk. Now I'm sober as hell. All I wanted was to black out. Maybe see if I could get drunk enough to go erase all of today. Get a do-over. Now here I am smack-dab in the middle of I don't *even* know what to call it. The further comedic adventures of Mutt and Jeff, crime-fighters extraordinaire? Or just Comedy of Errors?"

"Nobody asked you to volunteer," Harry pointed out. "There's the door."

Toni shot him a warning glare. "It's okay. Bobby's welcome. He's solid, Harry. I can vouch."

He cocked his head and stared at her. She raised one eyebrow slightly. After a second, he nodded. To Bobby he said, "Okay. You're in if you want to be. Welcome to the playpen."

Bobby blinked. "Just like that?"

"You don't get it," Gene said, still staring at the floor. "Even after seeing it, you don't get it. They're basically mind-linked. You didn't see it, you didn't hear it, but they just had a whole conversation about you. He questioned her, she answered, and he accepted her reasons and evidence. You didn't see their lips move because they've presumably evolved beyond the need for verbalization."

They all stared at Gene. He looked up. "What? I watch a lot of Star Trek reruns."

Bobby chuckled and said, "This is nuts."

"This is just daytime," Toni said. "Come on, you've been here before."

"Yeah," Bobby said. "I just... you know... I was hoping for maybe *two* weeks before the next near-death exp-"

Bobby broke off, and Harry looked over in time to see him sitting back, hand over his mouth. His eyes were far away, and as he watched, they glistened.

Toni saw it and went to sit next to him. She put a hand on his shoulder. Gold didn't react, but after a second he seemed to shake off whatever he was thinking and finished his sentence.

"...experience. But whatever. Okay," he clapped his hands, cleared his throat, and said hoarsely, "what's the first move?"

Toni squeezed his shoulder and stood up. She went to Harry and put a hand over his own. She pressed it, and he gave her a questioning look. She shook her head a scant inch, and he nodded.

Gene said, "I'm gonna go check on him." He got up and went into the apartment.

As the door closed, Bobby said again, "So what's first? Clara and her..." he glanced at Harry and changed his wording. "...partner? Kepner? Or is this Mills' territory?"

Toni gave Harry a wan smile. "Not this time, Bobby," she said.

"Why not?"

"Because first we have to figure out what's going on," Harry said. "That means I gotta go to the Aces and see Hendrick. Then out to Sal's place. See what I can turn up."

"We." Toni's icy tone was definite and final.

"That's what I said," Harry told her. "And if I didn't say it, you know I meant it."

"We," Bobby added.

Harry raised an eyebrow.

Bobby did the same.

Harry narrowed his eyes.

Bobby narrowed his.

Harry looked at Toni, who had to stifle a grin.

Bobby said, "Look, I just met you. I dunno if I want to put myself between you and a shit-ton of trouble-"

"That a scientific term?" Toni asked.

Bobby held up a finger and recited in a professorial voice, "One shit-ton. From the old English: Shite-tonnage. One shit-ton is the equivalent of twenty-four metric ass-loads, or to put it another way, one quarter of a fuck-ton. Therefore, one fuck-ton equals four shit-tons, equals ninety-six ass-loads. Literally. Your standard wild ass can haul up to one heck of a lot of shit. Ninety-six ass-loads equals four shit-tons, equals one fuck-ton. Interestingly, the way to get an ass to move quickly from farm-to-market was to insert a freshly-caught free range rabbit into the rectum of the ass. Hence the phrase-"

"Wild hare up your ass," Harry muttered. "Jesus Christ."

Toni barked laughter. "Tell me he's not worth keeping around, Harry."

"It's your call if you want to adopt strays," Harry said. "But you're walking him, feeding him, and cleaning up if he piddles on the rug."

Bobby barked sharply and let his tongue hang out, panting.

Toni put a hand over her eyes. "Bobby, for fuck's sake. I'm trying to convince him you're not an idiot or a tourist. You're not helping."

"Wait… I'm supposed to be *helping*?" Bobby asked. "Oh… that makes more sense. As I was saying, before being so rudely interrupted-"

"My apologies," Toni interrupted.

"…I don't know if I- thank you, apology accepted- if I want to put myself between you and a shit-ton of trouble," Bobby continued. He pointed at Toni. "But her? She's *earned* it. So I'm down for whatever. But I gotta tell you, man. Comes to a choice between saving her or saving you, I'm gonna leave you to fend for yourself and hustle her the hell outta the way."

Harry studied Bobby Gold's seamed face for a very long time. His melancholy eyes were unsettling to Bobby, who'd seen a lot of different eyes in his life. Furtive eyes, speculative eyes, crazy eyes. These eyes were not like the others. They were fearsome in their relentless hunt for track and sign across a stony ground. The eyes of a hunter with tireless legs and inexorable patience. *Jesus,* he thought, *What's with the flowery description? I'm not writing a fucking book.*

Harry said in a flat, definitive voice, "Okay."

"Okay?" Bobby asked, startled.

"Yes."

Toni smiled, having accepted the pronouncement as gospel. Bobby was suspicious. It seemed too easy.

"Just like that?"

Harry stood up. "What more do you want? A hug? I'm not a hugger."

Toni scooted up against him, and his arms enveloped her.

"Ordinarily," he amended. He hugged her. He said "I'm gonna check on Gene. Do me a favor?"

"Sure, Harry," she said.

"Run up and see how many girls we got in the apartment? We've been lucky, but I don't think we ought to be keeping them here. See if they'll lend us a bed and some cover."

Toni nodded. "Good call." She turned and kicked Bobby's feet. "Come on, you. Let's get some air."

Bobby stood. Toni unlocked the door and went around the right side of the office to a set of stairs leading to the apartment over the store. She and Harry owned the building and rented out the apartment to an ever-changing array of working girls from the neighborhood, making sure they had a safe place to stay. A good deed, Toni had called it. Harry considered it her version of atonement for her former life, but kept this opinion to himself. It was something he'd have thought of too, given time.

Gold zipped his jacket all the way up. He and Harry eyed one another. Bobby was uncomfortable. He was tall, gangly, and used to towering over everyone. He was taller than Harry DeMarko, but he had the uncomfortable feeling he was looking *up* at Harry. The man's demeanor projected a longer shadow and a taller profile than his physical form, it seemed like.

Harry said nothing, just watched him with those relentless eyes. Bobby seemed to make a decision. Bobby stuck out a hand. Harry took it and they shook.

"Bobby Gold."

"Harry DeMarko."

"Look… I'm glad you're back," Bobby said. "And… you know… me and Toni? We're just-"

"I know."

"Yeah?"

"Of course I do. She's *her*," Harry said.

Bobby grinned. "Yeah."

"You had her back," Harry said.

"Yeah, well," Bobby shuffled.

"No. You had her back. I *owe* you," Harry told the other man. "Thank you for that."

"You don't owe me anything," Bobby said. "She bought and paid for it. She had *my* back."

"Yeah. She does that. But what you and her did and said and what you and *I* do and say, those are two separate things. And I'm in your debt for keeping her safe," Harry said. His eyes blazed. "Whatever you need."

Bobby stared at Harry, dumbfounded.

"You just met me," Bobby said. "Why would you-"

"I met you because I'm not in prison," Harry said. "I met you because you helped *her* figure out that asshole Willoughsby's plan. I met you because Toni counted on you and you came through. I met you because you met *her*. I don't know why you're here-"

"Uh," Bobby began, and Harry cut him off.

"-and it doesn't matter. She's your friend. You're hers.

So… so am I." Harry gave him a half-smile. "Whatever you need, it's yours."

Bobby nodded, dazed. "Okay. Cool. I'm… uh…" he jerked his thumb at the door. Harry nodded and turned away. He went into the apartment, but not before Bobby gave him another long look.

I owe Sandy a beer, he thought as he hurried after Toni. *Damned if she wasn't right.*

CHAPTER THIRTEEN

The apartment was dim, the light came from the bathroom and one lamp by the door. On the bed, Johnny Abruzzi slept fitfully, sweat beading on his forehead. Gene was mopping at his brow with a damp cloth. In the corner Farrokh muttered something and rolled over in his doze. Starr was blinking sleepily up at Gene, worry on her fine features.

Harry asked in a soft voice, "How's he doing?"

"I don't like the fever, Harry. His temperature's three degrees high already. I gave him some penicillin just to be on the safe side." Gene dipped the cloth in a bowl next to the bed he'd filled with cool water. He handed the cloth to Starr. "Keep wiping his forehead. Try not to wake him. He needs to rest."

Taking the cloth, Starr asked, "Is he going to be okay? I thought it wasn't dangerous."

"Any time you introduce a foreign object into the human body through an orifice it's not meant to enter, you're rolling the dice. He *should* be fine. But we're going to watch him just to be sure. Try not to worry. Patients can feel worry. They don't respond well."

Starr stared up at Gene with wide eyes. "Is that true?"

"Documented. They can feel the emotions around them. Sometimes our minds are more powerful than drugs. If the mind is worried by the emotions around it, it can react in kind. That's why positive attitudes are necessary in a hospital." Gene patted her arm. "So try not to worry."

"Okay. Thank you, Doctor."

"Sure."

Gene led Harry to the sink, where he filled a water glass and drained it. He cast an eye on Harry's drawn face.

"You look like shit, Harry. When's the last time you slept?"

"I don't know… what day is it?"

"Saturday morning, I guess."

"Oh, Thursday, I think. We were out and about yesterday morning, just enjoying the feeling of being out. Went to the bank, fixed the shit with my pension checks," Harry said, leaning against the counter, arms folded.

"What's the deal?" Gene asked.

"Oh, they wouldn't let Toni cash 'em. The three that came around in the time I got sent up were just sitting there. No big deal. She's fearsome. She scrapped enough skip traces to keep the lights on and take care of the mortgage. So I went and talked to my union rep. I made her my beneficiary on my insurance, and put her on my next-of list so she gets my checks no matter what happens," he explained.

"Smart, given your line of work."

"Yeah. I don't want her worrying about it anymore."

"That's funny."

Harry gave him a sideways look. "What?"

"You, assuming you're gonna be dead and she won't be."

"What do you mean?"

"Come on, Harry, she's twice as reckless as you ever were. You should have seen her after the Terry Shoulders thing. She looked like she'd been through a meat grinder. She lost a tooth. Broken rib. That was two weeks ago. I bet her ribs still look like a rainbow," Gene said.

Harry shuffled his feet and glanced at Starr. The woman was busy mopping her husband's brow and didn't seem to be listening. "I made her an appointment to go to the dentist Monday. They're going to put a peg in-"

"My point," Gene overrode his protest, "is that she's not going to sit still if you go down. She'll be right there with you. And if she can't save you, she'll die trying. I don't expect her to live much more than five minutes longer than you do."

"I hope you're wrong," Harry said. "I don't want her throwing her life away. There's too much to do around here."

Gene snorted. "Figures."

"What?"

"You worried about the neighborhood while you were fighting off boyfriends in the shower, didn't you?"

"Nobody came at me that way inside," Harry said absently. "But yeah, I was worried. Farrokh's in the middle of this drug thing. Toni was all alone-"

"Bobby was here."

Harry was silent. Gene looked at him and said, "You're not jealous, are you?"

"Yeah I am," Harry said.

Gene blinked. "But… Toni's… well… Toni. She's not gonna-"

"Not like that. He was here, that's all. She was in trouble, and he was here. It should have been me."

"Harry, you were being tried for murder. They denied you bail. How in the world-"

Harry's fist thumped on the edge of the sink and Gene swallowed his words. Starr looked up with a frown, then went back to wiping Abruzzi's face.

"Sorry," Gene said.

"Don't be. I'm on edge. It should never have happened. And it was a *fluke*, Gene. A goddamned typo. If Kepner hadn't put my name down in a phony report, Willoughsby wouldn't have been outed. He wouldn't have come after me. He wouldn't have- Rachael Messner would still be alive. Toni wouldn't have been alone. Everything would have been fine," Harry said.

"Reasonable," Gene opined. "Reasonable and logical

and the biggest load of horseshit I've ever heard you spout, and I've heard you spout a lot of horseshit."

"Yeah, but I'm drunk when I do," Harry said.

"Sobriety doesn't exempt you from stupidity. Harry, you're the guy who went down an alley after a girl and got shot for your trouble. You're the guy who put himself on the line when hookers were being dropped all over your neighborhood. You're the guy stopped Porter Rockwell."

"Porter killed himself," Harry said.

"He killed himself, sure. And would he have done that if you hadn't figured out his sick game?"

Harry shrugged.

"No. Or maybe they'd have got him eventually. But you sped the timeline up and saved who knows how many lives. You didn't have to. You got no badge. You had no case. You had no reason to stick your great big Harry nose in the middle of things except that it's what your great big Harry nose is for. You and me both know you're going to be in the shit up to your neck for as long as there's shit to get into. And she's gonna be there right beside you. Hell or high water. And you know what?" Gene looked at him, stared up at him, watery eyes serious.

"What?"

"It's the reason we *all* do."

Harry shifted, uncomfortable. "I got some friends, sure. That doesn't mean-"

"Harry, you know how many laws I broke just walking in here tonight? Or how many Clara's broken, giving you her files? Or Mills? Or... hell... basically everyone you ever met? We've all broken laws for you, broken our word, or just done the wrong thing for the right reasons. Because of you. Toni's good at this stuff, but you're the *reason* she's good. We've seen her work, so now we trust her. But you? Harry, we've been watching you for *years*. We'll go to the wall for you because we know. You're the barometer. We may not be able to see the forest for the trees, but we all trust you'll burn that mother down if it means doing the right thing. So we put our faith in you. Always have. Always will."

Harry stared at the ground. "Maybe you shouldn't. That's a lot for one broken-down ex-cop."

"Yeah, well, if you ever get one wrong, we'll talk. Until then, shut up and do what it is you do. And take Toni with you. And hell, even Bobby. He's funny, Harry. Damned funny. And smarter than he lets on. Toni came up with the idea about checking the bullets against the card on file, but it was Bobby's idea to pull the old cases. That's how we tripped to Willoughsby's setup. He's weird, Harry, but he kinda, sorta fits right in. You know?"

"That's a shitty reason to put him in danger," Harry said. "Because he's weird."

Gene smiled. "It's better than being an innocent bystander and getting wiped out in a drive-by."

"I guess."

The apartment door opened and Toni stuck her head in. She smiled at Starr and joined Harry and Gene.

"Just two girls upstairs right now," Toni said. "Cherry and some new kid named Trix."

Harry grimaced. "You're kidding."

"That's what she called herself."

Gene raised an eyebrow. "After her clients, or the cereal?"

Toni shrugged. "Who knows? Anyhow, there's a bed up there for him."

Gene looked Abruzzi over. Starr looked up at him, and then Toni, and then at Harry. She said, "Thank you, Harry."

"Of course. Gene, is it safe to move him?"

Gene nodded. "He'll be fine, so long as we don't drop him. It's getting him up there that'll be tricky. We need a stretcher or something to move him. He's doped to the gills and he can't walk by himself."

"Will a blanket work? One on each end?" Harry asked.

"Maybe," Gene said. "It'll be heavy. Dead weight always is."

"Maybe you should get a body bag," Toni said with a smile. "At least those have handles."

She laughed, but Gene looked thoughtful. "That's not a bad idea. I'd have to run downtown, though, if you think he'll be safe here for an hour."

"No, I don't want to risk it. I want him out of the apartment. Bad enough keeping him in the building," said Harry.

"You can bring him to my place," Gene offered.

"No way," Harry said. "You're out far enough on this limb."

Gene nodded. "Okay, best do it quickly, then."

"I'll go have Cherry ready with the door," Toni said. "I'll send in Bobby."

"I've got it," Harry said.

"Not with that shoulder, you don't. I'll send in Bobby."

Harry watched her go and heard her say something to Gold, who appeared at the door. "Youse guys wanna make a body disappear?" he asked in a broad Jersey accent.

Gene laughed. Harry said, "Yeah. We're gonna tote him. Well, you two are going to. I can't risk dropping him. My shoulder."

Gene knew, but Bobby and Starr both looked puzzled. Harry grimaced. "I got shot. My left shoulder. That arm's not great anymore."

"No problem," Bobby said. "I Sherpa with the best of 'em. Gene?"

"Let me see the route," Gene said. "Get him ready. Heavy blanket under him. Tie knots in the corners. That'll make it easier to hold."

The diminutive ME went through the door to the office, and they heard him leave the office and then footsteps on the stairs. They returned. As he came into the apartment he said over his shoulder, "Toni, you're on doors. Harry, you go make sure no one sees us."

Farrokh, waking from his fitful sleep, looked around.

"Mr. Harry?"

"Farrokh," Harry said. "I forgot you were here. Don't worry…" he trailed off, looked down at Abruzzi, and looked back up. "Don't worry. But you're moving upstairs. I want you out of the way in case anyone lands on us and starts tearing the place part, looking for him. Okay?"

"As you say, Mr. Harry," Farrokh agreed in a desolate voice devoid of anything resembling a fight. He collected his backpack and gathered the bedclothes up. He put them in the hamper by the dresser and followed Harry. Harry grabbed his jacket and went outside, looking up and down Elizabeth Street. Traffic on Elizabeth Street was minimal on a busy day. This early, traffic was nonexistent. Shortly, Gene and Bobby came through the door, Bobby leading and walking backward while Gene brought up the rear. Outside, breath puffing in the cold air, Gene said, "I'll go first. You're too tall. He'll slide out."

Bobby nodded and they rotated. Abruzzi made a quiet noise as they jostled him, getting into position. And then they were up the stairs and into the apartment over the office. Starr followed with Gene's bag. Toni gave her arm a quick squeeze as she walked by, and Starr flashed a smile at her. It didn't change the haggard, worried look she wore much, but it was something. She hurried up the stairs after them, Farrokh on her heels.

Toni said, "I'll be right back." She hustled into the office and the apartment, came back with a broom. She busied herself sweeping the stairs and the snow in front of the office. Puzzled, Harry watched until he realized she was right; it looked like an army had marched from their office to the upstairs apartment.

"Good call, sweetheart. You'd have made an excellent tracker in the Wild West."

He followed her into the office. Toni set the broom inside their apartment door. "It's good as it can get. We better warn 'em to wipe the stairs down, if they're gonna be in and out. It's not foolproof, but it's better than hiding them in the bathroom if anyone comes looking." Alone for the moment, Harry pulled Toni into a quick hug. "Not the night I had planned," he told her, face buried in her hair.

She squeezed him. "You can't fool me, DeMarko. You love being in the thick of it. This is your real homecoming. You don't idle well. You're meant to run at top speed."

He leaned back and looked down at her, his faded blue eyes bright as he gazed into her green ones. "I would have liked one more quiet night, though. Maybe some sleep after."

She snuggled close, put her face up, and he kissed her. They were warming to the job when the office door opened. Harry disengaged without opening his eyes. "I swear to Christ, if one more thing happens-"

"I was gonna grab some coffee," Bobby said. "Should I go find a diner? You look busy."

Toni smirked. She stretched up, kissed Harry once more, and they parted. She kept her hand on his waist as they turned to look at Bobby. "Gene getting him settled?" Harry asked.

"Yeah. He started bleeding a little, but Gene said that's not unusual, after tilting him all over like a pinball table. The kid is curled up in the other bedroom." He moved past them and helped himself to a cup of coffee. He put it in a paper cup. Harry saw this and didn't say anything, but he glanced at Toni approvingly when Bobby filled, sugared, and capped two more. She grinned up at him. When Bobby turned to hand them theirs, both faces were solemn again.

"So what's the first move?" Gold asked.

"First things first, I'm going over to the Four Aces to drop in on Hendrick. He's gonna meet me there to fill out the details," Harry said.

Toni's face clouded over. "Maybe you oughta call first, Harry."

He quirked an eyebrow. "Why?"

Toni glanced at Bobby and said, "Surveillance."

Bobby swore to himself. "Shit. Forgot all about that."

"What?" Harry asked. He felt somewhat nettled that he didn't know what they referred to. Three months was an eternity on the street, in their lives, in their business. He needed to catch up.

"Mills and Capretti've been sitting on the Aces hoping for a hot tip," she told him. "Something to help with ongoing cases."

"Good to know," Harry said. "I'd have walked right in there. Good catch. We don't want them asking us questions. We don't want anyone asking questions. We have to be careful and think twice about every move we make."

"How do we let Hendrick know without tipping them to Mills? We don't want to blow their cover." Toni sipped her coffee.

"Does he know Bobby?" Harry asked.

"He does know Bobby," Bobby said. "He's met Bobby several times."

Harry bit down on a snappish reply. Instead he said, "Sorry."

"No big. You don't know me. She's your go-to for info. I get it."

Harry nodded. "We have to get a message to Hendrick without tipping Mills to what we're up to, without tipping Hendrick to what Mills is up to, and without giving away that we have Abruzzi. They'll have the phone tapped, naturally." Harry mused on this for a moment. Then he said, "Floor's open for suggestions."

"We could set their van on fire," Toni said. "Then send smoke signals."

Harry rolled his eyes. "Floor's open for intelligent suggestions."

She smacked him in the belly and he winced.

"Send flowers?" Bobby asked. "Put a note on the card?"

Harry thought about it. "That might work. Where's the nearest florist?"

Toni went to her desk and hauled the yellow pages out of a bottom drawer. She flipped until she found what she wanted. She didn't write a number down. She closed the book. "They're already open. I'll have a bouquet sent. What do you want the card to read?"

Harry thought about it. "Quiet. Public. Alone. What do you reckon?"

Toni gave it a moment's thought. "St. Patrick's."

Harry snapped his fingers. "Perfect. It's…" he looked at the clock. "Almost seven now. If you rush 'em… say we'll be there at ten A.M. till he shows. Between services will help."

"Can do. I'll run up to Dahli's."

"Something wrong with the phone here?" Harry asked.

Toni gave him a slanting smile. "I told you how we trapped Willoughsby."

"Oh. Right. The tap." Harry had been nonplussed to discover that his office phone had been primetime entertainment for a crooked FBI agent. "I thought they removed it?"

"Want to take a chance? Ordinarily," she said with a smirk, "we'd go to them first. Can't tip them off, can we?"

"No, you're right. Dahli's. Good idea."

"Back in a minute. Need anything?"

Harry shrugged. "I wouldn't say no to a bagel."

"Make it two, please," Bobby chimed in. He sipped his coffee. Toni gave Bobby a flat look, but said, "Okay."

She tugged the keys of the Chevelle out of her jeans. She took out her leather shoulder holster and shrugged into the straps. She checked her .38 and tucked it under her arm, snug in the holster. She shrugged into her suit coat and gave Harry a kiss on the cheek before walking to the car parked a couple of spaces away from the front of the office. They watched her fishtail around for a while as she tromped on the pedal.

"She does love driving in the snow," Bobby commented.

"Yeah she does. Scared the hell out of me when she whipped that thing around the corner. We did a donut and she just laughed the whole time. I can't believe it's been three months."

Bobby raised an eyebrow. "Three months?"

Harry looked at him. "Since she got her license."

Bobby blinked a couple of times. "Jesus. I didn't know that." He thought about it. He remembered the way she drove like she was intentionally crashing. "Holy Christ. How many angels does that woman have looking out for her?"

"I don't know," Harry said. "But I bet their wings have all gone gray."

"No doubt."

They drank coffee in silence, and Bobby refilled their cups once before Toni came back. She skidded to a stop in front of the office, a red streak in the Chevelle and sunlight.

She clomped into the office, pausing to kick snow off her boots, and brush off her pantlegs. She came in, face ruddy with the cold, a happy smile on her wide mouth. She tossed a paper bag on the desk.

"Mission accomplished and then some," she said. She went for Harry's coffee and held it. Her hands were red.

"Why do you look like you went for a roll in the snow?" Harry asked.

"Because I went for a roll in the snow," she said. 'I made the call, sent the flowers. Got bagels. While I was there, some kid tried to steal a candy bar and a soda."

Bobby said, "You chased down a kid?"

She nodded happily. "Two blocks. He was fast as all get-out. I dragged him back. Mr. Dahli put him to work sweeping to pay for the stuff."

Harry grinned. "I bet he gave 'em to the kid, too."

"Yeah he did," she said. "Mr. Dahli's a soft touch."

"I don't supposed you mentioned…" Harry jerked his thumb at the door of the apartment.

"Didn't seem the time," she said. "Mr. Dahli isn't worried about him, I figure, or he would have asked. My guess is the kid was out with Kilburn last night, so Mr. Dahli isn't worried yet."

"We need to ask him some questions. And maybe Kilburn, too. If Farrokh's off-page, Kilburn will come here looking for him."

"He's pretty shaken up, Harry. Give him some time to regroup," Toni protested. "He came here instead of going home. He looks like hell. You were a cop. Going undercover's part of the gig for a cop. But a civilian? His life's on the line, and he isn't trained for that. He came here because he knows it's a safe place. That we'll watch over him. I don't want to take that from him."

"That's a fair point."

Toni added, "He's freaking out. He's obviously in need of some down time and a place to hide."

"Don't worry, he's gonna get plenty of both. Whatever's going on with Kilburn and the sting, it's nothing to this thing with Sal. That's our priority." Harry rubbed the back of his neck. "What do you think? An hour's nap before we roll?"

Toni's eyes lit up. "I'm game."

Bobby said, "I'll stay here and guard the coffee."

Harry eyed him. "You eat my bagel and I'll shoot you."

"Harry!"

He said to Toni, not looking away from Bobby, "Like, in the leg. I wouldn't kill over a bagel."

"It's rye with lox and creamed cheese," she said.

"Like I said," Harry growled. "I'd kill you over a bagel."

Bobby nodded. "Got it. Don't eat the bagel. Go get some sleep."

"Tell me twice," Harry muttered, and went into the apartment. Toni winked at Bobby and tossed him the car keys. "Hey Bobby? Go for a long ride."

Bobby caught the keys awkwardly, looked at them, looked up, and nodded. "Yeah," he said. He grinned wolfishly at her. "You too."

To his considerable amazement, she blushed from the collar of her shirt to her hairline. She looked away with a bashful grin, but said nothing in return, and closed the apartment door.

Well now I've seen everything, he thought. He rooted in the bag for one of the bagels, checked it wasn't rye, and stuffed it in his mouth. One refill of coffee and he was out the door, locking it behind. He considered the Chevelle, but decided he didn't need getting pulled over. He hadn't had a drink in several hours, but he was still buzzing. Instead, he decided to go for a walk. He held the steaming coffee in one hand, bagel in the other, and went for a stroll.

CHAPTER FOURTEEN

After pounding on the apartment door twice, Harry and Toni shuffled out looking grumpy. Toni was combing her still-damp hair.

"Been an hour and twenty minutes," Bobby said. "I was feeling generous." The desk held fresh travelers of hot coffee, and the bag with Harry's bagel. Harry sipped the coffee. He stopped, leaned back to stare at the cup, and sipped again.

"Problem?" Bobby asked.

"Yes- well, no," Harry amended. "This is… good."

Toni tried hers and she uttered a startled noise. "What the hell?"

Bobby grinned. "I got some fresh-ground coffee and a box of kosher salt," he said. "Makes all the difference. Even in that piece of-"

"Don't speak ill of that coffee maker," Harry warned. "It's more a part of this outfit than you are. Besides, you have no idea how long it's been keeping us alive."

"I'm just saying. Not for nothing, but Folger's ain't what I call good coffee."

Harry sipped again. "And the salt?"

"I used to work with a guy who served in the Navy. He said that when the bridge pot started perking sailors would climb over their mothers for a cup. The secret, apparently, is to grind the beans right before brewing and throw some salt in."

Toni's face screwed up in disgust. "Salt?"

"Tell me that coffee's not a slice of heaven."

She sipped again, defensively, but said nothing.

"This guy… his name was Wade… told me it was tradition. They used to carry fresh water in barrels, once upon a time. Wooden ships, I mean. And when the fresh water ran low, you could face a mutiny if the coffee also ran low. So they started using sea water. Apparently, the salt does something to the coffee. To this day, they throw salt in the pot. And for whatever reason, it works," Bobby said. He sipped his coffee. "Stands to reason, I mean. Salt makes everything taste better."

"Not corn flakes," Toni said.

Bobby rolled his eyes.

Harry topped their cups. "Come on, you two. We have shit to do."

They filed out of the office. Bobby handed Toni the keys. "Here you go."

Harry raised a hand to object, but Toni glared at him, and he declined to say anything. She handed him her cup, which he took gracefully. Grinning triumphantly, she went to the driver's side. Harry held the passenger side open and waited for Bobby to climb into the back before slipping in himself. Toni gunned the engine, revving it happily.

"Go easy, Toni," Harry said.

"Why?" she asked, and dropped the gearshift. They skidded sideways as the tires sought purchase. They caught and the car lurched like a horse stung by a bee. She slowed at the corner, checked for oncoming traffic, and drifted around the corner, the back end of the Chevelle kicking out wide. She corrected, straightened, and did the same onto Bowery, gunning south for Houston, and St. Patrick's cathedral.

Harry held out her coffee to give her a sip, allowing her to keep both hands on the wheel. They pulled into a space on the west side of the cathedral with almost a minute to spare before nine. As they got out, the bells rang overhead.

They left the food and drinks in the car and followed a sparse Saturday mass crowd through the huge doors. After reconnoitering for a moment, Harry nudged Toni and pointed. Hendrick was in the back pew as far away from the pulpit as possible. They went to him and sat, Harry to his left, Toni on his right, and Bobby in the row in front. He craned around to listen.

Hendrick eyed him with suspicion. "Who's he?"

"Bobby Gold," Bobby said. "Head chef."

Harry rolled his eyes. "He's with us, Hendrick. He's safe."

"Ain't nothing safe," Hendrick said. "Why are we here? I ain't been in a church since my communion. We should have met at the Aces."

"If you want this done quiet," Harry said, "then we need to be out of the ordinary. Don't talk about it anywhere you normally go. Same goes for us. We're not using the phone in the office. Don't go to the Aces. Let's keep this between us, until we get answers."

Hendrick thought about it. "Okay. Makes sense. We could have met at Sal's."

"We don't know where Sal lives, Hendrick," Harry said.

"Oh. Right. Lemme tell you what happened. So-"

"This'll go faster if you let us ask questions," Harry cut him off.

Hendrick bristled visibly. "I ain't some lame on the street," he started.

"No, you're not," Harry said. "But you're not a detective either. You came to us because this is our job. Let us do our job."

"Fine, fine. Just remember: he gets turned over to us not the cops. You know I can make it hard on you."

"We know what's on the line, Hendrick," Harry said He and Toni exchanged a look. "Threatening doesn't help anyone. Don't cloud the issue. Let's start with facts."

He took a notebook and pencil out of his pocket, and

flipped to a fresh page. "First, when did it happen? Be as exact as you can."

"Higgins said it was midnight, almost straight up. He heard a ruckus and went over."

"How'd the guy get into Sal's house? Break a window, or-"

Hendrick colored. "The porch door was unlocked. Sal was having work done, and he left it for his company so they could work when he wasn't home."

"Who would know that?" Bobby asked.

Hendrick glared at him, but Harry said, "Good question. There's part of our suspect pool."

"The foreman, sure… me… Higgins…" Hendrick said with a thoughtful expression, "…maybe two or three other guys. I'll ask around. Normally we don't have to worry about things like this. People know to stay away from Sal's."

"Okay," Toni said. "What did Sal's guy do? He ran over?"

"Yeah. Well, not direct. He wasn't armed. He had to get his gun before he went in. He-"

"Hold it," Toni said. At the other end of the church, the organ wound up and the congregation began to sing. "He took his eyes off the house?"

Hendrick nodded. "Just while he got his gun."

She and Harry exchanged a glance.

Hendrick continued. "Then he ran across. Came in the back door, the kitchen door. Caught up with them in the… well… Sal was having a game room put in. It's all wood and stuff right now. That's where…" Hendrick paused. He swallowed, stared off into the distance, and gathered himself. He said in a toneless growl, "That's where the fucker killed Sal."

Harry jotted that down. "Higgins is?"

"Bill Higgins, Sal's bodyguard. One of 'em. The

other's Terry Shoulders," Hendrick said, shooting a sneer at Toni. "Or was."

"Don't blame me," she said. "It's not my fault he was too stupid to replace Terry."

Hendrick's face darkened.

"Sue me," Toni said. "Don't get me wrong, I wouldn't have chosen this. But one thing has nothing to do with the other. I'm not more to blame for Sal than Sal is. If he'd replaced Terry the same day, maybe we wouldn't be here."

Hendrick closed his eyes and took a deep breath. "Growing up, Sal was always around the house. My dad loved Sal best, of all his brothers, because Sal always took the least amount of risks. He wanted to come up, but he wasn't going to do it on someone's neck. He didn't make enemies he didn't have to. And he wouldn't have anyone around him he didn't trust with his life. He was still looking around. That's why he had just one guy on him. Normally he had two, he wanted three."

"Why weren't you one of his guards?" Harry asked. "If he's your uncle, he must have trusted you the most."

Hendrick sighed. "His rules. He didn't want family guarding him. Just in case of a hit. That way, we don't lose more than one family member. Sal hated funerals. Hated losing family. And he refused to put two family members at risk. Our line's hard enough, he said, without tempting fate."

Hendrick grinned, a feral, dangerous grin.

"Besides, he wanted to make sure there'd be someone left to get whatever son of a bitch took a shot."

Toni swallowed.

Harry jotted more notes. "Anything we should know about?"

"Just about everything," Hendrick said. "But you wanna narrow that down?"

"Internal beefs. Trouble with the other Families.

Anything that might give us a clue as to why someone would do this."

"Lots of people'd start shit if they could," Hendrick said. "That's the business."

"That's just it, though," Harry said. "Business. What you told me, this doesn't feel like that. It feels personal. It feels desperate. Makes me think there's another side to this we haven't seen yet."

Hendrick gave Harry a thoughtful look. "I was thinking the same thing. But no, no trouble as far as I know. But Sal being Sal, I didn't know everything."

"What did he have, aside from the Four Aces?" Toni asked. "How'd he cover his money? What were his fronts?"

Hendrick gave her a mild glare.

"Don't fuck around," she said. "We're past cutesy answers. You want us to figure this out, you gonna be ready to let us into it all, Hendrick. We know who Sal was, we know who you are, and we know who you work for. You came to us because we're now the law. You don't want to give us a chance to find them, no sweat. We'll give you back your deposit and go fuck yourself."

Hendrick twitched, like he wanted to go for a gun.

She put her tiny, pert nose close to his wide, flared one. "Listen, pal, you already made it clear: we find them so you can whack them out, or we're the ones get whacked out. Fine. I can accept that. But if you're gonna hobble us and then make us race, I ain't playing. Harry ain't playing. And just so you know, if you're gonna do it like that, we'll go to our cop friends. We'll go to our Fed friends. We'll go to our newspaper friends. In an hour we can have the law so far up your ass you'll taste blue polyester. So go ahead. Fuck with me."

"I oughta stomp a hole in your face," Hendrick snarled. "Just for threatening me."

"Go ask Terry how that goes," she said. She put a finger on his chest and pressed. "And remember, big guy… when Terry Shoulders went down, Harry was in the joint. It was my bust. So you want to dance? Pony up a quarter and name your tune, asshole."

She sat back, crossed her legs and her arms, and gave Hendrick a cool stare and a faint smile.

Hendrick's color deepened until he looked apoplectic. Then it drained away. Bobby watched the man struggle not to smile. To Harry, Hendrick said, "Your cookie's got a mouth."

"And a gun," Harry said. "Don't forget it."

"Oh, Sally loved talking with you," Hendrick said to Toni, and he gave her a surprising grin. "He thought you were a hoot. I can see why."

"He didn't take me seriously?" Toni asked.

"Oh, no. Sal took you really serious. He said you and this chump were the most dangerous characters in the Bowery. Said you didn't care if you lived or died. Didn't care if you pissed off the Family, or all the Families. Said all you cared about was giving your word and keeping it. And that made you dangerous. But he said he could work with you because of it. He trusted you, you know. I told him he was nuts, trusting you. That when you had to, you'd drop a Roosevelt dime on his ass."

Harry said, "He didn't buy it."

"No, he didn't. And after that thing with Jimmy Brown and that Afghani mutt running pussy to the far corners of the world, he said he'd trust you over some of the guys worked for him." Hendrick pinched the bridge of his nose with one hand, sighed, and blinked at Harry. "That's why I came to you. He said I could trust you."

Harry said, "You can. But it's up to you. And like she said, if you're not going to give us what we need to help, there's no point in even trying."

Hendrick sighed. "All right, all right. But," he warned, glaring at Toni, "no matter how tough you think you are, it wouldn't be just me coming for you. You might stop one of us. Or two. But we got more guys than Carter's got little pills."

She smiled wider at Hendrick. "Uh huh. Sure, big guy. Whatever you need to say. You want to get to it now?"

"Listen, Hendrick," Harry said. "You came to us. You hired us. Yeah, you threatened us. But you hired us, and we agreed. We didn't have to. Nothing on Earth could force us to do something we didn't want to. And since the police aren't knocking on Sal D'Amico's door asking all kinds of questions, you know we didn't rat you out. You're the client. Our job is your job. And your business is our secret. It goes no further. We use what we know to solve the case. You're the client, and that means you're protected. We won't talk about cases with anyone. Ever. But you have to make up your own mind whether to trust us or not. But stop with the threats.

Around them the congregation had settled, the singing had tapered off, and the sermon had begun.

Hendrick thought that over, shrugged, and said, "Sal has things all over. He has the Aces, for one, another jewelry place out in Queens, the construction business, a couple dry-cleaners. He has three funeral homes, as well as a cemetery."

"A cemetery?" Bobby asked. He'd been so quiet up to this point, Harry had forgotten the man was even there.

Hendrick didn't say anything, just stared at him. Bobby thought about it, breathed an almost silent "Ooooh," and nodded.

"You can imagine Sal's business was wide-spread," Hendrick said. "He owned or partnered with a lot of people in a lot of things, some bigger, like the jewelry stores, and some pieces of a lot of little stuff. Cash places.

You know."

"We're going to need addresses, and any information you have on the guys who run them," Harry said, scribbling furiously. Not yet, but maybe soon."

Hendrick said, "Whatever you want, I can get. If it's necessary."

Harry looked up at him. "We'll ask if something points toward it. Right now, all we have is something personal, something messy. Something that doesn't sound like a business beef. What about his numbers?"

"What do you mean?" Hendrick asked.

"Sal ran a couple bookies, right?" Harry asked. "Not to mention the hookers."

Hendrick gave a sidelong glance at Toni, who seemed to be watching the sermon. He said, "Cheddar would be a better person to ask about that. He ran all of Sal's pimps and whores."

Harry saw the muscle in Toni's jaw jump. "He gave Cheddar that much leeway? I thought it was just the Bowery."

Hendrick nodded. "He trusted Cheddar like he trusted me. Cheddar proved himself. He got it all."

"Who else did he have working with him that closely?" Toni asked. "Cheddar, presumably, knew he wasn't going to move up if Sal was gone. Maybe some of his other guys thought they might?"

Hendrick didn't think about it. "No one. Sal didn't have anyone ready to take his spot. Underbosses don't choose anyone. Mainly for just this reason. You don't want to make it too easy."

"Who did he hate?" Bobby asked.

Hendrick frowned at the lanky man. "What?"

"Who did he hate?" Bobby repeated. "If you can't think of anyone that had a beef with him, maybe come at it backward. Who did Sal hate? Someone who irked him."

Hendrick considered it, but said, "No one. If Sal had a problem, like Jimmy Brown, he took care of it. Like Jimmy Brown."

Hendrick's eyes seemed to blaze too brightly at Harry. Bobby watched this, the line between his eyes deepening. Harry returned Hendrick's look, with his bland, patient expression giving away nothing.

Bobby glanced at Toni, who shook her head a millimeter. He seemed to accept that and settled back.

"I don't know anyone who Sal hated. The people he didn't like didn't stick around long. Jimmy Brown. And a pimp he had on your turf. The one who was carving his name on his girls," Hendrick said. "But you took care of that, didn't you?"

Toni cleared her throat. "I did. The broken nose, the ribs, the pistol-whipping. All me, Hendrick."

Bobby shot her a startled look.

Hendrick chuckled. He looked at Harry. "What does she keep you around for?"

"Killing spiders," Harry said absently. "No other people he didn't like?"

"He didn't like a lot of people," Hendrick said. "You included. But that didn't mean he didn't respect you. You helped him get the job. He didn't forget that."

Bobby's eyes went to Harry, and to Toni, and back to Hendrick.

"I got the feeling Sal wanted us to lose his number," Harry said.

Hendrick chuckled. "Whenever you popped up he'd bitch and grouse about it, but I could tell he was looking forward to it. Too much of what we do is dealing with idiots. It's more dangerous to work with smart people, but it makes the boring jobs easier to handle."

Harry nodded. "All right. Before we start running down this stuff, there's one more thing."

Hendrick's eyes became wary. "What?"

"You know what. We need to see him."

Hendrick looked away, up at the stained glass windows lining the cathedral. He swallowed. Without looking back he asked, "Is it necessary?"

"It is if there's anything around his body or the scene that might help," Harry said.

Hendrick's eyes widened and he looked down. Tori had put her hand over his. Her hand seemed minuscule compared to Hendrick's gigantic paw, but she squeezed it anyhow. She said nothing. She kept looking up at the pulpit as the priest continued his sermon.

Hendrick stared at her hand, took a breath, and nodded. "Okay. When?"

"Now."

Hendrick stood up so fast Bobby jerked back. *Hendrick*, he reflected, *is a lot of guy to move like that*.

"I'll meet you there," Hendrick said.

"We don't know where Sal lived," Toni said.

Hendrick considered. He said, "Okay. Follow me. You got a ride, right?"

"Yep," Toni said. She stood and took out her keys. "I'm in a black Buick."

"Red Chevelle, out that way," she pointed. A few pews away, some parishioners looked around at the conversation. Hendrick glared, and they turned their attention back to the priest.

"I'll circle for you." Hendrick strode away toward the west exit.

On the way to the car, Bobby asked, "Should we bring our pet coroner?"

Harry didn't answer until they got to the Chevelle "No. If Hendrick's being straight, Sal died from an overdose of hammer. Don't need to expose Gene to confirm that. I expect it'll be obvious."

"You ever see someone die like that, Harry?" Toni asked as they got in. She started the engine and turned the heater up.

Harry let Bobby struggle into the back, then sat and slammed the door. "No. I was a beat cop. Most of the DBs I saw were vehicle-related. That was most popular. After that, stabbings. After that, guns. The occasional beating that led to accidental death. No hammers. Why do you ask?"

"I'm wondering how bad it's going to be."

Hendrick's Buick slowed behind them and honked. Toni backed out and followed as Hendrick began the drive to Queens.

"He's been dead, what… ten hours?" Bobby asked from the back.

"About that. It'll be bad. Not decomp, not yet, but he'll be stiff. And he'll be leaking," Harry said.

"Well yeah," Bobby said, "if they cracked him open like a coconut."

"No," Harry said. "He'll be leaking other things. It's not going to be pleasant. And believe it or not, it's worse when it's someone you know, good or bad."

Toni swallowed uneasily and followed Hendrick onto the bridge. Twenty minutes later they pulled into the cul-de-sac that held Sal's house and several others, flanking. Hendrick pulled into the drive and Toni parked behind him.

"Jesus," Bobby said. "It looks like my grandmother's neighborhood. Is this a joke? Or does being a Mob boss pay worse than the post office?"

"Nah," Toni said. "This makes perfect sense. Sal was low-key, and this place doesn't scream Mob."

"So he just lives here with people around him who don't know what he is?" Bobby asked. An edge developed in his voice, and Toni glanced at him.

"I doubt it, Bobby. We know his bodyguard lives on one side. The rest of these houses have family or at least friends who know," she said.

Harry said, "Sal didn't have a wife that I know of. And lots of the higher-ups live this way. They do it for camouflage, for security, or to plead poverty when they get caught."

"Security?"

Harry nodded. "Lots of these neighborhoods are generational. It's hard for strangers to sneak in. It's like an early warning system."

Hendrick heaved himself out of the Buick, which rocked a little on its springs. Toni shut off the engine and they got out. Harry waited until they were close enough to have a conversation in low voices.

"So this is Sal D'Amico's house, eh?"

"Forty years, Sal lived here. He loved this place."

"How is it he never married?" Toni asked.

"Some people aren't suited for it," Hendrick said. "Sal thought that he was one of those."

They examined the front of the single-story dwelling. It was very wide, wider than their shop on Elizabeth. There were paths in the snow on both sides leading to the back. Harry and Toni walked to the left, examined the single thread of tracks that led around a single bush halfway down the length of the house. The bush was an evergreen of some kind, snow dusting its branches.

The tracks led around the bush to the left and vanished, presumably, around the back of the house.

The path on the right side was a single set of footprints, more deliberately placed, someone walking steadily.

Harry asked, "Higgins' house?"

Hendrick pointed to the house on the right of Sal's. There were toys on the lawn, indistinct mounds under snow. A bicycle. A ball. What looked like a doll's house.

"Who's on the left?" Toni asked.

"Mrs. Carmondy. Nice old lady. She's about a million years old. Sal brings- brought- her groceries. I took her trash out when I came by. In fact," Hendrick said, "all these houses are owned by people Sal helped out. Some were here when he was little, some moved in later."

"Was Sal born here?" Bobby asked.

"No. This was his brother's house."

Harry frowned. "You said Sal was your uncle?"

Hendrick nodded. "Yep. This was my parents' place. After they died I sold it to Sal."

They stood silently, absorbing that.

"Didn't you want it?" Toni asked.

"Naah. I never liked it here. Too far away from the city."

Toni smiled at him. "I know what you mean."

"All right," Harry said. "Let's walk the scene."

He stepped in front of Hendrick and led the way. Hendrick watched him, nonplussed. Harry took a handkerchief out of his pocket as they caught up to him. "Don't touch anything," he instructed. "Hendrick, you been all over the inside of this place. But we were never here. Right?"

"No problem, Harry," Toni said.

"Hands in pockets," Bobby assured him.

Harry used the handkerchief to open the door and he held it while they tromped inside. It was warm in the house, but there was a faint odor already of something not quite right.

"Hendrick, take us through the attack," Harry ordered.

Hendrick led them to the kitchen. Higgins and Cheddar were sitting at the kitchen table. The smell of sour milk permeated the air. Harry put himself in the doorway and didn't let Bobby or Toni in. Higgins glared at Toni.

Cheddar raised a hand to the pair.

"Harry," he greeted. "Toni."

"Cheddar," Harry said. "Hendrick, go."

They watched as Hendrick pointed at the table, then the glass shards. "Sal was drinking milk when the guy got the jump on him. He threw the milk bottle and ran for it."

Harry examined the impact point next to the door. "No blood?"

"Don't think he hit the guy. Like he was trying to distract him."

Toni muttered, "He had a gun."

"We don't know that," Hendrick said.

Toni snorted laughter. "Come on, Hendrick. Sal was old-guard, right? Got his start in the forties. He came up the hard way, and he made his bones early. He wouldn't bother throwing milk at a guy holding a hammer. He'd have grabbed a knife. As far as I can tell, the reason he didn't is the guy had a gun."

Hendrick said nothing.

"Had a gun, but wasn't pro enough to shoot Sal right there," Harry mused. "He must have flinched away from the milk bottle. That gave Sal the time he needed."

He examined the casing of the door. He didn't see anything useful. "Toni? See anything else?"

Higgins' eyes flitted from Harry to Toni and back. "I thought you were the cop," he grunted.

"I was," Harry said. "And that means I see things one way. She wasn't, and she sees them differently."

Higgins didn't look convinced. Cheddar pointed at Bobby. "And him?"

Bobby grinned. "I'm the valet."

Cheddar looked at Harry and Toni. "He serious?"

"If he is, he better get me a coffee," Toni said, still studying the room.

"In that case, mawster, miss, I hereby tender my

resignation," Bobby said with a terrible attempt at a British butler's accent.

"You're indentured," Toni said. "You're not an employee."

"Ah. In which case, I'll fetch coffee and start a revolution."

Toni snorted. She said, "I don't see anything, Harry."

"Me neither. Okay, Hendrick. Where did they go next?"

Hendrick led them through the kitchen. Higgins and Cheddar followed. They picked their way carefully around the glass shards. Down the hall and through a sitting room, neither of which yielded results. They came to the in-progress construction.

In the middle of the floor lay the body of Sal D'Amico under a white, bloodstained sheet. There were pools around his corpse, blood and urine. The smells were quite strong, copper and vinegar, biting and pungent.

Harry looked up at Hendrick. "Get me a pair of tongs or something from the kitchen so I can move the sheet. Wrap it in a towel so I don't touch it."

Hendrick vanished and reappeared. He had a pair of claw-tipped tongs in his hand wrapped in a blue tea towel. Harry crossed to the door and took them, careful to touch just the towel. At the body, he gently plucked at a corner of the sheet. As he drew it back it resisted. It had dried to his body in several places. He pulled with gentle pressure, not wanting to move the body if he could help it. Once the sheet was away, he lifted it high, keeping it off the ground, and carried it to the doorway. He dropped the sheet in a heap to one side and handed Hendrick the tongs. He returned to his position over the still corpse of Sal D'Amico.

The damage to his face and neck were visible even from the doorway. His hand was curled against his chest, obviously broken. The back of his hand was dimpled and bruised, and the bird-like narrow bones under his papery skin were splintered. Behind him, a pair of sawhorses topped with a piece of junk plywood were in a heap, along with a toolbox and random scattering of tools. A crowbar lay a foot away from Sal's left hand, blood on the forked tine at the curved end. Dried blood had pooled under one leg.

Harry's face became a mask of emotionless observation. He walked widely around the body, looking at nothing else. Toni swallowed hard and stepped into the room, approaching from the other side of the body. Bobby watched from the doorway.

Minutes ticked by as they took in the details. The bathrobe, the disheveled hair, the awkward angle of his legs, one bent far sideways. The deep gouge along his inner thigh where the curled end of the crowbar had furrowed his flesh. Toni's eyes came back again and again to Sal's face. The right eye was closed, the left partially covered by dried blood, which had oozed from the several head wounds and pooled in the eye socket. There was a depression near the right temple almost a half-inch in depth.

Toni viewed all of this as dispassionately as she could. Unbidden, the image rose in her mind of the struggle. She saw the two men scuffle, she saw them fight for control. She…

She looked around. The rough plywood of the unfinished floors were not the most ideal surface, but.. there.

Her pulse quickened and she looked up at Harry with an exclamation that died on her lips.

He wasn't looking at the body. He was looking at her His eyes had faded to that remote, washed-out blue they took on when he was most deeply in thought. She whispered, "What?"

"What do you see?" he asked. His voice was devoid of emotion. It was hard-edged. It was professional.

It's his old voice, she thought. She shuddered. *The way he used to sound before... before us.*

She licked dry lips, stepped back, and said while pointing, "There's some kind of white dust there, by the door. It-"

"It's sheetrock dust," Higgins said. "They were putting in some-"

"Whatever," Toni said, waving his words away. "There's a swirling pattern. Like someone falling and scuffling. They fought over there."

Harry followed her gaze with his own but said nothing. Toni went to the scuffles and crouched. She pointed without touching. "Handprint. But… it's all smudged. Or…"

She nodded to herself. "Gloves."

Harry said nothing. He just watched. Bobby saw Hendrick and Higgins exchange a look. He saw Cheddar watching with a bemused but unsurprised look on his angular face. He watched her work. Then Bobby's eyes went to Harry.

Harry watched Toni with no expression, merely absorbing. Teaching her, Bobby thought. Then: No. this is… consultation. He's double-checking to see if she gets the same conclusion as he does.

His mouth parted in surprise, but he said nothing.

I'll be damned. He trusts her. He relies on her. They're… they really are better together.

He remembered what that feeling was like, when he and Nell had been so simpatico. He quashed the feeling, worried he'd open the door for other, less pleasant emotions.

Toni stepped around the swirl, face screwed up in

concentration. She looked at the body, measured the distance, looked at the scuffle, and turned sideways. Her arm shot out to the side. She froze, finger pointing, awkwardly resembling a bowling trophy topper.

"Harry?" she asked.

He went to where her finger was pointing, and a couple inches to the right found a series of scratches in the plywood.

"Something angular landed here and skidded," he reported.

"The gun," Toni said. She straightened. She looked at the body. "Sal gave as good as he got. He managed to knock the gun out of the killer's hand. That's why he didn't shoot Sal. They fought again. And then… they went at one another with what they could find."

She pointed at the pile of tools beyond Sal's body. "Sal must have knocked that over going for a weapon. They fell. The crowbar, that's a good one to grab. Looks like he fell on it, though. The thigh. He never got a chance to get in a swing. The killer was on him, crushed his hand, and then went for the head."

She knelt next to his body. She stared into his face. She put her hand out to close his eyes, which were half-open, but Harry said, "Don't."

Her hand jerked back a little. "Shit. Right. Sorry."

She stood up and looked at Harry, whose face still bore no expression. "Did I miss anything?"

"Maybe," he said. "But if you did, I did too."

"The reason it happened this way is that Sal put up a fight," Toni said.

Hendrick said, "Doesn't matter. I'm still going to crush every bone in this mutt's body, starting with his feet. Now tell me you got-"

"Wait," Bobby said. "Where's the weapon?"

Harry looked up at Bobby. "He took it with him,

Bobby. Either it was registered or it could be traced to him. He may have been an amateur, but he knew to take his gun."

"No," he said, and Toni looked up alertly at the thoughtfulness in his voice, "the hammer."

Harry looked around. "Hell's bells," he muttered. "Hendrick?"

"We didn't find nothing. What you see is what was here."

Higgins said, "He doubled back on me and I caught up with him outside. He was just running around the edge of the house. I got around the corner and put at least one hole in him."

Harry looked around. "Which way did he leave?" he asked. The opposite end of the room had another doorway cut into the bare lathe and plaster wall. Harry and Toni went to the far end of the room.

"I don't know," Higgins called. "When I came in the back, I saw him through the main hall. He was headed for the front door. When I ran after him, he cut back through here and went for the back."

Harry, followed by Toni, approached the ragged edges of the hole where a doorway would be when finished. As they neared, they could see a piece of cloth dangling from the protruding tip of a nail. Harry slowed and put himself between the door and the crowd behind him. "Grab it," he whispered.

She didn't slow down, merely exited the room through the hole in the wall. As she passed by the nail, the piece of cloth disappeared into one palm. Out of sight of the rest of them she pocketed it and continued down the hall. Harry studied the doorway. The nail was high, almost shoulder level. There was blood on the pointed tip. Harry licked his thumb and as he passed he rubbed the tip of the nail, hoping he got the blood off. He didn't stop to check.

They followed the short hall to the main entryway. The carpet runner on the floor was in disarray.

"Ran through here," Toni said.

"Seems so."

"Didn't get the front door open, or freaked out when Higgins saw him," she said. They were in the entryway they'd entered from, and they looked into the kitchen. It seemed a long way back. "He looks up when Higgins shouts. Higgins bolts toward him, he goes back the way he came?"

"Assume yes for now," Harry said. They walked back, retracing their path. The trio of men had not moved from the doorway, but Harry noticed Bobby was in front of them. He looked unhappy, and so did Hendrick.

"Trouble?" he asked.

"They wanted to follow you. I made them stay," Bobby said. "I think I came pretty close to getting thumped for the cause, truth be told, but I figured you wouldn't want them in there."

"Good thinking," Harry said. He and Toni circled wide around the body and rejoined them.

"Tell your pal here to-" Hendrick started, but Harry overrode him.

"He was right. Higgins, you're going to show us where you chased him around the house. Come on."

He brushed past the men, and Toni gave Bobby a thumb's up. Higgins scowled at her, and she thumbed her nose at the bodyguard.

"I oughta slap the smirk off your face," Higgins growled.

Toni just snickered and followed after Harry. They went into the kitchen. Higgins reached for the door, but Harry stopped him. "No. We're going out the front."

Higgins frowned. Toni said, "No more footprints than necessary. It's bad enough you ran all over them."

Bill Higgins bristled. "I'm just about through taking your-"

"Shut up," Hendrick said. "Do what they tell you."

"Hen, these fucking jokers-"

Hendrick seized Higgins by the throat. "You can follow their lead or you can follow Sal. Pick one."

Higgins' eyes widened. He choked, but managed to say, "O-okay, Hen. Okay. I'm sorry."

"Bobby, Hendrick, Cheddar," Toni said. "Stay here. Higgins, you're with us." She led the way to the front door. Harry followed behind Higgins so he wouldn't have to take his eye off the man.

Out front, Toni stopped him on the step. She faced the house. "Okay. First things first. You chased him out the back. Where did you come in?"

"I… the back. I told you."

"You came in the back door. Straight from your house?"

Higgins nodded. He pointed to the house on the right of Sal's. "That one's mine."

Harry was slowly scanning the cul-de-sac, not looking for anything, but looking all the same.

"Okay. You went in the back," Toni said. "You saw the guy by the front door down the hall. You yelled at him and ran after him."

"Yeah."

Toni scratched her head. "He ran back into the game room? Past Sal?"

"Yeah."

"Did you run through there?"

Higgins nodded. "Yeah."

"What color was your shirt?" she asked.

Higgins cocked his head. "What?"

"Your shirt. Have you changed?" she asked, impatient.

"What… no. This is what I was wearing. Coat, too,"

Higgins told her. Harry turned to look at the man. He was wearing a beige winter coat, down-filled. The collar of the shirt peeking through the neck was white. He went back to looking at the neighborhood. No faces watched them that he could tell. But something felt wrong. He waited, not forcing it.

"Okay. You both ran out the back door, the one you came in. You chased him which way?" she asked.

Higgins pointed to the left side of Sal's house. They could see the footprints in the snow, scuffled and indistinct. Harry had seen them on the way in and refused to start at the middle. Now he gave them a cursory look.

"Okay. Let's go." She started to move to the right side of the house. Higgins said, "But-"

"We're not messing up the footprints by walking over them," Harry said.

Higgins' mouth formed an 'ooh' of realization, and he started after Toni.

Sal must have been desperate, if he was relying on this chuckle-head to watch him, Harry thought. No wonder Hendrick thinks this is Toni's fault. Terry Shoulders would have been quicker, and that's saying something.

They rounded the house. Toni put a hand up. "You stay here and walk us through it." She swung wide out away from the house, making sure her feet touched fresh, undisturbed snow.

"I came out of the porch after him," Higgins said. "He was just at the corner there."

He pointed to the furthest corner of the house.

"I ran to it and saw him as he was about halfway down. I popped him one, fired a couple more times, but I missed. I ran down there after him in time to see the car pulling away. I put two into the car, I think. One in the back window. And they were gone. I came back to the house and went inside. It took me a while to call around and find

Hen. I hadda side-track him through Cheddar."

Higgins sighed. Toni looked at him sideways. "You knew Cheddar's phone number?"

Higgins shrugged. "Sure."

"Why?"

Harry arched an eyebrow at Toni. She screwed up her face.

"Oh. Because of his girls."

Higgins nodded, grinning.

Toni started to berate him, but gave it up. It wouldn't matter. Married or not, kids or not, it wouldn't matter. It never did. Not with Italian guys, not with Irish guys, not with any guys except for a very few individual guys. Like Harry. She swung wide around the house, still keeping to the snow. "Hey, Harry?"

"Stay here," Harry ordered Higgins, and followed Toni, keeping his feet in her fresh tracks. He joined her. Out of the corner of his eye, he could see, inside the house, Cheddar and Hendrick watching them. "What's up?"

She pointed. "Tell me what you see."

He looked. The broken tracks led down the side of the house, swung wide around a bush planted near the siding, and continued to the street. Harry looked more closely. No, it wasn't both tracks. One set seemed to slip between the house and the bush. Harry said, "Someone was in a hurry and didn't want to cut around."

Toni waited. The silence between them grew. Harry glanced at her, frowned faintly, and looked again. The track to the right of the bush was wider, no distinct footprints; more than one person had made that path. But the other tracks…

"Come on." he walked beside the heavily-trodden trail in the snow, keeping well clear. Toni followed him. They came to the bush. One set of tracks indeed slipped between the bush and the house. The other path swung around it.

Harry glanced at the bush. He crouched to get a better angle without crossing the treads.

On the siding of Sal's house, where the snow had been brushed away, was a faint tracing of blood.

Harry stood with a grin. He gave Toni a triumphant look. But she wasn't looking at the siding. She was looking toward the street. She walked a few feet further, looked back at the bush, then looked at the street again.

Harry whispered, "Sal's killer brushed against the house. There's blood."

She nodded absently but didn't answer.

Long accustomed to playing off one another, Harry didn't question her. He looked at the snow leading away from the bush, looked at the heavy tracks leading to the street, and looked back at the bush.

She looked at him. "What do you reckon, Harry?" she asked.

He looked at the bush, at the house, at the beaten path-

"Oh," he breathed. "Oh, I see."

"I thought you would," she said. She glanced over her shoulder, saw Higgins peering around the corner. At least he was in their fresh path, not tromping the evidence, such as it was.

"Come on," she said. "We got eyes on us."

He immediately started for the street. She trailed behind him as he followed the beaten tracks to the sidewalk. They became lost in the mush and grimy snow of the cul-de-sac. He looked back at the house, at Higgins peering at them still, and the bush by the side of Sal's house.

Whoever Higgins had chased around the side of the house had squeezed between the bush and the house to save time. Harry thought he might have just jumped it. *But if I had been running, and if I'd jumped it, I'd be dead. Higgins would have shot me in the back. Whoever ran down the side of the house was smarter than I would have been. Lucky for them. But then... who got to the street and jumped in the car?*

Toni and Harry started walking back to Higgins. As they passed the bush, Harry again looked at the fresh, unbroken snow that lay on the far side of where the blood smeared the siding.

As they passed the bush, neither looked back. There was no point in giving Higgins anything else to ask.

And the last thing they needed was Hendrick wondering who, if Higgins had chased someone to the street and saw them getting in a car, had hidden themselves behind that bush. Because the tracks showed someone squeezing between the house and the bush, toward the street, but the snow on the other side of the big, leafy evergreen, the side that led to the street, was clean and fresh and unbroken.

CHAPTER FIFTEEN

They stood in Sal's kitchen going over it a third time, but neither Toni nor Harry, or even Bobby with his sarcastic asides, could shake the story any further. Higgins insisted he'd told them everything, and after walking back into the house he hadn't left. Harry and Toni relented after three full repetitions.

"That's what we can get so far," Harry said. "Now we need to figure out how to find the guy."

"Where do you start?" Hendrick asked.

"Well, the best place would be hospitals, vets, and clinics for a gunshot wound. I also want to have you reach out to your contacts. Check all the back-alley docs you can. Anyone with any medical experience, someone your connections might go to for off-the-books help," Harry said. "We'll start scouting."

"Why not call your friends?" Higgins asked. "You still got people on the force, right?"

Harry gave the man a withering look. "I'm sorry. I was under the impression we were trying to not alert the authorities to any of this."

Hendrick gave Higgins a dark glare. "Shut up, Bill. Go home."

"But-"

"I said go home. You're not helping. Your job now is to keep an eye on Sal's place. Make sure no one comes snooping. Get the mail and the papers. Business as usual. Anyone important calls, Sal's got a stomach thing, he's in the city seeing his doctor. Understand?" Hendrick growled.

Higgins seemed about to argue, but thought better of it. Cheddar watched him walk back to his house with a sullen, hangdog expression on his heavy face.

"You know that guy is a liability, right?" Toni asked.

Hendrick shrugged. "He's what I've got right now. He's an idiot, but he's loyal. That's in short supply."

Harry said, "We'll get on our end, you get on yours. Let's meet up again tomorrow unless you find something or we do. What's Higgins' phone number?"

Hendrick looked blank.

"We can't call you at the Aces, and you can't come to our place," Harry reminded him impatiently. "The flower gag is too slow. None of our friends can know about this. And some of our friends are Feds. They're always watching."

"Right, right. Uh..." Hendrick looked at Cheddar.

Cheddar took a business card from his pocket. It was for some Chinese laundry uptown, but he'd scribbled a number on it. He read it off.

Harry didn't write it down. Cheddar gave a puzzled look until Toni recited it for him.

"Better than a Rolodex," Cheddar said.

"Better legs, too," Toni said. "Come on. I'm hungry."

"You're always hungry," Harry said. He raised a hand to Hendrick, who nodded.

"Well, feed me more," Toni said.

"Is there enough food for that?" Bobby asked from behind them.

"I'm not Clara," Toni objected. "It's not that bad."

"Jesus," Bobby muttered. "That woman."

Harry went to the passenger side of the Chevelle and held the door. "You met Clara?"

"Sure did," Bobby said, climbing into the back. "I may have nightmares for the rest of my life."

Harry chuckled. "Yeah, she can do that."

Toni revved the engine, they waved at Hendrick and Cheddar, who were still standing by the edge of the street, watching.

Toni gave Hendrick a big smile and said, "So, how fucked are we?"

Harry shrugged. "I'm not sure yet. Lemme think for a while."

"Okay. You think. I'm going to Katz's."

"My vote's for that second one," Bobby said. "I'm starving."

Toni steered the car through the snowy streets, sliding a little through turns with a grin. The day was full bright now, the sun overhead, and the day didn't seem nearly as bad as Harry was worried it might be. *At least we have some breathing room*, he thought.

CHAPTER SIXTEEN

They sat in the booth, Bobby and Toni across from Harry. Bobby had a Rueben, Toni had a roast beef sandwich, and Harry had opted for soup.

They ate in silence. Half of Toni's sandwich was gone before she asked Harry, "Now?"

Harry wiped his mouth on a napkin and said, "May as well."

Bobby's eyes opened wide as Toni brought out the piece of fabric she'd palmed at the scene. She set it on a clean napkin between them.

It was an inch or so long, half as wide, had a hemmed edge, and was black. The edge that wasn't hemmed was torn, and threads trailed from it.

Harry took out his notebook and a pencil and sketched a quick rectangle of Sal's house. He made a quick-and-dirty series of lines denoting the rooms and put a circle on the doorway they'd found the scrap on. He tapped it.

"This is where that scrap was. It was on a nail poking through the lath." He glanced up at Bobby. "They didn't see it."

Bobby nodded. "Just kinda freaked me out. I keep thinking about you like a cop. Cops wouldn't swipe evidence."

"I'm not a cop anymore. The rules are a little looser. Especially when our lives are on the line."

"I getcha," Bobby said. He took a bite of sandwich. He was well aware that Harry was using him as a sounding board. Toni didn't need the drawing. Harry didn't need the drawing. But it was always good to work out loud. He'd picked up on that with Toni. She liked to work through things verbally, and now Bobby could see where she picked it up.

"He came in the back door. The porch. But he must have wandered around the house. Sal's bedroom is here," he illustrated on the floor plan, "and the kitchen is here. Sal must have wandered out and they rotated around the house like this," he made a counter-clockwise circle on the diagram, "and then the killer came up the hallway and into the kitchen, which used to be a back porch. He confronts Sal, chases him into the game room, and they fight. He drops his gun here," again, he drew a circle, "picks up the nearest heavy object, and bam. No more Sal."

Harry sipped his Coke.

"Shortly after, the killer heads for the front door," he said. "He sees Higgins lumbering after him. Runs back into the game room, through the kitchen, and out the back. Higgins gives chase; he wings the guy as he goes around the corner."

"Remind me to ask Hendrick if any of the neighbors heard the shots," Toni said. "That close, Higgins is lucky he didn't accidentally shoot one of the neighbors. Those shots could have blown out windows, hit innocents."

Harry nodded. "You're right. They're lucky. Anyone else injured, cops and medics would have been all over the place."

"What happens if, you know, someone anonymously tips off the cops to Sal?" Bobby asked. "Out of your hands. Act of God. So sorry. Not your fault."

"Hendrick would take it personally," Harry said. "And try to have us rubbed out on principle."

Toni said around a mouthful of roast beef. "Although… dropping a dime ain't the same as giving up. And once the cops know, sure it'd be a hassle, but we might be able to convince Hendrick we can still work it. I mean, we could. And we could use the manpower and resources. Like, legit ones. It's not like tipping off the cops will immediately bring in the killer. We might be able to bring Hendrick around to that."

Harry thought about it. "Right now it's too risky. Hendrick's on edge. He'll make a snap judgment. He'd be right, too. Let's let it ride for a while. We're in no immediate danger, and that means we have time to think. Besides… if the force picks it up and the detectives on the case are decent, remember that we're harboring a fugitive murderer."

Bobby's face fell as he remembered that part of the tangle. "Oh. Right."

He put an X by the corner, then drew a line down the left side of the house. It swung around the corner and led to the front of the house, curving out away from the small circle Harry labeled 'bush'.

"The guy he chased ran this way," he said, drawing a line from the corner down the side of the house to the bush. "Higgins says he didn't see the guy running except for the short stretch toward the street here."

He drew an X at the street.

"When he got there, he saw the guy jump into a car and take off. He shoots out the rear window, but the car never stops. A couple hours later, we've got a bleeding houseguest."

Bobby sipped a glass of tea and fondly wished he had something stronger. "Sound straightforward."

"Yeah…" Harry trailed off. "Except."

"There's always an except," Bobby said.

"Yeah," Toni agreed. She bit half a pickle off and chewed it. Indistinctly she said, "We saw two sets of tracks." She pointed, and Harry drew a line. "They led from the corner to here."

She pointed to the bush. "The guy squeezed through here to save himself some time running."

"Might have saved his life," Bobby said.

"Maybe," Harry agreed. "We even saw a little smear of blood here, on the house, where he squeezed through."

Bobby said, "Still waiting on the except."

Toni flashed him a smile. She pointed at the far side of the bush, where the paper had no line. "There were no tracks on this side."

Bobby frowned. He stared at the map. "The fabric, here, right?"

"Yep," Toni said.

"With a blood spot."

"Looked like it," Harry agreed.

"The blood out here, on the house."

"Yep again," she said.

"But no tracks from the bush to the street?"

"Nope," Harry said.

Bobby frowned. "The blood on the house was from the shot?"

Toni and Harry grinned at each other. Harry shrugged. "No idea. All we know is, there was blood."

"And no tracks to the street, where the guy, your brother-in-law, ran to the car? Driven, presumably, by your sister, the bombshell redhead."

"Bombshell?"

Harry's eyes flickered to Bobby, who, without missing a beat, said, "A whole family of bombshells makes sense. I assume your mom is stacked, too. Must be where you got it. God knows you and your sister are gorgeous."

Bobby picked up his tea and sipped, a too-innocent look on his face.

Toni's mouth dropped open, but no sound came out. She turned to Harry.

"It was a good line," he said with a smile.

Toni shut her mouth, shook her head, and said, "Don't talk about my sister."

But Harry noticed a faint flush on her cheeks. He

grinned again and tapped her leg with his foot. She looked up and he winked. "He's right."

Bobby coughed and looked at the paper. "So... the guy jumps... what... eight feet? Eight feet to the beaten path?"

"If it's an inch," Harry agreed.

Bobby scratched his head. "I'm missing something."

"Give it a second," Toni said.

Bobby stared at the map, took the paper, turned it around, and said, "Okay, so Higgins comes around after winging the guy, sees him squeeze-"

"Hold it," Harry said. His voice was like iron. "Play that back, Bobby."

Bobby gave Harry a confused look. "What?"

"Start over. Where did Higgins shoot Abruzzi?"

"In the arm."

Harry closed his eyes and sighed. Toni said, "No, Bobby. Where was Abruzzi when Higgins saw him?"

Bobby tapped the X by the corner. "Here."

"And the next time Higgins gets eyes on him and shoots him, he's where?"

Bobby tapped the X by the street. "Here."

They waited. Bobby muttered, "Hold up."

He studied the lines. "You said he ran behind the bush, but the tracks don't lead from the bush to the road..."

He trailed off. He put his finger on the line at the corner, traced it to the bush. "I'd say he hid here, except Higgins saw him here. The blood on the siding was his... except, no. Wait. He hadn't been shot until... he must have... no. He... huh."

He pushed the sketch back to Harry. "Something's not right. Higgins isn't telling you something," he said.

Toni and Harry exchanged a glance. "Why do you say that?" Toni asked.

"Because in order for it to happen this way is-"

Bobby broke off, looked at each of them in turn. They

were both serious, quiet, and watching him with intensity.

"There were two guys," he whispered.

The triumphant flash of teeth from Toni to Harry and his approving nod filled Bobby Gold with a confusing mixture of emotions.

"Why are you guys fucking with me?" he asked heatedly. "If you already knew, why bother making me dance?"

Toni causally picked up the remaining half of her pickle and ate it. She didn't say anything. Neither did Harry. Bobby massaged the bridge of his nose. "Ah. Because you wanted to see what I could do with the clues. It's a goddamned audition. You wanted to see if I could keep up with you."

Harry shot a startled look at Toni, who said, "What? No, Bobby, that's not it. At all."

Bobby looked up at her. "Do tell."

"Scout's honor," she said, and threw three fingers up. "You wouldn't be here if you couldn't keep up. Loyalty's nice, but we don't need a Higgins."

Bobby gave first her then Harry a wary glance. Harry nodded. "She's right. She said you were smart. I wouldn't have you here if you weren't."

"If you say so," Bobby said uncertainly. "Then why this whole drawing? Why the clue-hunting? Why are you walking me through it?"

"Why would we do that, Harry?" Toni asked.

Harry sipped his Coke. "Dunno. You'd have to be pretty smart to figure out why we'd do that."

Bobby gave them both a middle finger. "Fuck you."

They all laughed at this, and the tension faded.

"Seriously," Harry said. "Why?"

Bobby shrugged, eyes on the diagram. "I can't think of…" He cocked his head. "A second guy," he muttered. He looked up at them. "A second guy?"

Neither Harry nor Toni said a word. Harry picked at the remaining half of Toni's sandwich, selected a morsel of roast beef and ate it.

Bobby's skin chilled, the hair stood up on his neck, and he said, hesitantly, "…you wanted to see what I thought?"

Toni nodded. "Not just that, though," she added.

Bobby frowned, and the sun came out on his long, lined face. He grinned at them. His voice was full of triumph, the joy of having solved a logical problem. "You wanted to see if I got the same impression you did. Came to the same conclusion with the same info."

Harry nodded. Glancing at Toni's beaming smile, he said to Bobby, "What do you know? She was right again."

"I'm always right," Toni said, crossing her arms. "Deal with it."

Harry let that pass. "Okay, so now we have two perps, both going into Sal's house to kill him-"

"Which one went in?" Bobby asked. "Abruzzi or the other one?"

"Good question," Toni said. "Someone was in Sal's house and caught themselves on the nail. And someone was outside hiding behind the bush. If it was the guy inside, or if it was blood from the nail, we can't tell. A piece of black cloth doesn't help. John's shirt had holes in it from the bullet, and besides, Gene cut it off. Maybe we can match it up, maybe we can't. But that's the next step. Figuring out who got shot, who snagged themselves on that nail, and," she looked at Harry and Bobby in turn, "and who beat Sal D'Amico to death with a hammer."

CHAPTER SEVENTEEN

It was nearly three when they got back to the office. The sun had vanished behind clouds, and the air had gotten noticeably crisper. They got out of the car, and as they headed for the door, Bobby asked, "Where did that car come from?"

Harry and Toni stopped and looked where he was pointing. It was the car Starr and Abruzzi had arrived in. Toni said as much.

"Yeah, okay," Bobby said. And as they went for the door, he asked, "Then why's it got a rear window?"

Harry's head snapped around. He peered closer. "Huh."

"They switched cars somewhere," Toni said. "The other car… Harry, if Hendrick finds it, it could be traced. We need to find that car."

Harry nodded. He unlocked the office and they went in. After coffee was poured, he said, "Who gets to run upstairs and ask Abruzzi the questions?"

Toni said, "Not it. This is going to get awkward. I don't want Starr angry at me because I'm standing on her husband's neck."

Harry nodded. "Okay. I'll take that hit. Why don't you-"

Harry broke off as a cab pulled up outside the office. Gene got out, saw them inside, and raised a hand. He paid the driver and hurried inside. "Hey, guys. How goes it?"

"It's been a day," Harry said. "Where did you go?"

"Hmm? Oh, I ran over to the office. Had to grab a few things," Gene said. He held up his bag. "Running low."

"How's Abruzzi?" Toni asked.

Gene's face darkened. He stood next to them, breath

pluming in the cold afternoon air. "I don't like the fever. He's high enough now that he's starting to hallucinate. If it keeps up, he's got to go to a hospital, Harry."

"That bad?"

"Infections kill every day," Gene said.

Bobby said in a thoughtful voice, "That's always a possibility."

Harry gave him a blank look, but Toni said, "Jesus. I guess that's a plan B. You're fucking dark lately, Gold."

"Yeah, well," he said, giving her a heavy look, "it's not without cause."

Toni looked away, dropping her eyes to the table.

"Excuse me," Gene said, "why is my patient dying a good thing?"

Harry caught up. "Ah. Yeah. If, on the off-chance, he does die, Gene, we can give him to Hendrick. No reason to hide him. We could say we found him in an alley or something."

"He's got stitches," Gene pointed out.

"Well, the truth of the matter is, if he dies from the infection, it doesn't matter," Harry said. "He got help and it didn't help. Case closed."

Toni said, "Doesn't change the fact that Starr will be devastated."

"Well, that's not our first option, sure," Harry said. "But it's a possible way out of this. First, we need to know where that car came from. I'll be right back. Gene, you want to come up, make sure he's okay?"

Gene stood. "I was going to do that either way. Come on."

Gene went to the door and looked up and down the street. "If we're being all clandestine, I figure a bunch of people running up and down the stairs won't help."

"Good thinking," Harry said. "When do you go back to work?"

Gene hesitated. He said, "I called in. Took five sick days. It's fine; I have about a bazillion of them; I never get sick. Lucky no one saw me raiding the supply closet."

Harry sighed. "I owe you, Gene. Thank you."

"You owe me for getting me into this. I'm committed to helping someone in need now. I don't normally treat live people. It's a nice change of pace. Of course, there's always the possibility that I kill him screwing something up. In which case I'm covered, because I'd do the autopsy." Gene laughed, Toni laughed, Harry laughed, Bobby Gold pursed his lips, eyes drifting up and to the left.

"I wonder how many people could get away with murder if they did that?" he pondered. "How many people have jobs they could use like cover?"

Gene looked up at Bobby and said tonelessly, "We had a detective murdering hookers a year or so ago," he said. "Kept getting himself assigned to the cases. Dead-ended a lot of investigations that way."

Bobby whistled. "Clever," he said. "What happened to him?"

"Harry killed him," Toni said.

Bobby's mouth dropped open. "You killed a cop?"

"Not just a cop. One of his poker buddies," Gene added.

Bobby looked from one face to the next, trying to work out if it was a joke or not.

"I didn't kill him," Harry corrected. "I tracked him down and told him I was taking him in or putting him down. Porter chose option C: he shot himself."

Bobby stared at Harry, who regarded the man with a look that Bobby would have been hard-pressed to define as other than remorseful. Anyone else would justify what they did to a friend, Bobby thought. Anyone else would make excuses.

But Harry said nothing. He and Gene left the office and went up to the apartment. Toni poured herself more coffee. Gold looked at her.

"Always does the right thing, huh?"

"Always, Bobby. Always."

Bobby nodded. "That's what's got you twisted up, isn't it?"

"What do you mean?"

"I can tell something's on your mind. The way you look at him."

She shrugged. "This is… this is different than anything else we've been into."

"You've… shall we say… skirted the rules before. Like shooting that guy that was beating on you."

"That was different," Toni said. "And so were all the other times. The rest of our work is on the side of the angels. We help the cops, or do what they can't. Even bounty hunting is helping them, in a way."

"And working with mobsters and pimps?" Bobby asked. "That's helping?"

Toni smiled wanly. "That's going along to get along. We do the most good for the most people. And we always include our friends. They know what we're up to. Clara and Kilburn and Mills. They know we're out here working to help. But this is different."

Bobby sat on the couch, unzipped his jacket, and scratched his chest. "How so?"

"Bobby, we're aiding and abetting a murder. We're hiding a killer. We're looking for someone that Hendrick can flat-out kill in retaliation," Toni snapped. "Seems like when we look over our shoulders now, the line we shouldn't cross is fading further and further back."

"Your sister needed your help."

"And that's what we're doing. But we're on the hook too, Bobby. We're just treading the water, trying to keep afloat. But even if we somehow get Starr and Johnny out of town without anyone knowing they're involved, even if we get 'em back home to Chicago, we're still complicit. We're always going to have covered this shit up." Toni crossed her arms and stared out the window at the street. "Once you get dirty, it's impossible to get clean."

Bobby watched the side of her face. She was somber and uncharacteristically introspective. It wasn't the woman he'd come to know the past few weeks.

"I know Harry's upset. He's good at not showing it. He's working the problem, but if I know him, he's already four steps beyond everyone else. He's already thinking about the endgame in this. And he's already realized that we're not getting out of this without lying to our friends," she told him. She shivered, staring out at the snow. "It's awful hard to come back from that."

"You'd be surprised what you can come back from," Gold said. His voice was bleak. "Sometimes you might wish you couldn't. Every time you slip, it's that much harder to come back. But if you've got balls you can do it. And you got the biggest pair I've seen outside of King Kong, lady."

Toni didn't smile. "It's not about me so much, Bobby. I know who I am, I know what I am. Nobody's opinion matters to me, not in my soul. It's cash on the barrel-head every time, I know that. I expect a lot from the people I know, but I give a lot in return. I wouldn't stiff a friend."

"But you ain't worried about you," Bobby said. It wasn't a question. "I've never seen you worry about anyone. Well, except one guy."

"Yeah," she breathed. "He's out on a limb here, Bobby. He'll do it, but it's because of me. And I'm doing it because of Starr. And she's doing it for her guy. Which is a motivation I can understand."

Bobby said, hesitantly, "You trust your sister? Is she

solid?"

He expected a withering stare, or a snappy retort, or even a fist in the nose, but she sighed. "Bobby... I haven't seen Starr since I left home. Four years? Five. I don't know who she is, not really."

She looked at him with steel in her eyes. "But she's a Bennett. She's my sister. And she gets the benefit of the doubt."

He nodded. "I getcha. But these aren't questions I'm the first to think of."

Toni's eyes rolled upward. She stared at the ceiling. "Yeah."

CHAPTER EIGHTEEN

Harry closed the door of the little apartment behind him. The smallish kitchen held a little table and four chairs. There were dirty dishes in the sink, but the counters were clean. He went into the living room, trailing after Gene. Cherry, her maraschino-colored hair in disarray, raised a hand to Harry. She was wearing a tee-shirt and a pair of red panties. Her legs were tucked under her and she was sipping what looked like soup from a big mug. The other girl, Trix, was waifish, skinny with huge eyes. She goggled at Harry. She was wrapped to her chin in a multicolored crocheted blanket.

"Thanks for the assist, girls," Harry said.

Cherry smiled. Trix nodded, her eyes huge and wide. "No problem, Harry," Cherry said.

"You keep it between us, you get a month's rent," Harry said. "You're doing us a huge favor."

Trix and Cherry shared a look. Cherry said, hesitantly, "Harry… you don't have to-"

Trix pursed her lips and glared at Cherry, but said nothing.

Harry smiled at them. "If we have to keep 'em up here more than a week, I'll make it two months. Okay?"

Glowing, Cherry said, "Whatever you need, Harry."

"Hey," Harry said. "You know Bobby Gold? Been hanging with Toni?"

Cherry's face became guarded. "Uh, yeah?"

"Don't worry about it," Harry assured her. "He's cool. But you tell him if you need supplies or anything, okay? I don't want you running out for extra food, or bandages, or stuff like that. The idea is to keep anyone outside from knowing you got guests. All right?"

"You got it, Harry," Cherry said.

He nodded at them and followed Gene into one of the three bedrooms, Cherry's by the look of the floor. It was covered with a myriad of undergarments, all her signature red.

Abruzzi lay on the bed, sweat beading on his face and chest. Gene was listening to his heart. Starr watched from a chair across from Gene, practically rubbing her hands together fretfully.

"What's the news?"

"He's still running a fever, but his pulse is steady. His blood pressure is still elevated, but he's stable, at least. I think it's just an infection. His lungs sound clear. No puncture, which is what I feared at first."

"You didn't say that," Starr accused. "You didn't say anything like that."

"Because I was worried it might be true. Now I'm not. Why worry you?" Gene asked.

Starr glared at him. "Asshole."

"Wait 'til you get the bill," Gene muttered. He checked Abruzzi's pulse again and pulled the stethoscope away from his ears. "He's asleep, which is the best for him. I'd rather not have to give him a sedative. He needs to recuperate. He lost a lot of blood. Not dangerous amounts, but significant. Has he eaten or drunk anything?"

"He woke up half an hour ago, kind of," Starr said. The worry was plain on her face. "He drank a glass of water, but wouldn't eat anything. He's been asleep ever since."

Gene nodded. "He'll be in and out for a day or two. Any longer than that and I may start to be worried, but right now," he said, staring into Starr's wide eyes, "I'm not worried about anything at all. Okay?"

She nodded, biting her lip. "Really? Or 'really, but I'm secretly wondering if his lung is punctured' really?"

"The regular kind."

Starr clearly didn't want to believe him, but she accepted it. "All right. What can I do now?"

"Right now, we keep him cool, monitor his heart rate and blood pressure, and let the body heal itself," Gene said. "He should be awake later today, or tomorrow at the latest."

"Is there any way to wake him up earlier?" Harry asked.

Starr stared up at Harry. "Why would you even ask that? He needs rest!"

"I ask because you won't answer any questions," Harry said, "and I'm getting tired of sandbagging. I understand he's hurt, but he didn't get hit saving an orphan from an oncoming car. He killed a Gambino boss. And I'm hiding him. I knew that boss. I've done business with him. He knew me, and his people know me. They know what I do. So when they need help, where did they come? That boss's people are on my neck to find him. Now I've got no goddamned time for games."

Harry squatted next to the chair and leveled his gaze at Starr, who flinched back a scant inch.

"If you want my help, you have to tell me everything. I can't hide what I don't know about. And since the guy he killed has a lot of nasty people looking for him, I need to be able to cover some tracks pretty friggin' quick. Especially in light of the fact that I'm one of the guys looking for him."

Harry gripped the arm of the chair. His fist closed around the wood, and knuckles cracked in the silence and whitened. Starr glanced down at them and back up. She cleared her throat.

"That the kind of man you are?" she asked with a wary look. "You gonna pop me one if I don't do what you want?"

To Gene's surprise, Harry grinned at her. "Oh, hell no

You have to know your sister better than that. That's not the kind of guy she'd give the time of day, is it?"

Starr, confused, shook her head. "No," she murmured hesitantly.

"Then don't insult me," Harry said. "But I'm up against it, and I'm starting to feel the pressure. And if you won't talk, he's going to. So you start talking, or Gene's going to give him something to wake him up. And if whatever he gives him doesn't work, I'm going to start poking that hole in him with a stick until I get the answers I need."

He looked into her deep green eyes, and his voice was quietly sincere. "Or are you going to tell me what you do know?"

She bit her lip, looked at Abruzzi, and looked back. "He… I'm not supposed to-"

Harry nodded. "I know. I know the whole party line. You don't know nothing, you didn't see nothing, you ain't gonna say nothing. But you're not talking to a cop, Starr, you're talking to someone who took you in with no questions, covered for you at least once, and who's currently giving a bunch of dangerous guys the run-around when he's supposed to be hunting your man. So maybe we dispense with the I'm-not-supposed-tos, and maybe just get on with the details. The more I know, the more I can cover up. And since your man isn't walking out of here today, getting him out of the city isn't much of an option. I need to put up a smokescreen, Starr. So talk."

He stood up and leaned against the wall, crossing his arms and staring at her.

She considered her words, glanced again at the restless form of Johnny Abruzzi next to her, and nodded to herself. She said without looking up, "I'll tell you what I know. I'll tell you what I suspect."

Harry waited, glanced at Gene, and Gene said, "I'll go

get a glass of somewhere else while you talk."

Harry nodded his thanks.

Gene closed the door, and Starr looked up at Harry. "Johnny's with the outfit."

"I figured. Chicago."

She shrugged. "It's what he does. He's... he's a soldier."

"Made?"

She shook her head. "No. Not yet."

The way she said it gave Harry pause. He narrowed his eyes. "Sal."

Starr nodded without looking up. "Yes."

Harry took a deep breath, a calming breath. He let go of his animosity for the moment. Sal knew what his life was, he thought. No reason to be upset about it.

"Why trust such a big job with a soldier?" Harry asked. "All alone? With his wife? That doesn't add up."

"Johnny... he did something a couple months ago. He... he was on house calls, you know?"

"B & E," Harry said. "Bird-dogging rich houses and ripping them off."

"Yes. And... he wanted his captain to notice him. So he started pulling extra jobs," she said. She looked up. "He kept meticulous records, though. He never kept a cent. He sent it all up the line. He wanted to make a name, not a profit."

Harry said nothing, and she colored a little.

"He... he picked the wrong house. The owner was home."

"Killed him?"

"Her," Starr said. "She drew on him and he had to put her down."

Harry's jaw flexed as he looked at Abruzzi. "He killed an innocent?"

"No!" Starr protested. "That's just it! She wasn't a

civilian. She was somebody's ex-wife. Somebody high up."

Harry stared at Abruzzi some more. "Did he know that?"

She frowned up at him. "Does it matter?"

Harry's eyes blazed. "Of course it matters! I don't give a shit what a bunch of gangster knuckleheads get up to between themselves. But innocent lives are a different matter. It's the line."

Starr swallowed. "I understand. And yes, he knew. The husband… he'd mentioned that his ex was keeping some things from him, some pictures of his parents, a high school ring, like that. Keepsakes. Nothing too valuable. Johnny wanted to get this man's approval. She wasn't supposed to be there. She was supposed to be out of town."

Harry raised an eyebrow. "Oh?"

Starr nodded. "That's what Johnny said. He said 'she was supposed to be in Florida.' That's what he was told. But when he went in, she was asleep in the bedroom. She came up firing. Him or her."

Harry's mind raced over the details. He was starting to get the picture, but he needed a few more facts. "Two explanations. Either the guy knew his ex was home, in which case he wanted her put down without ordering it, or the other thing: the guy wanted the stuff, but he took it poorly that his ex was gunned down."

"The second part, I think. They were… Johnny was in a lot of trouble, so he asked for a showstopper. Last-ditch," Starr said. "Something to get him right and give him an in. So they gave him this job. But he was cut off; no Outfit help. No resources. Just go pop the Gambino underboss. Pull it off and all is forgiven. And he gets Made."

Harry closed his eyes. "Everything he wants, all in one package. Very attractive."

"We picked up some supplies in Chicago, drove here and followed him until we had his patterns," Starr said. "And last night he did it."

Harry nodded. "Those supplies include a gun?"

"It's in the car," Starr said.

"Reminds me," Harry mused. "We need to get that car out of here. Keys?"

"In Johnny's jacket pocket."

"Okay, good. I'll get rid of the car. Anything in there to tie you to it?"

"No- wait. Probably some blood," Starr said. "And fingerprints."

"Uh huh. And where's the first car?" Harry asked.

"What do you mean?"

"I told you not to screw around, Starr," Harry said, voice hardening. "I understand the rear window was blown out. The car downstairs-"

"No, no, you're right. I forgot. I forgot. I'm not trying to hide anything," she protested.

"Okay," he relented. "I believe you."

Her relief was palpable. She said, "I know how much we need your help. You have my word, Harry. I won't lie to you."

"Please don't. Not after saying that. I'll be less inclined to help if I know I can't trust you," he said. "So what happened inside the house?"

Starr shook her head. "I don't know. I waited in the car, engine running. I was dozing, he was gone so long. Then I heard the shots. Johnny came tearing around the house holding his arm. He got in, we took off, someone shot out the back window. We came over the bridge, I camped out a porno theater until we saw some guy come out. He was married. I jacked his car-"

"Smart," Harry said. "Your idea?"

"Yes."

"Good thinking. He wouldn't report it. Not right away."

"That's what I was thinking. I jacked his car and we left the other one there. Then I drove here. You know the rest of it."

"Okay… the other car, anything to tie you to that?"

"No, it's a long-term parking swipe from O'Hare," she said. "No one's supposed to miss it for another three weeks, according to the tag."

Harry looked at her, his gaze thoughtful and probing. She said nothing, but met his eyes steadily. After a time he said, "You don't talk like a citizen. How long have you and Johnny been together?"

"Almost a year. We got married three months ago," she said. "Is that relevant?"

"Who knows? What did you do before that?"

"I went to the movies a lot," she said somewhat primly. "And read a lot of books."

He sighed. "You know what I mean. You don't talk like a civilian. You were on top of it with the getaway car, and that trick at the porno theater was too wise. You're not having a panic attack and you didn't seem bothered by the blood or the holes in your man. He was hurt in the car and you took the time to play that flirting game with me and Toni."

Starr didn't speak for a long time. Harry waited, counting heartbeats. She was testing his patience and he wasn't the sort to fail that kind of test. He counted three hundred before she said, "Small-time. Street hustle. Wheelman. I drove for a penny-ante crew outside Joliet. Ran a numbers book in Aurora for a couple months. Moved back to Chicago, met Johnny, and we've been together ever since. Why do you ask?"

"My reasons haven't changed. You've been on the grift since you were…"

"Fourteen. Us Bennett girls, we start early." She watched him process that.

He didn't bite the bait. Instead he said, "All right. Here's what happens now. I'm going to drop that car back off in the porno parking lot after a thorough cleaning. Then I'm going to lead Sal's people to the car you left. I'll-"

"What do you mean?" she demanded. "I thought you were helping us!"

Harry held up a hand. "Hold up. You may not know this, but I'm good at what I do. Toni and me together, we're very good at what we do. If we don't come up with something, it'll look suspicious. If I don't throw them a bone now and again, I'll look even more suspicious. I give them a real piece of gold now so they won't look too hard at the chicken feed I scatter later. Savvy?"

He was surprised how easily the street patter came back to him. He'd rousted plenty of grifters in the Bowery and they were all the same.

She nodded, still worried. "Okay. It makes sense."

"Good. I think that's everything for now. Where's your luggage?"

She turned white. "Oh, shit. It's in our original car. In the trunk."

"Okay, good. I'll grab it. Keys?"

"I left them downstairs," Starr said. "In Johnny's jacket in your apartment."

"All right. I'll get them on my way out. Your job is to stay here and wait until he wakes. And eat something would you? We don't need you passing out from hunger,' Harry said. "You need anything, you tell Cherry or... oh, yeah. Trix. They'll call down, and we'll run out. Don't leave the apartment. The idea is you don't exist. Don't do anything to fuck that up."

Starr bristled. "Yes, sir, mein herr."

Harry didn't laugh. "Starr, if you go down, we go

down too. I'll do what I can to keep you two out of the fire, but if it comes down to it, Toni's my priority. I'll take him to the cops myself if I think she's going to get hurt trying to take care of you."

"Why the cops?" she asked icily. "Wouldn't you rather give us to your friends?"

Harry gave her a cold stare. "Two things: one, they're not my friends. Two, if I take you to the cops, you stand to live longer than if Sal's men get you. Make no mistake, they want to do to you what your husband did to Sal. I'll keep you safe if I can; they don't know you were driving him. They'll turn your husband into an example for the ages. But if I take him to the cops, he goes down for murder. That means time in jail, that means a trial, that means he lives a while longer. Time is opportunity. The longer he lives, the better, right? Who knows? He might even beat the rap. But time in a cell is better than dead in a cellar, screaming his lungs out with his last breath. They'll take days to hurt him, Starr. The guys looking for him? They're not just Mafia. The guy that's sitting on me is Sal D'Amico's nephew."

Starr's already pale countenanced became further white.

"I don't need to explain to you what family will do when family is wronged. And you wronged a dangerous man. Hendrick is Made. He's got connections. He's got money. He's got men. And it might have been business for your man, but it's personal for him." Harry wiped his forehead and stared at his palm. "I'd burn down the world if something happened to Toni. I understand what Hendrick's capable of. And believe me, he's not even pretending to follow the law. I have to."

Starr looked at the floor. "I understand."

"I doubt it. You're a hustler. You got a sheet?"

"I've never been pinched," she said with sullen pride.

"Good for you. That means you haven't been in the game long enough," he said. "Me? I was a cop. Even if I'm not, that means I'm in the system. Being a cop is a lot like having a rap sheet. They know where I live, they know what kind of gun I use. They've got my fingerprints. And worse than that: I consult for them. Do you understand me?"

His voice had taken on an edge Starr didn't care for.

"The people that are looking for him, they're my people. Any one of them, I'd take a bullet for. And I have to lie to them. I have to keep Hendrick and the Gambinos in the dark, that's fine. But I'm used to having the law on my side too. Half the shit I do, I can do because I have access to the resources on both sides. Thanks to you being Toni's sister, now I have to fight both sides. I have to keep everyone in the dark, and try and pull a rabbit out of a hat I've never even worn. So do me a solid, would you? Stay here, shut up, and keep your head down. I'll do what I said I would. I'll help you. But you do what I say. Not because I'm power-tripping, but because it gives me the best chance to do what I have to do. Okay? Can you follow orders?"

"Ordinarily?" Starr asked. "Nope. Not even a little. And how dare you. I'd punch you just to watch you bleed for saying it. Just now? I understand. Harry, I get how far out on a limb you and Toni have put yourselves. I'll be a good girl."

"Fair enough. For what it's worth, I've been with Tori long enough to know that, under normal circumstances, I'd be in serious trouble, threatening a Bennett woman. But in normal circumstances I wouldn't have to be ordering you around, either. Just remember: this is my town. This isn't Chicago. Okay? You're a tourist; we live here. Give us a couple days, we'll figure this out."

Starr favored him with a warm smile. "Thank you,

Harry. You're a good sort."

He shrugged. "I have opinions about that. But the woman seems to like me. I figure I can't be far off the mark if Toni's still with me."

"You remind me of Daddy," Starr said.

"Was he a cop?"

The woman barked a sudden, unexpected guffaw. "Oh Lord, no. But he doesn't stop when he sets out to do something, either. And if the rest of the world thinks he's wrong and he thinks he's right, well... you better put money on him, because the world ain't nearly as stubborn as that man. But he loves Momma, and she hasn't kicked him to the curb yet. He told me once, 'Estrella, I can always tell if I'm doing right or wrong just by the look in your Momma's eyes.'"

Harry looked thoughtful. "Estrella?"

Starr's face became guarded. "Yeah. Estrella Marie."

"It means 'star', doesn't it? In Spanish?"

The redhead sighed. "Yes. But..." she glanced at Abruzzi and pursed her lips. "Well... if you repeat this, Harry, I'll cut off your balls."

Harry smiled and held up a hand. "Stays with me. On my word."

She narrowed her eyes at him, but smiled a little. "You better be serious. Anyhow... yes, it means 'star' in Spanish. But that's not why he named me Estrella. He... well... Daddy spends a lot of time in Arizona and Texas. Border states, you know? Near Mexico. And they make a beer down there. Estrella. He-"

"He named you after his favorite beer?" Harry asked. His eyes popped. "You're joking."

She shook her head. "Nope."

"Huh," Harry mused. He frowned. "Marie? That's Toni's middle name."

"Yep. All us Bennett girls have the same middle name.

It's Mom's name."

Harry smiled. "Neat."

"Kind of," Starr agreed. "It ties us all together, you know? Even more than blood. We're all the same brand. Different models, but the same make. Our last names might change," she said, looking down again at the unconscious Abruzzi, "but the 'Marie' is forever."

"So... Estrella. Antonia. You girls get unusual names," Harry said.

"You don't ask Toni about her past, do you?" asked as she cocked her head.

"Why would I? She doesn't ask about mine."

Starr's eyes widened. She gave him a piercing look, a probing look. "You're... you're not like I expected."

"What did you expect?"

"Not you," she said. "Not... I don't know... not so much like Daddy. I never figured Toni'd be the traditional type. Figured she'd go against the grain. But girls tend to marry their dads, you know?"

Harry shrugged. "No idea what you mean. I'm an only child."

"Oh," Starr said. "Well, I don't mean literally. But Daddy... well... Daddy's an outlaw. And..." she pointed at Abruzzi. "I hate to be stereotypical, but... if the leather jacket fits, right?"

"I'm not an outlaw," Harry protested.

Starr snorted. "Oh, please."

"I'm an ex-cop," he protested. "I wouldn't even give her a gun until she got a license. Or let her drive the car I'm all about rules."

"You're hiding a murderer, helping keep him from the Mob and the law," she pointed out.

"I... huh."

"You got an outlaw streak in you, Harry, I can see it a mile away. But that's not what makes you like Daddy. No, it's the other part. The honorable part. Daddy's an outlaw, but he has strict rules. His word means something. No," she frowned. "It's more than that. His word means everything. Right, wrong, or in between, it doesn't matter. If he gives his word, you can count on it. If Daddy gave me his word he was going to paddle a canoe to the moon, I wouldn't even ask questions. I'd just wait for the ten o'clock news to report it. You're like that. I can see why she's crazy about you."

Harry shuffled his feet. "Well, it's mutual."

Starr smiled at him. "I can tell. We're not in handcuffs."

"The day's not over," Harry said. "We'll have to see what happens from here."

She nodded. "Whatever happens, Harry… I'm grateful. We're grateful. And we're in your debt."

"I never kept track of markers before, and I'm not about to start now. Just keep an eye on him. I want to talk to him when he's awake and well enough, okay?"

"Will do, Harry," Starr said, and she smiled up at him through unshed tears. "Thank you."

He gave her a smile and left, shutting the door behind him.

Starr sighed, rubbed her face with both hands, and looked down at Johnny.

Johnny Abruzzi's eyes were open, and he stared back up at her.

CHAPTER NINTEEN

In the kitchen, Harry and Gene shared a moment of tense silence. Gene poured himself a cup of coffee from the cheap coffee maker on the counter.

"Give it to me straight, doc," Harry said. "Is the coffee worth it?"

"If you put enough sugar in it, it's palatable. These kids today, man, I tell you. No one makes a good strong cup of coffee anymore."

"Dying art."

"Aside from a few small, notable practitioners. That clip joint under us, for instance. They make coffee that'll peel paint. Almost good enough to drink."

Harry snorted laughter. "How's Abruzzi?"

Gene shrugged. "I don't know. It's worrying me that he hasn't come out of it yet. The pain meds shouldn't be keeping him out. They're just enough to take the edge off. The fever's high but not dangerous. But he won't wake up."

"At what point do we need to give up and take him to a hospital?"

"Well…" Gene considered, "not yet. If he stays stable, he'll be fine. But if his stats start tanking, I'm calling an ambulance. And then I'm going to Newark to visit my mother."

Harry nodded. "The last thing I want is for you to jeopardize your job or license. You do just that. Let us take the fallout."

Gene sipped the coffee. "So what's with the kid?"

Harry blinked, then nodded. "Right. Farrokh. He's Dahli's nephew. You know, at the market?"

"Oh, yeah. Nice guy."

"The best. His nephew got pulled into a drug thing a couple months back. We're helping him out from under it. I guess he's been working with Kilburn lately trying to get someone on a wire, but he showed up last night freaking out. We're giving him a place to sleep it off until he's ready to talk," Harry said.

"Harry, Harry, Harry. If I hadn't known you before she turned up, I'd say Toni had you trained to save the whole world. Instead, all I can say is, you put a lot on yourself, you know? You can't keep this up."

"I'll keep it up as long as someone needs me," Harry said. "I've never turned my back on a friend. I'm not starting now. When someone counts on you, you come through. Period."

Gene looked skeptical, but chuckled. "I guess me arguing with you is kind of insincere, after dragging myself into the middle of your mess."

Harry said nothing, but he looked troubled. Gene saw the look.

"Harry, you didn't twist my arm. You asked, I came. We go way back. You're my friend. I know what I'm doing."

"Do you?"

"Same thing you'd do if I called at two in the morning and needed help. Stop trying to scare me off."

Harry nodded. "So be it. But if he gets worse, you make the call and bug out. And if I tell you to go, you go. Deal?"

"One condition," Gene said.

"Yeah?"

"Start shipping industrial quantities of your coffee up here. This stuff is like water," Gene said, finishing the cup and pouring more.

"You tried just using more grounds?"

In response, Gene pulled the basket out of the top of

the coffee maker. Harry saw that it was full.

"Gotcha. Special coffee deliveries. I'll have someone running coffee, food, and medical supplies."

"Thanks, Harry."

"No problem. Do me a favor and keep an eye on Farrokh, too. He's sleeping now, but something's bugging him."

"No sweat."

"Oh," Harry snapped his fingers. "Where's Abruzzi's shirt?"

Gene looked smug. "I took it and all the other waste to work and incinerated it. No chance anyone's going to trace it."

"Crud."

Gene raised his empty hands. Harry said, "I was hoping to… you didn't see a tear in it shaped like this, did you?"

Harry pulled the scrap of cloth from his pocket. Gene examined it.

"I couldn't tell you. It was a rag when I-" Gene froze. "Oh, shit, Harry. Is this…?"

"Yeah. It's from the scene. I was hoping to match it to the shirt. It would have helped a little. I'm pretty sure Abruzzi whacked Sal, but there's a couple questions I have. It looks like it came from his shirt. But I'm damned if I can figure out when. I need him awake so I can figure this all out."

"Is it necessary? I thought the main idea was to lead the goons on a wild goose chase, get the guy upright, and wave goodbye," Gene said.

"Well, it's more complicated. If we don't get the guy that got Sal, I think Toni and I are on the hook for it."

Gene's round face paled. "You're kidding."

"I'm not. Now imagine that conversation. It's either your sister's husband, or it's us."

Gene blanched. "What are you gonna do?"

Harry sighed. "Well, the plan right now is to get some breathing room. Lead Hendrick and his pack on a chase. Make it look like we're doing everything we can to play nice and find the killer. I'm hoping that if we do a good enough job, maybe Hendrick'll relax a little and not put Toni and I in a hole next to Sal."

"Jesus, Harry… what are the chances?"

Harry turned his melancholy eyes to Gene and said fatalistically, "Sixty-forty, maybe. For putting us down."

"What are you going to do?" Gene asked, heart thumping painfully in his chest. The melancholy look in Harry's eyes hardened.

"Nobody's going to hurt Toni. Ever."

Gene wondered if that pimp and his bodyguard had realized that the look on Harry's face meant death. He shivered. No, he thought, or they'd still be alive.

"But there's many a slip twixt cup and lip," Harry said, and his eyes changed back to their normal bland, watchful gaze. "So we'll ride it out and hope we can keep above the water. Until then, it's business as usual. But we've got to do something about the cars, and Farrokh. He's scared and running, I think. And you know Kilburn's going to come knocking. We put him onto Farrokh, and he'll expect us to help him."

"Why oh why on Earth would he think that, Harry?" Gene asked. His voice was broadly sarcastic. "It's not like you make a habit out of sticking your neck cut."

"Yeah, yeah. Stay out of sight. I'll have Keen over running the stuff up, and fetching whatever you might need," Harry said. He tugged his collar high. "It's getting bad out there. I expect it to get worse."

Gene nodded. "A week away from Christmas, it's bound to get cold."

"Yeah," Harry said. "That doesn't help."

He had nodded to the women in the living room and closed the door before Gene realized he hadn't been talking about the weather.

CHAPTER TWENTY

In the office, he called Joaquin 'Keen' Hidalgo, another of their expanding circle of loyal friends. While they waited, Harry asked Toni, "Where's Abruzzi's jacket? And where's Gold?"

"In the apartment and in the bathroom, in that order. Why?"

"Keys," Harry said. She followed him into their apartment. He spotted the leather jacket on a chair and searched it. He found two sets of keys in the pockets. He set them on the table and continued searching the garment, but turned up nothing but an old piece of yellow lined paper, torn from a legal pad. It had a phone number on one side, and a faint '6' on the other, both in pencil. He showed it to her.

"Want me to call it?" she asked.

"Not yet," he said. "Just remember it."

"Harry, please," Toni said with derision. "When have I ever forgotten a phone number?"

"Yeah, yeah," he muttered. "If this is what I think it is, we can't call it."

Toni pursed her lips. "Backup?"

"I doubt it. Not if he was in as deep a bucket of shit as Starr indicated. No, I think it's a go-no-go number."

She raised one eyebrow.

"He would call to confirm the kill," Harry clarified. "Or not. Presumably, if he doesn't call, they know he either failed or died trying. If he does, they verify his kill. But if we call, it's possible we'll spook whoever's manning the number. Or confirm the kill accidentally."

"What if you don't say anything?" she asked.

"It's likely no one will answer anyhow. The call itself

could be the signal. And…" he turned it over. "…yeah. This could be how many times it's supposed to ring. That many rings, no more, no less, is the confirmation code."

She gave him an impressed look. "Pretty slick, Harry."

"Frisked a lot of street guys in my time. There's a million ways to pass along info that don't involve incriminating words," he said. "I wouldn't say it's a hundred percent, but I'd be willing to put twenty bucks on it."

She nodded. "So we keep it. Sit on it."

"Yeah. You want to take a ride?"

"Anytime, cowboy," She said, giving him a smile.

"Good girl. Keen's going to man the shop, and run out for supplies when they need them. I gave Cherry and Trix the rundown. Cherry was hurt I threatened her, but then Trix's reaction clued her in. Cherry's got our backs. They're squared. How about you? You packing, Annie Oakley?"

She lifted the edge of her jacket so he could see the revolver tucked just back of her hip, the way he carried his.

"Good again. I'm gonna sweep the place again, just to make sure if anyone comes sniffing, they won't find anything."

He was cleaning up the dishes when he heard Keen's voice. He finished and went into the office. Keen was about twenty-two, and he'd been shaping up under Harry and Toni's influence. Once an up-and-coming boxer turned neighborhood mugger and thug, he had become one of their most trusted friends and worked for them when they needed a hand. He had accompanied Toni and Bobby Gold on their now-infamous charge against the mountain of a man Terry Shoulders, although he'd sustained a concussion in doing so. His eyes were clear and bright, but he needed a shave.

"Morning, Harry," he greeted. "I figured you'd call before now."

Harry's hurt expression made Toni bark laughter. He said, "You thought I'd get into trouble before now? It's been a week, Keen."

"Yeah," Keen grinned. "You're overdue."

Harry snorted and made himself and Toni cups of coffee with lots of sugar. "Sit down, keep your lip shut, I'll give you a quick and dirty rundown."

Harry refilled the industrial Bunn coffeemaker. Coffee had become essential to the smooth running of the office. Harry was considering taking a picture of it and framing it, with a legend underneath the picture reading 'Employee of the Month", he explained about Sal, Hendrick, and the fugitives upstairs. As he talked, Keen's face became solemn. When he finished, the youth said, "Okay, you get some serious respect for this one, Harry. Most people would have taken a vacation after getting out of the joint. Did you piss off God, or does he just love you?"

Toni said with a grin, "Column A, column B. Come on, Keen. For us, this is a vacation. You know that."

"You guys party harder than any five people I know," Keen said. "Tell me what you need. Anything you want, I can do it."

Harry clapped him on the shoulder. "Thank you. You're not going to like it."

Keen gulped. "Terry Shoulders is the new 'ten'," he said. "On a scale of one to ten, how bad is it?"

Harry looked at the ceiling. "Oh, about an eight."

Keen laughed. "Then I'm good."

Toni held out a hand and Keen gave her a solemn slap with his own and caught her on the rebound. She said, "You're running interference. Literally. Answer the phones, man the office. Anyone comes around, no matter who they are, you stonewall. We're out on a case. No, you have no idea when we'll be back. Take messages, make notes, keep records of the times. We'll get a story straight for when we need it. But right now, no one can know we're working on anything big. Got it?"

"I got it," Keen said.

"They're going to call down here for whatever they need," Harry said, pointing up. "Get what they need, but make sure you're not seen going up and down the stairs. Oh, and Gene Kaminski's up there keeping the guy alive. He demands frequent coffee sacrifices, so keep the machine running at full speed."

Bobby strolled out of the apartment. He held out a fist and Keen bumped it with his own.

"Good to see you upright, Keen," Bobby said.

"You too. You're in this?"

Bobby shrugged amiably. "You know how it is."

Keen nodded emphatically. "It never rains, but it rains, sleets, thunders, lightnings, and earthquakes around here."

"Yeah. It's like they get bored if someone's not trying to kill them."

"I don't know about him," Toni said, jerking a thumb at Harry, "but I do."

"What is this, an improv group? We're on the clock.' Harry grubbed in his pocket, brought out a roll of bills thick enough to choke a healthy horse, and peeled off a bunch of twenties. He handed them to Keen.

"May as well make use of our fee," Harry said. "Bobby, you want to be a gopher? Keep the upstairs stocked. I told them to call down if they need anything."

Bobby sketched a salute.

"Better get on it before anything else happens, I guess," Toni said.

Harry stood and picked up their coffee. He handed one to Toni. "All right. We'll check in from time to time," he told Keen. "For now, look calm, be casual."

"You ought to get a radio or tv out here," Keen said, "you want to look like you're just killing time."

"I'll take it under advisement." Harry opened the door and held it for Toni. "After you, honey."

Toni patted his arm as she walked past. Harry nodded at Keen and Bobby and closed the door behind them. "You know the place they left the first car?" Harry asked as they walked to the Chevelle.

"Yeah, it's a skin-flick joint off Bowery and Canal. Quiet neighborhood, run-down."

"Okay. Let's stop at a market on the way, get a few towels and some cleaner, wipe this thing down quick. We do that, then we head to the first car."

"Why not just get rid of it?" she asked.

"Thought about it," Harry said, "but the guy she stole it from doesn't deserve that. He didn't do anything wrong. We wipe it down and put it back, he should be happy enough. I don't think it could be traced back to us, even if the cops wanted to investigate why someone would steal his car and then bring it back."

"Fair enough, I guess." She pulled the Chevelle's keys and unlocked the door. Harry went to her and gave her a quick kiss. "I'm right behind you," he whispered in her ear.

"Where it's safe," she agreed.

He snorted. "Keep under the limit. I don't want to get pulled over in a bloodstained getaway car."

"You're no fun. Fine."

She watched him walk around the back of the Chevelle, running his hands through the light accumulation of snow on the trunk lid. He ran his hands over the series of hilly dents in the lid. "Man," he said, "Terry almost busted out of this thing."

"I was afraid he'd just jam his feet through the gas tank and stop us, Flintstones-style," she said.

Harry looked up at her. "You need a safer line of work."

"You first, Harry."

"Safest place in a hurricane is the eye," he said.

"Sure," she agreed. "For a while."

"Yeah, well, there is that."

He walked to the Buick and unlocked it.

"Dahli's?" she called over the roof of the Chevelle.

"No. I don't want to answer any questions about…" he pointed vaguely upward.

"Gotcha. Someplace new, then."

"With a side lot. Or a back lot would be better. Fewer eyes."

"Can do."

She got into the Chevelle and he got into the Buick keeping track of where he put his hands. The bloodstain on the front seat had dried, and with the cold it hadn't had a chance to smell. Should be an easy cleanup, he thought.

He started the cold engine, revving it to reluctant life.

"Sure," he muttered. "Because anything about this is easy."

He waited until Toni pulled away before following, the Buick solid on the slippery packed snow. She hooked right at the top of Elizabeth, and then went left on Bowery. He followed at a reasonable distance, sipping his coffee.

CHAPTER TWENTY-ONE

An uneventful stop at a corner store and ten dollars' worth of bleach and towels later, and the stolen car was clean as Harry could get it. He followed Toni to the porno theater, and pulled into the furthest corner of the lot, wiping down the steering wheel and closing the door with a towel as he did.

In the opposite corner of the lot was a car half-covered with new snow, the rear window gone. Toni parked the Chevelle and Harry got out, slid the key into the lock on the trunk, and opened it. He tugged out a cheap suitcase, scanned the trunk, and almost closed it before stopping himself. He put the suitcase in their car and went back to the getaway vehicle. He lifted the trunk liner and searched underneath. Tucked into the crevice between the spare tire and the wall of the trunk was an envelope and a small gun. He picked up the gun by wrapping it in the envelope. He put them in the car on top of the suitcase. After replacing the liner he slammed the lid.

He checked inside the car. The snow had blown in, filling the rear deck of the car, cascading down into the back seat, and dusting the rest of the inside with powder. After glancing at the dried blood on the seat. He opened the glove box, rifling through the papers there. He found nothing. Under the seats, under the mats, nothing. He pulled driver's side visor down and a ticket fell out.

Long-term parking at O'Hare international. He nodded to himself and put it back. After a look in the back seat to make sure he hadn't missed anything, he tugged a small bottle of ammonia and another clean towel out of his pocket. He didn't expect to clean the blood up enough, but he hoped the ammonia would keep a trace from being possible. He slopped the vile-smelling, astringent liquid over the seat, rubbing it in with the towel. He upended the bottle and let it seep through the seat where, he hoped, it would destroy any blood that had run down and pooled under the seat. He wiped down every surface with the cloth and slammed the door.

In the Chevelle, Toni had the heater going full. He shivered as she turned the vents toward him.

"Now what?" she asked.

"We can tip off a tow truck, no problem. But how do we connect to it? Any plausible reason we'd be knocking on this particular door?"

She said, "I've been thinking about that. Maybe traffic?"

"I know a few people in traffic. But why would they call me about it?"

Toni thought about it. "Hey... the bullet hole?" she asked. "So, one of your traffic buddies gets a call about a car with a window shot out. You happen to ask if anything like that's turned up. They let you into impound to search it. And that's how we come to be knocking on this particular door."

Harry thought about it. "Okay. That's not bad. It's pretty good, actually. Hendrick is a lot smarter than he acts."

Toni nodded. "Harry? Do you get the idea that Hendrick's a bigger player than he acts like?"

He thought about it. "You know... he seems to be making a lot of moves a bodyguard wouldn't be, doesn't he? I was thinking that myself, after he said to meet him at the Aces. And giving Mills and his team the runaround. He's too savvy."

"Yeah. I don't like smart bad guys. It's too much work. Let's find a bar or a café or something and make a couple phone calls."

"You got it," Toni said, and she gave the Chevelle some gas. As she pulled into the street she asked, "We gonna be talking about the stuff in the back seat?"

"I'm waiting," Harry said. "I'm trying to decide if we have a right to go through their stuff."

"I think we're past being polite hosts, don't you? We're neck-deep in the water and the gators are snapping at our heels. Snooping through their clothes isn't the worst thing we've done lately."

Harry shrugged. "If it becomes necessary, we will. The gun is curious, but the envelope is worrying me. I think it's full of cash."

"Why's that worrying you?" Toni asked as she pulled into the parking lot of a small deli. She shut off the engine.

"Well, for one thing, why wouldn't it be in the suitcase? Why hide it?"

"Casual search?" Toni asked.

"Maybe, for the gun. But the envelope?"

"Huh. I got nothing." Toni leaned over the seat and stared at the brown envelope and the gun. "What is that?"

"It's a Colt .32. It's not a stopper. It's a paperweight. And it's bugging me."

"Why?"

Harry reached back, picked up the envelope, and wrapped it around the barrel of the gun. He showed it to her. The side with the serial number stamped into the metal was scarred. The number had been obliterated. Not simply scratched off, but etched somehow. "Acid," Harry said. "Someone went at the serial with a hammer and a punch, then rubbed it with acid. It would be nearly impossible to trace that."

"Well... don't killers want to keep from using easily-traceable guns?"

"They do," he said. He opened the glove box of the Chevelle and dropped the Colt inside. "But we've already seen Abruzzi's gun."

He got out and she followed, pocketing the keys. She said nothing as they went inside. Harry went to the cooler by the counter and grabbed out two Cokes. He paid for them with a five so he would get change. "You have a phone?" he asked the bored-looking clerk.

"Back by the deli counter," the man said, flipping a page in a magazine.

"Thanks," Harry said. He handed Toni a Coke and they popped the tops on the side of the cooler as they walked back.

"The gun's not Abruzzi's," Toni said, more to herself than to him. "It was hidden in the car."

He waited while she kicked it around. As he reached for the handset on the payphone, a dime ready, she said, "Oh, crap." She let out a giggle. "Oh, crap, Harry."

He gave her a tiny, tight smile. "What?"

"The gun and envelope… they're not Abruzzi's, are they?"

Harry dialed the office. "I doubt it. But the lightweight Colt, an envelope full of money? Add that to long-term parking, and you got a pretty clear message-" he broke off as someone answered.

"Yeah, I want to report an abandoned vehicle with what appears to be a shot-out back window. Yeah." Harry gave the desk sergeant the address of the porn theater. "Yeah. Yeah. What? My name? Sure, my name is-"

He pressed the disconnect lever and let the handset dangle.

Toni snickered.

After a minute Harry dialed the office. "Keen? Harry. How's that stray we took in? What did the vet say?"

Toni grinned.

"Still sleeping, huh? Well, getting hit by a car will do that. Okay. We'll see you when we see you. Thanks,

Keen."

He hung up.

"Well?"

"No change." He took the envelope they had found out of his pocket. He glanced around, then opened it. Inside was a thin sheaf of bills, a small black-and-white photo, and a glassine baggie of what looked like cocaine. Harry sighed. He pulled the photo out, examined it, but didn't recognize the man in the picture. He showed it to Toni, who shrugged. Harry tucked it away. He ran a thumb over the edge of the bills, fanning them. "Looks like two grand," he said under his breath.

"Jesus. I spent three months scraping by, now money's falling like rain."

Harry tucked the envelope away. "This is not great news. Our houseguests boosted a car meant for an out-of-town hitter. Someone's going to land in Chicago and go looking for this car. All hell could break loose."

"Yeah, but that's Chicago," Toni said, "and this is New York. What are the odds it gets traced?"

"Depends on how bad our luck is that day," Harry groused. He looked over the meat in the deli case. "You hungry?"

"I could eat."

"Pastrami?"

"Sure." She picked up the baggie of powder. "I'm gonna go use the bathroom. I'll drop this in the toilet."

Harry nodded. "I'll get sandwiches and cookies."

"You're a dear, sweet man." She patted his cheek.

"I do my best."

She stretched up and kissed him. He watched her walk to the back of the deli. As she sauntered off, he asked the woman behind the counter, "Can I get two pastrami-ryes, extra pickles, and a couple chocolate chip cookies? Say four of 'em?"

After he collected the sandwiches they sat by the window and ate, staring out at the snow. Around a mouthful of decent pastrami, Toni said, "Think the traffic thing is gonna work?"

Harry swallowed. "Maybe. But we need to be thinking about the next step. Because sure as shit Hendrick's either gonna ask us to trace it, or he'll run it through his own people. So step two's going to be covering that base."

"Can you run a plate without getting anyone suspicious?" Toni asked, biting into one of her cookies.

"I can pass it off as case-related, maybe. A hit-and-run. Something low-key," he said. "but the results will have to be real. That might draw attention. But I don't see what choice we have."

Toni sighed. "Yeah. If Hendrick and his crew run it and get different information than we give them, they might get the idea we're not being straight with them."

"Bingo."

"You want that last cookie, Harry?"

"Hmm? Oh, no. Go ahead."

She did.

Cleaning up, she said, "You're a good man, Harry DeMarko. You know that, right?"

He shrugged. "I do what I have to."

"Yeah, well, you're helping my sister. Right now, I feel like throwing her under the bus. This is a complicated caper, and it doesn't feel like it's going to get easier."

They walked to the door and exited, shivering at the chill in the air.

"I wonder," Harry mused, "if I would have been upset. Sal getting knocked off. If they'd just run for the border and we never knew who they were."

"I don't know," Toni said. "Sal was a decent enough criminal, but he was still a criminal."

"A useful one, sure, but yes, he was the bad guy."

Harry agreed.

They got into the Chevelle. "Where to?"

"Payphone on the way to the Office. Gonna call Hendrick, let him know what we 'found'," Harry said with a grimace.

"Okay," Toni agreed. Two blocks further on she spied a phone and Harry called Hendrick.

"Cops picked up the getaway car," Harry said. "The shot-out window flagged someone and they towed it. Bullet holes, blood, it checked out. My guy in Traffic let me poke around before forensics got to it."

"What do you know about it?" Hendrick asked.

"Well, it's not the shooter's car. It's stolen," Harry said. Hendrick grunted. "Yeah. But from where?"

Harry took a deep breath. "It was in long-term parking at O'Hare in Chicago. Way out of town."

"Chicago?" Hendrick mused. "That's going pretty far to find a clean getaway ride."

"What I thought," Harry said.

"Anything else?"

"Nope, unless they find a print or something, but it'll be days before they get to it. Far's they know it might have been a break-in. Some clumsy thief who wanted to boost it and cut the shit out of their hand or something getting in. It's a non-starter," Harry said.

"All right. Good work. Keep me posted," Hendrick said.

"Later." Harry hung up and went back to the car.

They were silent as Toni guided the Chevelle back to Bowery and rode it south. After a while, she said, "What's on your mind, Harry?"

"I'm worried about Farrokh. Something's off with him. More than just battle fatigue. You know?"

"Yeah," she said. "But it's a lot to put on the kid, having him wear a wire and trying to pull down his suppliers. Kilburn's watching out for him, though. You made sure of that."

"Yeah," Harry said, but something in his voice made her think he wasn't so sure.

"He's a citizen, doing his duty. He's going to be fine, so long as the 68s don't get frisky-"

They looked at one another. Harry's eyes were enough to make her stomach drop.

"Shit," Toni muttered. "You don't think-"

"I don't know for sure, but swing by Dahli's Market, okay? I want to see him, just to make sure he's okay."

Toni nodded, threw on the indicator, and slid into the right lane. A horn blared behind them and she flipped the bird without even looking back.

"Fucking cabbies think they own the road," she said.

"Well, they're the dominant life form on the streets. No wonder they think it's all theirs. Well," Harry amended, "theirs and the busses."

"Those busses," Toni swore. "Think they own the road. Jesus Christ, they do ten miles an hour half the time."

"They're on a schedule, Toni. Can't be too slow or too fast. Like Con Ed. If they get allotted four hours to fix a break, you know it's going to take four hours to the second, whether it's a fifteen minute job or not."

"Sure, sure," she grumped. They were coming up on Dahli's corner store. "I understand how unions work. And bus schedules. But still."

Harry chuckled. "As it ever was, as it ever shall be.' He stopped talking as they passed the market. The store was quiet, there were not people out front, and most importantly, there didn't seem, to be any trouble. The windows were still intact and the lights were on inside Through the myriad papers, bills, advertisements, and posters on the wall, Harry caught a glimpse of Malik Dahli, stiff and straight as ever, eternally behind his immaculate counter. He smiled at his customer, his teeth preternaturally white against his mahogany skin.

"Things look quiet," he said as they passed.

"No sign of angry bikers," Toni agreed. "Which is a good sign. You don't want to piss off a club. Hell hath no fury like a biker scorned."

Harry glanced at her out of the corner of his eye. "You speaking from experience?"

"First-hand," she said. "My daddy's a-"

She stopped midsentence.

He said, "You don't talk about family."

She swallowed, and said, "No."

"Bad?"

She looked at her hands. "Well… are you asking?"

"I'd be lying if I said I wasn't curious, Toni. But no. I'm not asking. If you don't want to talk, I'm not going to pry. You know that."

"You're awful sweet, Harry," she said. Her voice was quiet and thoughtful. "You've never asked me anything."

"Not my place."

"You're with me. And I'm with you. And it's not your place?"

"Toni, you've never asked me. Not a single question. Ever. You've seen me at my worst, you've seen me at my best. And you never ask. And you've backed me at every turn. You're all-or-nothing. Same as me. You get what you give, sweetheart. You know that. Your past is your own. Anything that happened before we got together is yours. I don't have a right to it. It would be… rude… if I were to quiz you." Harry put his hand out and Toni took it. "I don't know what you personally believe, Toni, but I believe that people shouldn't have to carry anything they didn't earn, and they don't owe anything they don't want to give up. If you want to tell me, I'm here. But all I need to know is that you're here and you're mine."

She squeezed his hand. "Thank you, Harry."

"Of course."

She drove slowly through the streets, contemplative and quiet. She passed Bleecker and kept driving aimlessly. He didn't ask why. He glanced at her every once in a while. As they turned back up Bowery, she said, "I hate rules."

He didn't say anything, just listened.

"Never cared for school. Not because I couldn't do it. Just because it was school. I started drinking for the same reason. Staying out all night. My parents... well. Dad is... he's like me. Mom, too. We're not rules-following people. It wouldn't surprise you to know that I got expelled from school. I was fifteen. Instead of going to the jail-with-books they wanted to send me to, I took off. I told mom and dad that I was going to New York. And I did. Hitched a ride, hid in a poultry truck, even gave a trucker a handjob to bring me the last fifty miles."

She glanced at Harry, but he was watching the road move by, face impassive. Not angry, she saw, or curious. Just... existing.

"I landed on my feet. Literally. Got a room at a youth hostel. Waited tables. Looked around to see what I could do that paid better. And one night I saw some of the girls getting dolled up. I asked 'em, and they told me. Times Square. Trolling. I'm not a prude. I wasn't a virgin even then. But I didn't understand it. Wasn't it dangerous? The usual new-girl questions. They said it wasn't dangerous if you're under someone's wing."

She turned the car up Elizabeth Street. They pulled up to the curb in front of the office. The sun had disappeared behind the buildings as the afternoon became early evening. The temperature dropped ten degrees when that happened. Harry shivered.

"They introduced me to their pimp. That was Mr. Jay.

You know the rest of the story," she said. "I was living. Nothing fancy. Jay wasn't so bad, as long as you had cash. I was doing whatever I wanted. I was outside all the rules. I liked it that way. And then I met you."

She smiled at him. "That's how I got here. That's how we met. That's my story. In case you wanted to know."

He took her hand. "I know what I need to," he said. "But thank you. You know I'd never ask."

"I know. I just don't want you to think I have some dark secret lurking in my past."

Harry squeezed her hand. "Even if you did, we'd handle it."

She smiled shyly at him and they got out of the car. The cold was as biting as Harry had feared. In the office, Keen had his feet up on Toni's desk and he was reading a newspaper.

"How'd it go?" he asked them.

Harry outlined what they had done about the car and why.

Keen screwed up his face. "Why would they ask?"

Toni gave him a withering stare. "Keen, you're smarter than that. Sure, maybe they won't ask. But what if they do?"

Keen didn't look convinced. "Okay."

"We're gonna go upstairs. Back in a minute." Harry and Toni checked the street for observers and went up the stairs. In the living room of the apartment, Cherry and Trix were chatting with Bobby Gold and Gene.

"Seriously," Bobby was saying, "even something like scrambled eggs can be a gourmet meal if you balance it right. A pinch of salt at the right time, low heat, some crème fresh-"

"Some what?" Cherry asked. Trix looked skeptical, but Cherry seemed to be taking notes.

"Oh... heavy cream. Fresher the better. Just a little,

maybe a couple tablespoons. You mix the eggs, then add the salt and mix again, then add the cream and mix again. Get it good and fluffy, lots of air. Melt some butter in the pan, pour in the mix, and let it sit for ninety seconds. As it starts to cook, drag your spatula through it, break up the curds that form first. Then let it sit. Then stir again. You want great big curds of egg. Something you can put a fork in. Once it's not liquid anymore, turn off your heat. Get the pan off it. Flip everything a couple times to cook evenly and aye viola," he said with a smile as he butchered the French on purpose. "The best scrambled eggs you'll ever have. Great after a night of hard… uh… drinking. Plus it's a good way to score bonus points, making someone breakfast the morning after."

Trix gave a half-smile. Cherry, on the other hand, was staring at Bobby with wide eyes, twirling her hair absently around one finger.

"Maybe you could teach me," she suggested with a hint of a smile.

Bobby grinned easily. "Come on. I had to pay for the education."

"Let's talk terms for lessons," Cherry said with a glint in her eye.

Gene looked from Cherry to Bobby and back. He raised a hand. "Uh," he said, "I can make a wicked bowl of cold cereal."

Bobby grinned at Gene. Cherry glared at him.

"If Julia Child and Marcus Welby here can tear themselves away," Harry said, "I could use a moment."

"I object," Gene said. "Quincy would be a better analogy."

"And I get stuck with Julia Child?" Bobby asked, pretending offense.

"You'd rather he said LaDiva Davis?" Gene asked.

Bobby pursed his lips. "Oooh. Yeah. That would have

been better."

Harry sighed. "Guys, come on."

Harry led the way to the kitchen, Bobby and Gene in tow. He explained about the car.

"What's the next move?" Bobby asked.

"As soon as he's stable, we gotta think about how to get him out of town," Harry said. "Any progress?"

"Naah. He's still out. Sleeping, I think, but he doesn't come out of it even when I change the bandages."

"Is that normal?"

"Not at all," Gene said. "I'm worried, Harry. Like, deeply worried. He's not in a coma as far as I can tell, but he's not coming out of it, and that's a great big warning sign."

"How long until I have to bite the bullet and take him to a hospital?"

Gene bit his lip. "Technically, yesterday. But I'd say you have another day at most before I risk killing him by not acting, and I don't-"

"No, no," Harry soothed. "That's not going to happen. You're not taking heat for this. It comes to that, you go visit your mother while we try to drop him off without being spotted."

Bobby said, "It's too bad they didn't go right to the hospital."

Harry and Gene looked up at him.

"What I mean is, they could have played it off as a mugging, or something. Maybe not the best excuse, but it might have worked long enough to get them clear. But now? He's got stiches. No matter how convincing a mugging story is-"

"Yeah," muttered Harry. "You're right. But if he'd shown up in any ER in the city, Hendrick would have known. He'll still find out, if we have to drop him. Hendrick has feelers out for anything medical at all, legit or not."

They all stood silently, digesting that.

"Do you think he's got enough feelers out that he could find out I took sick leave?" Gene asked.

Harry thought it over. "Highly unlikely. But still. After this is over, you're out of town, okay?"

Gene nodded, looking troubled.

Trix and Cherry came into the kitchen. They were wearing working outfits; tight skirts, tight blouses, Lycra and garish. They took heavy coats from the hooks by the door.

"You're not working," Harry protested. "It's gotta be 20 degrees outside."

"We have to," Cherry said. "We have a quota. And rent."

Harry grimaced. "I told you we'd-"

"Harry," Cherry chided gently, "we still work for someone. You know that. We have to work."

Harry didn't look like he accepted that, but he nodded once, saying nothing. The women left, Cherry giving Bobby an unreadable backward glance. He raised a hand and waved as she closed the door.

"Has Farrokh said anything?" Harry asked.

"He's still asleep, as far as I know," Bobby said "Something shook him to his core."

"Time's running out," Harry said. "I need to get him to talk. Listen, I'm gonna run down and get some coffee Bobby, see if Farrokh is awake. Gene, check on Johnny and Starr again for me."

"Can do," Bobby said.

Gene nodded. "No problem."

Harry tromped down the stairs and rounded the corner. He was opening the office door when a car turned down Elizabeth and approached. He recognized the type, a wide-bodied Dodge Diplomat in beige. Standard-issue unmarked cruiser.

Without surprise, Harry realized the driver was Rick Kilburn, a narcotics detective, and the one running Farrokh's undercover operation. After the local biker gang had pressured the young immigrant into selling heroin from the back of his father's store, Harry and Toni had put him on to Kilburn, who, in exchange for a green card and clean record, was using Farrokh as a mole. Harry raised a hand in greeting.

"Never rains but it pours," he said to himself. "Kilburn."

"Harry," Kilburn greeted.

"Come on in. Get some coffee. It's cold as hell out here."

Kilburn trotted to the door and Harry followed him in. Harry busied himself pouring while Kilburn shook off the biting cold.

"What brings you by?" Harry asked.

"Have you seen Farrokh?"

Harry handed Kilburn a mug. "Not for about a week. Why? Something happen?"

"Yeah. You could say that." Kilburn sipped the coffee and grimaced. "He's missing."

Harry snapped his head up. "Missing? What do you mean 'missing'?"

Kilburn raised a hand. "Easy. He's okay, I think. We just can't find him. He didn't show up at the... well. He was supposed to go to a meet two nights ago. He never showed up."

"Meet?"

Kilburn nodded his shaggy head. "He was supposed to meet with the 68s. There was a general meeting, the 68s, the Reapers, the Devils, and the Guns. They were holding a summit, like. Farrokh was supposed to go there early and pick up his week's supply. We... we sent him in with a key."

Harry's skin crawled. "You what?"

Kilburn had the grace to look contrite. "We thought we could get him to convince the 68s that he'd been approached by a dealer. A good-faith gesture, like. A gift."

"To lure them to a meet."

"Yeah." Kilburn sipped his coffee. "But he never went. We had eyes on the meet, all sides. We had eyes on Farrokh an hour before the meet. Then nothing. He got on a subway train and we lost him. He never showed up at the meeting, he hasn't been back to his uncle's store."

The street lights clicked on outside the office. Harry stared out into the growing darkness. "You're positive he's okay?"

"As I can be."

Harry turned his melancholy eyes to Kilburn. "I gave his uncle my word. I gave the kid my word."

"I know, Harry. I know. I'm doing everything I can. I know it's no consolation, but if anything happens to him, I'll come down on the 68s or whoever like the hammer of God." Kilburn set his coffee cup down gently. Harry saw his hand was shaking, and realized Kilburn was furious. At himself, he thought, and tried to ignore the twinge of guilt.

The door of their apartment opened and Toni stepped out. She smiled when she saw Kilburn, but it faded. She looked from Harry to Kilburn and back. Her left eye, shielded from Kilburn, winked at Harry. He gave her a perceptible nod.

She was listening, he thought. She's amazing.

"What's wrong?" she demanded. "What happened to Farrokh?"

Kilburn looked even more miserable. He explained.

Toni balled up her fists and put them on her hips. "Kilburn, if anything happens to that kid-"

"I know, I know," the detective intoned. "Believe me,

I'll help."

"Just do me a favor," Kilburn said. "If he shows up, let me know. And give him whatever he needs. But let me know."

"We will," Harry assured him. "Just find him."

Kilburn nodded. "I'm already on it. I'm hitting every place I knew for a fact he's been-"

Harry snapped, "You didn't tell Mr. Dahli, did you?"

Kilburn glared mildly at him. "Of course not."

"Good. He's most likely going to turn up safe and sound," Harry said. "He got scared and he hid somewhere, is my guess."

"I'm sure you're right. Okay. I'll talk to you."

Kilburn left the office and climbed into his car. Toni waited until he'd driven out of sight.

"Jesus, Harry."

"Yeah. Where's Keen?"

"Sent him home for the night. I didn't figure we'd need him much tonight."

"Good call. I need to think."

"What do we do?" she asked.

Harry busied himself fixing them some coffees. "We're going to go up and talk to Farrokh. We're going to try and talk to Abruzzi. We need information."

"What about Hendrick?"

Harry sighed. "We're gonna have to come up with something. The car buys us time, but he's not going to believe we aren't making any headway."

"Yeah."

Harry handed her a mug. She sipped. Meditatively she asked, "Why can't we just stabilize him and get him out of town, Harry?"

He didn't answer at first, merely stared out the front of their office at the darkness. Then he said, "We don't know what happened. We don't know the story, not completely.

We've made some educated guesses. But a couple things are staring us in the face right now. First, Abruzzi's still unconscious. It's too dangerous to move him. Second, there was someone else on the scene while Higgins was chasing Abruzzi. That means that, if Abruzzi did Sal, there might be a witness. In which case it's just a matter of time before the cops or the Mob go after Abruzzi, for the crime, or for retaliation. But... Abruzzi's in town why?"

"To kill Sal," Toni said.

"Yeah. It's his one shot to square himself with the Outfit," Harry said. "He's gotta kill Sal and get back to Chicago. But if there's a witness that can put him at the house-"

"Then it's just a matter of time before the cops land on Abruzzi for it, Chicago or no," Toni said.

"Alternative scenario?"

Toni thought it out. Her face fell. "Oh, shit. If he didn't take Sal out, he's just as screwed. It was his job. Which means he's done. His own people will whack him out if he shows up in Chicago without having done what they told him."

Harry nodded. "If the job was Abruzzi's and someone else got there first, Abruzzi's dead. If he tries to claim the kill and someone else already has, he looks even worse than if he just got there too late," Harry said. "So the one way Abruzzi gets home alive is if he makes it back alive and he was the one who did it."

"So Abruzzi's gotta find the witness, or find the killer," Toni breathed.

"Yeah. Which makes our position even worse than I thought," Harry said, sipping his coffee.

She raised an eyebrow. "How so?"

"We're looking for Sal's killer. If we don't come through, Hendrick falls on us. If we do and it's Abruzzi, we can't turn him in. If we do and it's not Abruzzi,

Chicago will find out. Abruzzi's dead either way."

Toni shivered.

"Honey," he said, and voice made her heart thump with fear. "I know she's your sister. I know he's her husband. But we might... we might not have much of a choice here. You know?"

"She's family," Toni said.

"Yeah."

Toni hugged herself, staring into the darkness. "If it comes to that... we need to get Starr out of town."

"If it comes to that, we need to get them both out of town," Harry said. "I won't let Hendrick kill him. Double that if Abruzzi is innocent."

"He came to town to kill Sal," Toni said.

"Yes. And the intent is there. But if he never got the chance, then I owe Hendrick nothing. If Johnny's not the guy, he can deal with Chicago on his own. That's not our problem."

"What if whatever they do to him they do to her?"

Harry's heart chilled. "I won't let that happen either, Toni."

"Okay. Okay. If you say it, it's so. But Harry... what happens when Hendrick comes for us?"

Harry turned to look at her. He put his hands on her shoulders and looked into her eyes. He smiled, and his eyes because cold, remote, and icy. "You know what will happen to Hendrick. And anyone else that tries to hurt you."

Toni shivered.

The door opened and Gene and Bobby came stomping in. They closed the door behind. Outside, a thick snowfall had begun, the air chocked with fat flakes of snow.

"Problems?" Harry asked.

"Grave," Bobby said. "We're out of coffee."

Harry sighed. "I'm going up to talk to Farrokh. How's

Abruzzi?"

"Still out," Gene said. He bit his lip. "Harry, any longer and we need to get him to a hospital. He's been unconscious way too long and I have no idea why. I don't mind helping, but I can't let him die willingly. I have an obligation."

"Yeah. Okay. Can you give it the night?" Harry asked.

"Yes, I think. As long as he doesn't spike a fever."

"Okay. I'll go up. Bobby, you cook. Toni, Gene, eat. Get some rest. Things will pick up in the morning and I could use you all at your best," Harry said. He topped up his mug and left the office. Snow swirled in as he opened and closed the door. Toni watched him go.

"What you got in there as far as food?" Bobby asked.

Toni shrugged. "No idea. It's been a couple days since I went to the market."

"I'm sure I can whip something up. Gene, come on. I'll show you how to cook." Bobby went into the apartment. "You can give up the unglamorous life of a respected medical professional. You're a sous chef now."

"Bitchin'," Gene said with a smile. "What's that?"

"You do all the shit I don't want to do," Bobby said. Toni went into the bathroom and Bobby rummaged in the walk-in cooler. He came up with a couple slabs of steak, some potatoes, and some broccoli. He looked in the fridge and found a block of cheese and some milk.

"Okay, kids, on today's show we're gonna learn how to make steak and broccoli, with mashed potatoes and a cheddar cream sauce."

"Doesn't sound too hard," Gene said.

Bobby looked down his nose at Gene. "You'd think so. You're on potatoes. Gimme a big boiling pot of water. Toni, shred the cheese and get some big bowls. Toni?"

He looked around, realized where she had gone.

"She's on taste-testing duty," Bobby remarked to

himself. "And bartending."

He began to assemble his kitchen, directing Gene as he went.

CHAPTER TWENTY-TWO

Harry peeked in on Starr and Johnny Abruzzi. He was still unconscious, and she was slumped in a chair beside the bed, one hand on his arm. He closed the bedroom door gently and crossed the small apartment. In Trix's room, Farrokh was curled into a fetal ball on top of the covers, both fists gripping the coverlet. Harry pulled the single chair over to the bed and gently shook Farrokh awake. The young man startled awake and sat upright with a jerk.

"What? Who-"

"Easy," Harry soothed. "It's just me. Relax."

Farrokh stared at Harry with wide, unseeing eyes, until the recognition came to him. "Mr. Harry?"

"Yeah. We need to talk. Take a minute, wake up, and get your bearings. You need the bathroom? Or water?"

Farrokh hesitated, then said, "Yes, please. Both."

Harry went to fetch some water while Farrokh used the small bathroom between the bedrooms. When he came back, Farrokh was sitting on the edge of the bed staring morosely at the floor.

Harry handed Farrokh the pilsner glass of water. The young man drained it completely, gasping for breath.

"Better?" Harry asked.

Farrokh nodded. He handed the glass back to Harry, and his hands were shaking.

"Kilburn was downstairs," Harry began.

Farrokh reared off the bed, eyes wide and hunted. "No, no-"

"Farrokh!" Harry barked. The young man froze. "I didn't tell him you were here."

Relief flooded Farrokh's face. "Thank you, Mr. Harry."

"Of course. But sit. Calm yourself. Let's talk."

"I-I cannot, Mr. Harry. I'm-"

"I'm going to stop you right there, Farrokh," Harry said gently. "You asked for a place to hide, I gave it to you. You asked me not to tell anyone you were here, I agreed. I've gone out on a limb for you. I lied to Kilburn. If he feels like it, he could jam me up. Me and Toni both. So need you to be straight with me. That's how you pay us back."

Farrokh stared at the floor. Harry saw tears drip from his eyes to splash on the carpet.

"Kilburn told me what you did," Harry said.

The look of shock on Farrokh's face took Harry aback. The agony he saw in the young man's eyes perplexed him.

"I-I did not want to," he said in a low, desolate voice. "I did not. But... they told me it was necessary. So... so I did."

Harry nodded. "Sometimes you have to do things you don't want to. I understand. I've been there. So has Toni. Everyone. That's no reason to run away."

"You do not understand, Mr. Harry. I did... I did as they asked. That is why I ran."

Harry frowned. "If you did as they asked, why run? Is it the 68s? Are they on to you? Is that why they're after you? I had a couple wanna-be biker trash show up last night looking for you."

Farrokh nodded. Harry noticed a wisp of jet hair peeking from under the ubiquitous turban the young man wore. "They want me to go to them once I'm done. I-I-I Just c-can't! I'm- I'm sorry!"

The boy burst into tears, covering his face with both hands. Harry frowned and put a hand on his shoulder. "It's okay. It's going to be okay."

Farrokh shied away. "No! It cannot be!"

"Stay here, Farrokh," Harry said. "I'm going to go get Gene, my friend. He's a doctor. Maybe he can help you calm down."

Harry got up and went to the door. The young man sobbed and slumped onto the bed, shaking with the force of his cries. Harry left the bedroom, turned, and found himself face to face with Starr.

"Harry?"

"Farrokh- the other friend I'm helping- he's in a bad way, poor kid. Would you sit with him while I run down to get Gene?"

"Sure, sure," she said. "No problem."

"See if you can get him talking. He got jammed up somehow, but he won't tell me anything. Is Johnny-"

"He's still asleep," she said, eyes flickering from Harry to the sound of Farrokh sobbing.

"Okay. Gene says if he doesn't wake up tonight he's going to the hospital. I know it's not ideal, but Gene thinks if he doesn't come to, there's a chance he might die."

Starr swallowed. "Okay. Go get him. I'll be here."

Harry nodded, let himself out of the apartment, and walked down the stairs. On the street the snowfall had worsened. The air was choked with thick flakes of snow and if it wasn't blizzard status yet, he didn't think it'd be long. He went into the warmth of the office, locking the door behind him. He let himself into the apartment and was confronted with the mouth-watering smells of steak and potatoes. They had just sat down at the table. A plate beside Toni awaited him.

"How's it going?" she asked.

"Farrokh is pretty upset. I was gonna ask Gene if he could sedate him or something." He went into the bathroom, availed himself of the facilities and emerged, drying his hands on a towel.

"I don't have much for that," Gene said. "But I'll see what I can do."

"Maybe he needs a few minutes, he's a mess. Give him

some quiet time," Harry said. "Me, too. I'm starved."

"If there's any left," Gene said around a mouthful of steak. "This is the best steak I've ever had."

Toni nodded. "He's right. Bobby, what kind of witchcraft did you use to make this?"

Harry sat down and Toni served him a portion of steak with a thick gold-brown crust that glistened, bright broccoli and beautiful yellow cream sauce, and the fluffiest mashed potatoes he'd ever seen, topped with a generous knob of butter. His mouth watered.

"This is how I used to make it on Friday nights," Bobby said. "While every restaurant in the city was trying to outdo one another with more and more elaborate dishes, I had four dishes a night done perfectly. Steak, chicken, fish, and lamb. Perfectly-cooked vegetables, perfectly-cooked meat. If you do something right, simple is better than complex. Most people pretend to have a vastly more refined palate than they do. Especially if you're rich. They're all pretending the food's mind-blowingly good when in reality it's average at best. Most of the chuckleheads in this city go places that are fancy and elite for the sake of being there, not the food."

Harry took a bite of the steak and his eyebrows climbed. "Dear God," he said. "This is…"

Toni chewed and swallowed. "Yeah."

"It's okay," Bobby said with a blush. "You should see what I can do with a proper mise."

Toni cocked her head. "A what?"

"Mise en place. Basically a cooking setup in a kitchen. All your ingredients prepared first, but bowls, spices, towels… everything you need so all you have to do is cook. You ever been to a concert or a club? Ever watch the drummer?"

"Yeah," Toni said.

"They don't have to look where they're drumming.

They just know, because it's all in the same place every time. That's when your music takes off. That's when cooking takes off."

They ate quietly, just enjoying the food and the quiet.

"How long were you a chef?" Gene asked.

"Oh, ten years or so as head chef. Ten years as a grunt. I worked shitty diners and greasy spoons for a while, summer jobs and spare cash in high school and college, until I decided it was the life I wanted. Went to the Culinary Institute, graduated, and that was that. I was in it up to my neck. I loved it."

A shadow flickered over Bobby's seamed face, and for a moment he seemed to age a decade. Then he smiled, a sunny, happy, and Toni was sure, fake smile, and the moment passed. They finished eating and Gene raised his glass. "To the chef. That was a meal I'll dream about for years to come."

"To the chef," Harry, Toni, and Keen echoed.

"Thanks."

Keen yawned, stretching and sighing as he finished. His eyes were half-open and he looked drugged.

Harry said, "Keen, there's nothing else to do tonight. You can get home if you want, before it gets too cold. We've got it covered for now. Come back around 8 or so, yeah?"

Keen nodded gratefully. "Will do. Good night, guys." He grabbed his coat and left. Toni started collecting dishes while Harry and Gene stood up.

"Bobby, can you babysit for me? Make sure they have everything they need, keep an eye on 'em?" Harry asked.

"Sure thing. I'll make a plate to take upstairs," Bobby said.

"Appreciate it," Harry told him. "Gene, are you sure you can't give the kid something? He's in a bad way."

"Sorry. I don't carry tranquilizers. No reason to have

any; most of my patients are dead. They don't need 'em. Have you tried alcohol?"

"I don't think he drinks. He and his Uncle are both... Hindu? Or... no. He told me once. Sheik? That's not right," Harry frowned.

"You mean Sikh?" Gene asked.

"Yeah, maybe."

"That makes sense, about the alcohol then," Gene said. "Maybe we can get him to count sheep."

"A meal will do it, too. Nothing better than a food coma to soothe your nerves," Bobby said. "I'll be upstairs."

He left, carrying several plates of food stacked along his arm. He looked perfectly at ease with a white dish towel over his shoulder and armload full of food in his steady grasp.

They finished cleaning up and sat again around the table. Toni produced a pack of cards and they played three-corner solitaire, some rummy, and a few hands of poker, letting the evening lull them into a sense of relaxation. After an hour or more of cards and coffee, Toni went into the walk-in and emerged with a bottle of whiskey.

"Harry?"

He eyed the bottle. "Maybe... no. Just in case."

He didn't finish the sentence, but Toni nodded. She put the bottle back and came out with three bottles of Pepsi. She stopped to pop the caps before sitting back down at the table.

"To a quiet night," Toni said, holding up her bottle.

"A quiet night," Harry and Gene echoed, touching their bottles to hers with a muted clink. They drank, and continued to play.

The clock showed almost 9 P.M. when Toni started yawning. Harry scratched his cheek and said, "My brain feels slow. Maybe a good night's sleep will jog something loose."

Gene said, "I want to check up on him before I go home. If he's not awake by morning, he's going to the hospital."

"Fair enough," Harry said. "Come on. I'll walk up with you. Make sure Bobby's got everything he needs."

They left the apartment, Gene carrying coffee mugs he had filled for Bobby, Starr, and Farrokh. They walked up the stairs. At the top, Harry came to an abrupt stop. Gene ran into him from behind. Hot coffee slopped on Gene's hands.

"Ouch! Damn it, Harry, what-"

"Quiet," Harry ordered. He drew his sidearm. "Gene, go back downstairs and get Toni."

Gene hurried back down the stairs and Harry heard the door of the office slam.

He nudged the half-open door out of the way, his pistol up and ready. The kitchen was empty and quiet. Moving carefully, he squared the corner, bringing his weapon up to scan the kitchen over the barrel. Nothing. He waited, weapon drawn, eyes cataloguing the room. A carton of eggs sat on the counter next to a mixing bowl. There were broken shells on a dish towel. A cast-iron frying pan sat on the four-burner stove near them. The stove was off. A moment later he heard Toni come up the stairs behind him. She had her own pistol up.

"Harry?" she whispered.

"It was open when we came up," he said. "Cover me."

"Got you."

He moved deeper into the kitchen, swung wide around the edge of the doorframe, and into the smallish living room. The chair closest to the room Farrokh had been in was overturned and the door of the bedroom was open. He jerked his head to his left, toward Johnny Abruzzi's room. Toni nodded and swung her weapon to cover that door, which was closed.

Harry approached the bedroom slowly, carefully. He put a foot around the edge of the door and swung it wide, stepping into the bedroom. The room was empty, the bed disheveled.

The closet was open, and he could see no one in it. He crouched and peered under the bed. Nothing.

Backing into the living room he turned and crossed to the hallway which led to the common bathroom and the second bedroom. A cursory glance into the bathroom gave him nothing. The shower curtain was half-closed, and the room was too small to hide anyone. He approached the bedroom door. Toni skirted across the hall, her gun momentarily rising to the ceiling as she passed behind him. She positioned herself and nodded. He stood aside from the door, put a hand on the knob, and turned it very slowly. He glanced at Toni and she nodded. He pulled the door open and stepped back. She swept what she could see of the room, shook her head curtly, and he stepped into the larger bedroom. The room was empty. He crouched, checked under the bed. Behind him, Toni nudged open the closet.

"Clear," Harry said.

"Clear," she agreed.

They holstered their weapons and stared at the room. The bed still showed bloodstains from where Abruzzi had lain.

"What the hell, Harry?"

"Got me," he said. He scanned the room. Nothing immediately registered as important. He walked back to the living room.

Toni followed him.

"Harry, where are they?"

"I don't know."

"We'd have heard a commotion," Toni said. "Or if they

were running, footsteps."

"Yeah," Harry said. He frowned in thought. He went back into the bedroom Farrokh had occupied. She trailed after him. The bed was rumpled, the water glass had been knocked from the nightstand, and had rolled partially under the bed.

Harry turned and stalked past Toni, back to the kitchen. He looked around in disgust, seething.

"Harry?" Toni's voice was urgent. He hurried back to the bedroom. He found her on her hands and knees peering into the blackness under the bed. She had the water glass in one hand.

"What did you find?"

Toni fished a crumpled knapsack from under the bed. She sat up on her haunches. "This is his, isn't it?"

"Yeah," Harry said.

She opened it and peered inside. She gave a tiny cry and reared back. She held it up. The inside of the bag was smeared with dried blood.

"Was he hurt?" Toni asked.

"No, I don't think so," Harry said, frowning down at the bag. "If he were, he wouldn't have bled inside the bag and not the outside."

Toni reached up and he helped her to her feet.

"Where's Bobby?" Toni asked. "We would have heard a struggle or something."

"I know."

This is getting weirder and weirder, Harry."

"You ain't kidding."

"Did they run, were they taken?" Toni asked. "How did we not hear anything?"

"I don't know," Harry said. The voice he used caused her to look up in alarm. He sounded… defeated. He looked forlorn. "Come on. Let's go call Kilburn."

Toni's eyes widened. "Harry-"

"This is too far," Harry said. "We need to tell Kilburn."

Toni sighed. "I guess you're right. He's gonna be pissed."

"He can join the club." Harry went into the kitchen. Toni handed him Farrokh's bag and said, "Hold on. I have to use the bathroom."

He waited as she went.

"Harry!"

He raced down the hall. She rarely sounded as panicked as she had when she called his name. He skidded to a stop in the doorway of the bathroom, gun drawn. Toni was crouched by the tub. She had pushed the shower curtain open to reveal the face of Bobby Gold, his skin a pallid grey, with rivulets of sweat running down his face.

Harry was on his knees beside her. "What the hell-"

A blood-streaked brick of heroin lay between his folded-up legs, one corner frayed and a few grains of yellow powder spilling from it. A disposable needle lay near his feet.

"Harry, he's still breathing," Toni gasped. "Gold, you stupid son of a bitch!"

She slapped him; his head rocked but he made no sound. Harry pushed the sleeve of his tee shirt up on his right arm. Nothing. The left, however, showed a dime-sized red hematoma on his arm above his bicep. Toni slapped him again. "Gold!"

"Toni, that's not helping," Harry snapped at her. "He OD'd. We need to call an ambulance."

"Gene-"

"He's out of this. I'm going to send him home." Harry looked around. He found a trash bag in a damp cardboard box in the cabinet under the sink. He put it over his hand like a glove and picked up the brick. He wrapped it up, stuffed it in Farrokh's bag, and said, "Stay with him. I'm going to clean up the bedroom quick, and then I'll call it in. You've got maybe ten minutes, okay? It won't be long."

Toni nodded, her hard, dry eyes glaring at the lanky, crumpled man in the tub. "Yeah. Yeah, okay."

"Be right back," he promised.

"You don't want the needle, too?"

He said, "They'll expect one. They'd ask questions if it wasn't here."

"Oh."

He hurried into the kitchen and looked in the trash. It was almost empty. He dropped the backpack, tugged the sack out of the bin, and went into Abruzzi's room. He stripped the bed and put the bloody bedsheets in the bag. In the closet he found a fresh sheet. He couldn't do anything about the blood on the mattress, but he could hide it. He worked fast, spreading the sheet over the bed. He put the blanket back on the bed. Luckily it was a dark burgundy. If it had stains on it, no one would notice. He made the bed neatly, tucked the pillow under the blanket, and squared the corners. He examined the freshly-made bed, then lay down on it. He rolled over twice, then got up and pulled the blanket back a quarter. Now it looked lived-in. He hurried through the apartment and down the stairs. He ran through the office and into his and Toni's apartment.

Gene looked up from the table. "Harry, what-"

"I need you to do me a huge favor, Gene."

"Sure," Gene said. "What?"

Harry held up the trash bag. "Take this and go for a walk. And be quick about it. Get a cab somewhere that isn't here. Be at least three or four blocks away when you do it. Okay? This is the bedclothes from the bed. They're bloody." Harry handed the garbage bag to Gene.

Gene had his coat on when Harry emerged. "Harry, what-"

"Don't forget your kit," Harry said.

Gene looked around. "It's upstairs by the bed."

"Stay here." Harry jogged back up the stairs and emerged a few moments later with Gene's medical bag.

"Harry, what's going on?"

"Farrokh's been planting heroin for Kilburn. He got scared and ran. He left a brick upstairs. Bobby overdosed on it," Harry said. "Please. This is time-critical, Gene."

"No shit, Harry!" He turned to go. Harry grabbed his arm.

"Gene, get out. You're done. I'm not dragging you any further down this rabbit-hole."

"Harry, if he's-"

"If he dies, he dies. Gene, they're gone. Farrokh, Starr, Abruzzi? They're gone. You're out. Please. I don't have time to argue," Harry said. Gene could see the frenzied energy in his eyes.

"Okay. Did you call EMS?"

"I will when I get upstairs. I didn't want the call coming from our place."

"Oh."

Harry walked Gene to the door. They stood in the cold, and Gene said, "Call me when you can."

Harry clapped him on the shoulder. "Absolutely. Thanks, Gene. For everything."

"No sweat. Stay safe, Harry. I hope Bobby's okay."

Harry's melancholy eyes sent a shiver down Gene's spine that had zero to do with the cold. "He fucked up. He lives, he lives. He dies, he dies. I'm done with him."

He turned to go and Gene grabbed his arm. "Harry, wait."

"What?"

"Just wait. What you said to me, keep it between us. Toni likes Bobby. He had her back. I like him, too. He seems solid. A good guy."

"He's a junkie. I can't count on a junkie, Gene."

"He got clean."

"Apparently not, if he's nodding out up there when he's supposed to be watching out for a kid I gave my word to." The disgust on Harry's face was ugly; Gene had never seen Harry look ugly.

"I get it, Harry. I do. But… a favor, for me? Just get all the facts first, Detective," Gene said in a flat voice. "You don't know everything."

Harry started to snap at him, held his tongue instead, and visibly his demeanor changed. His shoulders relaxed, the disgust vanished. "Okay. Okay. You're right. Let the evidence show you the truth, don't look for the truth you want."

Gene nodded. "First rule of detective work. Go. Fast."

Harry smiled at him and sped up the stairs. Gene hustled down the street, puffing and blowing hard after half a block. He was two blocks west before he stopped at a payphone and called for a Yellow Cab.

CHAPTER TWENTY-THREE

The ambulance made decent time, considering. But then, NYC EMS drivers had skills few mere mortal drivers could aspire to. Within ten minutes there were two paramedics crammed into the tiny bathroom, hefting Bobby out of the tub and onto a backboard. They got him down the stairs and into the ambulance while Harry and Toni watched from the street. They were in the car as the ambulance took off, and Toni tailed it all the way to the ER, committing every traffic offense for which NYC had laws. Harry, frankly, was surprised they didn't get pulled over. They were in the ER for most of an hour before a doctor came to talk to them. He had tired-looking eyes, frizzy brown hair, and betadine on a scratch on the back of one hand. He shook with them both.

"I'm Doctor Machenbaum. You're the family?"

"Friends," Toni said. "We found him."

"You listed yourself as next of kin," Machenbaum said.

"Had to," Toni told him. "He doesn't have any."

Her voice gave Harry pause. She sounded bitter. Angry. He glanced at her, but her attention was on the doctor.

"Very well. Your friend is going to be all right. He got lucky. Is he an addict?"

"Former," she said. "He's been clean for a couple years."

"It was a pretty light dose, all things considered. The medics gave him Naxalone in the bus; it may have saved his life. His breathing was worrisome for a bit. He's much better now," the doctor said.

"Is he being charged?" Harry asked.

"No. The evidence is gone, and besides, it was a

personal dose, not a large quantity."

Toni asked, "Can we see him?"

"They're moving him out of ICU into a temporary bed. It'll be a few minutes," Machenbaum told her.

Harry asked, "Is he being admitted?"

"When he feels strong enough, we'll give him the literature and send him on his way," Machenbaum told them.

"Literature?" Toni looked puzzled.

"Pamphlets about addiction, lists of meetings and services," Machenbaum explained.

A nurse came out to them and said, "The patient is in 203, Doctor."

"Thank you," Machenbaum acknowledged. Toni and Harry stood up. Harry shook with him, and then Toni did.

"Thank you, Doctor," Toni said. "Thank you very much."

The doctor nodded at them and he and the nurse left. Harry looked for the stairs. Toni stopped him.

"Harry… I can go alone, if you want."

He examined her face. She looked tired, careworn, worried, and frazzled. He put a hand on her cheek. "If you want. If you don't, I'm here."

"I always want," she said. She put her hand on his and closed her eyes, pressing his hand to her face. "But you seem pretty pissed at him. I get it; he was supposed to be watching out, instead he fell off the wagon, but Harry.. he's hurting."

Harry shrugged one shoulder. "So what? He put it above them. He wanted it more than he wanted to do the right thing."

She gazed up at Harry, the line between her eyes deepening. She said carefully, "You're angry because he let you down."

Harry said nothing.

"That's unfair, Harry, but you can't know why. I'll tell you. It's his story, but I'll tell you."

She sat. He took the chair next to her.

"Bobby was married. But she had a problem with the junk. She asked him to get clean, then told him. Then he OD'd on her. She saved his life, sent him to rehab, and he did it again. Three times. The third time, she left him."

Harry said nothing, but she saw approval in his eyes. It made her a little angry at him.

"When he came out the third time, she had left him. Divorced him. Moved away. Didn't even tell him. Because of the drugs. She remarried. And that's how he ended up where he is."

Harry didn't seem moved by this. "He shouldn't be surprised. Three strikes. He had plenty of warning."

"Yeah, and I don't disagree. But Harry... she left him. He didn't leave her. He didn't divorce her. And he's still in love. He never stopped loving her."

"He shouldn't have fucked it up," Harry said.

She lost her patience. "Harry, quit being obtuse. You're not stupid. Put yourself in his place. How would you feel if you lost me? If I didn't love you, but you still loved me? After Jay and Marvin, for instance. I knew who you were and what you would do. You're never going to stop being a cop, with or without a badge. That's who you are. What if I couldn't handle you being you? So I leave. After years of being apart, you still loved me. Imagine that. Imagine living with that, knowing you screwed it up."

Harry conceded, "It would be hell. I get it. But-"

"Harry, she died. Like, a couple days ago."

His eyes flickered. He didn't look away, but she could see he felt that. That he felt Bobby's pain.

"Okay. That's pretty bad. But is it an excuse?"

As he watched, her eyes glistened with tears. "Harry... she didn't just die. She overdosed. She left him because he wouldn't kick drugs, and she overdosed."

He felt like his breath had been knocked from his body. His stomach felt like a hole with a bottom that fell, kept falling. He felt sick. Harry DeMarko wasn't a deep man, but he knew one thing about himself: he owned up to his mistakes.

"Let's go," he said. He stood up. "A friend needs us."

Toni smiled gratefully up at him. He held out a hand and she took it. They walked to the stairs and found room 203. It was a four-bed room. Two were occupied. The window bed on the left held a sleeping octogenarian with a bandage over one eye. The other held the lean and careworn body of Bobby Gold. His curly hair was matted on one side. His skin, while no longer the grey it had been, was pallid and waxy. Toni went to his bedside. His eyes were closed. Harry went to the other side of the bed, opposite Toni. He looked down at Bobby Gold, fighting his disgust. He took in the man's pained face, his clenched teeth and the set of his jaw, his bony chest. Bobby's collar bones stood out in stark relief. If not for the gown, Harry thought, I'd see his ribs. He was very thin. Even his arms-

His arm.

Harry's demeanor changed. He exhaled, holding himself rigid and still as his eyes reassessed the body in front of him. Toni was about to touch Bobby's arm when she heard the knuckles of Harry's hands crackle and pop as they became fists.

She looked up. His face was calm-looking, almost placid, but she knew him, knew his face, and it sent a shiver down her back as she realized that the last time she'd seen this Harry, he'd killed two people.

She held her breath and watched his eyes. They were that distant, melancholy caste they took on when he was readying himself for action. When he'd already decided on a course and was simply slipping into the mode of mind he needed for it. She heard him swallow twice, the click of his throat loud in the quiet room.

He closed his eyes and she could almost hear him counting in his head. He opened his eyes and exhaled again, and his face didn't change so much as shifted from abstract to concrete. His eyes snapped sideways and he saw her looking at him. She raised both eyebrows.

Without speaking, his right hand rose and he pointed at Bobby's arm. From under the cuff of the hospital gown his bicep protruded. Toni looked at the hideous purple bruise on the side of Bobby's arm. She looked up at Harry. She shook her head slightly.

Harry said quietly, "That's the injection site."

Toni looked again. "Yeah."

"That's not a track mark," Harry explained. "That's what happens when you blow a vein or inject something under the skin too fast."

"He was skin-popping?"

"No. If he had, it wouldn't be this big."

Toni frowned at the bruising on Bobby's arm. "Then what?"

"This is what happens when someone who doesn't know what they're doing shoots someone else up," Harry growled. His control wavered. Toni looked up to see that Harry was very close to fury. "Or if they're in a hurry."

Bobby cleared his throat with a rasp. He opened one eye, looked at Toni, and he smiled a little. "Hey," he whispered in a rusted, clotted voice.

"Hey," Toni said, and put her hand on his arm.

He opened his other eyes and blinked several times. He winced and squinted. "Jesus. Headache."

"Bad?" Toni asked.

"I've had worse hangovers," Bobby said. "Can't remember when just now."

Harry said, voice strained by his rage, "What do you

remember?"

Bobby closed his eyes and said hoarsely, "'I remember a mass of things, but nothing distinctly; a quarrel, but nothing wherefore.'" He smiled for no reason they could see.

Harry cocked his head. Toni smacked Bobby's arm with an irritated snort. "Ain't the time, Bobby."

"There's always time for Shakespeare."

Harry made an impatient sound. "Are you ever serious?"

"Not if I can help it," Bobby croaked.

"What do you remember?" Harry asked again.

Bobby took a breath. "All of it," he said, his eyes on Toni's. "I remember the feeling. I remember the way it tasted. I remembered how good it was."

He looked up at Harry. "And I know what you want to know."

Toni frowned. "What?"

"It was Abruzzi. He stuck me when I wasn't looking."

Toni gritted her teeth. "God damn it."

Harry looked away, out the window, as Toni said, "This is my fault."

"No it isn't," Bobby and Harry said together. Harry smiled a little as he stared out the window at the snow-covered roof next door.

"I dragged you two into this. It's my brother-in-law that did this. He could have killed you!"

"He didn't," Bobby said. He tried to sit up. He slumped back, still sweating. The heartrate monitor beeped rapidly. "Jesus. I feel like I got curb-stomped by Terry Shoulders."

"You wish," Toni said. "You looked better than this after he got through with you."

Bobby nodded gingerly. "Yeah. This is worse. I hate to say it, but I've been here before. It looks awful, and it feels awful, but I'll be okay."

"You better," Toni said. She glanced up at Harry and asked, "What do you remember? Every detail."

Bobby said, "I was in the kitchen fixing dinner. Starr was in Farrokh's room-"

"Why was Starr in Farrokh's room?" Harry asked.

"She heard the kid freaking out," Bobby told him. "He wanted to leave, but I convinced him to stay. Starr said she'd talk to him, try to calm him down. They were in his room for half an hour, maybe more. I checked on Abruzzi. He was still out. I thought. I headed into the kitchen to make dinner. I heard Starr go into Abruzzi's room to check on him, I guess. I heard someone come into the kitchen a little later. I was whipping some eggs. I felt the sting, jerked around, and there was Abruzzi with a needle."

His eyes dipped away from Toni's earnest, concerned face. Harry watched them drop to the floor while he lied.

"I started to yell, but it was outta the blue, into the black. Next thing I know, I'm in an ER with a doc bending over me asking if I have any brain cells left." Bobby shrugged. "Everything else is a blank."

Toni patted his arm. "It's okay. You're okay."

Bobby cleared his throat again, and again. He looked around. To Toni he asked, "Could you find me some water? I'm parched."

"Sure," she said with a smile. She left the room in search of a nurse.

Harry and Bobby looked at each other.

"Starr," Harry said. It wasn't a question.

Bobby looked grim. "Yeah."

Harry nodded. "I figured."

"How's that?"

"You lied to Toni," Harry said.

Bobby grimaced and looked out the window. "I couldn't tell her. She feels bad enough. When her sister was into something she couldn't help, that was one thing. But now? Far as I'm concerned, she and Abruzzi deserve what they get."

"Yeah." Harry shoved his hands in his pockets. "I'm still on the hook for it, but you're clear."

A soft snort of laughter drew Harry's eyes back to the careworn, seamed face of Bobby Gold. "Yeah, like this is gonna stop me," he said.

"I'll stop you."

Bobby's genial eyes turned harder. "If I were doing it for you, I'd still tell you to fuck off."

Harry looked at Bobby, his unblinking gaze accepted and returned by the implacable stare of Bobby Gold. Harry nodded. His eyes flicked to the door and back.

"Toni told me," he said.

Bobby's steel gaze broke, his eyes glistening. He swallowed twice, sniffed, and gave Harry a sad smile. "'Love is real,'" he said. "'The most real, the most lasting, the sweetest, and yet the bitterest thing we know.'"

Harry's brow bowed upward as he raised his eyebrows.

Bobby shrugged. "Bronte. Doesn't matter."

Harry stood there quietly, unmoving. He fixed his gaze halfway between the floor and Bobby's eyes.

Bobby cleared his throat again. "You know," he said in a feather-soft voice, "she never even took a drink the whole time I knew her."

Harry listened.

Bobby shrugged one shoulder. "She didn't like being out of control. Ever. She was a practical woman, my Nell. Tough, fair, honest. It was her bad luck she fell in with me."

Harry glanced at Bobby's face. The man's eyes were closed. A tear wound down one cheek.

"She got a social work degree from NYU while I was cooking," Bobby continued. "She worked as a rehab councilor in Jersey. She didn't have to be, but she was."

Harry frowned. "Didn't have to be? That's a pretty specific calling. It ain't an easy job. I've seen things."

Bobby nodded, wiped the tear away with the back of his hand. "How much of me did Toni give you?"

It was an odd way to phrase the question. Harry considered. He didn't know Bobby Gold well at all. But he knew that the sun rose and set on Toni for him, and that was a feeling Harry could understand intimately. He realized with a disconcerting sense of alarm that he felt a strange kind of kinship with Bobby Gold. They were linked through Toni. But it was obvious Bobby liked to hide his depths. He gave the world a kind of comic buffoon because that's what they expected. Or he does, Harry thought. He considered that. Maybe the depths hidden within Bobby had led him to his own destruction. Now he does what he can to keep it away. A stirring on the back of his neck made his skin prickle. He acts like a clown because if he doesn't, he'll be who he used to be. Harry considered that revelation. So he thought about it very carefully before he answered.

"She told me you're solid. Good backup. That I can count on you," Harry said. He felt a twinge of guilt and reminded himself to buy Gene all the coffee he ever wanted. "That you used to be a cook, that you wrote some books."

"She never told you I'm a junkie?"

"She likely didn't think it mattered. It was in the past. Like I'm not a cop any more. And she's not-"

"Yeah," Bobby agreed.

"And about twenty minutes ago she told me about your wife."

"Yeah," Bobby agreed. "The books... that was something that rehab gave me. Nothing to do but sweat, puke, and write. Escapism, you know?"

Harry said nothing.

"They... they sell pretty good still," Bobby said. "The day I got out of rehab the last time, I found out she was gone. She'd meant it. I knew the deal: relapse again and she'd bail. I don't blame her."

Harry said nothing, but he swallowed a sudden lump that had gathered in the back of his throat.

"Couple weeks later I got served. Divorce papers."

Harry nodded. "Made it quick and clean. Didn't prolong it."

Bobby gave Harry a half-smile. "Yeah. She doesn't dither, my Nell. So I went to my lawyer with 'em. And we did the deed. And something else. I signed over my book rights to her. All proceeds. Anything they're worth, I gave it all to her. It's worth a bundle. She didn't have to work. Didn't have to do anything. But she chose to work in rehab. And look what it gets her."

Harry stared at Bobby now, his eyes held the melancholy, abstracted look they got when he was in work mode. His brain picked apart Bobby's words. His natural suspicion nibbled at the edges of the meanings. His trained processes sorted, filed, and selected the important pieces of information. If Harry DeMarko's mind existed in the physical world it would look identical to his office; desk, chair, filing cabinet full of manila folders.

The desk in his mind had a fresh sheet of paper tucked inside a brand-new open manila folder, and he was taking notes.

Toni came back with a nurse in tow. The nurse had a pitcher of water, a glass, and a thick sheaf of paperwork. She looked to be about forty, one of the battle-hardened veterans that could run the place without anyone's help, Harry thought. He'd known a lot of nurses, and if they made it that far, they were tougher than boot leather and had zero time for nonsense.

"You wanted water, Mr. Gold," the nurse said. She had a pin-neat white uniform, greying black hair, and a pinched expression. "I also have your discharge paperwork. You're cleared to leave. We need these beds for patients. You don't need to take up valuable space."

Bobby nodded and swung his legs over the side of the bed. "That's about all I'm good for," he said in a lighthearted voice.

The nurse's mouth pinched together as she glared at him. "We need the space for patients in distress. Not," she said with a sniff, "for people like you."

"Like me?"

"Junkies," the nurse all but spat.

Bobby hung his head a little. Toni's mouth opened and her face reddened.

Harry got there first. He stepped around the edge of the bed and snatched the paperwork from the nurse. She started to protest.

"Officer DeMarko, 9th precinct," he snapped. "This man's a witness. He was attacked. Junkie? This man was stabbed with someone else's needle. He's lucky to be alive and he's going to keep other people safe by helping me catch the bastard who did this. So maybe go away now. And keep your judgments to yourself next time. Thanks." Harry turned his back to the nurse.

The nurse jerked her head backward a little at his dismissal. "Mr.-"

"Officer," Harry said over his shoulder. "What?"

Her demeanor was subdued, less harsh. "Officer. He needs to sign-"

"We'll drop them off on our way out. Clothes."

The nurse looked around, found and opened a cabinet, and tugged out a mound of clothes; jeans, boots, a nondescript shirt, and a battered leather motorcycle jacket. She handed them to the bemused Bobby, who nodded his thanks. The nurse hesitated, said hurriedly, "I hope you feel better, Mr. Gold," and left the room with a single glance at Harry, who stared at her with flat, humorless eyes.

"Thanks," Bobby said as he tugged on his jeans.

"Nobody talks to my friends like that."

Toni gave Harry a brilliant smile. Bobby pulled his jeans up, rucking the gown aside. He didn't wear underwear. Toni turned to watch the nurses working like coordinated bees in a hive, efficiently shuttling around one another, weaving back and forth out of rooms and the central cubical. Bobby stood up and zipped and tabbed his jeans. He pulled the hospital gown off.

I was right about his ribs, Harry thought. Bobby's ribs did indeed stand out in clear ridges. His body was lean, muscled, and he had abs that Harry found himself jealous of. There was no fat on Bobby's body, he actually had heaps of stringy, wire-tough muscle under his skin. There were horizontal lines along both arms, from wrist to elbow, as well as oblong circles. The wounds of years in a kitchen, always moving, always behind the timer. Burns and spatters of hot oil had left their badges along his arms. Almost against his will, Harry found himself checking Bobby's elbows. There were no recent track marks, just the faded scars of another life, almost unnoticeable now. Harry felt another stab of shame for the check. He focused instead on a tattoo on Bobby's left shoulder. A skull-and-crossbones flag, except in addition to an eyepatch the skull wore a chef's hat. Harry smiled at that.

Bobby pulled the shirt over his head, sat again, and tugged on his boots. He laced them tight. He paused to drain the water glass, fill it, and drain it again. "I can't remember the last time I was this thirsty." He slid into his black leather jacket and zipped it to his chin.

"Okay, what's the move?"

"Home."

Toni saw Bobby's face when Harry said it. It was like the sun coming out. He glanced at Toni, who nodded and smiled as if to say welcome to the family.

"Home, and Kilburn," Harry said. "The subtle times are over. It's time to get loud."

CHAPTER TWENTY-FOUR

"I don't like it," Kilburn said. "I don't like it at all."

They were seated at the desks. Kilburn was stalking back and forth. Bobby had curled up on the bed, almost asleep. Beside the bed a bucket awaited further stomach contents. The Naxalone had brought about waves of nausea. On the edge of Toni's desk sat the brick of heroin in an evidence bag.

"Kilburn, what's he into?" Harry asked.

"I told you- he was supposed to try and lure his connections to a meet. That's it. Just get the 68s to agree to meet. Offer them the brick, get 'em to the meet. The last thing we needed before he was free and clear. We were going to arrest him along with his bosses so they didn't twig to his involvement. We were going to let him off on a technicality. But instead, he went AWOL. And now this." He gestured at the bag. "I don't like this one bit."

Toni gave Harry a dark look. Harry acknowledged the look with a solemn nod. "We're no happier than you are, Kilburn. Like I said, half an hour ago the kid's knocking on my door in hysterics, he drops his bag, and when we go inside to get him some food, he vanishes. He didn't even tell us what he was running from."

Harry repeated the story that he and Toni had worked up before calling Kilburn in.

"I know, I know," Kilburn snapped. "At least we know he's alive. I was worried he'd been snatched, or the 68s tumbled to him. This new thing is troublesome. I can't think why he'd run."

"We've been waiting for you before going up to the store," Toni said. "His uncle needs to know what's going on."

"You're going to scare the hell out of the guy," Kilburn said. "Let me figure out-"

"No," she said, a little angry now. "You've left him hanging already. He's already scared. This will at least give him something to hold onto."

"I could call-"

"No," Harry said. "This isn't a phone call kind of a situation, Kilburn. This is a face-to-face situation. He deserves to see our faces."

Kilburn opened his mouth, and Toni cut him off. "Ours. Not yours," she said. "He needs friends. He's just going to blame you. You don't deserve it, I think, and he doesn't need a scratching post. Not yet, anyhow."

Kilburn sighed, but nodded. "I get it. I told him I'd keep the kid safe. I'll stay away until I find Farrokh."

"Good call," Harry said. "He's one kid. How hard can it for the NYPD be to find one kid in this city?"

Kilburn let that pass. He picked up the evidence bag. "I've got to get this into evidence."

Harry had washed the blood off the package before calling Kilburn. The last thing they needed was the blood of an Outfit associate turning up on Kilburn's bait brick. Especially as it would eventually turn out that associate was married to Toni's sister.

The machinations involved in keeping everyone close and in the dark were wearing on Harry. He glanced at the clock on the wall. Almost midnight now. Fatigue washed over him. He couldn't remember the last time he slept.

Kilburn stopped at the door. "If he comes back, call me. After you handcuff him to a desk."

Harry grinned. "Two desks. He's wily."

"Two desks," Kilburn agreed. "See you. Thanks for the head's up about this."

"Anytime," Harry said. He locked the door behind Kilburn, and they watched him vanish into the gloom of the night. The dome light in his car lit up his tired, careworn face as he fished for his keys. Then the light was extinguished, and moments later the car vanished up the street. They went into the apartment. Bobby, head hanging over the edge of their bed, asked hoarsely, "We under arrest?"

"Not yet," Harry said, closing the door.

"What are you going to do now?" Bobby asked.

Harry scrubbed a hand over his face, sighed, and said, "I don't know. I guess we get in touch with Hendrick in the morning about the car, and go see Mr. Dahli. Then… wing it, I guess."

"What's gonna happen to the kid, do you think?"

Toni paced, marking the distance between the bathroom and the kitchen, brow furrowed. Harry watched her briefly, then looked at Bobby. "I don't know. There's a bunch of possibilities. Most of 'em aren't good. He either ran or he was taken. He's either in good hands or bad. He's either safe or…" he trailed off.

"Yeah," Bobby said. "What happens if it's the worst case?"

Toni uttered a startled noise. Bobby said, "I mean, I hope it doesn't go that way-"

"Farrokh." Toni's voice was flat and emotionless. Harry and Bobby stopped talking as she continued. "Farrokh was working for the 68s. Not willingly. But still. So… we have to go talk to them."

Harry grimaced. "Dangerous."

"You deal with the Mob, the Feds, and all manner of shady situations. You're afraid of a biker gang?" Bobby asked.

"Most everyone else has rules. We can get by within them. The 68s are drug dealers and thugs-for-hire. They don't need to operate by any codes. They're not run by the Mob. But they work with them. The 68s get to run their drugs in the City, the Mob gets a cut. Truce. Kind of. But the Families have to live here. They have to deal with us- the cops. The 68s are multi-state. No ties to any one place. No patterns. Try to pin them down and they'll just up and leave whenever they feel like it. That kind of mobility means they can be a lot louder and messy and get away with it. It's a shaky enough situation in that regard. They're not gonna want to give us anything. And if they find out we know Farrokh's running for them, they could decide scorched earth is the best solution."

"You guys are so much fun," Bobby said out of the side of his mouth. "You should sell tickets. Offer tours."

Harry said, "I want coffee, I think." He went into the office. Toni followed.

"He's right, you know. We're in a mess."

"Yeah, yeah," Harry grumped as he poured them each a cup. "So what else is new?"

Toni shut the apartment door and stood next to Harry. She took the cup he offered, wrapped her hands around it. It was chilly in the office.

"You were pretty fierce to that nurse, Harry."

"I didn't like what she said."

"Never seen you that way before."

He looked askance at her. "Yes you have."

She blinked, realized he was right. "Okay," she amended. "I've never seen you that way about anyone but me."

"Yes you have," he said again.

"Well, yeah… me and your friends."

He sipped his coffee and said nothing. She stretched up and kissed his cheek. "Thank you, Harry."

"He earned it," Harry said. "He had your back, he had my back, he took one for the team. He's solid. You were right."

And I was very wrong, he thought.

Toni's smile warmed him to his toes, and when she grinned at him his stomach seemed to writhe and flip like a kid on a rollercoaster.

"Come on," she said. "Take me to bed."

He shifted his feet. "I'm not sure now's the time-"

"You need sleep, Harry. And I do, too. A couple of hours isn't going to change anything. Unless you want to roam the streets like a stray dog hoping you run into Farrokh, Starr, or Abruzzi by accident, there's nothing we can do. Dahli's Market doesn't open until 6 anyhow. Come sleep."

She grabbed his hand and tugged him toward the door. He resisted long enough to lock the office door and shut off the lights. In the apartment, Bobby Gold was asleep on the bed, head still hanging over the edge. He was still dressed, still wore his boots, but Harry noticed he had been courteously careful to keep them off the coverlet.

"Right," Toni muttered. "Gold basically lives here now."

"He pulls his weight," Harry said. "We haven't eaten so well in… well… ever."

"Maybe you should give me a raise," Bobby muttered through slack lips.

"Hell, I'll double your pay right now if you go sleep on the couch," Toni said.

Bobby opened one eye. "You don't pay me."

"Triple, then," she said.

"Okay, but I have demands."

"Rating your value pretty high, aren't you?"

Bobby shrugged one shoulder. "You opened negotiations, not me. You want something, not me. I'm perfectly comfortable."

"Get to it," Toni said, "before I lose my sense of humor. What's it gonna take to get you off my bed?"

"First, I want a blanket."

"Done," she said.

"Second, I want a pillow."

"Agreed."

"Third, I want Harry to never make coffee again."

"Hey, how's this about me?" Harry protested from the bathroom. He was washing his hands.

"I'm not gonna work here if he's going to keep trying to poison me," Bobby said.

"Deal," Toni said. She hauled an extra blanket and pillow out of the wardrobe they used for storage and threw them at Bobby. He rolled over, sat up, and stretched languidly.

"I'll be in my office," he said, and left the apartment, shutting the door behind him. Toni shut off the lights as Harry sat on the edge of the bed. Toni joined him, finding her way in the dark by memory. The darkness was silent except for two distinct thuds as each of them set their gun next to the bed within easy reach. They undressed, snuggled together under the coverlet, and were deeply asleep in seconds.

CHAPTER TWENTY-FIVE

Sunday

"Tell the man we got his shipment in. We'll be at the club, same table we sat at last time, 10 o'clock sharp," Harry said and hung up the payphone. Toni hunched her shoulders in her jacket and shivered.

"That gives us three hours," she said, teeth chattering.

"Yeah," Harry said. "I guess we can't put this off any more. Come on."

He and Toni walked down the block until they stood in front of Dahli's Market. Harry pulled the door open and Toni scooted in, with him right on her heels. Inside the store was warm, and they enjoyed the warmth for a moment. And then Mr. Dahli greeted them.

"Mr. Toni! Mr. Harry! Good to see you this fine, brisk morning," The tall, dark-skinned man behind the counter said with a bow. The lights gleamed on his shiny-bald head.

"Mr. Dahli," Harry said. "Brisk is a way to describe it, I suppose."

Malik Dahli smiled at two of his favorite customers, his white teeth gleaming. As Harry and Toni stood there regarding him, the smile faded.

"There is a problem," Dahli said in a desolate voice. "Something has happened."

"First, we don't know that anything bad has happened," Harry cautioned. "We're looking for Farrokh. No one's seen him for a while. Detective Kilburn is looking, too. We're scouring the city, okay? We're going to find him and bring him home." Harry hoped he wasn't promising too much.

Dahli's head bowed, and he mumbled something under his breath. Harry realized the older man was praying.

"Farrokh was working on something for Kilburn, but before he could get it done, he seems to have panicked or been otherwise shaken by something, and he vanished," Toni said. "He got scared and he ran. We're trying to find him. We're going to find him."

Malik Dahli's eyes glistened, but he shed no tears. He nodded once, cleared his throat, and said in a low voice, "If you say it is so, then it is so. I trust you."

Harry's heart thumped once, painfully, and he took a deep breath to steady himself. He said, "We'll find him. And when we do, we'll bring him back here first. You have my word. Our word."

Toni's eyes roamed over the counter and walls behind the tall, thin man. She saw the pictures behind him, tucked low, of his wife and daughter, both back in India, of his elderly parents, of his sisters and brothers, and one of his whole family. Perhaps two dozen smiling, open faces; generations of the Dahli family.

She looked at the history before her, the lineage, the family. The shared experiences of a life together. She smiled to herself. Most of the men in the photograph resembled one another. It was obvious they were related. They wore similar clothes, similar beards, the same—

Her blood chilled. She shivered, looked up at Harry and Malik Dahli. She licked her lips. "May I ask you a personal question, Mr. Dahli?"

Dahli inclined his head. "You may."

"What are those head wraps the men in your family wear?" she asked. Harry glanced sideways at her.

"They are turbans," Malik Dahli said. "They are traditional headwear for Sikh men."

"Why do they wear them?"

"They are sacred coverings," Dahli told her, his face smoothing and lighting up as he warmed to what was obviously an important topic for him. "They are one part of our faith. One of five symbolic items Sikh men use to show their devotion and to demonstrate their belonging. The turban is a covering for the Kesh, the uncut hair of a Sikh. The hair is as important a part of the body as your arms, legs, or heart. In addition to the Kesh, we must always carry a Khanga, a wooden comb to remind us to be tidy," he said, removing a small comb from inside his shirt and displaying it for her before placing it in his pocket. "A Kara," he held up his hand and showed her the silver circlet around his wrist, "the circle represents the never-ending existence of God. The Kachera is… it is an undergarment we wear," he said with a look of embarrassment. "You will forgive me if I do not show you."

"Of course," she smiled at him.

"The last item is… problematic for a Sikh of faith in the modern world," Dahli said. He glanced at the door of his shop, reached beneath his shirt, and showed them a dagger about ten inches long. It had a curved hawkbill blade, and seemed to have been forged from a single piece of steel. "The Kirpan. A dagger with which we protect ourselves and others. The Kirpan reminds us to protect and defend those who are oppressed."

"That's a beautiful idea," Toni said. "I love it."

Dahli bowed his head as he slid the dagger into the sheath concealed at his waist.

Toni bit her lip, and asked shyly, "Why don't you wear a turban?"

Dahli gave her a wide smile full of white teeth. "The turban is to protect the uncut hair of the faithful, Miss Toni. But since the age of seventeen, I have had no need of one," he said, rubbing his hand over his hairless head. "I could still wear one, of course, but it would be symbolic, unnecessary and..." he looked around his shop again before finishing, "they are very uncomfortable in the summer."

She grinned at him. "I bet."

Harry got a pair of Cokes from the cooler, popped the caps on the metal bottle opener on the side, and carried them to the counter. He handed Dahli a dollar, ignoring the look of disapproval. Dahli reluctantly took the bill and put it in his register. Harry handed one of the Cokes to Toni, who sipped it.

"Is Farrokh in danger?" Dahli asked.

Harry hesitated, but said, "Yes, some. But he's got us, and he's got Kilburn, and he's got the NYPD looking for him. We'll find him and bring him home."

Dahli ducked his head again. "Thank you, my friend."

"Absolutely." He looked at Toni. "Ready? We've got places to be."

"Twice as ready as you are," she said.

They walked to the door of the store. "Twice? That seems unusually high."

"I'm always gonna be at least ten percent more anything than you are, DeMarko," she said, and bumped his hip with her own. They gave Malik Dahli a final wave and left the store.

Once in the car, Harry asked, voice devoid of humor, "What is it?"

Toni propped the Coke bottle in the Y of her crotch and fished inside her jacket for something. "What do you mean?"

"The questions about Dahli and his faith. What's on your mind?"

She nibbled the inside of her lip while she continued looking for something. "Dahli doesn't wear a turban."

"No sacred hair."

"Yeah," Toni said. She found what she was looking for, and from deep at the bottom of an inner jacket pocket she took a plastic bag with a swatch of cloth inside. She held it up. "But Farrokh wears one."

CHAPTER TWENTY-SIX

They pulled up to the church and went inside. The inside of the cathedral was far warmer than Harry would have guessed it could get. They found Hendrick in the same pew as the first time they'd met him. He was alone. He looked haggard, unshaven and unkempt, as though he'd either not slept in days or had slept in his clothes. He wasted no time.

"What did you find?" he asked, his voice raspy.

Toni and Harry slid into the pew next to him. "The car was empty, no belongings, but there was blood in it," Harry said. "Forensics is on it."

Hendrick's brow furrowed. "How long's it gonna take to run it?"

"No telling. Nobody was admitted to the ERs that we could find with a GSW," Harry told him. "So far, the guy's a ghost."

"Not until I get ahold of him," Hendrick said. "You ain't heard anything else?"

"That's what we've got so far. Figured you'd want to be kept in the loop."

"Yeah. License plate?"

Harry looked at Toni, who recited it. Hendrick fumbled a piece of paper out of his pocket and a pen, and scrawled it. "Anything else?"

"What does… what did Sal have to say about heroin?" Toni asked.

Hendrick gave her a mild glare. "Why?"

"Because someone's dealing in our neighborhood, and before we step on them, it would be nice to know if they're yours. If they're yours, we can do it nice and gentle. If not, we can do it hard. We don't like heroin in our neighborhood," she said with a slight snarl.

Hendrick nodded. "Yeah. Sal didn't like it either. He was trying to keep it out of the Bowery. Keep it up in Harlem. Out in Jersey. But away from the neighborhoods. There was gonna be a meeting soon about the whole thing."

Harry and Toni exchanged a look. "So no one's going to be upset if we come down on some lowlife dealers?" Harry asked.

"Look, long as you get me the guy who did Sal, I couldn't care less what you do. Hell, if you bring me the mook, I'll help you deliver the messages. But find the guy." Hendrick shoved the paper in his pocket. "Anything else?"

"No," Harry said. "We'll be in touch the second we have something."

Hendrick nodded and shuffled his way to the aisle. He left without a backward glance.

Harry sat back and sighed. Toni put a hand on his leg. They sat in silence. she said, "That's the connection, then."

Harry nodded. "Looks like it."

"It wasn't Abruzzi."

"No," he said. "It doesn't look like it."

"And he can't let anyone know."

"I gather that, if he doesn't pull off the hit himself, he's looking at a death sentence," Harry said. "And he's got to be frantic at this point."

"Because he didn't kill Sal," she said.

"No," Harry said. He sighed. "No, he didn't."

"And we know who did."

"Yeah, we do."

She took his hand. He squeezed it. They sat in silence until Toni asked, in a hesitant voice, "What do we do, Harry?"

She hadn't sounded that unsure for months, maybe a

year. It was the completely-lost sound of someone who didn't even know where to start. He squeezed her hand again.

"We figure out where Farrokh is. He's the priority. We promised Mr. Dahli. Once we do that, we figure out the next step."

Toni nodded. "Okay. Where do we start?"

"Well, we have a solid lead."

"The 68s?"

"It's the single solid lead we have," Harry said. "It's that or nothing. We need to find him now. Every minute lost is precious. In a kidnapping case, you have 48 hours of prime search time to recover the victim... alive, at any rate."

Toni put a hand to her mouth.

Harry said heatedly, "I should have thought of this earlier. I should have seen it! I screwed up, Toni."

"Harry, no," she said. "You didn't. You did everything you could. Farrokh came to us because he trusts us. But he didn't tell us what he did, Harry. I get it; he was scared, ashamed, the poor guy is in a huge bind. He's going to be deported if he's lucky. Years in jail if he's not. And that's just if the law gets him."

Harry nodded grimly. "If the 68s find out he's a mole, they'll grease him without a thought. And if they don't, Abruzzi will to claim the kill. We need to find him, Toni. I need to- I promised-"

He broke off. Toni stroked his cheek with her fingertips. "We will, Harry," she breathed. She leaned in and kissed him.

Harry turned his head and kissed her. She pressed closer, and they enjoyed a moment of respite before someone clearing their throat behind them broke in.

Harry and Toni turned to see a young priest carrying an armload of bibles frowning at them. Toni looked at Harry, looked at the priest, and back at Harry. She took his face in her hands and said, "Peace be with you."

Keeping his own face straight, Harry intoned, "And also you."

The younger priest tutted at them, but continued on his way.

"Come on," Harry said, standing. "Let's get out of here before you get burned at the stake."

"If I do, don't they martyr me?" she asked him with an impish smile.

"Possibly."

"Huh. And here mom always told me I was no saint."

Harry rolled his eyes. "It's not necessary."

"Why not?"

"They don't need to canonize you. You're already beautiful."

Toni blushed and slugged him in the arm. "Aw. You're just sayin' that so I'll save your soul."

He stopped so abruptly that she bumped into him. He turned to her, took her by the shoulders, and said, "You already did."

Her mouth opened, but she said nothing. Her eyes were wide with shock. He put a finger under her chin and closed her mouth. He took her hand and led her out of the church.

She said nothing all the way to the car. As they slid in and slammed the doors she said in a tiny voice, "Ditto, Harry."

She didn't have to explain. He smiled at her, and it was all the answer she needed. She revved the engine, put the car into drive, and they left skidding, curving tracks as they headed back to the office. On the way, Harry said, "Make a left. We need to get to the 9th. We have to talk to Clara, if she's in today."

She frowned. "Clara handles motorcycle gangs, too?"

"Organized crime is organized crime. They have a

separate task force, I think, but Clara's in charge."

"Okay," she said, and spun the wheel. They drifted through the turn and Harry tried not to grab for the door.

CHAPTER TWENTY-SEVEN

Clara Bowdler ran her department with a modicum of discipline, a modicum of fear, and a huge helping of mutual respect. Her lieutenant, Rick Kepner, abided by her style, and he'd come to develop almost as good a rapport with their officers as his boss had.

The discipline came from being not just cops but New York City cops. They were the line. The respect came from the countless times Clara had led them into situations herself. She risked her neck beside her people, often taking point, and once even getting shot for a rookie who had frozen like a jacklit deer when confronted with a drug dealer who seemed quite as surprised as they that he was home. Luckily her vest held. The rookie got over his greenness, and did quite well, rising through the department to become Clara's lieutenant.

The fear… that came from the countless times she and her people had shared meals. Clara Bowdler possessed an appetite unlike any other, and a bottomless storage space in her petite frame. She could (and did, regularly) win bets with her unrelenting passion for food.

Harry and Toni checked in at the front desk and made their way up to the fifth floor where Clara had her bullpen. As usual, the door was open and Clara was on her phone. She saw them and waved them in, still talking.

"No," she said. "No, that won't work. That's not- no. You told me you'd- if you'd let me-"

Harry watched her close her eyes, take a breath, and then bark, "Shut up! Listen to me for once! I want two on point, two on the roof, and four cruisers! You're running a box tail, not sticking a guy at the airport to watch for 'a guy'. I'm not taking a chance on losing them. And I'm not taking a chance on you losing them again! Get it done, or I'll make sure you end up on traffic."

She listened. Her face twisted in an amused, bitter snarl.

"Try me, buddy. I'll come down and stuff you in the dress skirt myself," she growled. "Get. It. Done. That's an order."

She started to hang up, heard the voice talking. She listened, smiled, and said, "Tell him what I told you. Don't forget to mention the part about the dress. Hasley can take it out of my budget; that's what it's there for. But get it done, or so help me God I will come find you wherever you are."

She listened, smiled, and said, "Thank you. Keep me posted."

She hung up the phone, sighed, and said, "I thought my day was rough, and you two walk in. What the hell is wrong now?"

She sounded irate, but she got up and pulled Harry into a rough hug. He returned it briefly and patted her on the back. Toni watched, wondered not for the first time what their history was, and let it go. He'd been gone a long time, and Clara was a good friend. Sure, she had arrested Harry for murder, but he'd told her to. Clara released him, pushed him out of the way, and gave Toni a hug as well. "You look better than last time I saw you," she said.

Toni grinned. "That was after Terry Shoulders. I couldn't look worse unless I was dead."

"Oh," Clara said. "That reminds me. Terry's on his way to Leavenworth."

"Leavenworth?"

Clara sat down and nodded. "Turns out old Terry was a soldier once. What I gather, he got fed up taking orders and left. Just up and left. We booked him in, and an old flag popped up. He's looking at five to ten for an AWOL charge."

Toni grimaced. "Yeesh. Leavenworth's rough."

"Yeah, but when you're a sasquatch living in a village full of gnomes, it's not that hard," she said. She pointed to the chairs. "Sit."

They settled in and Rick Kepner, his short brown hair tousled and unkept, stuck his head in. "Boss, did you- oh. Hey Harry. Toni. Good to see you. Did you get the-"

"Just got off the phone with 'em," Clara said. "Sondland is rounding up what we need."

Kepner grimaced. "Sondland? That prick is-"

"I know. I stood on him a little. He's doing it."

"Great. I've been sitting in a car for fourteen hours. I'm going home to shower and change," Kepner told her. Clara nodded. Rick didn't leave. After a second, Clara frowned, seemed to understand, and tossed him a ring of keys. "My place is closer. I need you back here as soon as possible."

Kepner caught the keys and grinned at Toni. His cheeks showed a little pink. He vanished from the door.

Harry shifted in his seat. Toni grinned at Clara. Clara lowered her eyes to her desk and picked up a pencil to fiddle with.

"So what is it I can do for you, Harry?" she asked, twirling the pencil between several fingers.

"We need some information on a gang," Harry told her. Clara raised an eyebrow.

"We're working a missing persons' and we need to know where the 68s are holing up."

Clara glanced at Toni, who was still grinning. She looked back at Harry.

"You're kidding. K & R?"

"So far just the K," Harry said. He looked at Toni "Kidnapping and ransom."

Toni nodded her thanks, absorbing the information into

her already considerable mental file of the shorthand and jargon that the cops and feds used around her.

"You're screwing around with motorcycle gangs now?"

Harry gave her a slanting smile. "Come on, Clara. It's winter. Most of 'em are down south, right? All that's left is the dregs. The prospects and the hopefuls. Yeah?"

Clara looked grumpy about it, but she nodded. "The ATF is monitoring the 68s in a joint deal with ATF. They're in Mexico, last I was briefed."

Harry nodded, and glanced at Toni. She wrinkled her nose at him.

"You think the halfwits are behind your MP?" Clara asked. Her eyes searched Harry's face. Toni saw her weighing his reactions, sizing him up.

"It's possible." He gave her a moment of his calm gaze before saying, "It's got to do with heroin."

"And there it is," Clara breathed. "Harry, I'm going to do you and her and me and this department a huge favor and warn you right the fuck off as of now. I just told you ATF and DEA are on this. You know what the D stands for. And it's a Fed beef. I can't even get near it. And if I can't-"

"We definitely can't," Harry agreed. "Clara, someone's dealing in my neighborhood. On my streets. The Gambinos aren't going to war over a street thug pushing their turf boundaries. But, as usual, I'm not cop, I'm not crook. They know me, or know of me. I can do things that won't start a street war."

"You're not cop, you're not crook. You're nobody. If you piss off everyone, Harry, sooner or later someone's going to unplug you," Clara said.

"Maybe," he agreed. He glanced at Toni. "But until they do, I'm going to do what I can to help who I can."

"Local dealer, huh?"

Harry nodded.

"Hooked someone you know?"

"Something like that."

He and Clara stared at one another for almost a full minute. Toni folded her hands over her belly and leaned back. She watched Clara's face while the other woman processed what she knew. she asked, "You're doing someone a favor, aren't you?"

Harry nodded.

Clara shook her head. "Damn it, Harry," she said with a sigh.

He said nothing.

Toni struggled to keep the grin off her face.

Clara's face showed exasperation, irritation, and resignation. To cover her capitulation, she growled, "You owe me two meals, Harry."

"Yeah, but I'll buy no more than three," he said.

Despite the tension, Clara's eyes lit up at the offer. "Fine, sure, whatever. Give me a couple hours," she said. "I'll call you when I know something."

Harry stood up. Toni followed suit. He held out a hand. Clara stared at it, looked up at him, with a new kind of look in her eyes. Disbelief.

She stood and took his hand. Harry shook with her solemnly. "Thank you, Clara. Look… I know I ask a lot. You know it's always appreciated, right?"

Clara nodded. "I do."

"And if it's the other way around, whatever you need, I'll do it."

"We," Toni said firmly.

"Whatever you need. Whenever you need it. Call us," Harry told Clara.

Clara stared at him with an unreadable expression. Toni thought it might be awe.

"I know, Harry. I know."

"I've asked a lot of favors. A lot. That makes me kind

of a shitty friend. So I'll buy you as many lunches as you need," he said with a faint smile. "But I wanted you to know how much your help means. And how much more your friendship means." Harry looked her in the eyes as he spoke, and the sincerity of his words caused Clara to smile.

"Thank you, Harry."

"Thank you, Clara. For everything," he said as he ended the handshake. He turned and left the office. Toni and Clara watched him go.

"Is he all right?" Clara asked in a low voice.

"Far as I know," Toni said in the same tone. "He's just… we're both spun out by this thing."

"He's been out a week now. How's he taking it?"

"You know Harry. He was more upset about the girl, Messner, than what he went through," Toni said. "Look, let's get together sometime soon. I'd like to talk."

Clara's attention turned to Toni. "Of course. Something up?"

Toni shrugged. "Oh, you know. Just dealing with a lot of stuff and I could use a perspective that isn't so close to it."

Clara narrowed her eyes. "Are you pregnant?"

Toni guffawed, such a genuine, honest reaction that Clara grinned by reflex.

"Jesus, no!" Toni gasped. "Why would you ask?"

Clara's lips twitched. "You wouldn't be the first woman to celebrate your man's return the best way, or to get carried away."

Toni gave her a big mock frown. "Clara… you know what I used to do for a living."

Clara didn't look away, as most people did when Toni mentioned her former life as a hooker. Clara accepted it as part of who she was, and wasn't the kind to judge. "Of course I do."

"Well," Toni asked, one hand on a hip and a slanting grin on her face, "You think I'd get pregnant accidentally? I'm smarter than that."

"True. Sorry."

"No sweat. Besides, when it happens it'll be because I want to," Toni said with a studied air of nonchalance.

Clara blinked twice. "I… have so many questions," she said. "But I'll hold 'em. If it isn't pregnant and you're not getting married, what's the deal?"

Toni's smile faded. "I worry about a couple things, Clara." She jerked a thumb over her shoulder. "Him and our friends, and family."

"Ah." Clara sighed. "And you ain't worried about him and us."

"You got it."

Clara came around the desk and she and Toni embraced, a quick, tight hug. "Anytime, Toni. Gimme a call. I'll kick Rick out and we'll get ice cream."

"It's a date," Toni said. "I better run."

"Yeah. You let him out of your sight he's gonna get in trouble," Clara said.

"Oh God," Toni moaned. "Trouble is all we ever get. See you, Fatso."

Toni hurried after Harry. Clara watched her catch up to him, catch his hand, and start tugging him forward like a five-year-old at the supermarket. Harry tugged her back, kissed her once, and they were in the elevator and gone. She shook her head. They're so good together, Clara thought. Way better than Harry and-

The phone rang. She slid from concerned friend to head of the OC unit for the NYPD, a transition that took less time than it took to reach over and grab the phone off the cradle. "Yeah?" she barked. "What?"

CHAPTER TWENTY-EIGHT

In the car, Harry asked casually, "How long have Clara and Rick been an item?"

Toni raised an eyebrow.

"Oh come on," he said. "I'm a detective. You're shocked I knew?"

She snorted. "Harry, I'm shocked you noticed. You're good at the hard stuff, not so quick with the soft stuff. Clara and Rick have been together a while now."

Harry nodded to himself as she started the car. "You knew," he said.

"Yeah, but I look at everything with different eyes than you do."

He felt like that was not a compliment, but he let it pass. She put the car in gear and asked, "How'd you figure it out, anyhow?"

Harry looked out the window as they left the precinct parking lot. "She offered Kepner her apartment keys so he could shower."

"Clara's place is closer," she said. "Rick lives over in Brooklyn."

"Yeah," Harry agreed. "But he didn't ask which key was her house key."

Toni smiled at him. She loved when he surprised her. Then she frowned. She had just lost a bet with Clara, and owed her a dinner. Clara had bet a year ago that Harry would tip to it at some point; Toni had bet against him ever realizing it.

They were quiet on the way back to the office. Toni drove more sedately than usual, not taking as much pleasure in the skidding and sliding of the car on packed snow. She parked and they were inside drinking coffee before either of them spoke.

"It's bugging you," Toni said. "Having to keep everyone on the outside."

"Clara especially," Harry said. "Sal's death is intel she needs. Things on the street are going to get hectic when it comes out. She'll be caught off-guard. And if she finds out we knew and didn't tell her-"

"Don't worry, Harry."

"How can I not?"

"By trusting that we're doing everything we can. When everyone finds out what we did and why, they'll-"

"They won't understand."

She huffed a frustrated breath, hauled the wheel over, and pulled up to the curb. She slammed the car into park and rounded on him, angry but controlled. "Do you remember standing over the body of Rachael Messner?"

He looked out the window. "You know I do."

"Do you?" she asked testily. "Because you may have forgotten who you called for help."

"Yeah, I called Clara because-"

"Because you needed help. And do you remember what she asked you?"

Harry swallowed. "She asked me if I wanted to run. If I wanted her to cook the scene. I told her no."

"Never mind what you told her. What did she ask you again?"

He turned to look at her. "I just said."

"Well say it again."

"Did you not hear me?" Harry asked, piqued.

Toni smiled mirthlessly. "Oh, I sure did. But you didn't, I guess. What did she ask you?"

He exhaled to cover his annoyance. To humor her, he said, "If I wanted her to cook the scene."

Toni waited, saying nothing. Harry cocked his head ever so slightly. "If you've got a point, I'm not getting it.

honey."

She smiled as she always did when he called her by a pet name. "I know. Harry, what is Clara?"

"She's a cop."

Toni waited.

"A detective."

She smiled at him.

Sighing, Harry said, "A good one. A very good one."

"Yes she is. And she was willing to compromise that, to break her faith. For you. Because you needed help. Even if it meant getting suspended."

"If she's lucky," Harry said. "Busted if she wasn't, back down to the streets. If they didn't just fire her outright."

"Her life, the meaning of it, would have been over. But you needed that. She was ready to offer her career up," Toni said. She poked him in the chest with a finger. "For you."

"Yeah, yeah," he groused. "I get it."

"Then explain it to me."

"Sometimes you have to go out on a limb for someone. Sometimes you have to put your ass on the line because that's what's needed," he said.

She patted his cheek. "See? You do know." She put the car into gear and pulled back into the street. A few minutes later they were in front of the office. Inside, Bobby Gold was behind Toni's desk, talking to someone on the phone. They shucked their coats; the office was practically a sauna.

"Any idea how long it would take?" Bobby asked. He listened. "No, no I get it. Thanks. I appreciate it, Gene. I owe you a dinner. Three-course. Later."

He hung up the phone.

"Trouble?" Harry asked.

"Naah. I asked Gene for a favor, that's all," Bobby

said. He didn't elaborate, and they didn't ask.

Harry poured them all coffee and sat. Bobby started to rise, but Toni waved him back down and perched on the edge of Harry's desk instead.

"How you feeling, Bobby?" she asked. "You look better."

He shrugged. His graying curls were sticking up in the back. The couch was comfortable, but his long, lanky frame didn't fit on it very well. "I don't want to crawl under a rock and die," he said. "I wouldn't want to run a marathon, either."

"That's good. I'm glad you're feeling better." Toni sipped her coffee. She cleared her throat and said, "You okay with the other part?"

Harry looked up at Toni with a puzzled expression. Bobby seemed to know what she was asking, though.

"It's not like I remembered," he said, and he looked at the floor. "I mean, it was definitely heroin, but it was maybe five seconds between the shot and the black." He rolled his head back and forth, the muted snaps and pops of his neck sounded like knuckles on glass. "I think I'm okay. I didn't feel the need to go find another fix, and I successfully made it from here to the bathroom and back without stopping to taste-test the whiskey. I think I'm okay."

Toni smiled at him. "Good. Because if you need anything-"

"I know," Bobby said. "Thanks."

They finished the coffee and were discussing what to do about lunch when a car pulled up in front of the office. Rick Kepner got out, left his door open, and bustled into the office. He handed Harry a slip of paper and nodded, hurrying back to his car and driving away.

Harry opened the folded sheet of paper. He read the address. He handed it to Toni, who handed it to Bobby.

They went into the apartment.

Toni and Harry exchanged a silent consensus and went into action. Harry opened his bottom drawer and took out his backup .32. Toni went into the apartment. She rummaged in a chest they stored in the bottom of the wardrobe, came up with a shotgun and two boxes of ammo, and four pairs of handcuffs.

She put them all on the table. She checked the shotgun and her personal weapon. The shotgun was unloaded. Her .38 had five rounds, hammer down on an empty chamber. Bobby and Harry joined her after a moment. Harry set his backup on the table, along with Toni's backup, a .32 colt in an ankle holster.

"So…" Bobby said as he watched them check their arsenal. "What are we doing for lunch? Because it looks like we're invading Guam."

Toni and Harry shared a glance. Harry nodded at her, and Toni said, "I know the answer but I gotta ask, Bobby," she said, racking beanbag shells into the shotgun. "In or out?"

Bobby feigned hurt. "Why, how could you ask such a thing? Have I not given my all for this team, time and time again?"

They stared at him. He said, "That's it. It was two times."

Harry rolled his eyes as Toni snorted laugher.

"Standard boilerplate warning, Gold," Toni said. "Can't guarantee your safety. This is life or death."

"'All that lives must die,'" Bobby quoted.

"Shakespeare," Harry muttered.

Bobby appeared nonplussed. Toni gave Harry a thoughtful look. "Was that a guess?" she asked.

"Hamlet," Harry said. "Act one, scene two. Line… hell if I remember."

He looked up to see both of them gaping at him.

"Had to read it in high school," he said a touch defensively. "I liked it."

"'He who studies old books will always find in them something new, and he who reads new books will always find in them something old.'"

They stared at him in silence.

"Lytton," Bobby muttered. "Doesn't matter."

"Seriously, Bobby," Harry said. "This is worse than going up against the Gambinos."

Bobby shrugged and took the shotgun from Toni. "'The tragedy of life is not that the beautiful die young, but that they grow old and mean. It shall not happen to me,'" Bobby said.

He waited, neither of them spoke.

"Oh come on," he said. "You guys don't know *Chandler?*"

"The beautiful die young, huh?" Toni asked.

"Yeah," Bobby said. "I'm pretty much immortal. Let's do this thing. I got a dinner date."

Toni and Harry exchanged another glance. They looked at Bobby, who said, "I mean... I assume we're eating dinner tonight."

Toni chuckled, and even Harry smiled.

"I thought you meant Sandy," Toni said.

Harry said, "I thought he meant Cherry."

"Are you guys ever serious?" Bobby asked.

"Not if we can help it," Harry and Toni said together. Toni scrounged a duffel from the wardrobe chest and put the shotgun in it. She and Harry slid their .38s into the belt holsters just back of their left hips, a synchronized gesture that unsettled Bobby for no reason he could name. The .32s went on the ankles, Harry's on his right, Toni's on her left.

Bobby watched them preparing, shrugged, and zipped his leather jacket to his chin. He picked up the duffel.

"What's the plan?"

Harry explained what he had in mind. Toni's eyebrows climbed. Bobby whistled.

"Are you sure, Harry?"

"No. But I can't see any other way to get Farrokh out, if he's still alive."

"Cops?" Bobby asked. "Clara?"

"They'll arrest everyone inside. And when they prove who killed Sal, his deal with Kilburn is going to vanish," Harry said.

"Jesus," Bobby said. "You're sure he'll go for it?"

"I don't know. I hope so."

Toni bit her lip. "Harry, Clara's going to find out. If what you think will happen happens, there's no way she won't put it together. Her intel leads to-"

"I know, I know," Harry said with a pained expression. "I'll explain it afterwards. I'm hoping the bonus will make up for it."

"You're still working with Mob guys," Bobby said. "Doesn't that mean this whole thing is dirty?"

Harry heaved a sigh. "That's always a danger. I could get heat for this that puts me back in jail. Accessory, if not present, certainly after the fact. But if I take the hit, Clara stays clean. There's any one of a dozen ways to have found out the location of their warehouse that doesn't lead back to Clara. And no matter what else happens, I'm not letting this get on her. Any of it."

Toni thumper her fist on the table, making them both jump. Her normally genial face was twisted with displeasure. She pointed at Harry with her other hand while thumping the table again.

"DeMarko, I ain't telling you again: it's we."

Harry smiled at her fondly. "We," he amended. "I won't forget again."

In the silence, Bobby asked, "What are our chances?"

Toni and Harry gave each other a long look. That answered it as far as Bobby was concerned, but Harry said, "If they're there, and if we get there in time… maybe forty percent we walk out whole."

"You have no cavalry you can call?" Bobby asked.

"Can't send in the cops. Farrokh, Starr, and Abruzzi go to jail, if they're not killed in a crossfire. Can't send in Hendricks. He'll kill everyone in the room just for being there. We've got no more angels."

Toni made a strange noise, halfway between a laugh and a hiccup. Harry looked at her, and she had a bewildered, puzzled, bemused expression on her face.

"What is it?" Harry asked.

Bobby started to grin. He knew that look.

Toni nibbled at the skin of her lower lip for a second. "I… I have an idea."

Harry's eyebrows rose. "Don't hold out on us, sweetheart," he said. "Give us what you got."

She told them. It didn't take long. When she was done, she looked at Harry almost in fear of what he might say. It was a good plan, an audacious plan, and it told Harry- and Bobby- more about her than she had told anyone in the world.

"What do you think?" she asked in a small voice.

Harry considered it.

"I think it's just about the best idea we've got."

Bobby gave her a thoughtful look. "You play it close to the vest, don't you?"

Defensively, Toni said, "I didn't see that it mattered. I still don't."

"It doesn't," Bobby said. Harry echoed the sentiment.

"It's just something else about you. It doesn't define you," he said.

She grinned. "Thanks."

"You're the one in this room with the best chance of

keeping us all alive," Harry said. "Thank you."

"No problem. I'm gonna go make a phone call," she said. She ran up to the apartment over their office while Bobby and Harry checked the gear. Rather, Bobby watched alertly as Harry explained the care and feeding of a shotgun to him.

"Remember to rack it all the way back. Don't get overexcited. If you short-shuck it, the breech will jam, and then you're screwed," Harry said.

"Got it," Bobby said.

Toni came back, and the look of troubled consternation on her face gave Harry pause. "Everything all right, Toni?" he asked.

She looked up. "Hm? Oh, yeah. It took a little while, but I tracked him down. He's digging into it."

"Timeline?"

"He said by two or so."

Bobby started to say something, but they heard banging on the office door. Toni peeked out, muttered a bewildered "What the fuck?" and went into the office. The men followed her in. Outside the office a thin, dark-haired man of about twenty-five was hammering on the door. He wore a white tee shirt, very tight, jeans, and sneakers. He was shivering violently. Toni hurried over and let him in.

"T-thanks, T-t-toni," he said, teeth chattering.

"What the hell, Chris?" Toni exclaimed. "Harry, get a blanket, would you? Bobby, coffee."

They did as she bade, while Toni led the shivering young man to the couch. Moments later he was enshrouded in two blankets and had his hands wrapped around a mug of steaming coffee.

"Thanks," he said.

"What the hell are you doing out in the snow with no coat?" Toni asked.

Chris shrugged. "It's what I was wearing when they

booked me in. They let me out, they gave me my clothes back."

Harry said, "Why didn't you get a cab?"

Chris gave Harry a sheepish look. "No money," he said.

"Look, Chris... I'm glad you're out, and I owe you for letting me use your car. But now's the worst possible time to take it back," Toni said as she sat beside him. "Let me keep it for a day or two, and it's yours."

Chris gave her a wan smile. "Thanks. For keeping it, I mean. And sure, you can use it. But when you're done, I'm going home. That's why I need it." He gave her a naked, lost look. "I'm done here. I can't take it anymore."

Toni gave him a fond smile and a hug. "I wish you all the best," she said. "Where's home?"

"Arizona. I was born in Phoenix, but my parents live in Flagstaff now."

Toni and Harry exchanged a look. "Uh, Arizona?" Tori asked. "What are you using for gas money?"

Chris stared at the floor. "I haven't gotten that far. Arturo owes me a little, I guess. I was hoping to scrounge some. If I have to, call my parents. Things... things didn't end well for us. That wouldn't be my first choice."

Toni shook her head. "Chris, you can't get to Ohio on one tank. This isn't a great plan."

"What else am I supposed to do, Toni?" Chris snapped. Harry could see the young man was on the edge of tears.

"You talk to us, of course," Toni said.

Chris blinked. "I-I don't need a loan," he said.

Bobby leaned against the desk and grinned. He could guess what happened next.

Toni glanced at Harry, who nodded. She said, "Let me make you an offer for the car. Get you home with some startup cash. It's better than going home broke, and I like the car."

Chris slumped his shoulders, sat back, and said, "I'm not in a position to argue. You've been more than nice to me."

Toni looked at Harry, who was already rooting through the desk. "What do you think, Harry? Two? Three?"

"Better make it four," Harry said. "We can take it out of Hendrick's deposit. Least it's good for something."

"Four hundred?" Chris asked. "I…I paid a grand for that car, Toni."

"No," she said, slipping an arm around his shoulders and squeezing him, "Four thousand."

Chris didn't want to believe her, he looked warily at Harry as though expecting a joke, but Harry had a roll of bills in his hand. He tossed it to Toni, who offered it to Chris.

"Lemme buy your car. Then we'll use it to take you wherever you want to go; airport, bus station, wherever. We'll get you home in style," she said.

He reached a hand out, Bobby saw it shaking. *She can't help herself,* he thought. *Her life should have made her tough. Should have beat the nice out of her. But she's just as sweet as pie.*

He remembered all the things he'd seen Toni do and shuddered.

Nice as pie until it's time to not *be nice. And when it's over, it's back to nice. How does she do that? It seems effortless.* He could hear her words in his head when he told her about Nell. "Anything you need. Anything we can do. You name it, it's yours, Bobby."

Chris Steudel's eyes welled with tears. "Toni…"

She shook her head. "Don't worry about it, Chris. The registration's in the glove box?"

"Y-yes," he whispered. He looked up at Harry, who was merely smiling at the young man. "Thank you."

"Any time," he said.

Toni jogged out to the car, fished through some notes, napkins, and assorted debris, and came up with the crumpled pink slip for Chris's '70 Chevelle. She came back into the office shivering. She and Chris filled it out, they both signed it, and Toni hugged him. "Thank you," she said seriously. "This is my first car."

Sitting back down on the sofa, Chris asked, "You never had a car?"

"Couldn't drive until a couple months ago. Never learned. And until I hooked up with him," she jerked a thumb at Harry, "I never had to tote bodies around. Can't drag a skiptrace through the subway."

"You tried," Bobby reminded her.

"Yeah, till you caused a scene and got the cops involved," she said with a smile.

"I caused a scene? You shot a car."

Harry's eyes snapped to Toni, who blushed. "I thought it was yours," she told Bobby with more than a note of defensiveness in her voice.

"That makes it better?" he asked.

"Bobby… shut up," Toni said.

He sketched her a salute, acknowledging the point he'd scored.

"I hate to break up happy fun time," Harry said, "But we've got other people to save today."

Toni nodded. "Right." She went to collect the duffel.

Bobby stood up. Harry pulled on his suit jacket, then pulled on his gray overcoat. Toni came back with the duffel of ammo and the shotgun, handed it to Bobbi, and put her own suit coat on. Chris watched them with growing alarm. He had seen the guns on Toni's and Harry's belts.

"Uh…" he hesitated. "What's going on?"

"Don't worry about it. But hey, do us a favor?"

"Sure, yeah," Chris said, eagerness crowding into his

voice.

Jesus, Bobby thought. *All of ten seconds, and they made another ally.* He looked at Harry. Sandy Redmay had been right about him. Harry DeMarko exuded a kind of calm and confidence that caused people to sit up straighter, smile wider, and go further than they would have under any other circumstances.

"Answer the phone?" Harry asked. "Write anything important down. There's some food in the back, and we got coffee out here. You get tired or anything, curl up on the couch so you hear the phone."

"Can do," Chris said.

"We'll be back," Harry said. "No idea when."

"What do I do if someone needs to get ahold of you?" Chris asked. "Where you going?"

Harry, Toni, and Bobby exchanged a look.

"Better you not know," Toni said. "Safer."

Chris's eyes became wide when Toni spoke.

His voice a half-whisper, Chris asked. "Are you- I mean… are you going to be okay?"

Harry and Toni exchanged another dark look.

"'There is no such thing as death,'" Bobby Gold quoted. "'though there be a thing called change.'"

Silence filled the office as each of them looked at Bobby. Chris looked puzzled, Toni and Harry were both raising one eyebrow, waiting.

"Uh… Haggard," Bobby said sheepishly. "Doesn't matter."

They followed Toni to the car. As he pulled the door closed, he said, "Lock this." Chris got up and locked the door behind them. He watched them pull away, shaking his head.

Whatever they're doing, I don't want to know, he thought. I'm done with this city. Everyone's nuts.

They drove up toward Bleecker, and Toni hung a right,

then a left on Bowery. After a few blocks, Harry said, "Next payphone, pull over."

Another block passed before they saw one. Toni wedged the Chevelle sideways between a tow truck and a VW Bug. Harry got out and fished in his pockets for quarters.

The phone rang four times before a voice answered, "Who's this?"

"Hendrick," Harry said. "Get him."

"I don't think-"

"Tell him I found his carpenter," Harry said impatiently.

"Er... one moment."

A thunk as the phone hit the counter. A moment later, Hendrick's voice came up the line. "Who's this?"

"Stupid question," Harry said.

"Whatcha got?"

"Not on this line."

Hendrick spoke aside for a second. "Try this one," he said. He gave Harry a number.

"Got it. Five minutes," Harry said, and hung up. He waited, counting patiently. At four and a half, he dialed the number Hendrick had recited.

"DeMarko," Hendrick said. "I've been waiting to hear from you. I'm losing my patience. Higgins said you found him?"

Harry said, "Heroin, Hendrick. It's all about the heroin. The 68s want their connection. My guess is they tried reasoning with Sal. When the official channels didn't work, they sent a guy."

Harry could practically hear Hendrick's teeth grinding as he growled, "So where are the right now?"

"There's an old warehouse in Alphabet City," Harry said, revealing what Clara's note had told him. "It's been abandoned for a couple years, as I understand it. The 68s are using it for storage."

"They're fucking dead," Hendrick ground out.

"Hold up there, Hendrick," Harry said. Now came the tricky part. "They've grabbed a neighborhood kid, a friend of mine. I want to go in and get him before you and your pals land on them. They're going to be twitchy is my guess. There aren't but one or two patched members in town now. The rest are down south somewhere. It's the prospects and hopefuls that did this. They want to earn their way in. Sal's their ticket."

"DeMarko-"

"No, listen to me, Hendrick. They pressured the kid into selling and muling. He's in deep. He's here illegally. A good kid, but the nimrods running the show leveraged his legal status to get him dealing in my neighborhood."

Hendrick chuckled. "And he came to you."

"And he came to me. I've been working it for a couple weeks. Then the thing with Sal happened, and I realized how bad it was getting. I'm trying to pull him out, get him clear. He's an innocent. Wrong place, wrong time," Harry said.

The recording of an operator broke in. "To continue your call, please insert-"

Harry had already dropped the change into the slot.

"Look, I understand, but I'm not taking any chances," Hendrick said. "Tell me where they are."

"Nope."

"What?" Hendrick's voice was clotted with rage.

"I said no. Not until you agree to my terms."

"Listen to me you little bitch," Hendrick snarled. "I don't-"

Harry hung up.

He counted to ten and dropped some more dimes into the slot, dialed the number again.

One ring and Hendrick picked up. "Don't you fucking

hang up on me," he practically bellowed. "I will find you-"

Harry hung up. His change rattled into the box, and he scooped it out. He dropped it back in and dialed.

When Hendrick picked up again after two rings, he sounded controlled, almost.

"Hendrick, you know I respect you," Harry said carefully. "But he came to me before you did, and I *gave him my word* I'd help."

Hendrick was silent, but Harry could hear his harsh breathing coming done the line. Harry held his own breath.

"I can respect that," Hendrick said. "And you *did* crack it. You got proof, right?"

Harry smiled. "Proof? Hell, I *know* who killed Sal. He told me himself."

Thunderous silence as Hendrick stopped puffing into the handset.

"You're not fucking with me, are you, DeMarko?"

"Hendrick, if it makes you feel better to threaten me, go ahead. You're the client. My job is to find what you tell me to find, uncover what you tell me to uncover, and get the results you want. You paid me; I work for you. So threaten me if you want. But you're wasting time." Harry took a deep breath. He was on the line- *scratch that*, he thought. *We're all on the line now*.

"Okay. Okay. Tell me what you need. Guys? Guns?"

"Appreciate it. But what I need is for you to be punctual."

"Okay."

Harry asked, "What time is it now?"

Hendrick said, "Straight-up one o'clock."

"Okay. It's gonna take us about twenty or thirty minutes to get there. Then we need to scout. If they were real 68s, the place would be locked the hell down. I'm betting on it being just a couple guys and they're not real heavyweights. So… figure on door-kicking at… let's call it two o'clock sharp," Harry said.

"Okay. I can do that. It'll give me time to rally bodies."

"You do that. I have a feeling I may need the help."

Hendrick chuckled. "When do you not?"

Harry grinned unexpectedly. He laughed and said, "True enough. Hendrick… don't jump the gun. I'm going out on a limb. I could have called you from the place, but I wanted to coordinate with you first. Okay? I'm showing you all the trust I got. I need you to do as you say. It's me and Toni's necks if you show up late, and it's the kid's life if you get cute and bust in early."

A long pause, and then Hendrick said, "I'll do it your way. As long as when the dust settles, I get to have a long chat with the guy that took a hammer to Sal."

Harry took a deep breath and lied, "I guarantee it."

"Okay. Two o'clock," Hendrick agreed. "We land with both feet. Where?"

Harry let out the breath. "There's an abandoned warehouse up in Alphabet city. The corner of East 12th and Avenue D. From what I understand, the 68s use it for storage. They don't receive or manufacture, so the cops leave it alone."

"How do you know that?"

"Please," Harry said. "Who are you talking to?"

Again, Hendrick chuckled. "Okay, okay. Two o'clock. And you better be right. Because you'll be there too. With me and my guys and a whole lotta guns. One way or another, someone's going down."

Harry swallowed. He had gambled everything on this stupid, insane plan. But that was his usual approach to everything. "Understood. And Hendrick?"

"Yeah?"

"Don't be late."

"Two o'clock straight up. East 12th and Avenue D. Who owns it?"

Harry said, "No idea. But the place is called Angel Street Imports."

Harry hung up. He blew on his hands and collected the nickel that popped out of the change slot. In the car he held his hands up to the heater vent and said, "It's done."

They had discussed the plan in detail after Clara's intelligence had arrived. Harry knew that, if the ATF and DEA were on the 68s, they could very well have the warehouse under watch. But it was a chance they'd have to take. Now for part two.

They found the warehouse, tucked away in the back streets near the East River. They parked a couple of blocks away to watch. There didn't appear to be anyone outside as guard, and there were no windows in the corrugated sides. Harry walked around two blocks, out of sight of the warehouse. It was one forty, according to the speaking clock. Toni gave him a questioning look. He nodded. "Yeah, it's time."

He dropped more change into the phone and dialed a number he knew by heart.

"Bowdler," the crisp answer came.

"Clara," Harry said.

"Hey, Harry," she said. She sounded like she was in a good mood.

"Detective."

"What's up?" Clara asked, voice devoid of cheer. He'd told her with a single word it was a business call, and she picked up on it.

"Do yourself a favor," he said. "Take a couple units to check on a guy."

"What guy? And why?"

"Sally D'Amico," Harry said. "And the why will make itself known."

"What is this?"

"An anonymous tip," Harry said, "from a concerned

citizen. Isn't that what you write? That's what I always wrote to protect my sources."

"Why are you tipping me off?"

"Because you deserve to know. Believe me. You're going to want to know before it goes wide."

Silence. Then: "Where?"

Harry gave her Sal's home address.

"Okay," Clara said. "I'll send some guys."

"No," Harry said, "you better ride along. It would be better if you were… if you were first on the scene."

In a dangerously quiet voice, Clara asked, "Is this like the Mercer case?"

"Nope. Nothing to do with me," Harry said. "Scout's honor."

More silence. He heard a pencil scratching in the background. "Then how do you know?"

"Officially? I don't."

"Unofficially?"

"I'll- *we'll*- take you out to dinner and explain."

Toni grinned at him.

"Should I expect dessert?"

"Bring handcuffs, just in case you don't buy the story."

He heard a soft thump, and could picture Clara leaning her head on the hand connected to the elbow she had just plunked down on the desk in resignation. "Jesus Christ, Harry-"

"I'll explain later. But you better hurry. I don't have any information from today; my intel is at least sixteen hours old."

Toni frowned at him, started to speak, but he held up a finger.

"All right. We're rolling. If you're in the vicinity, I'll have to haul you in, Mr. Anonymous," Clara told him.

"Not even on the same island, Fatso. Promise," Harry said.

"Okay. Be in touch."

She hung up.

"Harry-"

He held up the same finger. "One minute."

He dropped more change, dialed another number. After five or six rings, Cheddar picked up the phone at Sal's place.

"Yeah?"

"It's me," Harry said.

"What's up? Hendrick just called, told me to get Higgins and meet him at the club."

"Did you wipe everything down?"

"Best we could. Bill and I been sitting at the kitchen table playing poker. We touched the cards, that all."

"You'd better hope so," Harry said. "I just heard there's heat coming."

"Heat?"

"Cops," Harry said. "Someone tipped 'em off. Clear out."

"Shit," Cheddar said. Then: "*Shit!*"

Harry hung up the phone. He raised his eyebrows and Toni smiled.

"You knew what I was thinking."

"Great minds," Harry said. He bent down and kissed her. She leaned against him and they shared a moment of respite and affection. And then it passed.

When they parted, she found herself looking into those melancholy, remote eyes she knew so well. What she didn't know is that Harry was startled to see she had the same look in her own eyes.

"Ready?" she asked.

"As I'll ever be," he said.

"Let's go get him."

Toni led him to the car, where Bobby waited in the relative comfort of the back seat. "It's time. Come on,"

Harry said.

Bobby struggled out of the back seat as Harry tilted his seat forward. Bobby painted a comical figure trying to extricate himself from the car. He managed to get out, and tugged the duffel from the back seat.

They walked, single-file, keeping close to the buildings as they approached their target. The warehouse up close was faded and flaking white paint over bare rusting corrugated sheet metal. The front of the warehouse had two tractor-trailer-sized ramp-down loading bays with roll-up doors and no windows. Across the front of the building, centered over the two loading bays, was a block of red paint easily fifty feet long and twenty high that read 'Angel Street Imports, ltd.' There was a smaller entrance door on the left side of the building face.

Harry peered around the edge of the building. He leaned back. "There's two cars out front. Both empty," he reported. "Let's see if there's a back way."

They hurried down the alley between the warehouses, slowing at the corner. Harry again peeked out. "Nothing," he muttered.

They crossed the back of the building and followed the other alley to the front. After yet another peek, Harry said, "Okay. This is going to be interesting."

"What?" Toni asked.

"We're gonna have to go in the front door."

"Is that smart?" Bobby asked, eyes wide.

"It's what we got, unless you have a better idea," Harry said.

Bobby shrugged. "It's your game, boss, I'm just batting clean-up."

"How do we do it, Harry?" Toni asked. "Guns up? You go left, I go right?"

Harry thought about it. "I don't think so. Let's try asking nicely for a change."

Before Toni or Bobby could stop him, he walked to the door, opened it, and went inside. Toni said, "Ask nicely, he says."

Bobby nodded. He unzipped the duffel and put his hand on the shotgun's grip. "Let's go ask nicely."

"After you, Cisco," she said with a gesture.

"Don't mind if I do, Pancho," Bobby said, and he followed Harry through the door with Toni on his heels.

CHAPTER TWENTY-NINE

He heard voices before he saw anyone. Toni and Bobby rushed in behind him. He hadn't drawn his weapon. He held up a hand. They could hear a jumble of arguing voices as well as sobbing in the distance.

They formed up on Harry's shoulders, Toni on his left, Bobby on his right. The warehouse was full of empty shelves in a grid pattern, wide-open spaces for shifting cargo to and from trailers, a machine shop toward the left rear and a huge office enclosure toward the back, surrounded by walls that went only halfway to the ceiling. The walls were mostly glass, probably had once had blinds on the inside, but were now bare.

Harry looked around before leading them toward the enclosure. His amazement at there being no door guards or lookouts increased as they got within ten feet of the office enclosure before anyone noticed them. To Harry's complete lack of surprise, he recognized three of the men in the office. Cad, along with his buddies Ham and Def had been looking for Farrokh. There were three other people with them. They were all scruffy-looking, and none of them looked older than twenty-five. None of them was wearing a vest that would indicate they were fully-patched members of the 68s MC. Ham glanced up and yelled, pointing. Cad turned to look and gave a start of surprise. Harry grinned and waved. They stared as Harry led Toni and Bobbi to the doorway of the makeshift office. The room held only a couple of old chairs and a rickety table off to one side.

"What the hell do you want?" Cad barked. Harry tried not to smile. He was obviously trying hard to look tough, but Harry could see he was fraying around the edges.

"I'm looking for someone," Harry said. "Looks like I found someone."

A glint of recognition in Cad's eyes, and he glowered. "You're that smartass from the other night."

"I am indeed."

Cad's buddies formed up on Cad's shoulders, spreading out. "What are you doing here, man?" Cad asked. "You don't belong here."

"You've got something of mine, and I want it back," Harry said.

"That so?"

"That's so. Good-looking kid about twenty-two. Dark skin, kinda stringy. You know who I mean."

Cad sneered. "You thought you were being cute, didn't you? Shining me on, playing dumb. Didn't know him, huh?"

"Didn't know you. And there was no reason in the world to give you anything, let alone a friend," Harry said.

"You and your asshole friends need to leave," Cad said. As if by prearranged signal, the crowd around the younger man began to produce knives and guns from their belts. Harry didn't move, and neither did Bobby or Toni.

"Very shrewd," Harry said. "Now what?"

"Now you leave or we put you down," Cad said. "Get out."

"No."

Cad blinked. "What?"

"I said no. But lemme ask you this: did your club give you permission to make a move on Gambino turf? And did you think it would go unanswered?"

Before Cad could speak, Harry pulled his .38 with one hand and seized Cad by the throat with the other. He pressed his gun against Cad's temple. Behind him, Harry knew Toni had just drawn her gun and Bobby had pulled the shotgun from the duffel. Staring at the crowd behind

Cad, Harry growled, "Wanna see what his last thought is? No? Then back up."

Hesitantly, they looked at one another. Harry dug the barrel of his pistol into Cad's head, making him yelp.

"I said back up. Son, you better reason with your idiot friends before I air out your skull."

Cad stared at Harry with wide eyes and said, "Back up! You hear me? Back up!"

"Into the office. We're gonna have a little chat." Harry spun Cad around and pressed the gun to the back of his head. Pushing Cad ahead of him, Harry steered him in the direction of the office. Cad's friends fled before him, frowning and muttering. Cad said, bravado seasoning his words, "Man, you screwed up. Stepping on the 68s is gonna be the last thing you-"

"Shut up."

He pushed Cad into the office ahead of him. Cad and his crew turned to face the trio of intruders. "Man, I don't know-"

He broke off as Harry looked down at the floor. The warehouse office held a few folding chairs, a cheap folding table laden with some food and bottles of beer, and three bodies, hogtied and gagged on the floor. The sobbing Harry had heard was coming from Farrokh. The young man was shuddering and gagging against the bandana tied in his mouth, and his eyes were bloodshot and terrified. The turban had been knocked from his head, and his long, wiry black hair had fallen from its plait to cascade around his shoulders.

Beside him lay Johnny Abruzzi, his face swollen and bruised, but his eyes blazed with defiant fury.

Beside Johnny lay Starr, who didn't look hurt, but was unconscious.

Harry's eyes became remote and his vision took on a crisp, clear aspect. His calmness betrayed his anger to Toni and Bobby.

He looked up from the three figures on the floor and directly at Cad. "You're lucky they're still alive."

Cad gave a nervous chuckle. "*I'm lucky?*"

"Somewhat lucky. If you'd hurt them, you'd be bleeding out right now," Harry told him. Still pointing the gun at Cad, Harry crossed the office to stand on the far side. Bobby and Toni spread out a little more for better cover. Toni made sure her field of fire didn't include Harry. The shotgun held beanbag rounds, so she wasn't worried about Bobby.

Cad and his friends focused on Harry. Cad said, "You get the hell out of here, and you'll be the lucky one, old man. You beat it now and I won't sic the club on you."

Harry lowered his gun, to everyone's surprise. He said, "What are my guarantees?"

Toni and Bobby exchanged a look.

"You don't get no guarantees," Cad said, confidence growing as Harry's gun arm relaxed. "You get out, and I'll consider it."

Harry stared at the floor, brow furrowed in thought. He said, without looking up, "Hey, Toni?"

"Yes, Harry?"

He looked at her. "Do I look old to you?"

She grinned at him. "Hell no. You're in your prime."

"What I thought," he said. He looked at Cad. "Here's the counter-offer. I walk out of here with my friends, including Farrokh, my sister-in-law, and her husband."

Toni blinked. Abruzzi craned his head up to stare at Harry.

"You let me do that, and I'll keep what I know to myself."

Cad and his pals exchanged amused glances. While their attention was away from him, his eyes flickered to Toni, and over her shoulder. They were back on Cad's grinning face before he looked back.

"What the hell do you think you know, man?" Cad asked. "You got shit."

"Oh," Harry mused, "I know more than you think I do. I know you're pushing heroin into the bowery. I know it started recently, since the fall. I know you're pushing up on the Gambino territory and against their rules without your boss's say-so."

"Yeah?" Cad said. "That what you think you know?"

"I know two other things," Harry said. Out of the corner of his eye he saw movement near the door of the warehouse.

"And they are?"

"Well," Harry said, "I know you killed Sal D'Amico."

Startled silence filled the room as Cad and his friends exchanged another look.

"Oh yeah?" Cad asked. His voice wavered a little, but steadied as he continued. "And the other thing?"

"You didn't have the go-ahead from the 68s to do it. You're all on your own," Harry said. He raised his gun a little, clicked the safety on, and pulled his coat away from his side. He holstered the gun. Uneasily, Cad and his buddies exchanged yet another worried glance. Emboldened, Cad pulled a knife from a sheath at his waist. It was a Marine-style K-Bar, Harry saw. He was familiar with the weapon. His friend Porter Rockwell had carried one just like it.

"You've used up all your chances," Cad said. "You have no idea what you're talking about."

"So I'm wrong?" Harry asked. "About what part?"

"All of it."

"So you *do* have permission to push smack on my streets?"

"Shut up," Cad said.

"So you *do* have permission from your club to do it?"

"I said-"

"Did you get permission to start a war between the Gambinos and the 68s by whacking out Sal D'Amico?"

"I said," Cad snarled, pointing the knife at Harry, "to shut up."

"Let him talk," said a voice from the dimness beyond the office. "I'm just getting interested."

Harry ducked his head in greeting. "Good timing. I was running out of stalling tactics."

Everyone except Harry, Toni, and Bobby turned toward the doorway. Hendrick, Cheddar, and two other men approached. Toni and Bobby joined Harry standing over the three tied figures. Toni holstered her weapon and checked Starr's pulse.

"She's still alive, Harry."

"Good," he said. When she moved to take their gags off, Harry told her, "Don't. Not yet."

She nodded and remained crouched by her sister. Bobby loomed over her like a guardian angel, shotgun at the ready.

Cad, eyes wide, started to speak. Hendrick pistol-whipped him, a high curving blow that caught Cad across the nose, snapping the cartilage. Cad screeched and dropped to the concrete, clutching his broken nose in both hands.

Hendrick kicked him hard enough to lift him into the air and drop him a few feet away. Cad gagged, and curled into a ball.

Cheddar pointed an automatic at Cad's coterie. "Drop the gear. Against the wall."

The half-dozen men dropped their weapons on the folding table and shuffled backward against the far wall of the office, hands up. Hendrick kicked Cad again, this time in the knee. His howl of pain drowned out Harry, who had to wait for it to subside before attempting to speak.

"Hendrick," he began, but the huge man cut him off.

"Get out, DeMarko. You don't want to be part of this."

Harry glanced at the huddled crowd of wanna-be biker thugs and sighed. "Have to be, though."

Hendrick turned his rage-filled eyes on Harry. "We're even. You found 'em. And I'm gonna do what I said I was gonna do, and you're not going to stop me."

Harry raised both hands placatingly. "Hendrick, I'm not trying to stop you. But I need to speak to you before you make a mistake."

"What mistake?"

"Killing the prospects of a biker gang," Harry said. "That's gonna cause ripples."

"So what?" Hendrick snapped. "They started it, shoving the smack into our territory-"

"Yes, and that is absolutely true," Harry said, trying to keep his voice low and reasonable. This was the most delicate part of their plan, and it involved being absolutely precise. His goal was to keep himself and his people alive. To that end, he had to feed the idiots to Hendrick. But he couldn't do that, because he knew what kind of trouble it would stir up. "But I would like you to wait."

Hendrick was practically vibrating with repressed rage. He took a step toward Harry and raised his pistol. "You have five seconds to explain before I stop being happy with your work and start being angry at your mouth."

"If a rival gang wiped out a bunch of your connected guys, no made guys, just the connected bottom-feeders, what would you do?" Harry asked.

Hendrick spat the words at him. "Level their fucking houses and piss on the ashes," he snarled.

"That's what you're about to do," Harry said. He pointed at the prospects. "They're the connected guys. They're the 68s connected guys."

Hendrick rolled his eyes toward the crowd.

"That one, right there," Harry said, pointing at Cad, "is the one who masterminded this whole thing. He's behind the heroin and Sal."

Hendrick quivered at the name.

"But Hendrick, are you sure you want to start a war? The 68s won't care who started what. They'll be obligated to answer the statement with like-minded statements. They'll put your guys down, you'll put their guys down, and no one wins," Harry said.

"You telling me he doesn't deserve to die?"

He glanced down at the three still, bound figures. "Nope," he said. "I'm just saying you can't kill them. Not yet, at least."

Hendrick squeezed the gun until his fist shook. Harry wondered if Hendrick could explode the bullets through squeezing them. He looked up, over Hendrick's shoulder, and his heart hammered a little faster. Hope surged over him, a giddy, welcome jolt of adrenaline.

"Why not?" Hendrick all but bellowed.

"Because," said a voice from behind all of them, ' a man should have a chance to shoot his own dog."

CHAPTER THIRTY

Harry and his friends froze.

From the office they could hear Hendrick's low growling, and Cad's screech: "We didn't make the hit! I swear!"

Harry closed his eyes. There were footsteps now, approaching them. Harry turned and looked over his shoulder. Crow's men, Hendrick's men, and Cheddar were all hurrying toward them. Harry debated for an instant, but decided against it. "Shit," he muttered.

"Harry?" Toni asked.

"We almost made it," he said to her. "Ten goddamned feet." He put up his hands as Crow's enforcers flanked them.

"Maybe don't run off just yet," The one on the left said. He had a long dark ponytail of gray and brown hair, and his eyes were feral.

"Yeah," the other one said. "Stick around." The other one was bald, except for a patch of scruff at the peak of his forehead.

"Come on," the first one said, waving his pistol. "Let's go have a chat."

Single file they walked back to the office. Cad's mouth was bloody, and Toni saw that he was missing a tooth. Hendrick was examining his fist. He plucked a piece of enamel out of his knuckle and tossed it aside.

"Explain," Hendrick snarled.

Sighing, Harry said, "Nothing to explain. Farrokh was blackmailed into dealing for them, then muling. Finally, they put him up to the kill. He didn't want to, but he did. They threatened to kill his family."

Hendrick stared at Farrokh, who shied away from

Hendrick's glare.

"DeMarko," he breathed, "you *knew* about it?"

Harry said nothing.

"How long?"

Harry said nothing.

"How fucking long?" Hendrick barked.

Harry shrugged. "Couple of days."

Hendrick grabbed Harry by his shirt and dragged him close. He put his face close enough that their noses practically touched, and whispered, "You're a dead man."

The sound of a gun being cocked broke the spell. Toni leveled her pistol at Hendrick. "You first, big guy," she said through clenched teeth.

"You better put me down with the first shot," Hendrick promised. "You won't get a second chance."

Crow watched the exchange with a bemused look on his face. He said, "You might have forgotten, but the fact is, they're under my wing," Crow said.

"What are you talking about?" Hendrick snapped.

"The women are daughters of a close friend of mine," Crow said. "They and their men are under my protection. I can't let you kill 'em."

Hendrick struggled for control. His eyes went to Farrokh. "What about him?"

Crow scratched his cheek. "I haven't made up my mind if he's a part of that deal."

Hendrick shot a glare over his shoulder. "Better make up your mind quick."

"The kid's innocent," Johnny said.

More silence as Abruzzi's words registered. Hendrick and Harry and Crow all stared at him.

He shrugged, winced at the flash of pain from his stitches, and said, "*I'm* the one who killed Sal."

"Why the mighty fuck did you do that?" Crow asked.

Abruzzi turned his eyes to Crow and said, "I'm with

the Outfit."

Crow's eyes flicked from Abruzzi to Hendrick and back. "Chicago?" he asked.

"That's right."

Farrokh stared at Abruzzi. He said, "No! You cannot do this!"

He turned to Hendrick. "I killed him! *I* killed the man! Not him!" The young man's eyes went to the huddle of prospects. "They made me and I did it so they would not hurt my uncle!"

Abruzzi snorted. "Sure you did."

"You disagree?" Crow asked.

"I straight-up call him a liar, man," Abruzzi said. "Whatever they did to make the kid go to that house that night, he was terrified and hesitant. I got there first and ran into him as I was coming out. Sal was already dead when he got there. I guess your guys here threatened him with something heavy if he failed. That's why he tried to take credit for it; to keep them away from his uncle or whoever."

Harry stared at Abruzzi with a thoughtful frown. Hendrick noted this, and narrowed his eyes. He said to Crow, "Lemme borrow the kid for a second. I want to ask him some questions."

Crow nodded. "Long as you don't kill him yet."

"No problem." Hendrick pointed his gun at Farrokh. "Come with me."

Farrokh shook harder, but nodded his head jerkily. He walked out of the office with Hendrick behind him.

Harry watched them go. To Abruzzi he said, "What are you doing?"

"What's right," Abruzzi said over his shoulder.

"Why start now?" Toni asked.

He had the self-awareness to look abashed. "Look, what I did, it ain't personal. It's just a job."

Crow stared at him. "*Chicago* wanted him dead?"

Abruzzi nodded.

"Why?"

"Beats me," Abruzzi said in a bored voice. "You know how it is; they don't tell you if you don't need to know, and you don't ask. He was just a name to me."

Hendrick came back, pushing the terrified Farrokh ahead of him. He pointed at Abruzzi. "Your turn."

"Sure thing," he said, and joined Hendrick. They walked into the depths of the warehouse.

Farrokh stood between Harry and Toni. He was still shaking, eyes on the floor. His hair spilled around his face like a curtain.

Hendrick and Abruzzi came back. Hendrick shoved the man hard enough toward the door that, if he hadn't caught the edge of the doorjamb he would have fallen headlong. He stumbled back to his place next to Bobby Gold.

Crow looked over at Hendrick. "Well?"

Harry closed his eyes.

Hendrick said, "He was telling the truth."

"Which one?" asked Crow.

"That one," Hendrick said. Harry opened his eyes to find Hendrick pointing his gun at Abruzzi. He and Tori gave each other a puzzled look.

"What?" Harry asked, confused. "He did?"

"You lied to me, DeMarko," Hendrick chided. "But I get it. You really thought the kid did it."

Crow asked, "How do you know?"

"The kid got everything wrong about Sal's murder. But him?" Hendrick said, still aiming at Abruzzi's nose, "he knew everything. The layout of the house, the robe Sal was wearing. Everything."

Harry stared in shock at Abruzzi, who gave Hendrick an even look, his eyes on the barrel of Hendrick's gun.

"So what now?" Crow asked.

"Now? Now I find a sledgehammer and show him how I feel about what he did."

Crow cleared his throat. "I can't let you do that."

Hendrick turned to the biker, whose thumbs were still hooked in his pockets. "What're you talking about?"

"I can't let you kill him. He's protected."

"He killed my uncle!"

"I know he did. But I'm against it here. I said it's a favor to a friend, keeping them alive."

"I don't give two shits about your favor!"

Crow held up his hands. "I know. But you should, considering who asked."

"I have had as much of this shit as I'm going to," Hendrick said. "I'm killing him."

"You do that, and every MC in the country, every MC in the Collective, is gonna turn up here asking why," Crow said quietly.

Hendrick faltered. "What?"

"Every single one of them. The 68s, both chapters. The Reapers, *every* chapter. The Tacoma Guns. The Sun Devils. The Bastard Riders. All of them. Every club we have is going to come rain down hell," Crow said. Hendrick turned to him, face slack with surprise.

"Why?"

"Because it is what it is," Crow said. "You gonna risk an all-out war with every outlaw club in this country?"

Hendrick glanced at Abruzzi. Crow gave subtle hand signals to his men. They each pointed their guns at Hendrick.

Hendrick told Crow, "You turn on the Gambinos, they'll call in markers from every other Family. You'll be taking us *all* on."

Instead of acknowledging the threat, Crow said, "You know, if this one hadn't been sent after your uncle, Sal would *still* be dead. It looks like a coincidence they both got there when they did. If it wasn't him, it would have been the errand-boy. We wouldn't know the whole story. Most of the 68s are down south. I stayed here to handle the day-to-day and keep an eye on some investments. These prospects fucked everything into a cocked hat. They didn't ask permission, they didn't ask for advice. It would have been a bold move, I'll admit. Stupid and counterproductive, but bold. I know Cad; I sponsored him. He's dumb as a rock, but he's got guts."

Cad brightened a little, but it didn't last.

"Problem is, his guts made him write a check we wouldn't have been interested in cashing. Even leaving Chicago out of the equation, we'd still be in the same spot, dealing with the same shit, if it wasn't for your detective and his crew."

Toni smiled a little. Harry watched everything. Bobby was staring down at the woman in his arms. She made a soft noise and her eyes fluttered, but she didn't wake.

Hendrick's lip rose and fell. Harry thought he sounded remarkably calm given the situation. "So what?"

"So what? So what is… maybe in this particular matter I don't need to shoot my own dog."

Hendrick, eyes still pinned on Abruzzi, didn't respond right away. Then, with effort they could see, he turned away from Abruzzi.

"Consider it doing *me* a favor," Crow said. "Saves me the trouble of having to explain why we're all of a sudden beefing with one of the most powerful Families in New York. Consider it payment in full for a stupid mistake. Consider it a goodwill gesture. Whatever you want. Them for him."

Hendrick licked his lips. "I just let him *walk*?"

Harry held up a finger. "Hendrick, if Chicago sent someone for Sal, isn't that business?"

"So?"

"So it's just business. It's not personal. He's not a villain. He's a tool."

Abruzzi spoke up. "I'm sorry it went down how it did," he said. He sounded abashed. "It was supposed to be quick and clean. Two in the head. I didn't go in there with a hammer, you know. I'm a professional. But the reason it went so hard is because he fought like a banshee to the end. He was one hell of a scrapper, old as he was. I got lucky or it would have been me on that floor."

Hendrick closed his eyes. Cheddar watched him nervously. Hendrick exhaled and stared at the floor. "Get out, DeMarko," his voice a whisper so soft it could have been the wind. "All of you. Get out. And you-"

He pointed at Abruzzi without looking up from the floor.

"If you ever set foot in New York again, nothing on earth will save you."

Abruzzi nodded. "Understood. Thank you."

"We're in your debt," Harry said to Crow.

"No, you're not." He looked at Toni. "'Shine is."

"You know who he is," she said, raising her chin. "You know it's as good as an edict from God himself."

"That's why you're still alive," Crow said. "Now vanish."

They wasted no time in hurrying to the door. The last thing they heard was Hendrick asking, "Who's got the hammer?"

That and a faint scream as they closed the door behind them.

CHAPTER THIRTY-ONE

Harry and his friends froze.

From the office they could hear Hendrick's low growling, and Cad's screech: "We didn't make the hit! I swear!"

Harry closed his eyes. There were footsteps now, approaching them. Harry turned and looked over his shoulder. Crow's men, Hendrick's men, and Cheddar were all hurrying toward them. Harry debated for an instant, but decided against it. "Shit," he muttered.

"Harry?" Toni asked.

"We almost made it," he said to her. "Ten goddamned feet." He put up his hands as Crow's enforcers flanked them.

"Maybe don't run off just yet," The one on the left said. He had a long dark ponytail of gray and brown hair, and his eyes were feral.

"Yeah," the other one said. "Stick around." The other one was bald, except for a patch of scruff at the peak of his forehead.

"Come on," the first one said, waving his pistol. "Let's go have a chat."

Single file they walked back to the office. Cad's mouth was bloody, and Toni saw that he was missing a tooth. Hendrick was examining his fist. He plucked a piece of enamel out of his knuckle and tossed it aside.

"Explain," Hendrick snarled.

Sighing, Harry said, "Nothing to explain. Farrokh was blackmailed into dealing for them, then muling. Finally, they put him up to the kill. He didn't want to, but he did. They threatened to kill his family."

Hendrick stared at Farrokh, who shied away from

Hendrick's glare.

"DeMarko," he breathed, "you *knew* about it?"

Harry said nothing.

"How long?"

Harry said nothing.

"How fucking long?" Hendrick barked.

Harry shrugged. "Couple of days."

Hendrick grabbed Harry by his shirt and dragged him close. He put his face close enough that their noses practically touched, and whispered, "You're a dead man."

The sound of a gun being cocked broke the spell. Toni leveled her pistol at Hendrick. "You first, big guy," she said through clenched teeth.

"You better put me down with the first shot," Hendrick promised. "You won't get a second chance."

Crow watched the exchange with a bemused look on his face. He said, "You might have forgotten, but the fact is, they're under my wing," Crow said.

"What are you talking about?" Hendrick snapped.

"The women are daughters of a close friend of mine," Crow said. "They and their men are under my protection. I can't let you kill 'em."

Hendrick struggled for control. His eyes went to Farrokh. "What about him?"

Crow scratched his cheek. "I haven't made up my mind if he's a part of that deal."

Hendrick shot a glare over his shoulder. "Better make up your mind quick."

"The kid's innocent," Johnny said.

More silence as Abruzzi's words registered. Hendrick and Harry and Crow all stared at him.

He shrugged, winced at the flash of pain from his stitches, and said, "*I'm* the one who killed Sal."

"Why the mighty fuck did you do that?" Crow asked.

Abruzzi turned his eyes to Crow and said, "I'm with

the Outfit."

Crow's eyes flicked from Abruzzi to Hendrick and back. "Chicago?" he asked.

"That's right."

Farrokh stared at Abruzzi. He said, "No! You cannot do this!"

He turned to Hendrick. "I killed him! *I* killed the man! Not him!" The young man's eyes went to the huddle of prospects. "They made me and I did it so they would not hurt my uncle!"

Abruzzi snorted. "Sure you did."

"You disagree?" Crow asked.

"I straight-up call him a liar, man," Abruzzi said. "Whatever they did to make the kid go to that house that night, he was terrified and hesitant. I got there first and ran into him as I was coming out. Sal was already dead when he got there. I guess your guys here threatened him with something heavy if he failed. That's why he tried to take credit for it; to keep them away from his uncle or whoever."

Harry stared at Abruzzi with a thoughtful frown. Hendrick noted this, and narrowed his eyes. He said to Crow, "Lemme borrow the kid for a second. I want to ask him some questions."

Crow nodded. "Long as you don't kill him yet."

"No problem." Hendrick pointed his gun at Farrokh. "Come with me."

Farrokh shook harder, but nodded his head jerkily. He walked out of the office with Hendrick behind him.

Harry watched them go. To Abruzzi he said, "What are you doing?"

"What's right," Abruzzi said over his shoulder.

"Why start now?" Toni asked.

He had the self-awareness to look abashed. "Look, what I did, it ain't personal. It's just a job."

Crow stared at him. "*Chicago* wanted him dead?"

Abruzzi nodded.

"Why?"

"Beats me," Abruzzi said in a bored voice. "You know how it is; they don't tell you if you don't need to know, and you don't ask. He was just a name to me."

Hendrick came back, pushing the terrified Farrokh ahead of him. He pointed at Abruzzi. "Your turn."

"Sure thing," he said, and joined Hendrick. They walked into the depths of the warehouse.

Farrokh stood between Harry and Toni. He was still shaking, eyes on the floor. His hair spilled around his face like a curtain.

Hendrick and Abruzzi came back. Hendrick shoved the man hard enough toward the door that, if he hadn't caught the edge of the doorjamb he would have fallen headlong. He stumbled back to his place next to Bobby Gold.

Crow looked over at Hendrick. "Well?"

Harry closed his eyes.

Hendrick said, "He was telling the truth."

"Which one?" asked Crow.

"That one," Hendrick said. Harry opened his eyes to find Hendrick pointing his gun at Abruzzi. He and Toni gave each other a puzzled look.

"What?" Harry asked, confused. "He did?"

"You lied to me, DeMarko," Hendrick chided. "But I get it. You really thought the kid did it."

Crow asked, "How do you know?"

"The kid got everything wrong about Sal's murder. But him?" Hendrick said, still aiming at Abruzzi's nose, "he knew everything. The layout of the house, the robe Sal was wearing. Everything."

Harry stared in shock at Abruzzi, who gave Hendrick an even look, his eyes on the barrel of Hendrick's gun.

"So what now?" Crow asked.

"Now? Now I find a sledgehammer and show him how I feel about what he did."

Crow cleared his throat. "I can't let you do that."

Hendrick turned to the biker, whose thumbs were still hooked in his pockets. "What're you talking about?"

"I can't let you kill him. He's protected."

"He killed my uncle!"

"I know he did. But I'm against it here. I said it's a favor to a friend, keeping them alive."

"I don't give two shits about your favor!"

Crow held up his hands. "I know. But you should, considering who asked."

"I have had as much of this shit as I'm going to," Hendrick said. "I'm killing him."

"You do that, and every MC in the country, every MC in the Collective, is gonna turn up here asking why," Crow said quietly.

Hendrick faltered. "What?"

"Every single one of them. The 68s, both chapters. The Reapers, *every* chapter. The Tacoma Guns. The Sun Devils. The Bastard Riders. All of them. Every club we have is going to come rain down hell," Crow said. Hendrick turned to him, face slack with surprise.

"Why?"

"Because it is what it is," Crow said. "You gonna risk an all-out war with every outlaw club in this country?"

Hendrick glanced at Abruzzi. Crow gave subtle hand signals to his men. They each pointed their guns at Hendrick.

Hendrick told Crow, "You turn on the Gambinos, they'll call in markers from every other Family. You'll be taking us *all* on."

Instead of acknowledging the threat, Crow said, "You know, if this one hadn't been sent after your uncle, Sal would *still* be dead. It looks like a coincidence they both got there when they did. If it wasn't him, it would have been the errand-boy. We wouldn't know the whole story. Most of the 68s are down south. I stayed here to handle the day-to-day and keep an eye on some investments. These prospects fucked everything into a cocked hat. They didn't ask permission, they didn't ask for advice. It would have been a bold move, I'll admit. Stupid and counterproductive, but bold. I know Cad; I sponsored him. He's dumb as a rock, but he's got guts."

Cad brightened a little, but it didn't last.

"Problem is, his guts made him write a check we wouldn't have been interested in cashing. Even leaving Chicago out of the equation, we'd still be in the same spot, dealing with the same shit, if it wasn't for your detective and his crew."

Toni smiled a little. Harry watched everything. Bobby was staring down at the woman in his arms. She made a soft noise and her eyes fluttered, but she didn't wake.

Hendrick's lip rose and fell. Harry thought he sounded remarkably calm given the situation. "So what?"

"So what? So what is… maybe in this particular matter I don't need to shoot my own dog."

Hendrick, eyes still pinned on Abruzzi, didn't respond right away. Then, with effort they could see, he turned away from Abruzzi.

"Consider it doing *me* a favor," Crow said. "Saves me the trouble of having to explain why we're all of a sudden beefing with one of the most powerful Families in New York. Consider it payment in full for a stupid mistake. Consider it a goodwill gesture. Whatever you want. Them for him."

Hendrick licked his lips. "I just let him *walk*?"

Harry held up a finger. "Hendrick, if Chicago sent someone for Sal, isn't that business?"

"So?"

"So it's just business. It's not personal. He's not a villain. He's a tool."

Abruzzi spoke up. "I'm sorry it went down how it did," he said. He sounded abashed. "It was supposed to be quick and clean. Two in the head. I didn't go in there with a hammer, you know. I'm a professional. But the reason it went so hard is because he fought like a banshee to the end. He was one hell of a scrapper, old as he was. I got lucky or it would have been me on that floor."

Hendrick closed his eyes. Cheddar watched him nervously. Hendrick exhaled and stared at the floor. "Get out, DeMarko," his voice a whisper so soft it could have been the wind. "All of you. Get out. And you-"

He pointed at Abruzzi without looking up from the floor.

"If you ever set foot in New York again, nothing on earth will save you."

Abruzzi nodded. "Understood. Thank you."

"We're in your debt," Harry said to Crow.

"No, you're not." He looked at Toni. "'Shine is."

"You know who he is," she said, raising her chin. "You know it's as good as an edict from God himself."

"That's why you're still alive," Crow said. "Now vanish."

They wasted no time in hurrying to the door. The last thing they heard was Hendrick asking, "Who's got the hammer?"

That and a faint scream as they closed the door behind them.

CHAPTER THIRTY-TWO

Back in the office, Chris was curled up on the sofa asleep, blankets over his head. His light snores were a gentle rhythm in the background. Harry poured coffee into a mug, and he noticed his hands were shaking. He set the mug down. Toni came up behind him and slipped her arms around his waist. For a while they said nothing. Then she said against his back, "Close one today, huh?"

"More than close," he said. "I thought we were dead for certain. When Abruzzi confessed-"

"I know," Toni said. "What made him do that?"

Harry's fists crackled as he clenched them. "Let's go ask," he said.

She followed him into the apartment. Abruzzi was shirtless in a chair, with Gene examining him. Bobby Gold was slumped in a chair, staring at nothing. Starr was in the shower. They had taken Farrokh back to his uncle's store. Their reunion had fixed a lot of anger for Harry, but not all of it.

"Gene?"

"Hmm?" The M.E. grunted without looking up.

"How fragile is he?"

Gene shrugged. "He popped two stitches."

"If I hit him a couple three times, is he gonna break open like a pinata?"

Gene chuckled. "I wouldn't go for any body shots. You'll pop more stitches. But no, if you hit him, candy won't come out."

"Good," Harry said. "Stick around just in case, okay?"

Abruzzi was watching Harry with lidded eyes, not speaking. Gene chuckled again, looked up, and the smile on his face faltered. "Wait… you're serious?"

"As can be. And Gene… I'm sorry I dragged you into this. I didn't know you'd be helping someone like him."

Gene raised an eyebrow. "*You* helped someone like him."

"Because Toni's sister was in trouble. I should have-' Harry made a fist. "I should have known better."

"It's all over now, though, right?"

"Thanks to him, I've lied to everyone I respect. People I owe debts I can't pay, who trust *me* because I always do the right thing. I burned it all when I agreed to help *him*. I blew it. I made a bad call and I blew it. I don't know how to square that."

"Is thumping on him gonna do that?"

"No," Harry said. "That's just for me. Call it payment for services rendered."

Abruzzi swallowed, but remained silent. *Wise of him*, Bobby thought.

Gene put a hand on Harry's shoulder. "I get it. I *do*. But Harry… we *do* trust you. You and Toni both. You're… you're kind of the best of us. You don't let *anything* go. You don't let things stand as they are when it's not fair. You do the very best you can, every single time. Look, I'm not a priest. I can't speak for anyone else. But *talk* to them. Same as you did me. Tell them what you did. Tell them how you screwed up. I bet you'll be surprised how fast they forgive you."

Harry didn't say anything, but Toni saw something hopeful in his eyes. "Why?" he whispered.

"All things being equal, maybe you *did* screw up. But you did it doing what you always do: you helped someone. And family is… family. Nothing you could have done, from what I've seen, except what you did."

Harry looked skeptical but Toni swatted him on the arm. "Pay attention," she said. "He's talking sense."

Gene said, "I'm done with that. But Harry… the reason

they'll all understand is… well…" he gave Harry a sad smile. "We know- we *all* know- that you'd do it for any one of us. That you'd put everything you have into it, and everything on the line to fix it. For every one of us. You don't stay mad at people who will do that for you."

Starr came out of the bathroom wrapped in a towel, her red hair still damp and hanging down her back like the tail of a comet.

Toni went to her. "You feeling okay?"

Starr nodded. "Just a clock in the head. I'm hardheaded. It's fine."

"Good." The loud smack of an open palm on Starr's cheeks resounded through the apartment. Starr's head snapped to the side, her cheek already dark red with Toni's hand print. "How *dare* you do this to me!" Toni snarled. "How *could* you? We could have lost *everything*!"

Starr pressed a hand gingerly to her cheek. "Toni, I didn't have a choice."

"Yeah, you did," Toni sneered, her green eyes blazing with anger. "You could have kept driving."

Harry watched but did nothing else. Gene looked anxiously between the women and Bobby Gold, who watched with a remote, almost vacant expression. Johnny Abruzzi stood up. "Hey, now hold on a-"

Both women rounded on him. "You keep your goddamned mouth *shut*!" Toni snarled.

"Sit the hell down or I'll reach through that hole in your side and pull your friggin' heart out!" Starr snapped. "You've done enough!"

Abruzzi fell back a step. He looked at both women, took a second step back, and all but fell into his chair.

Toni loomed over him, hands on her hips. "We all but had you out of there! Free and clear! And you had to open your mouth. Why? Why the fuck would you put us in the crosshairs? Huh?"

Harry was considering intervening if Toni landed more than two or three punches. *Or maybe four,* he thought. *Five, max.* But Starr made an embarrassed sound. She said, hesitantly, "Because I made him to it."

Toni turned to her sister. "You *what*?"

"Wait a minute…" Bobby said. They all looked at him. "He *didn't* do it."

Nobody spoke. Then Harry got it, too. He looked at Toni, whose face held a mixture of indignant anger and sudden thoughtful confusion.

"No, he didn't, did he?" Harry mused.

Abruzzi said nothing. Toni, Harry, and Bobby exchanged looks.

"How'd you know about the inside of the house?" Bobby asked.

"And how'd you know about Sal's bathrobe?" Toni asked.

Harry said, "Farrokh lied to Hendrick. He purposely flubbed the details. Why would he do that? Why would *you* do that?"

"Like I said," Starr told them, glaring at Abruzzi. "I made him do it."

"What, did you threaten to shoot him?" Toni asked.

Starr shook her head. "No. Divorce him."

"Ouch," Toni said.

"Well, it was better than the alternative," she said. "You got some whiskey in here? I could use a shot."

Harry went to the walk-in and got two bottles of scotch. He handed one to Bobby and pulled the cork from his own with his teeth. He upended the bottle and took a deep swallow, then handed it to Toni, who did the same. Bobby opened his bottle and tipped it up. His Adam's apple bobbed as he swallowed three, four, five times. He set the bottle down, a third of it gone. Abruzzi reached for it and Bobby smacked his hand away. "Get your own, asshole," he growled.

"Bobby doesn't like you," Harry said. "And I think he's a good judge of character."

"It's not that I don't like him," Bobby said, "it's that he's laboring under the mistaken apprehension that all men were created interesting."

Toni, Harry, and Gene looked at each other. Toni said, "Okay, I'll bite. Who said that?"

"I did."

"Yeah, but who said it originally?"

"Me," Bobby said. "I said it. First book. *Zero Registration*. The good guy says it to the bad guy at the end of the book."

Harry made an impressed noise. "That's a good line."

"Yeah. Then he shot the bad guy."

Abruzzi looked at Bobby.

"I take it back," Harry said. "It's a *great* line."

Gene took the bottle from Toni and sipped, handing it back. "Someone please explain what just happened?"

Starr sat down. Harry looked at the table instead of down the front of her towel. Out of the corner of his eye he could see Toni watching him, but she was smiling. "I don't know how much..." Starr began, trailed off, and gave Bobby an apologetic look. "I don't know how much you remember."

"You were chatting up Farrokh, then you were sending a rocket up my arm," Bobby said.

Toni's eyes went from Bobby to Starr. The momentary confusion gave way to understanding, anger, and then resignation.

Bobby saw it, hesitated, and mouthed, "Sorry."

Toni, lips pressed into a narrow line, gave him a curt, single nod.

Starr blushed. "Yeah. I'm sorry about that. But I wasn't sure you'd be quiet. I sat with the boy for a while, got him to open up. He told me about killing Sal. He was crying and just a wreck. I was shocked when he told me. I went into Johnny's room and told him. Johnny said we had a golden opportunity-"

"Kill him and run. But the 68s got to you first," Harry said.

Starr gave him an icy glare. "Actually, no. I explained to Farrokh about Johnny's… assignment. Farrokh, Johnny, and I discussed it. We came up with the idea to get him off the hook. Johnny would go to the Outfit and claim the kill. Once he confirmed it, he would be practically Made. He would have some protection against the factions here. Maybe enough to get us out of here in one piece."

"Farrokh agreed with you?" Harry asked.

"He's the one who recognized that if Johnny were going to convince anyone, he needed to know every detail of the hit. So they collaborated. And we went to the 68s to get Farrokh off the hook."

Toni blinked. "We thought you'd jabbed Bobby to put him down and Farrokh rabbited on you. We figured…" she looked at Abruzzi. "We figured you'd know your best chance was to kill him. Then no one would doubt you did the job."

Abruzzi shrugged. "Actually, that *was* my first thought. But I wasn't gonna do that to Starr. Her *or* her family," he said. "So we came up with a better plan."

"Why didn't you just sap Bobby?" Gene asked. "Shooting him up was risky as hell. You could have killed him."

Abruzzi gave Gene a dark look. "That was my idea. ' I wasn't in any shape to fight anyone. Starr wouldn't do it, and Farrokh couldn't. Besides, I knew how much junk to use. I have experience. I kicked a couple years ago."

Bobby's hand gripped the neck of his bottle. His knuckles whitened. "So did I," he ground out through clenched teeth.

Abruzzi looked chastened. "I'm sorry about that. But we needed to move fast. It was a matter of time before it all hit the fan. So we dosed him, snuck out, and high-tailed it to the 68s club. We meant to pull the switch on them and get clear. They panicked and clocked us. We all woke up at the warehouse, and I thought for sure we were dead. Then you came in. After they spilled the beans about Farrokh killing D'Amico, I had to do something. So I confessed. Luckily, that kid's got some balls. He played right along, and we fed that walking side of beef the bullshit we'd planned from the start. Done, done, and done."

"Why not just *tell* us that?" Harry snapped. "We could have-"

"You were already in deep enough. You put yourself on the hook for me, and for Starr, and for Farrokh," Abruzzi said, voice icy. "We all agreed; you did enough. If we sank or swam it was on us. We knew the danger, but like you told *him*," Abruzzi pointed at Gene, "we couldn't let you risk anything else for us. You did enough. It wasn't your debt anymore."

Harry, nonplussed, said nothing.

"That was risky," Toni said, trying not to be impressed. "Very risky."

"They could have killed you," Harry said very quietly. "They could have dropped you right then and there. We got you out by the skin of our teeth. But they could just as easily have put two in your head."

"I know that," Abruzzi said. He looked up at Harry. "It went bad, and yeah, you saved our asses. But it needed to be done this way. Look, I'd love to say I was doing it to save the kid, but the fact is, I was doing it because I *had* to. I can't go back to Chicago without confirmation. Now, the people that need to know it *here* know. And when I get back, I can prove it to *my* people."

Harry didn't say anything. Toni took a sip of whiskey. Bobby asked, "Prove it how?"

Abruzzi hesitated. "The hammer."

Harry closed his eyes. "I thought Farrokh would have dumped it somewhere. I've been waiting for it to turn up."

"Naah. It was in the kid's backpack along with the gun they gave him to use on Sal, and that brick of H."

"Where are the gun and hammer now?" Toni asked.

"In a garbage bag under the kid's bed upstairs."

Toni went up and got the gun and hammer. She came back down with it, saying, "Cherry is *pissed*. The new girl had it up to here with our shitstorm. She moved out. Cherry's worried she won't be able to make rent."

"We'll work something out. We owe her a couple months free anyhow," Harry said.

Johnny Abruzzi was dressed in an old shirt of Harry's, and his leather jacket. Starr wore a blouse and slacks Tori had given her. Toni took the shotgun out of the duffel and put the hammer in it, under a bunch of their dirty clothes. She handed the gun to Harry, who started to clean it with a rag.

"I'll dispose of this later. No telling what it was used for or what it's tied to." He remembered something, reached into his pocket, and pulled the crumpled yellow sheet of paper. He handed it to Abruzzi. "We'll drop you, Starr, and Chris at the bus station. Make your call then." Harry said. "We've got to get you all out of town tonight. Now."

Abruzzi started to speak. "Look, I'm sorry-"

Harry punched him in the mouth, a solid right that spun the man around. Abruzzi stumbled backward, tripped over his chair, and fell heavily to the floor. He yelped as he landed on his wound.

"Jesus, Harry," Gene chided. He bent over Abruzzi to check the stitches. "I told you to stay away from the body."

"Gene, I hit him in the *mouth*."

Abruzzi shook Gene off. "I'm fine. I'm fine."

"You heard Hendrick. Stay out of New York," Harry said.

"I know." Abruzzi climbed to his feet. No one offered to help.

"I know you *know*," Harry growled, and he grabbed Abruzzi's jacket and yanked him close. "I'm telling you again. You get the fuck out of my city and you *stay* gone. I ever even *hear* of you coming back here and I'll find you, wherever you are, and I *will* kill you."

"I'll help," Bobby chimed in.

"I'll make it look like an accident," Gene said, appearing pleased that he could participate.

"And I'll make the body disappear," Toni promised.

Abruzzi gulped, nodded, and started to speak, but Harry held up a finger. "Not a word. Not *one*. You speak again, I'll put you in the trunk."

Abruzzi nodded. Starr pushed him toward the door. "Come on, you," she said. "Before you get yourself killed."

"Starr," Toni started.

"No," Starr said. She gave Toni an abashed look. "I know. And believe me, it won't happen again. Promise."

Toni nodded. Starr cocked her head and said, "'Shine went to bat for us. Had our back in a big way. The biggest."

"Fathers," Toni said.

"Yeah."

Bobby and Gene sat down at the table as Toni closed the door behind her. Bobby sipped from his bottle again. Gene looked at the second bottle. He shrugged and sipped. He reached into his bag, crouched by his feet, and took out a manila folder.

"I got it," he said.

Bobby stared at the folder. "You work fast."

"Told them I was a friend of the family."

Bobby smiled wanly. "'It is a melancholy truth that even poor men have great relations,'" Bobby quoted.

Gene thought about that for a moment. Bobby stared to give his usual disclaimer, but to his surprise Gene said, "Dickens. *Bleak House*."

"My man!" Bobby exclaimed with a grin.

"But you screwed it up, didn't you? Isn't it the other way around?"

Bobby shrugged. "It sounds like hubris if I call myself a great man. It's easier being poor."

Gene sipped from his bottle again and Bobby opened the coroner's report. He read twice and then closed it with a sigh. Without looking up, he said, "I don't suppose…"

"No," Gene said. "It looks legit. Nothing odd or out of place. Sorry."

"Yeah. Me, too," Bobby swiped a hand across his eyes.

Grimacing, Gene asked, "You okay?"

He didn't have to explain what he meant. Bobby got it.

"I guess," Bobby said. "I won't know until I am. You know?"

Gene nodded. "I hear you." He looked around the apartment. "You wanna play some cards?"

Bobby smiled. It wasn't a sarcastic smile; it was warm and his eyes were grateful. "You're a good man, Charlie Brown."

Gene shrugged, smiled, and said, "Nickels and dimes. Nothing wild."

CHAPTER THIRTY-THREE

Two hours later the door opened and Harry and Toni came inside. Harry shucked his coat with a long-suffering sigh. Toni fell over on the bed and stared at the ceiling.

"What a friggin' day," Toni said.

"Agreed," Harry said. He and Toni each kicked off their shoes. Toni slipped out of her jacket and put her gun on the side table on her side of the bed. After scrounging a couple of sandwiches, they joined Bobby and Gene at the table. Both of them were bleary-eyed and at least three sheets to the wind. With a chuckle, Harry scooped the cards off the center of the table and started to shuffle.

"I want to sleep for a week," Toni said.

"Second," Bobby said.

Gene mused, "I could sleep."

Harry said, "I hear you. But a week isn't gonna cut it. We have a new client. New case. We start in the morning."

All eyes went to Harry. Toni said, almost fearfully, "You're kidding."

"Nope."

"Harry DeMarko," she said, her voice becoming stern, "you haven't left my sight all day. *When* did you get a new client?"

"I didn't," he said. "You did."

"I did?"

"Yes, you did." Harry dealt the cards out, three to each of them. "Gene, you said you took some time off, right?"

"Uh... yeah?" Gene sounded uncertain, but he said, "What's the case?"

"First, let's play some cards. But one hand. That's it. Then bed. Get some good sleep tonight. I can't believe I'm actually saying this," Harry said, shuffling the cards with a snap. "But first thing in the morning, we leave for Jersey."

Bobby froze. He stared, dumbfounded, at Harry. Toni glanced at Bobby, and back to Harry. Gene smiled, put a hand on Bobby's shoulder, and squeezed.

Toni said, "You mean…"

Harry picked up his cards and arranged them in his hand. When he looked up, his eyes were flat and had taken on a melancholy aspect. "We're going to find out what happened to Bobby's wife."

THE END

Author's Note

This was a fun book to write, but a harder one than the first four. It does, however represent the culmination of four years' worth of plotlines being resolved. That is very satisfying. Insofar as the stories are an unbroken string of really bad days, this book represents a clean break, a new beginning, and a whole new set of characters and problems in which to tangle Harry, Toni, and Bobby Gold. The first five books represent a more-or-less closed set. Time to start a new one.

Bobby Gold is an interesting character to write. He was supposed to be a one-note sounding board for Toni while Harry was in jail, so she'd have someone to talk to, and toward whom she could demonstrate her own personality quirks without the overarching love between her and Harry. But the best laid plans, as the Bard said. Bobby became a much more interesting character than I intended, and even caused a virtual re-write mid-book. Long about the middle, I realized that, in order to grow, Bobby needed some tragedy. Nothing brings out character like adversity, and Bobby Gold has it in spades, both of them. Bobby Gold is, of course, my tribute to the late Anthony Bourdain, from whom I borrowed his look, his occupation, his penchant for literature, and his heroin addiction.

If you've read the first four Bennett & DeMarko books (I hope so, they're intended to be very linear), you're familiar with Toni Bennett already. The Bennett family is a creation I've been slowly introducing in my work as a way to tie everything together into a shared world. Although written out of order, the timeline of appearances of the Bennett sisters runs thusly:

Set in 1970, my novel Nomad, a story about a biker gang, features Baby Bennett.

Set in 1980, the Harry and Toni series continues this line with Toni, and introduces Toni's younger sister, Starr, as well as her husband, the would-be Mobster Johnny Abruzzi.

Set in 2000, twenty years from Harry and Toni's now, my novel Pros, features an older (and hopefully wiser) Starr, her ex-husband Chicago Outfit Capo John Abruzzi, and introduces a third Bennett sister, Angie.

Forty years of Bennett women so far, and I doubt we've seen all of them just yet.

I owe my eternal gratitude (and an unspecified amount of homemade cookies) to any number of people, not the least of which is my publisher, Lisa Orban, who gets (along with cookies) the official title of Author Whisperer. She's kind and supportive, and only makes fun of me a little. Jennie Rosenblum, my long-suffering editor who, despite being from New Jersey, is one of my favorite people in the world. She is also owed my gratitude (not cookies, though; she's a gin girl) for keeping me from spinning out when my workload is burdensome. My four oldest friends Ian Bullard, Jason May, Phil Tivis, and Shaun Collins are always ready to take the piss out of me if I'm getting to rambunctious. One cannot ask a higher service from such good friends.

My kids, Gabe, Zach, and Beanie. I wasn't ready to be a father. I can't imagine my life without them.

My wife, Cara, who, despite living with me for a decade, has never made an attempt on my life.

That I know of.

And always my gratitude to my readers. Your kind attention is very much appreciated. Thank you for giving my world a try.

Aaron S Gallagher
April 8th, 2020

Also by Aaron S Gallagher

Pros
Return Fire
The Veiled Earth Book I - Magician
The Veiled Earth Book II - Martyr
The Veiled Earth Book III - Savior
The Other Side of the Atmosphere
Dirty Wings and Other Stories
Orphan World
The Long Way Home
What You Wish For
Bennett & DeMarko 1 - The Bleecker Street Bodies
Bennett & DeMarko 2 - The Delancey Street Disappearances
Bennett & DeMarko 3 - The Mercer Street Murder
Bennett & DeMarko 4 - The Elizabeth Street Epiphany
Nomad
Blue Sail

CPSIA information can be obtained
at www.ICGtesting.com
Printed in the USA
LVHW082337180820
663571LV00018B/344/J